Sophistry
(For Alex)

Part 1 of The Sabia

Book I of Mathan: Mad Bear of the Western Dearth

Dedicated to my own personal Sabia –
The Julie

By: S. Marshall Wilson

Lyrics to Heather Dale's song "I Follow My King" are used with
permission. Originally recorded on her CD "The Hidden Path"
(copyright Amphis Music 2006). Her recordings are available at
www.HeatherDale.com.

ISBN: 0-9974957-0-7
ISBN-13: 978-0-9974957-0-6

NORTH MOUNTAIN
PUBLISHING

I AM PROFOUNDLY INDEBTED:

To my own, personal Sabia – my staunchest ally and truest friend – Julie, for the inspiration, encouragement, support, and tea that drew this tale from my heart and onto the page. Absent you, I would long ago have been crushed beneath my many burdens.

To those who walked the Dearthlands with me and brought me home again. The Truth is far greater than we are, and it requires no defense. IRONHORSE

To my children whose mere existence demands better of me than I have.

To Mom for keeping me alive until I figured out how to do it myself.

To Dad for the mythos.

To Heather Wilson Kammers for seeing the value in most of my mad schemes.

To Aunt Joanie for the idea that I might have a tale worth telling.

To Connie Denicola for telling me I did.

To the Roundtablers – C. A. Hocking, Jess Alter, Christy King, Kathy Campbell, Ron Shaw, Libby Rosengren, Angie Carrera, Efrona Mor, Lena Stark, Mar González, and Eve Rabi for convincing me that I could do it then showing me how.

To my friends who read and considered and commented – especially Lea Ann Day, Cindy Neal, Nick Olsen, Barb Close, Dorothy Wilson, Dana Bourque, Marilyn Kinyon, Courtney Ronshausen, John Dicks, J. Lowell Wilson, and Qamrosh Khan.

To Derek Murphy at Creative Indie for his fine books, excellent guidance, and beautiful cover design.

To Clive Johnson for his graciously persistent editing and conscientious text formatting.

To Thomas Riepenhoff for permission to quote the chorus to "The Outhouse Song"

To Heather Dale for permission to quote her stunningly beautiful lyrics to "I Follow My King".

To Master Smith Danny Trenary of VinTin Welding and Fabricating for allowing me to beat on hot metal while I picked his brain. He would have been better served had I left him alone. The finest thing we forged was an enduring friendship. Any and all inappropriate elaboration on the process is mine alone. Danny is not responsible for any mistakes.

To Ann Feuerbach, PhD for her technical consultation on ancient steel production methods... especially the idea for the wind towers. Any and all inappropriate elaboration on the process is mine alone. Dr. Feuerbach is not responsible for any mistakes.

To Daniel Lerch for his expert recommendations on steganography. Any and all inappropriate elaboration on the process is mine alone. Mr. Lerch is not responsible for any mistakes.

To Tim Gonzalez Photography for the beautiful cover image.

To Countess Kallista Morganova (Denise Zavala) for the expert costume design.

To the Great, Good God. "For in Him we live and move and have our being; as certain also of your own poets have said..."

To many others who should surely send me notice to include them in the Acknowledgements for Philosophy Part 2 of The Sabia.

APOLOGIA

I lay aside now my truest love, my clarsach, to frame my tale as the Sabia taught me. In the discipline of writing I marry my capricious heart to my ordered mind so I may record an account that is faithful to the soul and true to the facts of all that we saw, all that we did, and all that we were.

I have heard the whispers. I am not deaf, though old, blind and lame. I have heard them say that I hope to defend his memory from the imperious impeachment of those who call themselves wise, but you've no call to doubt my motives. My only ambition is to publish the truth. The truth is far greater than the man, and it requires no defense.

For forty years I stumbled beside him, carried his burdens, and fought his wars. I was there in his youth; I was there at his death. Since that day, I have traveled widely to speak with those who knew the tales of his father's mad ventures, of his mother's wild beauty, of the fall of Dunglaun, of the Fair Ones, of the Brown Ones, and of his assault on the High King's keep.

Know you this: I will lay him bare before you as not

even he could. You will know his oafish buffoonery, his preposterous rage, his infantile brooding. Bound up with these flaws which his detractors delight to publish, you will find ample evidence of his gallant humor, his generous compassion, his forthright courage and his humble grace. You will likely find evidence of more as well.

It may be that some who read this account will be worthy to judge the man. Whether he was good or no, I've no right to say. He was a man. He was great and greatly flawed. He was a man.

Pay heed then to the testimony of the bard. If you are wise enough to own your weakness and strong enough to claim your folly, perhaps you will find in this man Mathan, known as the "Mad Bear of the Western Dearth", a brother and a friend.

CHAPTER 1
Who Are You, Then?

"Out of suffering have emerged the strongest souls; the most massive characters are seared with scars."
Khalil Gibran

On a day of days in late autumn, when the silver sun rolled down the slope of the leaden sky, a wee lad of eight summers sat screaming in the muck in an alleyway beside his family's home. Before him, his mother lay twitching as she reached out for him. She tried to speak, but only blood passed her trembling lips. The boy scrambled backwards until his back was pressed against the stone wall and screamed until the scream was all he knew; then, he knew no more.

He woke to muffled voices and a door banging open and slamming shut. He peered about. He knew the house but it was not home. The faces of the rushing people were familiar but distorted with unutterable grief. Each paused to study his face, to speak a word, or to lay a hand on his head, but among them he could not find the one he sought.

The lad's father burst through the door, snatched him from the bed where he lay and jogged outside before the door could slam shut. After laying him onto a pallet of blankets surrounded by crates in the bed of a wain, Ardal caressed his son's cheek then kissed the crate beside him. He faltered for a moment then looked over his shoulder and spoke into the darkness. "Ach, Orin, and what would we do without you?"

"Same as we would have without you, my lad. Go now. Look for us with the thaw."

Ardal laid his hand on his son's cheek again then stepped off the back of the wain to embrace his friend. "If you can't bring our gear without bringing others behind you, don't come. You'll accept my wain as fair trade for this one you've given me?"

"Think not on it, lad, only get you to the vale. Your tools and belongings will follow you in the spring."

Ardal strode to the side of the wain to climb into the driver's seat but turned at the sound of stifled sobs behind him. He enfolded Orin's willowy wife in a crushing embrace, and she bore the weight of him as he buckled beneath his grief. Once he was able, he stood upright, placed his hands on her shoulders and looked into her inflamed eyes. "Keva. Ai, Keva. She loved you as no other. And now, what will we do? We who were so loved by such a one as she? What will become of us?"

Keva slapped Ardal as hard as she could. "That's how she'd answer your self-pity. Get the boy home. Spare no thought for aught else, including us."

She caressed the welt that rose on his cheek. "And, Ardal, let no charge of blame for this horror fall on your shoulders. You are a good man and a worthy husband to such as she. Go now. The boy needs you." She pushed him toward the wain.

Ardal mounted and drove into the night. He continued through daybreak and into late morning until the horses stumbled in their weariness. He halted in a glade beside a spring-fed stream where he unhitched the team and hobbled them. He filled his skins and returned to the wain. As he approached, he noted the odor of corruption that came from the long crate in spite of the quantity of salt he had packed in with his wife's remains. He stumbled.

Ardal lifted his son to lay him on the driver's bench but discovered he had fouled himself. He stripped the child then carried him to the stream and lowered him into the cool water. The boy immediately awoke and darted a glance about the glade, like a hare cornered by hounds. His gaze found Ardal's and rested for a moment; then the boy howled and attacked the hands that held him. Ardal lost his grip and the boy fell onto his back in the water.

He flailed and spluttered frenetically until his mind settled into a single sense – a negation of all he had come to know. "Noooooooooo. No. No. No no no no. NO!" He stood naked, defiant, clench-fisted and shivering as he flung his negation into Ardal's face.

Ardal sat in the mud on the bank, his elbows on his knees, and held his head in his hands while the boy continued to flail and shout. Even after the shouting stopped, he did not lift his gaze until he felt a small, impossibly cold hand on his cheek. The boy stood, blue-lipped and shuddering, before him.

Ardal wrapped him in a clean blanket then set him on the driver's bench with bread, cheese, water, and apples. After he had washed his son's clothes and spread them out over an apple crate to dry, he hitched and un-hobbled the team and left the glade behind.

The journey from Shallowford to Taermun lasted the better part of two weeks. In that time, the stench of the crate increased despite the salt until it was nigh intolerable, but then had begun to abate. Still, when they drove into Taermun, death billowed behind them like the train of a gown.

Enervated by grief for his lost wife, worry for his catatonic son, and the rigors of the journey, Ardal drove the wain to the home of his brother, Alistair, for Alistair would do what Ardal could not.

While Alistair dug beneath the oak atop the knoll that rose behind the smithy, he decried the foolishness of his younger brother. The grunts of his efforts punctuated his words. "Told him to settle down. That aught like this might happen. Why'd he bring her all the way here? Only a fool would carry a corpse halfway across the land. The boy'll never recover, and who'll care for him? I've plenty to occupy my time. Ai, lass, you deserved better than my fool of a brother for a husband and an end like this." His muttering continued even after he had lowered the crate into the grave and covered it.

Alistair ambled down to the river to wash away the fatigue and the stench of his duty before he returned to his home to find his brother and nephew under the pall of profound slumber and the sure ministration of a small, plain woman.

Alistair noted the well-tended fire, the steaming kettle and the general order she had imposed upon his home. He assessed her as a handsome and capable woman, which tempered his suspicious agitation when he addressed her: "Who are you, then?"

The woman glanced over her shoulder then continued slicing vegetables. "You should know me, Alistair Wainwright, son of Ivor Smith of the Northern Marches. At the least, you know of me for Ivor knew me well. I am here to ensure no further harm comes to the lad for a season."

"I did not send for you."

"You cannot command my presence, Alistair. I go where I go and do as I do."

"Aye, that much I know. Whether you are wanted or no, you enter a man's home and drive him mad. You've destroyed more doughty men than an army of invaders might. Here lies my brother, laid to waste by your scheming. His son, no doubt, will fare no better."

The slight woman gazed expressionlessly at the burly man. "Imagine that. A son of Ivor himself stands before the heir of the House of Killinchy, the rightful ruler of Dunglaun, and speaks of armed invasion. Which of us, Alistair, is mad?"

She allowed the question to hang unanswered for a long time before turning away from the wainwright and speaking over her shoulder. "Allow them to rest, Alistair, and to eat. Allow me to salt the stew, then will I prepare their place in the smithy house and you may send them away into my charge. We'll no longer burden you with duties to your family."

"Seems a sensible plan." Alistair shouldered open the door and walked out.

***

Quiet voices and a hand on his brow raised the boy from his frigid emptiness, and he raised his eyelids enough to allow a sliver of light to enter. A man stood beside his bed and leaned down to study him. He looked away and spoke quietly in a rich voice. "Fear not. He'll be well, and better than well, he'll be good."

A small, plain woman stood beside him and laid her hand on his shoulder. "Ai, Josiah. I feared I'd lost him."

The lad carried with him the image of Josiah's smile as he sank again into the darkness.

***

The wan sunlight caressed his brow but brought little relief from the chill breeze that entered with it through the open window. The bracing draft and the pale light cajoled him, along with the gentle tones of a woman's voice. They called him to rise.

"Mathan. Mathan, my child. Darlin', you must not lie here in your grief. Arise, m'love. Your deliverance will come, but you must rise to meet it. Mathan. Mathan, my son…"

The lad opened his eyes against the dark foreboding that held them shut and studied the gravely merry mien of the small, plain woman who insistently called him to rise. He peered about, scrutinizing the darker corners of the room in search of something he had lost.

The woman sat beside him and brushed his hair away from his brow then laid her hand on his cheek. She gazed into his eyes, as though to draw out his suffering. "She's not here, child."

Her pronouncement of his loss settled onto him, frigid, dense and massive. After an interminable moment, his defiant rage erupted into a wordless wail and poured forth in bright, hot tears. She leaned near to speak soothingly to him, and he left a weal on her cheek.

Unperturbed, she took his hands in hers and considered his wild glare. Her placid gaze became for him the only fixed point in all the world. Mathan gradually focused all his senses on that gaze and stepped away from the mad void that yawned beneath him. He shuddered as he drew in his last sob.

His voiced creaked from disuse. "Where's my mam?" It was a demand rather than a question.

"She's gone before you on the adventure all men undertake whether they will it or no." Her gaze never wavered.

"Bring her back."

"I cannot, though I would with all my heart." She spoke the last as though to herself but continued her frank appraisal of Mathan. "It is not within my purview."

"Who are you, then?"

"My name is a secret. Some day, perhaps I'll tell you when it will mean something to you. Men here call me by names that mean something to them. Your mother called me 'the Sabia'. You will learn to know me."

"Sabia?" Mathan repeated and returned her studious

stare.

The Sabia maintained eye contact as she pressed her lips together in a tight smile and assented with a slight nod. "That I am."

They sat silently for a moment, knowing each other until Mathan's eyes widened as bits of remembered horror rampaged through his mind. He drew his knees to his chest and huddled in the corner at the head of his bed. His eyes roamed the room again, peering into the darker corners. "Sabia, where are the monsters?"

"They've gone, m'love." She laid her hand on his cheek and looked him in the eyes again. "They've gone away."

"They've gone with Mam?"

"Ach, no, dear one. They've gone their own way and will vex your mam no more."

"What about me? Will they vex me again?"

"Aye, Mathan. I fear they'll vex you for many long years to come, but you'll be strong. You must be courageous. I'll be with you."

Sabia stayed with Mathan even when his father, the formidable Ardal, did not. She cared for him much as his own mother would have. She provided simple food, unaffected affection, and compassion unsullied by pity. She walked or sat with him for hours, recounting fantastic tales of the exploits of great heroes in the face of overwhelming opposition.

She kept her word to his father and never told him aught of the Fall of Dunglaun, the Battle for Hart's Pass, the Mad Foray into the Dearthlands, nor any of the others tales that came together to form the foundation of his own.

***

A dozen years later as he stumbled across the threshold of manhood, Mathan also stumbled upon Sabia where she spoke in the common. Stepping into the shadow of the market stall of Amir, the spice merchant, he listened in on her soliloquy.

Around Amir's sales pitch, gossip, and questions, Mathan was able to catch snatches of Sabia's discourse with passersby. She stood in the market calling them to set aside their foolish ways. "How long?" she asked them. "How long will you mock knowledge and remain in your ignorance?"

Most of the villagers ignored her, but she had collected a devoted following of hecklers, a group of five idle young men who followed her through the marketplace, jeering at her and anyone with the temerity to pause and consider her words.

Abruptly, Sabia rounded on her tormentors. "Because you wouldn't listen, because you ignored my extended hand and mocked my advice, I will mock you when your terror seizes you. Your own mockery and complacency will destroy you utterly." She held the gaze of their leader, a lad called Nikko, for an eternal moment then concluded simply, "And I will laugh." Nikko shuddered.

Turning to the small crowd witnessing her wrath, Sabia extended her hand in invitation and cajoled them, "But you... You are not so foolish as they. Come, hear my word, learn to pursue wisdom and you will have naught to fear."

Mathan surprised himself along with everyone else when he stepped out into the open from behind Amir's stall to answer Sabia's invitation. "I'd like to have a whole lot of naught to fear." He spoke to Sabia as though no one else were present.

Sabia's smile suggested he had spoken words of incredible beauty. Taking his hand, she drew him to her side and whispered intently, "I've a message for you alone, m'love." She continued to hold his hand as she began to instruct him, there in the street in front of everyone, including her mockers. "I will pour out my spirit on you and teach you my words."

Overhearing this, one of the hecklers jeered, "Ol' Bear – he don't know what a woman's spirit is *for*. Pour it out on me instead." Mathan's massive fist hammered into the blackguard's offending mouth snapping his head back so it struck the wall of the shop behind with a sharp crack.

Sabia exploited the resulting chaos to pull Mathan through an open house across the lane and into an alley beyond. His hopes that she had been impressed by his unsolicited defense of her honor were extinguished along with his residual anger when she fervently pulled him on and admonished, "A fool gives full vent to his anger, but a wise man holds it in check."

"He was implying–" A sharp look from Sabia stilled him.

"Worse has been said of me by better men. Do not trouble yourself with what others think of me… nor of yourself."

She held up her hand. "Hush. We have no time for your folly. Listen, learn and practice what I tell you. I will come when you call me, but you must learn to recognize wisdom's voice.

"The onus is on you. The time for your departure has come. The culmination of the age is upon us. You have been and will be called. Go where you are called.

"Pay close attention to what your father tells you; never forget what you learned at your mother's knee. Wear their counsel like flowers in your hair, like rings on your fingers.

"Do you hear me, Mathan? Heed the call. Remember your father's words; never forget what you learned at your mother's knee. Tell me you understand," she insisted, her strong, tiny hands grasping his upper arms and her fierce eyes boring into his.

Mathan looked away then took her hands in his. He smiled and re-engaged her gaze. "I understand your words, Sabia." He released her hands. "But I don't know what you're talking about."

Sabia's countenance bespoke such severe antipathy that

it confounded the flow of Mathan's words. "I told you we've no time for your folly, child. Learn to recognize my voice. I will come when you need me, but you must learn to know wisdom." With that, she sauntered away, leaving him alone and very much bewildered in the alley behind a stranger's house.

With a disconcerted shrug, he turned to find the gawky, desultory village minstrel sitting and muttering to himself on the back doorstep of a bakery whose proprietor was known to be generous with day-old bread.

When Mathan asked what troubled the storyteller, Tigue pointed a shaking finger in the direction Sabia had gone. "That woman spins seductive tales of glory and honor which compel otherwise normal people by her dark art to fantasize madly of braving great dangers to combat phantasmagoric enemies in hopes of accomplishing abstruse goals in the name of an obscure prince – she…" His rising rant ended as a befuddled and thoughtful look settled on his countenance. "She troubles me greatly," he muttered as though that thought itself troubled him.

Mathan chuckled, laid a copper dada into the habitually upturned palm of the minstrel and turned away. He had only gone a few paces before Tigue collected himself and glanced down at the unexpected offering. He snorted his derision and shouted after Mathan, "A single dada? You insult me, you colossal lout."

"Your tale of Sabia merited less. Now, you can buy a loaf for your dinner rather than wait here for the baker to pity you with his refuse. A pint, however, will cost you a sweeter song." Mathan ambled off, pleased with his own cleverness.

For his twin acts of valor and cleverness in defense of Sabia he experienced the heady pleasure of the approval of his own conscience. He had crushed one of her detractors with his mighty hamfist and eviscerated the other with his quick, sharp tongue. He wondered, "What more could be asked of a man?"

Sabia had denounced his quick anger, but she was not to be the only person to denounce him. At sunrise the next day, Mathan answered a knock at the front door of his father's house to find Cian, the oldest member of the town guard, looking wanly back at him. "Where's your da?" he asked diffidently.

"Dunno. He was gone when I woke."

"You're to come with me," the guard intoned, as if reciting a line from an oft-repeated ceremony.

"Well, and a fine 'Good morning' to you as well, Guard Leader. Am I, then? And shall I invite my trousers to come along?"

The elderly guard leader sighed long and hard as he withdrew a rolled parchment from his pouch and presented it to Mathan. "This document directs you to come with me."

"Are you certain, Cian? It could be a recipe for Mag Petty's rhubarb pie." He unrolled the scroll and took in the pertinent facts at a glance. "Ai, no. It seems it's an invitation to a party."

Cian lifted the pike he had been leaning on and leveled it at Mathan. "It's a warrant, oaf. Trousers or no, you're to come with me."

Mathan lifted his hands and stepped back into the house. "Come in, Cian. Come right in. Make yourself at home. The water's on. Have some tea while I see to my trousers."

Mathan was soon mildly surprised to see Cian take his invitation literally, preparing himself a cup of tea. He was a bit more surprised when the old man gingerly lowered himself into Ardal's chair and propped his feet on his stool. "Take your time, lad. Take your time. Once, back in Shallowford, your da scolded me for taking my ease in his home. And see now, I've been invited to do just that by none other than his only son."

Mathan entered the room, his boots in his hand. "As I remember, old scoundrel, you had crawled through the

13

window and were eating his dinner."

Cian's leathery face cracked into a broad grin. "It was good, too. Your ma was a good cook, boy."

"Do not speak of my mother. You know nothing of her." He smiled. "She was a terrible cook."

Mathan leaned against the wall while he pulled on his boots. "If you intend to drag me off to the guardhouse, you had best do it soon. Who knows how long you have left? How did you come to be so very old, Cian?"

The leader of the guard fixed him with a sharp glare. "It ain't the years, lad. It's the miles." He glanced at his tea, still steeping on the table, sighed and clambered out of Ardal's chair. "Let's go then, shall we, lad? Cap'n ain't patient."

As they passed through the doorway, Cian reached for his pike, leaning upon it like a staff, and shuffled toward the guardhouse, never once glancing back to see if his charge had followed. Mathan, meanwhile, walked behind for a while, wondering at Cian's shambling gait, before catching up and clapping him on the shoulder. Cian glanced at him from under his heavy brows and nodded curtly.

Upon their arrival, Cian entered the guardhouse, knocked on the door to the captain's office and pushed it open without waiting for an answer. Then he waved Mathan through and shuffled over to take up his accustomed position on his own chair, tilted back against the wall, his feet propped on his desk. He closed his eyes, sighed and allowed his head to droop.

Elgin, the one-eyed captain of the guard, bellowed an affable "Ho" when Mathan entered. "Come in, Bear. Make us some tea," he ordered without looking up from the documents that covered his battered desk.

Mathan obliged while Elgin attended to his papers and mumbled in agitated bemusement, "You hafta keep an eye on Joe. You never know what he'll do next." Mathan knew that Elgin habitually referred to the men under his command as "Joe" but did not ask, nor did Elgin explain which particular Joe might have committed what particular offense.

Remembering Cian's tea cooling on the table at home, Mathan made three cups and gently set one on his desk so as not to interrupt the old man's soft snores.

The Captain looked up from his papers to accept the cup from Mathan's mammoth hand. "Thank you for coming, Wildman."

"I didn't interpret the old man's message as an invitation, Elgin. It was a legal order to appear before the captain of the guard. There was never any question I would come."

"Old man?" Elgin shook his head. "'Fear the old man in a profession in which men often die young.' The way I got it figured is you were lookin' for an excuse to come drink all my fine tea; so, you near kill the one fella in town likely to draw attention to his own cowardice by denouncin' you officially."

"'Near killing?' Elgin, I only hit him once, and that was in passing. Besides, I don't need an excuse to drink your wretched tea. I think the quartermaster issues you tins of swamp grass—"

The import of Elgin's words now struck Mathan. He foundered in a wave of dismay for a moment as he wondered aloud, "'Likely to draw attention to his own cowardice'? Nikko? I hit the Teshak's son? Ah, scrios, Elgin! I didn't even see his face."

Elgin chuckled, "Well, you should see it now. In my estimation, a man should never 'near kill' a fella like Nikko. You either kill him or leave him be." He leaned forward and peered intently into Mathan's eyes. "Meanwhile, there is the question of how to address this situation."

The Captain leaned back and propped his boots on the desk, clods of dried mud flaking off them onto his documents, and he fixed the younger man with a steely, one-eyed gaze, "as I see it, you have precious few

15

options."

He ponderously lifted a crooked index finger and enumerated. "The first is to admit fault and pass a few pleasant nights here with my lads, drinking wretched tea and swapping tales of your many manly exploits."

Mathan bristled. "I'll admit nothing except that Nikko is a fool and a coward, as well as a poor hand at a job. I've done naught amiss."

He lowered his eyes and his voice, "Besides, I have no manly exploits to tell of."

Elgin raised an eyebrow at the interruption. "No, not a one? But Anyah..." but then he saw Mathan's embarrassment. He cleared his throat, seeming to rethink his words.

Elgin set his feet on the floor so he could lean across the desk and watch Mathan's face. Now lifting his thumb, he continued enumerating. "The second would be to deny wrongdoing and defend yourself before the council. This is the only option that holds the potential to restore your good name."

"Don't reckon I'd stand much chance with that option, not given it was the teshak's boy I hit."

"Lad, I believe you sell our chieftain well short of his rights." Elgin leaned back, plainly allowing Mathan room to consider his options.

"So, I could 'admit' I'm in the wrong." Mathan's expression was that of one smelling a foul odor. "Or I will stand before the council." He snorted derisively.

"What do you advise, Captain?" Mathan said, glancing askance at Elgin.

The captain sighed. "A wise man would make his case before the council and clear his name. In clearing his name, he might call into question the character of his accuser and perhaps thereby save this village the potential ignominy of a generation with Nikko as teshak." He considered the young man before him. "What'll you do, lad?"

"I would certainly like to be the one who saves the village from Nikko, but only the teshak can do that. I'll be teshak the day Nikko volunteers to carry my tools."

"So, then, you're to become my guest here at the Guardhouse Inn, and you'll make restitution to Nikko. I didn't think you had it in you to apologize to him, lad, but I suppose you've learned some humility since yesterday."

"It seems to me I have a third option that you neglected to mention, Captain. I have spoken with you for a dozen years now of my desire to fight with the Western Division against the Dearthmen. As soon as I am free to decide my own path, I will inscribe into the army. I'll make my way to Shallowford and present myself to the inscriptor there. This is my decision. Then, no one will care to try me for striking a fool."

It required only a moment for the Captain to regain his composure. "Such may be your decision, but it occurs to me that Ardal will have a great deal to say on this as on every subject. Truly, lad, you should lay this idea before your dad."

"I'll not allow another to decide this issue for me."

"Sure, I can hear him now. 'No, Bear, you mad child,' he'll say. 'The army has no need for an oaf such as yourself whose fists work faster than his brain.'" Elgin's chuckle developed into a deep belly laugh. When it subsided, he wiped drops of merriment from his eye and stepped around the desk.

Elgin offered Mathan his hand, but then, in one motion, pulled him to his feet and spun him to face the door. "I'll report to the counsel that you are considering submitting to a term of service. They will withhold judgment while you discuss your ideas with Ardal. I'm certain he will have strong opinions on the matter of your potential inscription."

Mathan scoffed heartily. "What does my father know of fighting?"

Elgin laughed until he choked. "Why do you trouble

me with questions whose answers are best known by your own dad?" He wiped a tear from the corner of his eye. "Go home, Bear, I've no need of a clown." He placed a hand between Mathan's shoulder blades and impelled him toward the door.

"Some say you are mad, Elgin – that the wars took more than your eye."

"Perhaps, you great lump, and perhaps I bought something with the loss of that eye. Get out of here before I make you drink more tea." Mathan dodged Elgin's poorly aimed kick and opened the door.

Cian lifted his cup and grinned. Mathan nodded and stepped outside, deciding to take the long way home through the common. He walked around the open space at the center of the village several times while rehearsing the conversation he intended having with his father. By the time he had been around twice, he had begun to put together a strategy he believed would convince his father that his proposed inscription would well serve them all.

He would focus on the good it would bring Taermun for one of its citizens to serve in the High King's army. He would emphasize how Ardal could then be proud that a son of his had risen above his humble beginnings to do great things for the whole land. He would, though, not mention his desire to acquire the skills necessary to hunt the men responsible for his mother's death. By the time he had turned off Market Street into Polecat Alley, he was almost prepared to face his father's sharp inquisition.

Only a few steps into the alleyway and he paused midstride, surprised by the absence of the normal din arising from the smithy at the end of the row. All thoughts of his inscription fled when he realized that the heavy wooden slab doors at the far end of the alley were shut. The building stood strangely silent – and yet stranger still, no smoke rose from the forge.

He could not remember a time when he had entered this alleyway during daylight hours and not seen those doors flung wide open, his father – or, as Mathan called him, his daddo – in full view bludgeoning some piece of red-hot metal into submission. Mathan lifted the latch, pulled open the door and stepped inside, finding the forge cold and his father's tools all neatly arranged, as if they had not been used all morning.

He did not realize he was holding his breath until he released it in relief at hearing his father's voice coming through the door at the back of the workshop. He called out, "Daddo?" as he went to pull open the door to the blacksmith's cottage.

Ardal rose from the table he was sitting at, calling back, "All's well, boy. Quieten yourself and wait for me outside."

Realizing he had interrupted a serious discussion between his father and Cavan, the Teshak of Taermun, also sitting at the table, Mathan feared he knew what they were talking about. He took a deep breath, ready to speak in his own defense, thought better of it and quickly withdrew to the workshop.

The old chieftain's ragged voice, though, followed him: "Come in, boy, this concerns you as well." Mathan slipped back into the room as quietly as his bulk would allow and pulled down a milking stool from its place among the rafters. He sat, a hangdog look on his face as he waited for the axe to fall.

When Mathan was settled, Cavan picked up his thread with Ardal. Noting that the two men spoke of matters concerning the administration of services to the town rather than the administration of justice to local miscreants, Mathan allowed the sound of their voices to dwindle steadily to a drone.

He pursued various half-remembered ideas, meandering through imagined future battles and those ancient ones Sabia had told him about. Mathan's attention had slid well away from the present when he caught a scrap of the conversation. "We came here to escape notice."

Abruptly, the two men rose from the table and moved toward the door into the workshop. Startled, Mathan also rose and held open the door ahead of Cavan.

The man halted before passing through. "I know you must think on it, Ardal, for it is no small matter, but you are the man. We both know the boy is unfit to serve. This recent business," and he inclined his head toward Mathan, "makes that plain. Good afternoon, old friend. May you find wisdom to decide well." Cavan clasped Ardal's forearm with his hand, and Ardal returned the gesture of respect.

Mathan led Cavan through the workshop then held open the outer door for him. Cavan grasped Mathan's upper arm and looked intently into his eyes. "Sometimes, lad, one man standing outweighs a thousand fleeing." He spoke as though the words had immediate import then shambled slowly away. Mathan watched him pause at the end of the alley and peer both ways down Market Street for a long while before turning the corner.

When Mathan went back into the room, Ardal stirred from staring into the cold, dark hearth and asserted that the recent discussion was for the ears of none but those present until he had made a decision. As Mathan had not understood the small bit he had paid any heed to, he was certain he would not disclose anything to anyone.

To his father's manifest relief, Mathan changed the subject. "Daddo, what would you make of Sabia?"

"I don't suppose it's my business to make anything of her, Son."

"What I mean to ask is, 'What is your opinion of her?'"

His father eyed him askance. "It seems fairly apparent that you have your own strong opinions of her. Why do you require mine?" Ardal's demeanor indicated to Mathan that his father did not entirely disapprove of his activities of the previous day.

"You'll want to be careful, lad, that you know why you fight. You've the capacity to do great damage, and the passion to back it, but you've no wisdom to restrain it."

"Yes, Daddo, I know well your thoughts on my temper and on fighting," then he sighed, "and on my lack of wisdom."

He bowed in mock courtly propriety. "What I asked, Sir, was your opinion of Sabia. Some say she's mad, and others that she's a great wise woman. I'd know if I may, O Daddo – great and wise, if she can be trusted."

Ardal snorted in shocked bemusement at his only son's strange choice of words. "Can she be trusted?" He grinned. "Well, there's no doubt about that, I reckon. She can certainly be trusted to do what she will do. She's either far worse than they say or far better than we can imagine. Whichever it is, she's more of it than a man should have to bear.

"Your mother, now, she used to say, 'The Sabia's mind is full of light and her heart is full of truth'. She passed many a strange and interesting evening beneath our roof. Your ma would laugh and cry, and sometimes she'd sit thinkin' so deeply she seemed barely to breathe.

"When we lost your mother, I was a shambles. I couldn't care for you. I couldn't decide which boot to put on first. Sabia came. She bathed you. She fed you. She told you stories – sang you songs. It took months for me to become useful again. One day, she returned to find that I had cooked us a stew, formed a set of terrets for a new breastcollar harness and taken you to the cobbler to be measured for shoes.

She knelt and embraced you, and looking over your shoulder, told me, 'I'll visit when I can, Ardal. This one will stand alone. He will stand when no one else can. Teach him to stand, my brother.'

"After that day, she would visit when I was least prepared to accommodate her, and spend her time telling you stories. This continued until you preferred running the woods with Anyah over sitting with Sabia. When I began to teach you our trade, you had less time for either Anyah or Sabia. Whenever she was in the village, Sabia spoke in the marketplace where she developed a retinue of fools and scoffers, and you apparently developed an aversion to her at that point."

He paused for a moment then spoke in a ragged whisper. "I've seen her break from a crowd in the market to pursue you. Mathan, I've seen you deliberately walk away when she approached you. Why would you do that, Son?"

Mathan glanced at his clasped hands. "I dunno, Da." He flinched. "She mothers me. She questions me about the lads – in front of them! Once, when I was talking with Anyah, Sabia strolled straight up. 'She's a fine girl, Mathan, but you'll walk different paths.' Why would I wait around for her after that?

"Dad, you've seen her standin' out in the streets and shoutin' that 'The wise will become kings and the foolish will fall into a hole' or some other similar nonsense. I love her, Daddo, but it's impossible to have a serious conversation with her. Besides, I *did* stand up for her yesterday."

Ardal heard all his son had said but addressed him on one point only. "What you mean to say, lad, is that it's impossible to have a frivolous conversation with her." Ignoring the comment about standing up for Sabia, he offered his son a loaf of dense, dark bread and a wedge of hard cheese.

Mathan laid the bread and cheese aside, took an earthenware pitcher from the shelf above the table, and stepped out the front door of the cottage into the small garden. He returned with a pitcher of cold, clear water. Stirring the coals, he brought the hearth to life then sliced the loaf onto a wooden platter. He laid the platter on the hearth and sat on the stool with the cheese between his knees. He scraped the softened cheese from the wedge and spread it on a slice of bread until only a sliver remained. He popped the sliver into his mouth then sat at the table with the platter. Through all of this, Ardal had remained seated, clearly transfixed by his own thoughts.

"I'll leave you to think, old da," Mathan almost whispered, "only have a bite while you do."

Ardal nodded his thanks, took a slice of bread and ate silently. Mathan followed suit after he had filled two wooden cups from the pitcher and set one on Ardal's side of the table. The two sat silent and still as stones while each considered his own mind. Finally, Mathan roused himself, left the dishes so as not to rouse Ardal, and, glancing back once, slipped out the door.

In his preoccupation with Sabia, Mathan stubbed a toe on the way through the workshop and scraped his knuckles on the door latch. By the time he had closed the door behind him, he had determined that the one thing he knew about Sabia was that she was bad for his health.

Lumbering down Market Street, he sank more deeply into his Sabia-filled thoughts. He had known her since childhood, but she had shown no signs of aging. His father, though, had a beard that was now mostly gray and hair beginning to match, but Sabia seemed to have grown more winsome as Mathan had matured.

According to the oldest of Taermun's citizens, their grandparents had told them tales of the amaranthine madwoman of the mountain who from time to time had descended into Dunglaun and incited otherwise sane people to pursue strange and appalling destinies. It seemed that Sabia and the fabled madwoman had more than a little in common. Mathan mused a while on the possibility that the two might in fact be one then discarded it as whimsical.

Some had demanded that Cavan banish Sabia from the vale. His only response had been "Not I – not for anything will I consider the vale without her." Then he had shaken his head, chuckling, and muttered, "To think she *could* be banished."

For his part, Mathan could not picture his life without

her. His imagination would take him only as far as visceral reactions rather than as far as solid thoughts. He called to mind that she had told him "I will come to you when you need me". His feet carried him to the common where he assumed his accustomed seat on the third step of its dais. He filled and lit his pipe.

CHAPTER 2
The Calling

"Great necessities call out great virtues."
Abigail Adams

"Stand aside, please." The imperious demand interrupted Mathan's deep musings. He started and looked up at the liveried stranger who waited somewhat impatiently for him to move from the steps where he sat. "Permit me to pass. I am an emissary sent from Maldren Keep."

Mathan's baffled smile provoked the messenger's already chafed fervor even as Mathan stood slowly and stepped aside, gesturing to the steps with his outstretched hand. The courier thanked him – a terse nod – and pushed past, mounting the steps. While all around the common merchants opened their stalls and laid out their wares, the messenger unslung the trumpet that hung diagonally across his back. He blew silently into its mouthpiece to warm it and to prepare his lips to draw sound from it.

When Mathan sat down again, he fell immediately back into that well-rehearsed fantasy of his in which he joined the fabled western division on their most dangerous missions. He passionately desired one day to become a legend in his own right.

The courier again interrupted his reverie when he stooped to ask Mathan for the name of his village. He loudly and carefully enunciated, "My friend, what is the name of this village?"

Mathan rose from his seat. "Welcome to Taermun."

The courier smiled broadly, offered his hand and winced as Mathan grasped his forearm. "I am glad to know you, friend," he said through his wince. "My name is Evan. I am required to present the High King's message once a day for three consecutive days at each place I encounter."

He tugged slightly against Mathan's hold. "Do you intend to keep that?"

Mathan released Evan's now throbbing forearm and grinned. "I'm Mathan," he growled. "Some call me 'Bear'."

"I wonder why. Excuse me a moment while I discharge my duty; then perhaps you would be so good as to show me to decent inn if you have one. Afterwards, I need to meet with any notables of the village. If you would care to join me this evening, we could talk over dinner. The pleasure of paying would be mine, or rather – I should say – the High King's, as it is he who has made provision for my journey."

"Forbid that I should deny him such a pleasure," rumbled Mathan. "Get to work."

"Excellent." Evan grinned. He raised his trumpet and blew a short flourish that drew a number of villagers onto the green. Once they had gathered, he addressed them.

"Dear friends of the worthy village of... um, Taermun, please, hear me. I am Evan, an emissary of the Royal College of Heralds and Couriers, sent with a message from the High King himself." With a flourish, he unrolled a scroll.

"What does the High King look like?" shouted a woman.

Evan's brief gaze failed to find who'd called out, before

he went on to announce, "This message is for all who will receive it."

"He doesn't know what the High King looks like," guffawed a man. Indicating all those present, he demanded, "How are we supposed to believe you've got a message from him when you can't even say what he looks like?"

This left Evan utterly flummoxed. "You must understand, his appearance has no bearing on the content of his message."

"What? You mean the High King of all Tierasal has a message for *me* - for Alistair the wainwright of Taermun? Is his carriage in need of repair? Is the royal carter ill?"

Taken aback that a mere craftsman could be possessed of such insolence, Evan pointedly told him, "I did say the High King sends this message to any who will receive it."

The wainwright made a show of placing his hand on his cheek. "So… it's not actually a message for *me* then?"

"Well, no … not specifically for you personally," stammered Evan.

"If whoever sent you—"

"The High King," insisted Evan.

"Whoever sent you intended you deliver a message to 'any who will receive it' then it ain't for me."

Alistair stalked away, shaking his head and loudly muttering, "Message from the High King. For Taermun. Not likely. What fool would send a message for 'whoever cares to listen'?" The sound of his muttering finally died away as he crossed Gristmill Lane.

Mathan watched as most of Evan's audience followed Alistair's lead. A scant few remained to hear what news had been brought to them from the Keep of Tierasal's remote and sequestered High King.

Mathan's curiosity held him, as did his desire to atone for Alistair's rudeness toward his new friend. He was also deeply compelled by a sense that Evan's message for "any who will receive it" was somehow inexplicably and inextricably linked to the message Sabia had said was for Mathan alone.

The others who stayed included a small group of children, Sabia who stood silently and patiently some dozen steps behind Mathan, and a few others, each of whom Mathan recognized as somewhat dispossessed.

While Mathan scanned the small remnant of the audience, Evan rerolled the parchment, bound a silver ribbon around the scroll and turned to descend the steps.

Mathan blocked his path. "One moment. You've not read us the notice."

Evan gazed levelly at him. "Nobody cares; there's no one here to listen."

"Well, there's a handful of folk here. I don't think all of us together quite equals 'no one'."

Evan shrugged, untied the ribbon, unrolled the parchment, struck a dramatic pose, and in a loud, trained voice, read the open letter from the High King of Tierasal to Mathan, Sabia and the handful of dispossessed villagers:

His Royal Majesty,
High King of Tierasal,
Sovereign Lord of the Bractlands
And
Lord Protector of Arenstock and Calasia
Invites you to come and dine with him
at his seat
In Maldren Keep.
Provision has been made for the journey.

Evan then turned the parchment to display the seal it bore, and added, "Friend, do not delay."

The motley bunch stared at the fine parchment silently then drifted away in several directions.

Only Sabia remained, and although the questions that filled Mathan's heart had not yet formed fully in his mind, she answered them nonetheless with a small smile and an even smaller nod of encouragement before wandering away, barefoot into the gathering dusk.

Incongruously, Evan leapt from the platform and landed beside Mathan, chuckling. "Look at them." He slapped Mathan's shoulder. "It's like they've never heard a royal proclamation."

"We haven't," asserted Mathan quietly. "Come with me. I'll show you to the inn then to the Seat of the Teshak. You owe me dinner … and an apology."

"Apology? Whatever for? I have said nothing untrue, but it does amuse me to think there are those within the realms of the High King who have *never* heard a simple royal proclamation." Evan went to a tall, dappled gelding tied to a post at the edge of the common.

"This particular proclamation has been circulated since before my grandfather was born." He indicated that Mathan should lead the way. "How is it you have never heard it?"

Mathan's stare drew Evan up short. "How is it your grandfather did not bring us this proclamation before, so we might have heard it?" They continued walking. 'Friend, do not delay' you said. If it was published before your grandfather was born, why should I not delay? Does the invitation close at some point?"

"I am uncertain. It is how we are trained to present the message."

"You are 'uncertain'? Then why do you speak?"

"I believe the idea is for you to complete your pilgrimage while you yet live. No man knows the count of his days."

"You 'believe?' Are you not trained in these matters? Is this not your livelihood? If you do not know, who does? You have dined with the High King, have you not? Did you never ask him?"

"Mathan, I think you misunderstand. The High King has his ministers and representatives who entertain his guests. As did my father and his before him, I approached the High King's gate, was met by such a one, and taken to a feasting chamber where my arrival was celebrated.

In Galantamhor, the arrival of a seeker at the High King's gate warrants a great ceremony during which he is sworn into the High King's service and symbolically washed then dressed in the robes of a novitiate of his chosen service."

"Ceremony? I care not for your ceremony. Did you dine with the High King or no? Did you pass through the gates and look him in the eye? Can a man enter his court and speak to him of the grinding and tearing of life?"

Evan seemed embarrassed but also amused by his new friend's unsophisticated outlook. "There are many educated and experienced ministers at the gates who will gladly explain to you their understanding of the various proclamations of the High King."

"Why should I want their understanding explained to me when I may talk with the High King himself? Sheer foolishness."

Evan shook his head. "My friend, you are not to be faulted for your ignorance in matters of the court." He leaned nearer, as though sharing a great secret. "There are those among the most learned who postulate that there might not actually be a High King but that the Primate rules in his stead."

Evan chuckled at Mathan's apparent shock. "Oh, yes. It is conceivable. Is it not? We have the laws laid down by the High King generations ago. He allowed his ministers to maintain the land in his name according to his dictates. When he failed to produce an heir, and his reign ended, the ministers continued in their duties. Is it so abhorrent to consider?"

Mathan halted and indicated the open stable door ahead. Evan fumbled with his kit a moment before he managed to remove it from his tall horse and drop it to the ground. Mathan tossed the kit over his own shoulder.

"Evan, you see the long, two-storey building up against

the hill? That is the inn of Mag Petty. There you will find a room. Finish your business here then meet me there," and he walked off before Evan could say a word.

A while later, Evan strode up the street toward the inn, greeting each person he passed. At the inn, Mathan greeted him with exasperation in his voice. "Next time, I'll let you carry your own kit. Anyway, it's now all stowed in your room, which is locked. Mag has the key. Just to the side of the inn is the Seat of the Teshak. I'll return for your promised dinner at sunset."

Mathan turned on his heel but then immediately turned back. "One last question, Evan. If I were to go to the Keep and meet one of those ministers, would I be made into one of them before I could look the High King in the eye?"

"I believe that is the intention."

"I'll have none of that," said Mathan and strode away.

CHAPTER 3
Provision for the Journey

"Wise men speak because they have something to say; fools because they have to say something."
Plato

Anyah, the innkeeper's daughter, was a formidable woman. She was taller than the average man and bolder than most. Her thick braid was the color of a sand bar in the sun, and her penetrating eyes a cool slate blue. After demolishing his defenses with her modest glance and ready smile, she could impale a man with her intense gaze and eviscerate him with her apt wit. Profound compassion, agile banter and a merry heart, though, more than tempered her imposing presence.

Evan waved the back of his hand and sneered at the voluminous tankard of ale she had offered. "Remove this trough of swill posthaste."

Anyah bristled. "Mister," she plunked the tankard onto the table, "*this* is the finest ale in all of Tierasal."

Evan's derisive snort belied his words. "I am certain, Miss, that you have traveled widely and sampled much, but my preference is for wine – the dryer the better. Please serve it chilled. I thank you for your kind attention. After you return with the wine, you may prepare our dinner. Bring only your finest fare – such as that might be."

Anyah shut her mouth with a snap when she saw the bemused look on Mathan's face. He chuckled and placed his large paw over the tankard in front of Evan when she attempted to remove it. "It'll save you the trouble of bringing me another." Anyah spun on her heel – a fury and a flurry of skirts and tresses – then flounced off to the kitchen, inspiring Mathan to release an explosion of deep laughter.

"You simply must keep these provincials in their place." Evan sighed as Mathan wiped his tearing eyes and reached for the first of his two tankards. "Otherwise, they become unmanageable."

Mathan observed his companion over the rim of his tankard for any sign he had made the comment in jest. After a moment's consideration, though, he realized that Evan had meant exactly what he had said. "We provincials don't appreciate being 'managed'."

"Pardon my effrontery. It was not my intent to insult your neighbors, and I certainly did not intend to classify you with that woman, my friend."

"'That woman' is my best friend … and has been for as long as I can remember."

Mathan's ire clearly left Evan flummoxed. He allowed himself a moment to calm down then asked Evan to tell him about the High King's city.

Evan employed each of his well-honed rhetorical tools to recount the many virtues of the high-minded and liveried worthies who attended to the daily administration of Tierasal from their well-appointed offices within the courts outside the Keep. He described his plans to rise through the ranks to a position of influence in the Royal College of Heralds and Couriers.

As Evan's florid description rambled from the

ornamental furnishings in the office of a certain official to the fine horsemanship of another, Mathan wondered if such things could truly matter to anyone. He suppressed a yawn and interrupted the herald's litany to ask, "Is this the message the High King sends?"

Mathan caricatured the pose he had seen Evan employ and mimicked his voice, "Come to the keep so I may give you an ivory-inlaid desk and teach you to affect a lordly air in the saddle," then opined, "It seems to me a poor cause for him to send you on such an arduous journey."

Evan's only response was to fix Mathan with a look of intense scrutiny that Mathan pointedly returned. Anyah chuckled sardonically, and the spell was broken. The men looked up simultaneously to realize that she was standing close by, holding a tray bearing their meals.

Anyah served Evan with an exaggerated flourish. His eyes followed her hand as she set before him a dainty porcelain plate with scant portions of white bread, broiled fish and steamed vegetables followed by a glass goblet of blush wine.

When she attempted to lay the folded linen napkin beside his plate, Evan pushed back his chair, lifted his hands slightly and looked down at his lap. She tilted her head and raised an eyebrow before dropping the napkin on the floor beside the table.

Evan ignored both the napkin and Anyah and focused his attention on the hearth at the far side of the room, as if the mantle held some fascination for him.

Laughing, Anyah turned to Mathan and plunked down a wooden trencher piled high with roast beef; boiled, spiced potatoes and carrots; and a loaf of dense, dark bread with fresh butter. She caught Mathan's eye, again raised an eyebrow, indicated the messenger with her chin and whispered intently, "What have you got to do with this bit of foppery?"

Mathan opened his mouth to explain, but Evan had shifted his attention to survey the table studiously before protesting, "Miss, you wrong me to prefer my companion with a full, hearty meal while laying before me a morsel barely sufficient to sustain a young girl."

"Sir," she replied in a piquant tone, "you demanded only our 'finest fare'. I had little enough of that, but a bounty of our commonest, which I have now given to your common companion. Besides," she added with a wry grin, "you so whinge, gossip and preen like a young girl that I assumed you'd prefer to eat like one."

Mathan cut a generous portion of his own beef and covered Evan's plate with it then grinned at him. He jerked a thumb at Anyah. "The man – no matter his station – who could 'manage' this 'provincial' would be a king indeed."

He pushed the chair between them away from the table with his foot and gestured for Anyah to take a seat. "Show her the invitation, Evan. She'll be interested in what you have to say ... not, mind you, about the brass door knockers or linen curtains in Galantamhor but certainly about the invitation."

Anyah sat and broke off a bit of the dark bread. Evan removed the scroll from his satchel, unrolled it, struck a theatrical pose – awkward in his seated position – cleared his throat, and began to read dramatically. He stopped when Anyah sniggered. He ceremoniously re-rolled the scroll and reached for his satchel, but then gasped when Anyah snatched the scroll from his hand.

Anyah ignored Evan's imperious look as well as his outstretched hand and settled back into her seat to read, a deep solemnity resting upon her. After she had read it through a few times and studied the seal, she laid the scroll aside.

Evan snatched it up, inspected and rolled it then put it away as if he were hiding a treasure. Through all of this, Anyah stared at the rafters, clearly lost in the enormity of the few words she had read.

Finally, she lowered her gaze to meet Mathan's. "What

do you make of this, Bear?"

"I don't suppose it's my business to make anything of it."

Anyah snorted derisively. "You sound like Ardal." Without raising his eyes, Mathan shrugged.

Anyah touched his elbow. "I need to know if you think this is real."

Mathan reluctantly met her gaze. "I'm goin' to the Keep, but not the now. I've some promises to keep. But when I do go, it'll not be as a supplicant."

"I know, Bear, and I'd see those men suffer horrific pain and humiliation as they die, for what they did to your mother." She laid her arm across his shoulders and spoke in a low, intense voice. "The High King invites us to his home. You could lay your complaint before him. He has vast resources to find and punish your mother's murderers."

Mathan looked up at Anyah. "What if it's hogwash?"

"Does it seem hogwash to you? Can you afford to leave that question unanswered? If the High King himself invites us, can anything be more important than that?"

"Only one thing I can think of," he said morosely, but then raised his voice. "Come with me, Anyah. It'll be like when we were kids running around the Vale, exploring the wood and the Dolewash–"

"Ai, Bear," but she sighed. "I'm no more a warrior than you are a bear. I know you think you must do this, but my life is here. If my way leads me from here, it must lead to the Keep. I too have been laid waste, and know the High King can answer my own affliction…" She glanced at Evan apparently to indicate that she didn't wish to discuss such private matters within earshot of strangers.

Smirking, she teased him. "Besides, I'll not have it said of me that I ran off with the likes of you."

"What sort *would* you run off with?"

"Oh, he'd be half again as tall as you but only half as ugly. He'd have steel in his bones, fire in his heart and silver on his tongue. If you meet him in your travels, direct him here to the inn for a pint."

"I shall bear your duty, Lady." He bowed. "I shall seek your wandering deity and compel him with my vast store of strong words and grappling maneuvers to hie him forthwith to the Inn of Mag Petty in Taermun of the fair Avinn Vale, wherein awaits one mug of fine amber ale and another of fine amber flesh set with cold gray eyes and fitted with a whiplash for a tongue."

"Oh, you're a fine ass to bear such a burden," and she patted his head.

Evan's evident astonishment sent the other two into a fury of loud, deep laughter. "Your conversation confounds me. You speak gravely of absurdities and mock fair truth."

Mathan cocked his head. "Evan, my friend, I *never* mock truth. The fact that I laugh in its presence does not negate my obedience. I have known men who would prostrate themselves in abject humiliation before some idea they called 'true' yet fail to obey it. Which of us mocks?

"Besides, as Daddo often says, 'There's a noteworthy difference between a thing that makes no sense and one that makes no sense to you.'"

Anyah stood at the call of four patrons who had entered the common room. She extended her hand to the herald and smiled sadly at him. "I cannot thank you for coming. Your visit, I'm afraid, will cost us all before long. I will thank you for your service to the High King and for your friendship if I may have it."

"I'm certain I do not understand—"

"Accept her hand and her friendship," Mathan urged. "She offers neither lightly, and each is precious."

Evan stood and took Anyah's hand in a courtly manner, bowed and lightly brushed it with his lips, as though swearing fealty rather than merely accepting an offer of friendship. "Lady, it is an honor." Evan watched her for a moment then laughed, as though, for the first time in his adult life, he had been inundated by a wave of pure merriment.

"She has that effect on people," Mathan told him, grinning as Evan took his seat. "Eat your 'fine fare'. It seems Tigue plans to sing for his supper." Mathan pointed his chin to the far corner of the room where the minstrel sat, tuning his harp.

Evan observed Anyah as she moved through the crowd. Mathan heard him say quietly, "These people are not who I believed them to be."

Mathan got up and went to the kitchen as a couple of dozen patrons trickled through the door in small groups and shouted their greetings to Anyah before finding their seats. A while later, Mathan returned with a foam-topped tankard for his companion, who grinned wryly and lifted it in salute.

Tigue nodded to Alistair, seated nearby, who bellowed, "Hush, lads. It begins."

As the din died away, Tigue strummed a haunting ayre. He repeated the first few notes until silence reigned in the inn. The frenetic miscreant Mathan had met in the alley had been transformed into a bard and a prophet by the process of tuning his small clarsach. Now he gained momentum and anointed his audience with lyrical fire.

Ere the far West sank beneath the restless deep,
Lived a maid whose father, the king, taught her well
How sunlight cascades through the rainfall
And streams of singing water flow ever downhill.

Each night, they'd dance ere she lay down to sleep
The dances of high courtiers and rude folk in the dell;
He'd tell her great tales in which a wise lass
Defeated the scheme of some sniveling shill.

The maiden grew more prudent and dutiful 'til
She was known through the land as the wisest of women.
She taught nobles modesty and the folk to be sage.
She made enemies friends; and friends, she made brothers.

Temperance made her lovely, Wisdom more beautiful still:
An idol for neighboring lords she called kinsmen.
Competing suitors converted ardor into rage
Intoning dire threats against each of the others.

She pressed her advisors to guide her to peace,
But her ministers, captains and counselors failed.
She consulted the shepherd, her father's old friend
Whose apt counsel furnished a plan.

Hearing his proposal, the lady wept with release,
Swallowed her fear and, shuddering, exhaled;
Then, climbed the herd's path to his crude lodge at its end
And hid herself there from the company of Men.

Three princelings stormed the city each demanding her hand.
Our shepherd called out as he closed the garden gate,
"How, lords, can you hope to claim love by your might?"
One prince demanded; one bartered; one pled,

"Where does she hide? With which king? In what land?"
The answer he gave sealed the old herdsman's fate.
"You won't find the Lady though you search day and night."
A moment's sharp violence and the pastor lay dead.

High on her mountain, riven and taciturn,
The wise Queen stood empty
And watched her city burn.

Tigue continued gently to play the remains of the ayre
while the echoes of his words drew an antiphon from the
hearts of his congregation. Not a soul stirred, though all
their souls stirred until the faintest reverberations of the lay
died away. For an eternal moment, breathtaking joy
threatened to shatter each attendant heart.

Alistair woke first from his reverie and decreed that all
should wake with him. "Anyah. A ditty to lighten the

mood. We mean to be merry tonight."

Anyah spoke somberly from the rear of the crowd. "Alistair, I'd sooner feed my mother's cooking to the hogs than to croak a ditty on the heels of that splendid ballad."

Seeing the ire rise in Alistair's face, Mathan rose and jostled his way to the hearth beside Tigue and announced, "Since Anyah must busy herself with serving our bard the meal he's earned, I'll howl for you long enough for him to eat. Perhaps he'll want seconds and sing for us again." The bard's fire took up residence deep inside Mathan.

"Now, this is a rhyme that is meant for a lesson but which to me serves more for a laugh. You see–"

"Shut your noise and sing," came a shout from the dark corner at the rear of the room.

"Both at once, eh? Hmm, I'll attempt your challenge, Madoc, when you prove yourself able both to speak and not sound a fool."

As the roars of laughter died down, Mathan caught Anyah's eye and sobered a bit at what he read there. "My friends, please lend me your ears for a while–"

"I wouldn't lend you a dada, much less my ears." Madoc shouted in an ale-inspired attempt to recover his dignity.

"I vow in the presence of a representative of the High King himself," and he indicated the embarrassed Evan, "that I will return them to you undamaged and only slightly soiled. I am fairly certain, friends, that I can warble nearly as tunefully and twice as loudly as Master Zane's fine tabby tom on a warm summer's eve."

"Not likely, lad," Zane chuckled from his table to one side.

Mathan cleared his throat and began to sing a tune of his own composition in a rich but uncertain baritone.

I sat in the grass
As I watched you go past,
Stumbling beneath your great load.

"My Brother," I said,
And you turned your tired head,
"You're blockin' my view 'cross the road.

"My friend, I'm merry today.
I must sing songs and play;
Lay aside your great burden of sorrow.

"Come, sing your own song.
Perhaps I'll sing along.
If needs be, I'll help you tomorrow."

As Mathan chuckled, Alistair grumbled, "Anyah would have served that tune better."

"Aye, Uncle, maybe she should have served the tune rather than your fourth pint of bitter."

"You will come to ruin, lad, as have better men before you if you don't learn your place and some respect for your elders." Alistair's warning had the force of a threat.

The inn fell into a deep silence as they all sensed the rising tension between Taermun's chief dissident and his malapert nephew. An insistent point of incandescence glowed from the shadowed corner behind the spectators causing Mathan to forget the apt rejoinder that had risen in his mind. He stood, transfixed, as the light resolved itself into the compelling serenity that emanated from the gravely merry mien of a small, plain woman.

Willing his mouth closed, he then pushed his way through the crowd towards Sabia and demanded, "Why are you here?"

"I am here more often than you would think. Do you come here to escape me?" She smiled sadly. "Tigue called me. He and I have not spoken for a while, but I still count him among my friends."

"Step outside with me." She walked out into the late evening, only glancing over her shoulder to smile warmly at the bard. He lifted his glass in salute.

Outside, the relative chill of the night air raised goosebumps on Mathan's arms as the din of the inn gave way to the chirping of crickets. The volume of his own rumbling voice startled him. "I'll only follow so far to hear you speak, Lady."

"Come away a little farther, Love, so I may speak plainly, with no fear of interruption."

Mathan followed her dim silhouette out onto the deserted greensward and up to the dais at its center. The sable sky threw the constellations into sharp relief, each individual star shone like a balefire. Their frigid brilliance pierced Mathan with an almost violent longing for something he could neither name nor describe.

When she had reached the foot of the steps, Sabia rounded on him. "It is time, my love." She spoke quietly, rapidly and intimately. "Set your feet on the path. Go where you've been called. The High King calls you."

"If there is a High King, and if he calls me, such a one would call me to more than gilt brocades and buckled shoes. Anyone who calls himself a High King and calls me to be a mincing ninny is no king for me."

Sabia countered Mathan's impertinence with her silent contempt until he ducked his head. She then spoke over her shoulder as she turned back to the inn. "I was called here by a man who has become wiser than you. I go to him now. When you need me or when you merely want me, seek me. You will find me."

Mathan followed a few paces behind but did not speak. Once back in the inn, he found his comrades, called Evan to join them and together they fell into their cups.

CHAPTER 4
Blood, Fire, and Steel

"...it is a wise father that knows his own child."
<u>The Merchant of Venice</u>
William Shakespeare

Mathan woke to the ringing of Ardal's measured hammer strike. He rolled from his bed and stumbled rapidly to the privy. As he handled his business, a tune ran through his mind. It was a ditty he had heard Tigue sing on occasions when he was only mildly drunk. Pushing open the door with his foot, he emitted a short, loud bark of a laugh, and bellowed the chorus as he stepped down onto the well-worn path to the workshop.

> Don't linger too long in the outhouse
> 'Cause there's creatures that live in the hole.
> HEY.
> When your work there is done,
> Pull your pants up and run
> If you want to be savin' your soul.

He paused on the pathway, threw back his head, spread his arms wide, and drew out the last profound syllable.

Ardal glanced up at Mathan's approach but maintained the rhythm of his swing, showering the floor with molten slag each time he slammed his eight-pound maul into the white-hot, doubled-over bar of steel. Mathan could feel the heat on his face, radiating from the blank Ardal now welded. Mathan leaned back, half sitting on the worktable behind him, and waited for his father to lay aside his work. Instead, the smith continued to hammer the heat from the steel before again shoving it into the coals. He worked the double bellows until the forge fire roared.

Using a pair of long tongs, Ardal pulled the lightly sparking bar from the forge and laid it on the anvil. Indicating that Mathan should take the maul, Ardal sprinkled potash along the bar and held it steady. Mathan folded it in half and pounded along its length until he had welded the two halves into one shorter bar. Ardal reheated it, and they folded the bar four more times then drew it out until it was as wide as a man's wrist and would reach from his elbow to the ground.

While he waited for an opportunity to broach the topic of his intended inscription, Mathan stared into the gouts of flame jetting between the clods of coal at the heart of the forge. The hammer rang on.

Gradually, Mathan became aware of an insistent gnawing in his gut. He managed to slip from the shop to the kitchen door without interrupting Ardal's clanging reverie. Inside the kitchen, he stoked the ingle's coals and added kindling then larger sticks until the heat from the flames became ferocious; then he stepped out the front door with a water bucket in hand.

A quarter of the water he brought back went into the kettle and half of the remainder into the pot. Mathan set the bucket aside and hung the pot and kettle on the trammels of a crane which he then swung over the fire. When the water began to boil, he donned a rawhide glove then swung the crane out and lifted the kettle from the trammel. Placing the kettle on the hearth, he removed the lid, threw in a measure of tea leaves, replaced the lid and left the tea to steep while he turned his attention to the pot. After stirring in two large measures of oats he rotated the crane arm with a flesh fork so the pot hung again over the fire.

Occasionally reaching into the ingle to stir the gruel, Mathan reviewed his strategy for his imminent discussion with his father. Each scenario he imagined ended in some sort of sharp rebuff and left Mathan wondering how he would ever convince Ardal. He needed to make him understand and accept his need to saunter off alone to Shallowford, and thence into the western borderlands as a soldier of the High King.

Mathan had, for years, indulged himself with a profound desire to join the Western Division, to "hunt the monsters" responsible for his mother's death. Standing now on the verge of acting upon it, the idea that he, the lumbering bumbler of Taermun, could serve the High King and wreak justice on the monsters from his nightmares seemed asinine. Ah, well, it wasn't the first asinine thing he had done. It likely would not be the last.

After ladling half the oats into a wooden bowl, Mathan poured the remainder into another then dipped two spoons in turn into a honey crock and stirred each into a bowl of porridge. He placed the two bowls onto a plank the length of his forearm, added the kettle, two crockery mugs and a small earthenware ewer of goat milk and carried them out to the shop in time to hear an explosive hiss and see dense vapor rise as Ardal quenched his steel bar in the nearby trough.

"Ho, Daddo," Mathan bellowed, "lay aside the fruits of your grueling labor and sample the fruits of my own." Ardal left the bar cooling in the trough and turned with a nod to receive a bowl and a mug from his son.

"Milk?" Mathan offered, raising the pitcher.

"A scosh in the cup and two in the bowl, thanks." Ardal extended the vessels to receive the milk then placed them on the table at his side. After stirring the honey into his porridge, he placed the spoon into his mouth to remove the clinging gruel then used it to stir his tea. Returning the spoon to his bowl, Ardal lifted his cup to his lips and blew perfunctorily before sipping the tea.

"I thank you, Son. Perhaps a bit more salt next time."

"What? In the tea?" and Mathan feigned astonishment.

Ardal lowered the spoon before placing it in his mouth, and with a puckish glimmer in his eyes, advised his son, "When you arrive at the inscription office in Shallowford, be sure to entreat for the position of Captain's Fool. You are more than qualified."

Mathan's chuckle was cut short by the realization that his father was well aware of his intent … and that he apparently approved of it.

Clearly noting Mathan's chagrin, Ardal threw him a wry smile. "Do you think I don't *know* you, boy? You're my son." He considered the bar in the trough then set his mug aside and kneeled down. For a moment, Ardal's face displayed intense concentration as he fumbled under the table. Intrigued and confused, Mathan leaned across to get a better view.

Grinning wildly, Ardal rose with a wrapped bundle across his upturned palms. He laid it reverentially on the table. It was narrow and rigid and enveloped in a worn woolen cloth of the multi-colored checks of a tartan. Its length extended beyond the edges of the table.

Mathan stared curiously at it, then at his father who stared raptly at the bundle. After a short pause, Mathan reached to release the thong holding it wrapped, but then stayed his hand.

"You'll not loose that knot, lad," and offered him a shop knife. "Cut it instead. I honed the edge this morning for this very purpose."

Mathan slipped the blade under the thong and slit it

apart. He parted the woolen cloth to reveal a large linen cushion, some four feet long by about one wide. It was embroidered with the emblem of a dead family from a ruined city in a wasted land.

"Daddo?" Mathan looked to Ardal.

"Aye, lad. Yes. I'll make it plain, but first, open it," and Ardal waved his hands at the cushion in his frustration at the delay.

"Open it?"

"Open the... Bah!" and Ardal snatched up the knife from the table and slit the sewn seam nearest him. He opened the cushion as if it were a treasure chest. "There, now," he sighed. "Take it."

Mathan lifted the mass of cotton bandages that filled the linen cushion and began to unwind them. With each layer he removed, his fascination grew until his hands shook so much he had to lay the bundle on the table to finish.

Finally, lying upon the tattered tartan, upon the linen ensign, upon the mass of bandages was an unadorned black leather scabbard with a brass chape and locket. Extending from the locket was a leather-wrapped handle, long enough to allow Mathan a double-handed grasp. A half-moon shaped pommel capped the handle. Between it and the locket, ran a cross-bar that curved down toward the scabbard and tapered to a barb at each end.

Mathan drew a violently shaking hand across his pale, sweating brow and then laid it on the scabbard, taking hold of the handle with his other. He lifted both to eyelevel and yanked them apart. The oiled blade slid easily from its scabbard until the blade tip cleared the chape and rapidly pivoted down in Mathan's hand, striking the tabletop with a dull thud.

"You'll want to be careful with that, lad. If not for the table, you'd have lost a few toes." Ardal appraised his heir and grinned. "Aye, you make a pretty pair, you two — my young son and my old bastard."

Mathan's shock must have been manifest. His jaw worked in a vain attempt to deploy any one of the legions of questions mustering in his mind. He gingerly laid the hilt on the table noting the deep gouge the tip of the blade had left in the table and the gash in the linen and plaid. "Sorry 'bout that," he muttered.

"Think not on it, Son," Ardal said affably, "only don't do it again."

"What's the pattern in it? Why's the steel look this way? Why do you have a sword?" Mathan's mind now stumbled across the most troubling of the questions whirring through his mind like a flock of startled starlings. "Why's the Ensign of Killinchy on the linen?"

Ardal waved his hand before his face palm outward to silence Mathan, then paused, as though taking stock of his son's state of mind, before forging on. "On a day of days, when I was a stripling of a lad and a freshly minted soldier with my eye set on glory—"

"A soldier? You were a soldier?"

"Yeah, I was," replied Ardal inscrutably. "Now, shut it and 'Hearken to my tale', as Tigue would say. And don't look at me in that tone of voice. It's not I who's mad; it's you who's ignorant. Is that so hard to believe?"

Mathan stared dubiously at his now enigmatic father.

"As I believe I was sayin'," Ardal continued, "On a day of days, when I was a stripling of a lad and a freshly minted soldier with my eye set on glory—"

"You've rehearsed this."

"Shut it, boy, or I'll shut it for you." Ardal made an all too evident show of trying to figure out where he had got to in his story. "Ach. I've not the patience for telling this tale. I'll leave it to Sabia. She'll serve it better."

"Da, you were a Soldier and never told me. What did you… Why?"

"Go you now, lad. Your Release will take place this eve. Go you now, and prepare for it. You are maddening thick at times, boy."

Mathan stood for a moment, thinking how to cajole the tale from Ardal then remembered that his father was not a man who could be cajoled, nor bribed or threatened. He grabbed a hatchet and headed to the birch grove to collect deadfall.

CHAPTER 5
Release

"Does anyone dare despise this day of small beginnings?"
Zechariah 4:10 (MSG)

On the steps leading to the dais in the center of the lush greensward at the heart of Taermun sat its keeper – a fair lummox of a man. As he sat, Mathan thought; as he thought, he drew on his clay pipe. The earthy smoke from the red-brown sweetleaf drifted lazily earthward in the torpid evening air.

Mathan glanced over his shoulder to the center of the platform where lay a hearthstone on the flattened summit of the small hillock around which the dais had been built. Since Ardal had dismissed him he had labored to build the bonfire required for his Release. The Release was a simple, ancient ceremony in which the men of the village assembled on the green at sunset to witness the declarations of a father releasing his son and of the son accepting sole responsibility for his own provision, obligations and decisions, as well as the consequences of those decisions.

The men of Taermun drifted into the green from all sides and formed a loose circle on the dais around the hearthstone. Ardal brought forward a small hardwood box and a pair of tongs. Mathan took the tongs and withdrew an ember from the box then used it to light the kindling at the base of the meticulously arranged stack of wood. Before long, the wood began to catch fire.

Alistair broke through the circle on one side and threw a punch in passing that connected with his nephew's sternum and knocked Mathan back a step, then he shouldered his way into the far side of the circle of onlookers. A chuckle ran through the crowd until Cavan, the old Teshak of Taermun, nodded to Mathan's father and intoned, "Begin."

Ardal reached up, placed his right hand on Mathan's head and recited the words of the ancient rite, "I am Ardal, son of Ivor. Before me stands my son, Mathan, known as 'Bear'. He has been instructed in our ways, learned a trade, proven himself industrious, and accepted responsibility for his actions. He will be my staff and support in my dotage."

Cavan stepped forward as Ardal stepped back. He reached up, and Mathan bowed his head to allow the chieftain to touch its crown. Speaking in high, strong, measured tones, the chieftain repeated the question he had posed to each of the assembled men as well as many of their fathers, "Young Mathan, son of Ardal, will you now accept as your right and responsibility the great burdens and blessings of freedom and manhood, to be exercised and defended in life and in death?"

Mathan raised his head, met his father's eye and recited the oath that Ardal had taught him. "With the tools I've been given, in the time I now live, as wisdom guides me, I will endeavor to serve, to strengthen, to build, and to defend my brothers and their families, my village and its people, my land and our ways. I call upon myself the consequences of my own actions and the burden of my own sustenance. I will allow myself to become a burden to no man through my sloth, inattention or cowardice. You are my witnesses."

Sabia appeared from the encircling darkness and averred, "Aye, my love. You are and shall be surrounded always by a great cloud of witnesses." She went on to speak passionately of his "Calling". She told him he would travel far and experience wild adventures in which he would accomplish great feats and suffer much. She did not elucidate beyond that, but the young man had own visions of the great feats he would accomplish. He had dreamed long and thought much of the moment when he would hold in his hands the throats of the men who had sent butchers to kill his mother.

The assembled men maintained a respectful if uneasy silence while Sabia spoke. After she stood to the side with the air of a soldier who had discharged a duty, the men perfunctorily congratulated Mathan and Ardal. Some clapped Mathan on his back and offered a congratulatory handshake, but none remained behind to discuss with him his plans to join the Western Division. None asked him if he had any intent for a certain bright, strong girl. Each meandered home, leaving Mathan behind to tend the fire until only ashes remained.

Ardal clapped his son on the shoulder and looked past him to where Sabia now stood. He nodded to her and then to Mathan. Sabia embraced Ardal as he walked past her on his way home, then she settled in and prepared to pour out to Mathan the tales she had so long withheld from him at his father's request.

They sat in deep silence until the light of the sun began to overtake the balefire. Sabia took a deep breath and released a long, shuddering sigh before turning to Mathan. "Would you hear now the tale of one of the best of men?"

"It would do my heart good, Lady."

"Aye, Bear, that it would, but not in the way you mean." She perched on the top step of the dais, deliberately arranged the folds of her skirt and raised her face to the sunrise while Mathan stood, bemused.

When she lowered her gaze to him, it seemed as though Sabia had just returned from a distant place. She began formally. "I will tell you now of a fierce warrior, a passionate poet, a discerning prophet, a lustral priest and a magnanimous king."

He sat cross-legged at her feet, like he had done as a child, and murmured, "Such great men, this is sure to be a fine tale."

"Hush, Bear, and listen. This is no mere tale; it is the faithful testimony of a scrupulous witness ... and a legend of the truest sort. It recounts some of the more notable deeds of not five men but one, for how can one be called a man if he is not in some measure warrior, poet, prophet, priest and king?"

CHAPTER 6
The Fall of Dunglaun

"You may abandon your body, but you must preserve your honor."
A Book of Five Rings
Miyamoto Musashi

Finnbarr, son of Uvar, Lord of Hebron Heath, came into this world on a night like no other. The cloudless sky loomed profound and vast, legions of stars shone resplendent and keen and the pregnant moon rose buoyant and luxuriant. In the keep of Dunglaun, a temperate breeze ruffled the white lace curtains of Lady Maeve's chamber while lullabies emanated from a harp as the lady labored to bring forth her firstborn son.

Throughout the land, he was lauded, even by some enemies of the realm, as the child who, according to an ancient augur, would grow to bring peace and prosperity to all of Tierasal through the ultimate defeat of the Dearthmen and of the wild Bracties.

He was a beautiful child who thrived on the attention he received. His cleverness astounded his instructors, and his prowess amazed his trainers. He quoted the poets while besting older boys in feats of strength and skill. He saw far and heard distinctly. What he could not claim by skill, he would win by charm. Only his tutor maintained that perhaps he would be well served by learning the value of humility, but her he rather disdained.

He wrote pretty ditties which pleased the young ladies. Then he captured live mice and released them into the parlor while those same ladies took their tea. He tortured his mother by climbing trees and chasing snakes and his father by declaring that one day he'd "tear down the wall to make Dunglaun a friendlier town". Finnbarr, son of Uvar, never encountered fear. He never doubted that his desires were good, his will sufficient or his rights assured to attempt any task or attain any prize.

Upon reading the fine words of poets and the wise, he would build a shrine to them in his mind, but they never entered his heart. He cavalierly spoke those fine words into the ears of others to his own edification and often to their great detriment.

Once, when Finnbarr should have been beside him, Uvar rode with his retinue to face the war-band of Fardorcha, Lord of Carragaener. Finnbarr defied his father and remained behind to entertain himself with a new toy he had found. She was the only child of a lord of the Fair Ones of the North who had come to negotiate treaties with Uvar's trade minister, Lew. Within a few moments of their arrival, Dieterick's daughter had caught Finnbarr's imagination, if not his heart.

Mairyam was her name. Sharpness defined her features, her wit and her tongue. She radiated a compelling energy which enveloped those around her and left them either intrigued or incensed – and often both.

Her agile mind and canny speech piqued young Finnbarr's interest. He mistook her cleverness for wisdom, her presence for beauty, her impudence for courage. He decided rather than discovered who she was, and multitudes have born the price of his fatuity.

While Mairyam trifled with Finnbarr, Dieterick haggled with Lew and Fardorcha wrangled with Uvar. Ultimately, the defenders of Hebron Heath each succumbed to his own respective rival.

When the Hebronite warband appeared silhouetted along the eastern ridge at dawn on the third day, the Warders on the walls of Dunglaun shouted for their captain, Mawnus. He careered across the wide bailey and jostled up the stairs to the gallery, his cuirass unbelted and his sword bare in his hand. Squinted into the rising sun, he minutely analyzed the distant shadows to discern their import.

Lowering his gaze to buckle his cuirass, Mawnus laconically addressed the leader of the first watch. "Agrona, muster the full watch. I want everyone, even the sick, lame and lazy, bearing arms."

"Yes, Captain. And the gates?" Agrona snapped back.

"You've enough to do. I'll handle the gates. Rouse the watch and bring the other watch leaders. I want all three of you here now." Noting the question in her eyes, Mawnus fiercely whispered, "Go!"

Agrona was halfway to the armory by the time Mawnus released his next breath. She exploded through the door in a frenzy that drew curses, then questions and finally action from the Warders working there. "You three, on the wall. Now!"

As they sprinted from the room, Agrona sent the armorer's assistants to the homes of the other two watch leaders, to carry word to muster their crews and meet Mawnus on the east wall above the gate. Agrona pushed past the startled armorer to return to Mawnus.

Ossian intercepted Agrona near the stable master's house, and they reported to Mawnus together on the wall beside the gate. The captain ignored them and continued his instructions to the gate master. "The southern door is bolted fast above and below, Ellar. Throw wide the northern to admit our war band to ride through in column, but prepare to secure it rapidly."

Ellar strode to the gatehouse by way of acknowledging the captain's orders.

Mawnus continued ignoring Ossian and Agrona while he watched the gatemen begin their preparations. When Faelan finally joined them, Agrona stepped before the captain, prepared to speak.

Mawnus forestalled the storm of inquiries brewing in her mind. "Lass, I know the status of *your* positions. Now, be you patient while the lads report." He looked to Ossian.

The evening watch leader gave his report. "Captain, I have thirty able-bodied Warders, including eight tyros, manning assigned positions on the western and northern walls and three injured or ill Warders and five tyros to run arrows and water to the Warders on the wall."

Mawnus nodded and turned to Faelan. "And you?"

Faelan straightened his shoulders and looked his father in the eye. "Captain, the third watch is alerted and preparing. Within a quarter hour, twenty-seven able-bodied Warders, including five tyros, will man the positions on the western and southern walls. On the ground, in support, I'll have four tyros under the charge of Mad Dog. That leaves our lines thin, but we will hold."

Mawnus considered for a moment, then issued orders. "Ossian, take over the right-center position on the western wall from Faelan. Faelan, put Mad Dog in your last post on the southern wall and disperse the tyros among your positions with experienced Warders. Oss, disperse your supply runners to support all three watches. 'Grona, consolidate your entire watch on the eastern wall. Each of you will send a runner to my position in the east gate tower. I will send you further guidance by your runners. Move!"

Mawnus indulged himself a moment's reflection. Agrona was a fierce and intelligent leader, but she lacked foresight and follow-through. The Warders knew her as "Zephyr". Ossian was also intelligent and capable. He always prepared meticulously, but he was often inflexible in execution. To the Warders, he was the "Architect". Faelan lacked the sharp intellect of his comrades and often missed the finer points of any given situation, but he would never be moved once he had taken his stand. The Warders called him "Bastion". The captain knew his watch leaders would stand, fight and lead; he also knew that each would die rather than fail. He hoped their dedication would suffice.

The watch captain's reverie was broken by the arrival of Faelan's runner – a slight, young tyro who showed no sign of having sprinted from the far corner of the town. "Captain," she snapped and sharply nodded in salute.

Mawnus returned the nod. "Aderyn," he replied and resumed his scan of the eastern ridgeline. He missed the flush of pleasure that had colored the tyro's face when he called her by name. "Tell me, lass, what you see out there."

Aderyn flushed again. "Captain, I see only shadows. By the movement of them, though, I would say they are engaged in battle. I cannot say who prevails, but I have a guess."

"Say on, lass."

"Captain, it seems to me they've approached no closer than the eastern ridge, which indicates that our war band holds the attackers at bay for the now."

"Aye, Aderyn, 'for the now', as you say, they hold–"

Ossian's runner tripped on the top stair and fell between the tyro and the captain. Aderyn shouted in surprise and turned in a fighter's crouch, her short blade naked in her hand. The tension left her when Mawnus offered the messenger his hand. "Feargas is it?" The young man nodded.

Mawnus cast a cursory look about him, "And where is the runner I asked of Agrona?"

"Here, Captain." Agrona stepped around an archer who stood watch at an arrow loop. "I had none I could spare, and I was close enough to come myself."

Mawnus raised an eyebrow then succinctly laid out his assessment of the situation. "As you all know, the daughter of Alan the Tall came four days ago to report that her father had been killed and his farm razed by riders from the war band of Fardorcha. Our Uvar kindled his ire and roused his own war band to answer the incursion. They have returned sooner than expected, and in seeming disarray. It appears to me they are presently engaged in an attempt to hold Fardorcha at bay so we may prepare for the coming assault.

"We have roused the Watch and manned the wall. Until we know more, we will watch and stand ready."

He turned to Feargas. "Tell me, lad, what will you tell your watch leader?"

"Captain, you did not tell me to say anything to him."

"Fool!" Aderyn whispered fiercely.

Feargas clenched his fists and flushed, but Mawnus ignored the outburst. "Boy, all that I told you is a message for your watch leader."

The aspiring Warder repeated all that Mawnus had said in exact detail. The captain nodded, impressed, and turned expectantly to Aderyn. "Lass?" It was her turn to look uncomfortable.

"Captain, you said you don't know what is going on, and that we should wait until you do," she stammered.

Mawnus shook his head. "Feargas, you have two minutes to teach Aderyn the message I send to her watch leader." The young man nodded and looked doubtfully at his unwilling pupil. Mawnus laid a hand on his shoulder. "Tell him also that Ellar has shut and secured the northern door of the gate and is set to secure the southern."

"Captain, a rider!" a Warder shouted, stepping away from his post to allow Mawnus a view.

He peered between the battlements into the shadow of the eastern ridge and bellowed toward the approaching hoof beats: "Halt!" but the horseman's pace only increased.

Mawnus signaled to Berach, the bow master, who sent a shaft into the darkness to thud, quivering in the ground mere feet ahead of the advancing rider.

The horse reared, dumping its rider, and fell to its side before staggering to its feet. A moment passed before they heard a high, clear voice in bright humor say, "Master Berach, you have missed your mark, and I thank you most sincerely for it."

"I found my mark well enough, Mistress Eimhir. Are you injured?"

"Alas, yes, but you'll not see the weal," she quipped.

"Cease your banter, lass, and speak the word you carry from Uvar," Mawnus snapped.

"Aye, Captain. It is this: 'I will part my forces, allowing the dark one to pass as far as the wall where you will hold him until I can bring my might to bear upon his rear, so as to crush him upon your anvil with my hammer'." The herald paused. "Do you receive this, Captain?"

"We stand ready and will stand fast."

"Aye, Captain." With lithe grace, Eimhir swung herself into the saddle and turned away from the wall.

Berach called her back. "You can't mean to ride back into that."

The sprightly woman grinned, though unseen by the Warders on the wall. "Can't I, though? And where should I be but beside my king?" With a light tug of the rein, she whirled her mount about and urged him on, back toward the skirmish.

Chagrinned, Berach turned to Mawnus. "Captain, why did you not hold her here?"

"Hold her?" Mawnus scoffed. "Berach, she is my wife, but she is also her own woman. I'll hold her as she wills and bless her as she rides." He peered into the darkness after the fading hoof beats, then called to the gate master, "Secure the gate!"

Ellar signaled a gateman atop the wall who pulled a lever to release the gate's counterweight. The open one of the two massive doors ineluctably swung shut. Gatemen then freed long iron shafts, the diameter of a man's wrist that dropped through the doors into mortices at intervals across the gate's threshold. Finally, thick chains, secured to the walls, were passed through loops on the inside of the doors.

Satisfied that the gates were secure, Mawnus turned his attention again to the striving figures silhouetted on the ridgeline. A short while later, the Hebronite horsemen broke and ran, leaving the attackers a clear path to the city. A hoarse, triumphant cry broke forth from the warband of Fardorcha, and as one, they raced ahead to besiege the city.

Mawnus bellowed over his shoulder. "Warders! Stand to!" and felt the focused response of his company.

The watch leaders reported their readiness. In a clear, level voice, Ossian called out his unit's status. "Second Watch stands ready, Captain."

Agrona half-shrieked her report. "Pity the orphans of the invaders for First Watch stands ready."

"Third Watch stands ready, my Captain." Faelan intoned from the far side of the keep.

As Fardorcha's horsemen thundered along the ridgeline, his infantry charged into the valley while his archers took up positions just below the crest of the ridge. Mawnus bellowed, "Ware, Ossian, cavalry maneuvering north."

"Ho, Captain!" The Watch Leader peered across the undulating plain, clearly alert for any signs of horsemen moving through the wheat fields.

"They must have dismounted. We'll need to burn the crops," he muttered to himself.

His assistant watch leader must have overheard. "What was that, Oss?"

"It's all I can see to do, Cam. They're usin' the wheat to screen their movements while they mass to attack. If we burn the crops, we'll disrupt their movements, delay the attack and deprive them of the element of surprise. Go 'head, Cam. Tell 'em to light the pitch bolts and loose on my command."

Cam shook his head resignedly. "It'll be a hard winter … if we survive the summer." He turned to carry his leader's message but then paused and said, "Lower me outside the wall, Oss. I'll smell 'em out and fire a pitch bolt back into the air to signal their location."

Ossian considered this for a moment. "Nah, Cam. It's brave, no doubt, but futile and foolhardy. Meanwhile, we're wasting precious time. Do it. Do it now. No more palaver, do you hear?"

Cam ran along the wall, shouting, "Make ready pitch bolts!"

Ossian gestured to a tyro nearby. "Spread the word, Malchi," he said, intensely and quietly. "Make ready pitch bolts."

She dropped her crossbow and sprinted along the wall in the other direction, shouting the order.

Ossian shook his head as he chuckled and stooped to recover the weapon. "I'll need to train her to hold onto this … if she survives … if *I* do." He again looked out on the fields.

Faelan walked the wall, encouraging his troops, guffawing in response to a boast from a wiry ginger lad. "Aye, Kyran, we'll each owe you a pint when you've whipped your mob of breachers."

Young Kyran grinned. "They'll not breach it, not in Bastion's sector."

Faelan clapped him on the back and returned his grin. "No, my friend, not so long as Kyran, son of Dublain, stands 'pon it."

Ossian, the architect, was not at all surprised to see a flaming bolt fly skyward from the field where he had told Cam not to go. Cam had clearly found the enemy, and it seemed they had found Cam. He broke from the cover of the wheat, burbling incomprehensibly through his blood-filled mouth and fell at the base of the wall.

"Light and loose!" Ossian shouted, so he could be heard all along the wall.

A cloud of flaming bolts flew into the dry standing wheat. A moment later, another cloud followed. Before long, cries of "Fire!" arose as raiders ran from the field to take cover among the boulders on the ridgeline to the north. Ossian and three of his longbowmen, harassed any invaders who showed themselves until he heard the ringing of Kyran's cry from Faelan's sector. "Ware ladders!"

Ossian ordered his watch to turnabout and direct their bolts and arrows across the common in support of the beleaguered Third Watch. His own shaft soon thudded into the chest of one of four men now pressing Faelan, flipping the attacker over the rampart, to fall outside the wall. Drawing and nocking a fresh arrow, Ossian watched Faelan heft another of the attackers over his head and toss him from the battlements. Ossian chuckled but then watched Faelan fall backwards into the bailey, each arm firmly around the neck of one of his remaining assailants.

Lying beneath them he managed to snap their necks and roll them aside. He stood, but then shuddered and dropped to his knees, pierced by three bolts fired from the bailey behind him.

His father saluted him from the far wall as he toppled onto his side.

Ossian drew his broadsword and shouted, "Second Watch! Tyros on the wall. Maintain vigil. Warders, follow me," and he loped down the steps to the bailey, to stem the tide of foreigners now somehow pouring out from inside the great hall.

His dismay at encountering invaders inside the walls of the town did not hinder Ossian's attack. One man lay maimed and dying at his feet, another stood looking stupidly down at his severed left hand by the time the Warders caught up to their watch leader. With a backhand motion, Ossian slit the man's throat and carried through to block another's descending mace.

Appearing at Ossian's side, Galchovar thrust his blade between the ribs exposed beneath the raised mace. "What is this, Oss? These men are none of Fardorcha's. They are Northerners by the look of them. How did they get into the Hall?"

"Treachery," Ossian grunted and stepped back to allow the corpses to roll down the steps. "These men are the 'trade goods' that filled the wains brought by the northern lord."

"Then we are lost." Galchovar took up the fallen man's mace and hurled it at a rapidly approaching attacker. The man dodged it and advanced.

"Aye, friend, lost and also preserved for we are freed from hope and so from fear. Die well and make them pay for it."

More invaders poured over the wall and into the bailey, then across the common before the Warders halted their advance, but another wave pressed its way along the parapet walk. The head of the first man snapped back as Malchi's bolt pierced his eye. The men behind stumbled over him, two falling into the bailey. The tyros held the wall for eight lifetimes, but then the invaders held northern parapet and used the position to send volleys into the defenders below.

The men of Carragaener who had hidden among the boulders to the north were now no longer under threat from archers, so they mounted and rode to the site of the breach, adding their mass to the attack. Ossian organized the decimated Warders to fight a rear guard action across the town, to the base of the eastern wall where First Watch could support them from above. Meanwhile, the remainder of Third Watch, which had manned the southern wall, came roaring through the town and slammed into the flank of the foreign infantry.

Each warder extracted a toll from the invaders but young Aderyn who faltered at her first kill and so was left squirming and mewling as her innards spilled into the mud.

"Go and fight, fool!" she screeched when a fellow tyro, stopped to attend her. He grimaced and returned to the fray.

Eventually, the defenders came to be crushed between the wall and the invaders, as a ship driven upon the rocks in a gale. Ossian shouted for assistance from Mawnus. Agrona's reply came through her grunts of exertion. "The Captain awaits us in the Great Mead Hall with our fathers, my brother. I will join you there soon."

Ossian turned his attention to earning his own seat at the fabled Table of the Mighty. "Faelan precedes us. Perhaps he will hold our seats," he quipped over his shoulder.

At the base of the wall, Ossian heard Agrona's prolonged belly laugh from above him. "If he holds no place for me, I will perch me upon his spacious lap and there stay until we are called out to the Last Battle. Think on that, if you dare."

Chortling at the image of staid Faelan importuned by aggressive Agrona, Ossian surveyed the mass of invaders for one among them who was worthy of his life. Locating his target, he grabbed the nearest Warder and shouted into his ear while pointing his sword. "That man. Do you see him? The giant with the axe. Him! He must die today. I will have him ere I fall! Take me there."

The Warder, one Tieg, grunted his assent, and never taking his eye from the quarry, shouted for select Warders by name to come to his side. "To me, my friends. Let us die with our brave Ossian."

Tieg and Ossian fought their way through while the others battled to join them. Presently, they assembled around the Watch Leader who quickly explained, "I have seen a man who kills with each blow. Take me, my friends, and introduce me to him."

Drustan stood before Ossian and directed, "Hand on my shoulder, Oss, so I know you're still there." Ossian gripped the Warder's shoulder and raised his naked broadsword in his other hand. The small knot of Warders moved through the invaders like a coracle against the tide. They made little ground that they did not then lose, but the dead piled about them, forcing them to push on to avoid stumbling over the fallen.

Mad Drustan dropped, his head crushed by a cudgel. Ossian lunged forward and skewered his assailant then Faydelm closed the breach, and they again pushed nearer the axe-wielding captain Ossian had chosen.

Faydelm blithely dispatched six men before a spear split her thigh. Groaning, she stumbled. Ossian lifted her to her feet and Brann stepped in to take her from him. He held her fiercely, his tears flowing as freely as her blood. She caressed his lips with her bloodied hand. "You were a good friend."

"I am what you've made me, m'love," Brann insisted. Faydelm swooned and he laid her gently down then waved Ossian forward. "Leave me, for surely I'll not leave her."

The shrinking sortie pressed on. Ossian spared a glance back at wild Brann, still astride his wife's crumpled body, howling his fury and hacking to pieces any who came within reach. When Ossian again looked ahead, it seemed they had come no nearer the axe-wielding invader.

Strangely, he came to them.

The five were sorely pressed now, encircled by fierce men and sharp steel. Each was exhausted, bloodied and athirst. The axeman strode toward them through the mass of striving bodies as a harrow through well-tilled earth. "Ho!" he shouted and held his axe at arm's length, pointing it at Ossian. "Let us test ourselves each 'pon the other."

"That's no hoe, friend. It's an axe, and this," he said, raising his blade in salute, "is the spade with which I will dig your grave."

"I thought to challenge a great warrior, not a great fool," the giant sneered.

Ossian threw his arms wide and his head back. "Can a

man not be both?"

"Come then, we will laugh together." The foreigner gestured Ossian forward with one hand as he raised his axe in the other.

Ossian passed through the protective cordon of his sword-brothers and broke into a sprint. Just as he entered the axe's reach, he sidestepped and switched his sword into his other hand. As he passed his adversary, Ossian chopped at him. The foreigner leapt aside with an alacrity his size belied and swept his axe blindly behind him. It connected with Ossian's sword, swung around to shield his back. The force of the blow knocked the watch leader to the ground, and the invader charged.

Ossian rolled, jumped to his feet, and thrust his blade before him just in time to impale his adversary up to its hilt. Embracing Ossian, the monstrous man crushed him against himself, snapping Ossian's ribs. His eyes popped open, and the hilt that protruded from the giant's belly punctured his own.

The two men tumbled into the muck, writhing together as Ossian's impromptu bodyguard ran past them, now in search of their own worthy ends.

Of all the Watch, Agrona was the last to remain. When all of her fellow Warders lay dead or dying, she knelt, panting, atop the wall, her arms pinioned behind her by two mighty men. Fardorcha himself stood before her, the point of his sword resting in the notch just above her breastbone.

"Do you know," he asked balefully, "why you still breathe? Do you wonder why I stayed my archers' hands when you stood alone? Would you like to know?"

In answer, Agrona rocked back on her toes, marshalling her remaining strength, and thrust herself onto Fardorcha's blade. The triumph that shone in her eyes maddened him. He set upon the men who had held her. "Could you not hold a wee lass?" he screamed while punching and kicking at them. One fell from the wall in his surprise. The other curled into a ball to protect himself while shouting for mercy as the king continued to kick him.

Once his rage had been sated, Fardorcha pointed to the man at his feet, speaking to no one in particular. "See to him. He is a good man." He wiped and sheathed his blade then lifted Agrona and carried her like a child down the steps to the bailey where he laid her across his saddle, then led his beast away.

A sweet, wordless dirge drifted above the destruction, meandering through the moaning wails like an antiphon. A naked ocarina player wandered through the rubble in the misty twilight.

All was lost that day – none of the notables survived the assault against Dunglaun but for the prince, his tutor, Mairyam, and Dieterick. The people who remained were scattered, leaderless and defenseless.

Dieterick took Finnbarr to the North Country and trained him to serve as a paladin in his own house. There Finnbarr and Mairyam were married. Before long, she ceased to enthrall him and began instead to gall him; so, he found reasons to wander afield in service of arms.

Ten years after he had entered Dieterick's house, Finnbarr left Mairyam and their infant daughter there and rode south with a warband of the Northmen under his command. He had sworn to wreak his vengeance on those who had bereft him, beginning with the mad king Fardorcha. In the lands of his father, he turned aside from his fell task to seek what he had lost among the relics of his former life. He found his tutor where he had left her – among the ruins of his old home.

She ran out to meet him, and he near rode her down. Leaping from his mount, he caught her up in his arms, buried his face against her neck, and she christened him with a lavish spate of tears. "Ai, dear Finnbarr, I welcome you home."

He lifted his eyes to hers. "Finnbarr is dead," he

whispered then stood back and addressed her in the formal manner of the Northmen. "I am Fintan. Finnbarr was a fool, so I killed him. I beat him bloody in the grappling pit; I cut him to shreds on the practice glebe; I ran him to ground each morning for years. I laid him low remorselessly for the ignorant cur he was. Now, I stand in his place to pay his debts and to conquer where he crawled. Lady, send me to Fardorcha."

"You know the way, you have the means, and there is much for you to learn there. I will accompany you." She swung up and rode behind him, to call Fardorcha to account.

They thundered along the highway for three days, camping in the open. Neither Fintan nor any of his men displayed any fear of discovery or of resistance. Everywhere, they were met with miserable apathy and abject poverty. These folk scarce had the will to live and certainly none to attack.

After crossing the moors, they crested a rise which, on the far side, dropped away into a vast depression. From the north end of this leaf-shaped basin a glacial river flowed then sundered into myriad streams before rejoining into a single torrent that dropped into a narrow gorge to the southeast. Amid the many streams stood a low plateau upon which Fardorcha's grandfather had built his caer.

It was accessible by only one route – a narrow road built along the ridge of an esker that rose near the gorge wall and wound up from the marsh along the river's edge until it was joined to the face of the plateau by a short timber drawbridge. On either side of this stood a square tower that housed a windlass and was surmounted by a covered archer's nest.

Before they could take it all in, they heard crashing sounds coming from the precipitous slope of undergrowth to one side. Presently, a horse and rider broke from the gorse and rapidly descended away from them.

"Hold!" Fintan commanded laying his hand on the

elbow of the mounted bowman beside him. The archer tracked the fleeing sentry with the tip of his arrow until the man had disappeared into the fold of the next hummock. The archer lowered his bow and released its string's tension before turning a scrutinizing eye on his captain.

"I intend to quarrel with none here save Fardorcha himself." Fintan never lifted his studious gaze from the panorama before him. "Let them warn him. Perhaps he will come forth to face me and so save his people from ruin. If he does, there will be more honor in him than I supposed, but I have no stomach to shoot a fleeing man in the back."

Fintan nudged his mount with his heels and guided him toward the trail the fleeing sentry had taken down to the foot of the decline. The war band followed quietly in file, deftly loosing the keepers on their scabbards.

They descended for a space then dismounted, to lead their mounts where the path narrowed to wind through a broad scree field. Fintan heard the yowl and caught the tawny flash of a catamount as it disappeared among the hillock-sized boulders at the bottom of the defile.

They remounted among the boulders and rode on at a leisurely pace, marking the sentry's progress as he climbed the esker. He never slowed, even as he entered the gates. Fintan shook his head. "He'll lame that beast."

They never made it to the esker. They halted, to watch the gates close behind a small contingent of emerging horsemen who escorted a wain across the bridge. They met the horsemen and their wain in a marshy field below the stony rise. A man, riding beside the wain, hailed them then detached himself from the others and approached. Fintan told his Northmen to remain behind, and rode out, his tutor still mounted behind him, to meet the herald.

They exchanged curt pleasantries, then the herald asked Fintan to state his business before telling him to leave the witch behind.

Fintan was incensed. "This lady is family to me. She

stays with me."

Fintan looked beyond the Herald to the wain. "Come, you old coward. Come and meet your fate. I am Fintan, son of Uvar, come to destroy you."

A wheezing laugh rose from the wain. "Let him pass. What kept you, lad? I expected you long ago."

Fintan dismounted and approached the wain, his tutor following behind him. What they found there was a dissipated, foul smelling lump of a man. He clambered out of the wain, waved a broadsword about and repeatedly accused Fintan of murdering his daughter. Each time he spat an invective, he lunged at Fintan

Fintan circled the old wretch and parried his blows as he would a child's. "I have killed nary a woman, save only the vile witch of Echtmoor, and she was barely a woman and could in no way have been your daughter. Tell me what you mean by this accusation."

Fardorcha lowered the point of his sword and slumped against the wain. "Tell you what you already know? Why do you mock me?" He turned to a man who stood nearby. "Kill him, Odran. Kill him. He murdered your princess and mocks your king. No ... no, merely hold him a moment, for I'll do it myself."

Odran glanced at Fintan and lowered his eyes. "Not so, my lord. This man is here under truce. Do not dishonor yourself, my lord."

Fintan sheathed his blade and nodded at Odran. "Tell me, Fardorcha, how is it you believe I killed your princess? You are the murderer, not I. You razed Dunglaun. I saw you. I killed no one that day ... to my everlasting shame."

Fardorcha drew himself up and spoke haltingly between wheezes. "Years before, your father, Uvar, and I, we fought, Dunglaun and Carragaener. We were beaten. He offered terms. Demanded a hostage. I had only one daughter. He offered to make a pact – trade, protection." The old man was now breathless. "We would wed our two kingdoms through our heirs. You and Agrona were betrothed so we'd have peace between us."

Fintan sucked in his breath. "Agrona? Agrona wanted naught to do with me. She was two years my senior and pursued the attention of older pages – those who excelled with arms. There was one Faelan she favored – a great hulking lad… She would have none of me and joined the watch with Faelan. She was killed when *you* attacked. *You* killed Agrona."

Fardorcha pushed himself away from the wain. "She was to become the queen of the combined kingdom. Instead, Uvar made her a tyro." He descended into a spate of coughing that brought up blood.

Fintan waited for the paroxysm to pass before he laid his charge on the broken king. "Fardorcha, you gave your daughter to Uvar as a hostage, with hopes she and I would rule a combined kingdom. But she did not choose me. The truth is that I was as unworthy of her as she was impatient with me. You deceived Albrecht, king of the Fair in the North, through his emissary Dieterick, and convinced him to help you destroy Dunglaun. Then, when you'd achieved all you wanted, you killed your only daughter with your own hand."

A ragged sob tore loose from deep inside Fardorcha. "Because you were a fool … because you were a wastrel, my daughter and many others better than you died in ignominy. Who do you think you are? Kill me then. I will die at the hands of the man who killed my only child."

"You must do it yourself, for her blood is on your hands rather than mine. I will not kill a sick old madman."

"Your pity wounds deeper than your blade ever might." Fardorcha dissolved into a fit of rattling coughs.

Fintan nodded to Odran. "See to your king. I will trouble him no longer."

And so Fintan remounted and retraced his long journey back to the ruins of Dunglaun, to rally his people to begin again.

In the midst of his labors there, while born down by

the weight of responsibilities and weary beyond belief, his tutor one day came to him with a beaker of cold water in one hand and a folded piece of linen in the other. She bowed slightly from the waist and offered him the beaker and the linen. "Today, dear one, you have become the Lord of Hebron Heath."

Fintan nodded his gratitude and greedily drank the water, then wiped his brow with the linen. He shoved the linen through his belt, handed the beaker to his tutor and returned to his labors.

That evening, Fintan realized that the linen cloth she had given him was the same one on which Maeve herself had embroidered the ensign of Killinchy and that Uvar had carried as a standard into battle on the day he and Dunglaun had fallen. It had been found, laundered and repaired, and now he held it and had been named "Lord of Hebron Heath". He washed the day's sweat and dirt from it then folded it away, wrapped in his family tartan.

He dispatched the Northmen to the house of Dieterick with a message to Mairyam, bidding her come and bring their child to help him rebuild their home.

She sent word back by two of the men that her home was in the house of her father, that she would not have her daughter live in a shack surrounded by swineherds, with a nameless soldier for a father.

Fintan gathered as many of his scattered people as would follow him, and led them westward to find new lands. They passed isolated farmsteads and lonely sheepfolds but no villages. As they traveled, they heard mention of a place where Fintan hoped they could find rest.

West of their ruined city, hidden deep in the fair Avinn Vale and nestled between the outstretched arms of haunted Mount Doleram, the sons of old Dunglaun laid their hearthstones and began to thrive. They came to know their new home as "Taermun", their sanctuary.

CHAPTER 7
The Battle for Hart's Pass

"Cowards are cruel, but the brave love mercy and delight to save."
<u>Fables</u>
John Gay

Two of the Northmen accompanied Fintan to Taermun. Ivor the smith had two sons, but Erdman the wainwright had none. When his older son, Alistair, had come of age, Ivor apprenticed him to Erdman. The younger, Ardal, took to smithing with a passion. The brothers differed in many respects. Alistair had a taste for mutton and an appreciation for good, stout walls. Ardal preferred venison and broad perspectives. Alistair mastered his trade and left Erdman's house to build his own. Ardal mastered his trade and left Ivor's house to wield a sword in the service of the High King.

On a day of days, when he was a stripling of a lad and a freshly minted soldier with his eye set on glory, Ardal was assigned to a small unit at a minor outpost on a high, barren plain reached only by a goat path that crossed through a narrow pass between two mountains on the southern end of the western frontier. It was called, "Stonebreak Pass." Of course, now it has another name.

The endless rotation of patrols and standing watch on the wall left Ardal bored and restless. Since he was a fully apprenticed blacksmith thanks to his father, and a curious lad thanks to his mother, he began to hang about the armory shop. There he found occupation for his hands though his mind often wandered.

By the time he'd been at Stonebreak long enough to begin to believe that boredom would kill him long before an enemy blade, he'd earned his ratings as a blade-smith and as an armorer. Soon, the standard repair of armor and weapons wasn't interesting enough. He began to play with ideas for its improvement. Most of his ideas were useless in the long run, but he learned quite a bit from the process.

Very little happened for a very long time, then a great deal happened in a very short time.

This day of days began early enough, with Cian, Leader of the Thirty of Light Footmen, rousting his men in preparation for a patrol at first light. Their mission was to secure the pass to allow the Thirty of Horse to pass safely through in search of the supply wains they'd been expecting these past three days

Elgin, Thirty Captain of the Light Footmen, inspected his unit then told Cian to send a lad to the gate master, to request he open the gate. Cian sent Ardal who mounted the ladder beside the gate and, in the gray dawn light, made for the gate master's lookout.

As he walked the wall and looked out across the plain, he imagined that he saw dark shapes darting about in the thick mist. 'We're bein' watched,' said Moreley the lookout. As though his words had conjured them, they appeared, whooping and leaping through the mists like foul spirits come to take the defenders' souls rather than just men intent on slicing them open. Something flew past Ardal and ripped out Moreley's throat.

Ardal jumped from the wall and hit the ground rolling

in front of Cian who was on his way up. Cian pulled Ardal to his feet, shoved him toward the ladder and shouted for him to climb.

It was fortunate for all on the post that the invaders struck when they did, with a third of the strength of the caer on the wall and another third standing ready to fight. If they had assaulted after the gates had been opened for the patrol, it would have been the worse for all of Tierasal.

After three days' chaos and pain, the Dearthmen pulled back into the high ground surrounding the plain and shouted threats and taunts at the defenders, hoping to draw them out from behind their walls. What they didn't expect was that they would come out in the way they did.

Cian sent word to Ardal through Ekurn, his Ten Leader, that he was to meet Thirty Captain Elgin outside the Hundred Captain's Seat. He ran by the horse trough to wash his face on the way. When he arrived, he found Elgin leaning against the corner of the Seat, his helmet under his arm, tapping the toe of his boot against the ground.

Ardal jogged over to his Thirty Captain and nodded sharply in salute. Elgin returned the nod. "Your Ten Leader claims you can write and accuses you of being smarter than you seem."

Ardal acknowledged that he could write, at any rate, and asked how he might be of service. His Captain asked if he'd be willing to take notes for a meeting of the captains so they could focus on developing a strategy. Ardal said he'd do his best, and they went in together. Elgin pulled out a chair and told Ardal to sit down. He left for a few minutes and returned with some writing supplies and a cup of tea.

The Hundred Captain, Elgin's commander, came in a few minutes later, trailing his orderly. "Initiate final inspection on Horse as soon as they are assembled. I will be out shortly to conduct spot checks." The orderly nodded curtly and almost smashed down the door on his way out.

Hundred Captain Hart scanned the room, taking the measure of each man. Each Thirty Captain or, in this context, each 'Thirty' sat at the table except for Elgin who stood behind Ardal. When Hart's eye met Ardal's, he nodded then raised his gaze to engage Elgin behind him. Then he took in the Gatemaster, the Armorer, and the Quartermaster who had also attended. "Welcome, Swordbrothers. Begin."

Each of the assembled leaders reported his unit's or section's situation in as few words as possible. Beginning with the Horse Thirty, then the Heavy Footmen Thirty, and finally the Light Footmen Thirty, they rapidly and clearly informed all present of their strength, capabilities and any issues which might interfere with their ability to fight. It became apparent that the seemingly informal meeting was conducted according to an established protocol. Ardal recorded everything even when it seemed unimportant.

Upon receiving all the reports, Hart waited for Ardal to complete the sentence he was writing. "Check on your Thirties. Meet back here in half an hour, prepared to brief changes and to receive orders." The meeting rapidly dispersed.

Hart looked at Ardal then at Elgin while he addressed Ardal. "Give me your notes, and bring us some tea." Elgin nodded curtly, signifying that he understood Hart's intent that he leave Ardal with him. Elgin turned on his heel and strode out to meet Cian while Ardal went to see the cooks.

When Ardal returned, he set Hart's tea on the table within his reach then walked to the far side of the room to take his seat. "Footman," Hart said quietly without looking up from Ardal's notes.

"Hundred Captain?" Ardal stood up straight and rigid.

"Your handwriting is atrocious."

"I offer my apologies, Captain."

"Your observations, however, are excellent."

"I offer my thanks, Captain." Ardal nodded.

"No, no. I thank you. Relax. It will be your last chance for a while."

"Yes, Captain." Ardal returned to his chair.

The Hundred sat intent on Ardal's notes and on his own thoughts for a long while. Occasionally, he added notes of his own. Then, without lifting his eyes from the pages, he asked in a distracted tone, "Your name, soldier?"

"Ardal, my captain," he replied, adding, "of the Avinn Vale," as though it would matter to him. The Hundred nodded, made notes, and continued reading. The room began to fill again, and Hart sent Ardal to find more paper so he could continue taking notes.

The assembled leaders went through a rapid version of the previous meeting, merely updating the previous reports. When it came to Elgin's turn, he reported, "No change, except that one of my best sword arms now serves a pen."

A chuckle went round the room, and Ardal's face turned red. Hart smiled. "Happens to the best of us, Elgin. Won't be long before you occupy your own Seat and see more paper than any decent man should ever see."

Glendon, Captain of the Mounted Thirty, appeared shocked. "Did the Captain just call Elgin a 'decent man'?"

Hugh, Thirty Captain of Heavy Footmen, shook his head. "That can't be right. Have the scribe read it back."

Ardal took a deep breath but Elgin cut him short. "I curse the day you see me behind a desk, Captain."

The Hundred replied levelly, "Elgin, you curse every day."

Raucous laughter broke out and shattered the severity that had previously pervaded the room, then the leaders settled into their business. Hart stated the situation clearly for his Captains of Thirty. "Gentlemen and Elgin, I am not lying when I say that today will be rife with opportunities for you and your men to earn everlasting glory. The Dearthmen hold the pass. We are near a week past the anticipated arrival of our supplies. I expect no one to come this way from the Three Hundred until they realize - in another day or so - that their supply wains haven't returned to them. Were we to wait on them, none would remain to tell how the rest of us earned everlasting glory.

"Now, we might hope that the supply trains turned back and so returned with word of the Dearthmen in the pass. In that case, we could expect help at any moment. There's a problem with this plan, however, and that is—"

"Hope is not a method,' quoted the Thirties in unison, like schoolboys. Apparently, it was something they had heard the Hundred say on more than a few occasions.

Hart nodded. "Right, but there are methods we might employ based on the likely assumption that we are on our own for a while longer. I believe our best option lies in a rapid, aggressive assault coupled with an effective deception plan supported by archery from the battlements. The problem with this idea is that there is no flexibility. We have no reserve force. We do it once; we do it rapidly; we do it right, or we fail and earn everlasting glory.

"Horse will ride out at a full gallop." He looked at Glendon, Captain of the Mounted Thirty. "You must give every indication that your only thought is to escape the pass and go for reinforcements."

Hart fixed Glendon with his intense gaze. "Glen, I am well aware that the restricted terrain within the pass will not allow you to maintain a gallop once you cross the plain. You will fly out of the gates, headed straight for the trailhead, enter the pass and move as rapidly as you can down the trail without allowing the enemy to draw you into a fight. Just move, move, move. This is our deception plan."

He held Glendon's eye until he received an acknowledging nod.

"The purpose of the deception is to draw them into the open so we can slaughter them. A smoke arrow will signal you to turn like the tide and smash the enemy repeatedly against the rock formed by the phalanx of the Heavy

Thirty.

"They will pursue Horse with the majority of their force, leaving the rest behind to watch the post. As Horse departs the caer, Elgin, you rope down the southeast corner of the battlements and use the streambed to cover your movement. From there, move rapidly into the surrounding high ground. Your purpose is to locate the enemy commander and his support personnel who will likely be among the stay-behind force.

"You must destroy their leadership as rapidly as possible. Once that is done, they cannot long sustain the attack. Until this is accomplished, yours is the primary mission. A smoke arrow will signal mission accomplished. Fire it as you fight your way down to join us on the plain."

Hart addressed the Captain of the Thirty of Heavy Foot. "Hugh Mor, I have this insane notion that you might form your unit into a new terrain feature in the center of the plain, against which Horse may drive the enemy, there to crush them repeatedly until naught is left of them but the stench of their fear."

"Aye, Captain, it does seem the mission we were made for. We'll head out when Horse enters the pass, yeah?"

"That's it." Hart's grim satisfaction was evident in his tight smile and terse nod. "Though you may be buried in bodies and drowned in blood, you must not move. Fix the enemy in the center of the plain to allow Horse to maneuver against them repeatedly. You grab them by the throat and Light will decapitate them, then Horse will smash them to bits. All hinges on you."

"We will stand, Captain." Hugh spoke simply, as though informing the Hundred of his intention to take a walk.

"That, gentlemen, is the plan." Hart looked around the room and received nods of understanding from all.

"I will ride with Horse if they will have me." He glanced toward Glendon.

The Horseman nodded curtly. "My honor, Captain."

Certain now that the captains of his fighting units understood their missions, Hart instructed the leaders of the support sections to harry the enemy from the battlements and to stand ready to open the gates of the caer if necessary.

"Any questions, lads?" Hart met the eye of each man in turn, then dismissed them. "Go in the strength of your brothers and quit you like men. I will meet you on the plain or in eternal glory. Horse rides within the half hour."

The leaders rose to rejoin their units, and the Hundred stretched out his hand. "Ardal of the Avinn Vale." Ardal placed his notes into the Hundred's hand. Hart thanked him, laid the notes on the table and extended his hand again. Ardal grasped his forearm and the Captain reciprocated. "Ardal, it is my honor to fight alongside you, brother."

"The honor, Captain, is all mine." The next time he would see Hart, Ardal would discover what honor really looked like.

Ardal's notes from that meeting, as well as his observations of what followed, were later submitted to the historic record of what was to become known as "The Battle for Hart's Pass".

Ardal soon watched Horse ride out, then roped down from the battlements with Light. They separated into Tens and moved through the high ground, hunting the enemy commander's Seat, hidden among the rocks and draws. Elgin moved with Ekurn, Ardal's Ten Leader, as they picked their way through gorse, stones and defiles toward the point of convergence for the Tens' designated search patterns. Elgin had previously identified a particular high meadow as the most likely location for an encampment. A field of springs filled a small pool that ran off to a waterfall at its lower end. Rather than approach from the lightly wooded gentle southern slope, Elgin led his sword-brothers to climb the narrow, treacherous defile under the waterfall to the east of the meadow.

As he reached the top of the climb, Elgin quietly slipped behind a sentry who had been posted there to watch the southern approach. He caught the man from behind and hefted him over the waterfall. Ardal watched the Dearthman bounce down the ravine then he climbed quickly into the fray. He rushed an approaching Dearthman, sliced him open and left him squirming and screaming.

Elgin called out for his men to join him. "Light. To me." Ekurn impelled Ardal with a shove to follow Elgin. As they arrived in the center of the camp, a foeman crushed Cian's thigh with a steel-bound cudgel. With his claymore, Elgin removed the man's forearms before pursuing the fleeing enemy captain.

Ardal broke clear of the skirmish and ran to the rear of the camp where the horses were tethered. There, he found the enemy commander cutting one free of its tether. Ardal ran toward him, as he shouted for Elgin.

The enemy commander mounted, so Ardal was able only to tickle the man's ribs with his broadsword. If he had held a longsword instead, the commander would have been done for. The Dearthman kicked him in the chest. Ardal hit the ground hard, scrambling out of the way as Elgin pulled the horse down by its bridle. The rider rolled free and Ardal kicked him hard in the head.

Three enemy soldiers came to their commander's aid. Elgin ran toward them, shouting over his shoulder, "Do him." Ardal slid his blade in between his adversary's ribs and twisted it. The Dearthman spasmed wildly, a gout of blood shooting from his mouth. Ardal ran to assist Elgin.

By the time he had run the twenty yards to where Elgin stood against three men, one was already retching, holding his innards in his hands. A second was sitting on the ground, moaning and watching the blood pump rhythmically from the stump of his leg. Elgin trembled violently as he pressed his hand over the gory side of his face, attempting to hold the third attacker at bay with his broken claymore. Ardal ran screaming at the attacker who then broke and ran directly onto the pike of Ten Leader Hai who had come up behind him. Elgin fell to his knees.

Ardal knelt beside him. The man was apparently mad with pain given that his words seemed to make no sense. "Take to heart the head."

"Calm yourself, Captain—"

Elgin slapped him hard and gasped, "Take … the head … to Hart," and he indicated the corpse of the enemy commander.

"Aye, Captain, with a will."

Hai knelt beside Elgin and tried to pull his hand away from his face. Elgin slapped Hai's hand away then poked him in the chest with his finger. "Hai. Thirty Captain. Leave two for wounded. Take horses. Ride to fight." He blanched and shuddered then reared back to fix Hai with his remaining eye. "Don't look at me. Go."

By this time Ardal was mounting the enemy commander's horse, his naked blade in one hand, the topknot of the severed head in the other, and the reins in his teeth. He rode hard toward the plain, guiding the horse with his knees. The signal arrow rose up from behind him and passed over his head, as if guiding him to the fight.

He heard the battleclash long before he saw aught. He rode to outstrip the wind before and so the wind behind could not catch him. As he broke from the woodline and out into the open valley floor, he oriented on Heavy Foot's phalanx near the center of the plain.

The Dearthman war band's fore was sore beset by Horse while Heavy mangled their flanks and rear. Ardal rode directly for Horse, shouting for Hart.

Drawing nearer still, he could now recognize individual soldiers and their feats. Each strove mightily, goaded by Hart's audacity. Repeatedly, he drove in, wrecked men, withdrew, whirled, and drove in again. He was a beautiful horror.

Finally, above the din, Hart heard Ardal call his name.

Breaking free of the mob, Hart rode to meet him, drawing alongside so Ardal could have touched his mount's heaving flank. Ardal displayed his loathsome offering.

The Captain grimaced and shuddered as he leaned across to inspect the head of his enemy. Noting his pallor and that he bled freely from numerous gashes, Ardal realized that what he had taken for revulsion had instead been a disciplined response to grievous pain.

"Well done, Ardal of the Avinn Vale. Much earlier than expected. I did not note your signal arrow fly, though. Hold the head securely."

Ardal laid his blade across his lap so he could hold the head in both hands. Hart drove his spear point beneath the chin and up into the head so it was now firmly impaled at an angle of submission.

Hart handed Ardal the shaft and indicated he should follow before he whirled his mount and charged back into the fray. Taking up his sword and lifting the speared head aloft, Ardal followed closely but with no idea of his commander's intent.

Hart drew up on the edge of the fight and indicated to Ardal that he should hold his trophy high. Ardal stood in his stirrups and, grasping the butt, lifted the spear high above his head then rode twice around the writhing mass, screaming for them to look upon him. The Tierasalan captains and leaders took notice and drew their troops into a cordon about the invaders while the Dearthmen pointed at Ardal and shouted unintelligibly.

By the time Ardal had returned to Hart's side, an uneasy truce reigned on the field. He lowered the spear butt to rest on the toe of his boot, the severed head on a level with Ardal's, the shaft below the head now heavily encased in congealed gore.

"Who speaks for the Dearthmen?" Hart wheezed at Ardal.

"Captain, I can't know that."

"You can if you ask them." Ardal found that if he

listened closely he could just make out Hart's words. "Ardal, speak for me. My voice is gone."

"Even then, Ardal did not realize how dire Hart's condition must have been. "Aye, Captain. I will relay your words."

"Nay, Ardal, use your own. Show them that their commander is dead. Offer them food and drink, rest and shelter if they will lay down their arms and come to the caer."

The import of his message struck Ardal dumb. He wracked his mind for words to end the killing. Hart urged him on. "Ardal, you have their ears. Use them before they begin swinging blades from boredom."

Ardal nodded and raised his voice. "Dearthmen, who speaks for you?"

A high voice from within the crowd replied half-heartedly, "He is dead."

"Then come forward and represent your brothers." Ardal searched the crowd for the man who had spoken.

"These pigs are not my brothers." The man laughed then swore. "Do not look shocked. They would say the same of me."

Ardal located the speaker and settled his gaze on him. "I am sorry to hear it. You do not strike me as a pig."

The speaker shrugged. "What do you want?"

Ardal lifted his voice along with the spiked head to ensure that all could see and hear even if they could not understand. "My Captain offers you your lives in return for your weapons. What does your Captain offer?"

The man raised his voice and addressed the Dearthmen in their native tongue. A heated debate ensued. It raged until, prompted by a gesture from Hart, Ardal shouted, "Decide."

The spokesman shrugged and addressed his response to Hundred Captain Hart. "I for one am willing to become your slave if it means I might live. Who knows? Perhaps my new master will be gracious to me. Some others agree

with me. Still others ask if they might not return home."
He scoffed. "Others yet have threatened to kill any and all
who lay down their arms. I, as I have said, know I will be a
slave in whichever country I live and gratefully accept your
offer." He looked warily about at the Dearthmen around
him.

Ardal spoke again for Hart. "There will be no slaves."

The spokesman bowed his head and cursed vehemently
in his own language, but then raised his head enough to
glower from beneath his brows at Hart. "So, you will
execute us." He spat the accusation as though it poisoned
him.

"Nothing of that." His misunderstanding had shocked
Ardal. "We will take your arms not your lives or your
bodies. We are free men and have no use for those who
are not."

"Hostages for a while." Hart grunted wanly, and Ardal
nodded.

"All who lay down their weapons will be conducted to
the caer as our guests and as surety against another attack
by your countrymen. Any man who does not, today, lay
down his arms will himself be laid low."

The spokesman relayed Ardal's words to the
Dearthmen. A great racket ensued. Ardal allowed the
discussion to continue until it seemed it might come to
blows among them, then he shouted for calm.

"Any who choose to live may come and stand to my
left where a contingent of our soldiers will accept your
weapons and conduct you in safety to the caer. All who
choose otherwise will be cut down where they stand."

The Dearthman warband began to unravel, and the
newly arrived Light Thirty, mounted on their recently
acquired horses, dismounted to receive weapons. Ardal
turned to observe and pulled alongside Hart, to request
further guidance. The man sat upright and rigid, staring at
his mount's ears, his mouth slightly open.

"Ardal gestured to Glendon, the Captain of Horse,

who drew near and inclined his head, as though to hear his commander's words. He glanced up at Ardal from under his brows. "He's dead, you know."

Ardal nodded. "Yes, Captain. How do we return him to the caer and keep this knowledge from spreading?"

Glendon considered for a moment. "Leave it to me, Footman. Next chance, you'll have a dram on me." He clapped his hand on Ardal's shoulder then rode off to confer with his Thirty Leader.

A few minutes later, a Ten of Horse approached. Gerritt, the Ten Leader, casually walked his horse alongside the captain's, so the toe of his own boot extended through his stirrup and connected with the heel of the captain's boot. Another mounted soldier did likewise on the other side. Two others galloped back to the caer, to prepare for his arrival. The six remaining horsemen rode three before and three aft of the captain, like the personal guard he had never before required.

All the while, as they walked their horses back to the caer, Gerritt carried on an animated discussion with their dead captain, thereby maintaining the illusion of strength he had established. All in all, it was rather nicely done.

Ardal turned back to the field to find that nearly all of the Dearthmen had surrendered to Light and were being herded toward the caer. His soul welled up inside him at the wisdom of the fallen captain who had turned their doom on its head. Meanwhile, a small knot of Dearthmen had formed a tight perimeter, bristling with blades. Heavy Foot and Horse had surrounded them, but they remained at a stalemate.

Ardal rode to the head of the ragged column making its way to the caer, then back down it, looking at their faces. When he found the spokesman, Ardal drew him out and up onto his horse and rode hard for Heavy. On the way, Ardal asked the interpreter why some held out.

"They are stupid animals."

"They are men just as you are a man. Are you not all

Dearthmen?"

The man scoffed then spat. "They call me their slave, yet they haven't the wits to recognize how that word applies to them."

Ardal turned in the saddle to see the man more clearly, but they had already arrived at the standoff. "What sort of man are you, then?"

"I was 'Partlan,' a free man and scholar of The Bractlands. That was before I became 'Boom – the Owl', a slave with too many questions according to my master."

"Partlan, you are your only master now. I hope to talk more with you soon. For now, though, we have work to do."

"Aye, Captain, with a will." Partlan said like a true Tierasalan.

They dismounted, and Ardal looked into Partlan's clear blue eyes and explained that he was no captain but the least and poorest of the High King's soldiers. Partlan stared back doubtfully. Ardal clapped him on the shoulder. "Come, my friend, we must end this travesty if we can."

Ardal jogged quickly with the impaled head, his bloody blade and his disarmed enemy to Hugh, the Thirty Captain of Heavy Foot, and spoke his name. Without lifting his gaze from his trapped quarry, Hugh Mor told Ardal to name his errand.

"It is three-fold, Captain. First, Hundred Captain Hart is dead."

Hugh scoffed. "I saw him ride to the caer."

"A ruse, Captain. I was there. Glendon, Captain of Horse, arranged to remove him from the field without revealing he had fallen."

"A wise ruse." Hugh nodded but never looking away from the duty before him.

"As for my second errand, Captain, it is to ask your leave to dispose of this repugnant thing." Ardal moved the spiked head into his field of view and noted the revulsion on Hugh's face.

"And why would you trouble me with such a bothersome thing?"

"Forgive me, Captain, but it seems to me that in the current situation you must become our acting Hundred Captain."

Hugh nodded. "Perhaps, but, as you see, I am otherwise engaged. Elgin will do for the now."

"He is currently unavailable, Captain."

"Ah, worse and worse." Hugh spared a glance at Ardal's face. "I suppose you saw that happen as well?"

Ardal winced but spoke plainly. "I did, Captain. His face was ruined."

"His face, eh? No great loss then." Hugh Mor sighed.

Bitter regret crept into Ardal's voice as he explained that Elgin had held off three men while he had fiddled with killing one.

The Captain nodded in commiseration. "Go ye back to your sword-brothers, lad, and do your duty by them."

"Aye, Captain, only let me discharge my third duty here." Ardal noted that the soldiers of Hart's Hundred who remained on the field had gathered in a loose perimeter around the tight one of the Heavy Thirty, to observe and support if the need arose.

"Do so and leave me to dispatch these stalwart foemen." The Captain returned his baleful gaze to their recalcitrant adversaries.

"I have brought you Partlan the Bractie to assist in your negotiations for their surrender."

"Hart has already offered them their options. They have chosen. We will now execute them. Take your Bractie to the caer with the others," he said through clenched teeth.

A moment later, Hugh sighed and relented somewhat. "Truth, lad. I have no heart to murder such men. Gladly did I face them in battle, but the battle is ended and they are but desperate men who must lose their lives or their honor. I would do the same if I stood where they do."

Ardal considered the situation for a moment. "Hundred Captain, may I have your leave to negotiate with the foemen an honorable path to life for them?"

Hugh flicked an incredulous look at Ardal. "You might try. You'll no doubt fail, but you might try nonetheless. It'd be a boon to at least make the attempt. What'll you say to them, I wonder."

"I am uncertain, but I've an idea that Partlan will be useful. I'll draw their leader here so you may overhear the discussion and offer your guidance."

Hugh pressed his lips firmly together and nodded. "Aye, lad. Do it, but first, give me your name."

"Ardal, Captain, of the Avinn Vale.'

Hugh thought for a moment. "Not a place I've heard of, but I will know it hereafter. Put your Bractie to it, Ardal. Find me a way through this."

"Aye, Captain." Ardal turned to Partlan. "Call their leader forward."

The former slave stepped forward and raised his voice. Ardal intently studied the response of the Dearthmen and noted that many glanced toward a grizzled man who stood on the edge of their group. He returned their glances furtively.

A young man in the center spoke up, and Partlan translated: "And why should we allow you to butcher our chief when you should face us instead, blade to blade?"

Ardal stepped forward, thrust his blade into the soil, raised his hands and turned about to show that he intended no treachery. Slowly, he walked to the grizzled man he had observed communicating wordlessly with his men. Partlan followed him.

Ardal again turned about to show he bore no weapons, and then looked the man in the eye, extending his hand. After a long pause, the invader switched his sword to his other hand and tentatively grasped Ardal's. He raised and lowered it slightly a few times holding Ardal's gaze all the while. When he released Ardal's hand, Ardal grasped his forearm in proper greeting. The Dearthman leader returned the gesture before Ardal finally stepped back.

The leader spoke, and Partlan translated. "This is a respite for parley, yes?"

Ardal agreed. "Only you and I will be unarmed. Neither will surrender his weapon; both will leave them behind."

The enemy chieftain turned to address his soldiers. At his words, they looked about, then, one by one, stood down.

Partlan and the man spoke, then the man handed his sword to someone behind him and displayed his empty hands, turning about as Ardal had done. He looked into Ardal's face and made a sound he did not understand, something like a cough. Ardal looked quizzically at his translator. Partlan explained: "It's his name – Kaff."

"What does it mean?"

Partlan sneered. "What does your name mean? It's just the sound someone makes when they want his attention."

Ardal explained: "In my home, our parents give us names with meanings they hope we'll live up to."

Partlan nodded. "In my home as well, but his parents did not give him this name; his master did. It is, I suppose, because his face is as dark as the black drink that the Dearthmen favor. It is known as 'kaff'."

Ardal urged the enemy chieftain and the liberated slave to walk with him to a position midway between the lines and directly before Hugh. Once there, he gestured to Kaff who began to talk loudly enough that the men behind him could hear. Partlan focused on him for a long while, nodding occasionally. He spoke twice to Kaff who gave a lengthy response each time. Ardal listened intently but understood nothing.

After what seemed an eternity, Partlan turned to Ardal. "First, they will not surrender. Second, they will die first. Third, you cannot take their weapons from them." The translator paused, clearly expectant of a response.

Ardal considered for a while. "Is that all he said? You two talked quite a while. There must have been more."

Partlan sighed and shrugged, holding his palms up. "He is a Dearthman. They are prone to flowery prose when a simple 'yes' or 'no' would suffice. There was, however, something else, but it was mostly nonsense, talking in circles. He said they were sworn to the death to serve their master, who is now dead, and you seem to be the man who killed him. I believe he might be indicating that they will die before they surrender—"

"Aye, Partie, I believe I got that bit," Ardal fumed.

Partlan repeated the words pedantically. "I believe he might be indicating that they will die before they surrender, but there might be another way. They took an oath that imperils the spirits of their families. The oath was to serve their master or his successor unto death. He did note, however, based upon the evidence you carry, that their master is now dead and without an appointed successor."

Ardal looked over his shoulder at where the Captain stood listening. "Captain? What shall I say here?"

"So, they keep their lives, their arms and their honor by transferring the onus of their oath to a new master?" The Captain screwed his face up for a long while and then finally said, "Tell them I accept, and let's get back to the caer."

Ardal nodded at Partlan, indicating he should translate the Captain's words. After another intense conversation with Kaff, Partlan turned to Ardal, somewhat disconcerted. "He says they will not merely join your army; that is surrender. They will, though, here and now, swear service to their new master or they will fight to the death... And the new master must be the one who defeated the old one."

Ardal glanced from Partlan to Hugh and then to Kaff. "Elgin led the mission to destroy the enemy leadership. When he is able, I am certain he will attend to this matter."

The Captain sounded exasperated. "Elgin, if you

remember, did not take the commander's life. You did, and you bear his head. More importantly, for the current circumstances, you are here. Accept their oath and be done with it. We will work out how to handle the situation once we're back at the caer. Only let us go there soon."

Ardal glared at Hugh. "Captain, I'll have no man make such an oath to me."

Hugh's voice took on an edge. "Footman, you will do as your Captain orders and take the oaths of any of these men who offer it. Then you will take the lives of any who refuse. Understand well that their wise leader has divined a way for them to live, to retain their honor and protect the spirits of their families. You will honor his wisdom."

Ardal bowed his head at the disgrace of the thing, wondering what had happened to corrupt the sovereignty of these men so they allowed it to be turned against them. He lifted the impaled head of their former master high above his head and raised his voice so all could hear, even if they couldn't understand. "If you will offer me your oath, I will accept it, and you will retain your arms in my service."

Partlan spoke to Kaff who then turned and shouted to his assembled men. All but two kneeled. Kaff stared at the young men still standing, horrified, and shouted a command at them. One shouted back, defiantly. The other pled, tears in his eyes, gesturing for Kaff to join them, but Kaff shouted again. Both looked away – one stoic, the other now weeping freely.

Kaff faced about rigidly, tears in his own eyes, and muttered under his breath. Partlan translated: "The proud fools will lose their heads."

"I don't believe he meant that to be translated, Partlan." Ardal reproached him for invading Kaff's private commentary. "Tell him to make the vow and be done. I've no stomach for more of this."

Partlan made a "get on with it gesture" toward Kaff who then kneeled before Ardal and laid his sword on the ground. All his men, except the two who had refused, followed suit. They bowed to the ground, touching their foreheads to their blades and intoned a monotonous chant. After prostrating themselves three times, they remained kneeling. Kaff murmured from his kneeling position, and Partlan translated: "They are waiting for you to accept their vow and allow them to rise."

Ardal looked back at the captain who gave him the same signal Partlan had given Kaff. "I gratefully accept your offer of service," Ardal said feebly, Partlan translating his every word. "Rise and join us in the caer."

Some twenty Dearthmen, including Kaff, rose. Ardal told him to bring the two dissenters forward. He nodded slowly and went to fetch them, but then stopped and turned back to asked if Ardal might consider a substitution. He almost begged him to accept his own head in place of the two.

"Bring them to me." Ardal's command was unequivocal. Kaff nodded and obeyed.

Partlan sneered. "Congratulations. You now own two tens of slaves. So are fortunes built."

Ardal glared at Partlan. "I'll have no fortune built on the sweat of other men."

Kaff and the two dissenters approached. The first stood defiant before Ardal, so close he could hear him breathe. The prisoner's hand then darted out and backhanded Ardal across his cheek, bringing tears to his eyes. Partlan and Kaff grabbed him, and Kaff bloodied his lips with a punch.

The other seemed younger and more frightened than angry, but seemingly as determined. He said something to Kaff that sounded like a reproach. Kaff merely looked into the boy's eyes for a moment before kneeling in front of Ardal. He briefly looked up at his new master and then threw his head back and spread his arms wide before prostrating himself at Ardal's feet, babbling and grasping at his ankles, repeatedly striking his forehead against the toes of Ardal's boots.

Ardal reached down and touched the top of Kaff's head to stay him, but the man only sobbed more loudly, moaning and raising his tear-streaked face to Ardal. He threw dirt in the air and began rocking on his heels while the two young men looked on in loathing. He rocked more forcefully slamming his forehead into Ardal's boots while he howled unintelligibly. Partlan said, "He keeps repeating the same words: 'Take my head. Take my head'."

Through Partlan, Ardal asked Kaff to bring him his sword, still stuck in the ground near Hugh. Kaff rose laboriously and shuffled to obey. Ardal then asked the captain to loan him four stout lads who would hold the dissenters in submission. When Kaff, turned with the sword now in his hand, and saw the two boys prostrate, he dropped the sword and threw himself across their necks, sobbing and shouting. Partlan translated: "Mercy, my lord."

At first, Ardal was dismayed, then he surmised that the dissenters must be the old man's sons. He retrieved his discarded blade then directed Kaff to kneel facing his sons. He addressed the boys through Partlan. "Today, you have earned death, not because you fought against us, not because you kept your oath, but because you despised your father. You have earned the death sentence I am now prepared to execute upon you."

He raised his sword above the exposed neck of the older boy and slowly brought it down, drawing it lightly across the skin, a trickle of blood in its wake. "Your head now belongs to me."

The prisoner shouted, and Partlan translated: "You are weak." Ardal slapped the back of the prisoner's head with the flat of his blade and he slumped forward. He was soon trussed and secured across the back of one of the captured horses.

Ardal spoke to the other boy as he raised his sword. He told him he had earned a death sentence by despising his father. The prisoner agreed. "It were better had I called down utter destruction on myself and let no other man – especially this one – bear it for me. Take my head."

Again, Ardal used his blade to draw a trickle of blood. "Your head too is mine. I may claim it at will for any or no reason at all." The boy nodded and sobbed.

Ardal now stood beside Kaff and raised his sword. "I spared your sons' lives, Kaff. They are mine to do with as I will."

Kaff's countenance was serene. "Take my head. I gladly give it because you have saved their lives."

"Your head is mine, Kaff. You took a vow to serve me. You cannot offer me what is already mine." Ardal waited a long while for his response.

"What then can you want of me?" Kaff almost whispered.

"I want your heart."

Trembling erratically, Kaff tore open his shirt and screamed, "Take it."

Ardal touched the tip of his blade to Kaff's chest and once more drew a trail of blood. "Your heart is mine. Give me your true name and those of your sons."

Between sobs, Kaff recited a long litany of sounds that Ardal did not recognize. "You'll need to write that out for me at the caer. For now, I need a short version."

Placing his hand over his heart, Kaff enunciated his name. "Amir."

Indicating the unconscious form of his older son, he said "Nabal", and then "Hakov" as he placed his hand on his younger son's shoulder.

"Amir, your service to me is two-fold. You will be my Thirty Leader as I am their Thirty Captain, and you will teach me your language and ways. All of you will learn ours." Ardal planted his sword in the ground, lifted Amir to stand, shuddering, before him and embraced the man.

Amir bowed and touched his forehead, then his chest with the tips of the first two finger of his right hand. "I am yours, head and heart. However I may serve you, I shall."

Ardal asked that the younger son be released, and he too was soon prostrate before him, making his own vow of service. Ardal helped him to his feet. "Hakov, you will never again touch a weapon. You will study the healing arts. You will become expert in all forms of treatment for wounds and illness that you might serve your brothers."

Hakov bowed. "I will do my best".

Ardal noticed the older brother stirring. "You, Nabal, will never touch a weapon again. You will serve any and all. If potatoes need peeling, you will peel them. If a chamber pot is full, you will empty it. If a burden must be carried, you will bear it."

Partlan assured Ardal that Nabal's response was nothing but a litany of curses.

Ardal turned to Hundred Captain Hugh, exhausted in mind and body. Hugh nodded his grim satisfaction and also turned toward the caer. Lumbering home, Ardal mourned Hart's loss and Elgin's wound. He dreaded the moment he would learn what else he must mourn.

Ekurn rode up, leading Ardal's forgotten horse. Reaching for the reins, Ardal's felt sudden shame at his evident relief. Hart would never have allowed such weakness to show.

"Ai, Ekurn, and you've saved me for sure. It's always looking out for the men, you are. Thank you, my Ten Leader."

There was no hint of mockery in his reply. "My honor, Captain." Ekurn then rode back to his Ten - the Ten that was no longer Ardal's.

Ardal gratefully mounted and rode alongside his Thirty of formerly foreign invaders and wondered if he could ever think of them as his own, in the same way that Ekurn thought of his Ten.

Two of the Dearthman Thirty were being helped along by others. Ardal dismounted and indicated that they should ride on his horse. The men stared, incredulous and bewildered. Ardal wondered again, and for what would not be the last time, what sort of men had owned the service of these, that such a simple response to a need should seem to them a great deed. He bellowed Partlan's name, repeatedly.

"Lord?" Partlan answered from just behind him.

"Three things, Partie, old pal. One. Never call me that again. I'll have a hard enough time adjusting to 'Captain'."

"Yes, Captain."

Ardal winced. "Two." He reached back, took hold of Partlan's wrist and pulled him up to walk alongside him. "Don't wait for me to call. Assume I want you with me when I'm with these men. You see, Partie… Do you mind if I call you Partie?"

Partlan studied Ardal's face and replied cautiously. "It is my own name spoken as though by the voice of a friend. I was known by my slave name for so long that this is now a mercy and a boon."

"Right," and Ardal wondered why he could not have simply said "It'll do".

"You see, Partie, I cannot talk with my Thirty; so, I'll need you with me until I can."

"Captain, there are other Bractmen among those who surrendered who might serve as translators."

"That is good news; however, I'll need you with me, and the others can serve as they are needed with the other Dearthmen."

They walked along in silence for a while. The new captain glanced occasionally up at the wounded soldiers mounted on his horse. Partlan cleared his throat. "Three, Captain?"

"Eh?" Partlan's voice had shaken Ardal from his lethargic reverie, one centered on a pint of the finest ale in all of Tierasal, and taken in the homely inn of Mag Petty. "What is it, Partie?"

"The third thing, Captain?"

"Oh, aye. Number three is this: before settling in

tonight, I'll want a list of the complete names and common use names for each of the men. If there are any who currently fill leadership roles, I'll want that information as well."

Partlan smiled broadly and inclined his head. "I'll gladly do your will in this, Captain, and will carry the list with me at all times. I am grateful you recognize my value as a scribe."

"I suppose you'll serve as well as any other man for scribbling. It's your knowledge of the Dearthman language that makes you the one for this job."

"'As well as any other'? You say it as though writing were a common skill, Captain."

"Common enough I reckon. My mam taught me. Dad said I'd better learn before he'd allow me to work the bellows."

Partlan paused. "Captain, earlier you told me you were a simple soldier in the High King's army, and now indicate that you were a blacksmith." It was more a question than a statement.

"Yes, Partie, and?"

"Captain, do all the High King's soldiers read and write?"

"I dunno, Partie. Many, perhaps most. Why is that a bother for you?

"Merely because it seems to me that the High King's men are lordly men ... even the lowest among them as you claim to be. You are lettered, you speak your own thoughts, and even when under authority, you are not subjected to it, rather it is born as an honor. It's as though you are an army of kings."

Ardal scoffed. "'Kings'? We are farmers, merchants, laborers, and even a smith or two who have offered ourselves for a time to serve the security of our land. If we are sovereigns it is each man of himself and his home as well as a space the length of his arms about him. If that is lordly, then call me a king, for my arms are longer than most."

"You jest, Captain, about something that most men have never known. To be sovereign of your own mind, body and home – that makes a man a king." Partlan was clearly vexed, but fatigue was taking Ardal's mind, and he missed the point.

"We are not kings, Partie, just free men by natural right, as all men are. There is nothing remarkable about it." He spoke laboriously as to an inattentive child.

"If you will forgive me, Captain, you bear such a burden and esteem, such a blessing lightly because you were born to it. That seems to me an extremely foolish position that, if pursued, places your self-sovereignty at risk. If you truly believe your ownership of yourself and your home is an 'unremarkable natural right', you might be unwilling to take remarkable measures to protect it. I am certain the enemies of your self-sovereignty have not missed this point." Partlan apparently spoke of a matter of some importance to him.

Ardal's thoughts were a jumble. He was exhausted in mind and body. He had recently, quite against his will, become the "owner" of two dozen men. He was far from home and the best ale in Tierasal. To top it all, a recently freed slave was now lecturing him concerning his life as a free man. Perhaps Ardal could have been forgiven for what he did next. He halted, turned to Partlan, looked deeply into his eyes and allowed his ire to show. "Shut you up, Partie, or I shall shut you myself."

"Yes, Captain," and Partlan gave a slight bow.

Ardal now growled, "Ach. My name is Ardal."

They walked on to the caer in silence. Along the way, they began to note the bodies of individual Dearthmen within bowshot of the walls. Apparently, the Quartermaster, Gatemaster and Armory sections had contributed to the battle from atop the walls. Upon their arrival, the mourning began in earnest for they'd lost a tithe of their brothers.

The process of consolidating his new unit – feeding, housing and establishing a chain of command – occupied Ardal's mind but not his heart. It separated him from his brothers; so, he mourned the dead alone.

The next day, they buried Hart and ten others in the meadow where they had taken the enemy commander. One of them was Clunie, not only Ardal's Tenmate, but his mate, as well. He was the fellow who'd watched his back and expected him to watch his own in return. No matter where they were or what they did, Clunie would have a story, or a song, or a prank that would get them all laughing.

Ekurn informed Ardal that Clunie had been skewered with a spear through his back during the raid on the enemy encampment, after Ardal had broken from the unit to cut off the enemy commander's retreat. There was no note of accusation in Ekurn's voice, but Ardal heard it nonetheless. He put his face into his hands and shuddered. "Ai, my heart. Ekurn, what'll I do?"

"Remember and honor him." Ekurn pulled Ardal's hands away from his face. When Ardal raised his eyes, Ekurn nodded, sharply. "Honor, Captain."

"Honor, my Brother," and Ardal returned the nod.

Ekurn turned on his heel and left Ardal with the weight of his loss and his responsibilities.

CHAPTER 8
Onward and Upward

"Come further up, come further in!"
<u>The Last Battle</u>
C. S. Lewis

Three days after the battle, Hugh, the Thirty Captain of Heavy Foot recently become Hundred Captain, called Ardal to his Seat and instructed him to "Take a few things to the Captain of Three Hundred for his consideration". The "few things" included the arms and armor of two hundred forty-one Dearthmen who had surrendered or been killed, seventy-three of the surrendered Dearthman who had chosen to remain in Tierasal, twenty-two Dearthmen who had willingly pledged their lives to Ardal, one who had done so less willingly, and one prisoner who had remained recalcitrant. Hugh also entrusted to him a copy of his notes on the battle and the personal effects of their fallen sword-brothers. Seven men with grievous wounds who yet remained alive would journey with them by wain to the surgeon at the caer of the Three Hundred. Two of the seven were men of Ardal's Dearthman contingent.

Hugh attached a Ten of Light Foot and a Ten of Horse to the company. He said it was all the security he could give them and more than he could spare. Ardal protested that Hugh would need them to defend the caer and that he had his Thirty of armed Dearthmen. Hugh scoffed. "Aye, you have them, or they have you. Have you never known a man to break his oath? I've no fear of the whole lot turnin' on you, but one or two here or there might have strange ideas." He placed his hand on Ardal's shoulder and spoke fiercely. "Ardal you're a fine lad, and fate has made a Captain of you, but you cannot rely on fate and must develop some wits of your own. Go, now. Honor, my friend."

"Honor, my Captain." The two men clasped forearms. "I will return the two Tens with a full report."

"Aye, just make sure it ain't full of dung."

Ardal was much heartened to find that the Ten of Light Foot that would accompany them was his own. Like him, they were mounted on captured horses and they led the remaining ones. It was disconcerting but encouraging for Ardal when Ekurn reported to him as any Ten Leader to any Thirty Captain. "It's I that am glad to have you here, Ekurn. The presence of my sword-brothers gives me the strength of Ten."

"To a man, they volunteered to accompany you. Once my men were committed," Ekurn grinned and shrugged, "I had no choice but to come along. We are, of course, only nine, but we will suffice for twenty. More importantly, we will ever be vigilant for any sign that the Dearthmen might turn against you. I have tasked two men to guard our prisoner who is secured to a pulling shackle on one of the wains of the wounded.'

At that moment, Gerritt rode up and Ardal greeted him heartily. "Ho, Gerritt, and it is a boon to see you this fine day."

"Honor, Captain." He walked his horse alongside

Ardal's so they could talk in private. "When we heard that a Ten of Light had stolen mounts for themselves and aspired to join the ranks of Horse," and he looked somberly at Ekurn, "we thought it fitting that we volunteer to come along and test their horsemanship."

Ekurn chuckled. "Gerritt, I have seen you move with your mount as one creature through the battleclash with nary a tug on the reins nor any sign you guided him. I'll not challenge you but will gladly learn from you where horses are concerned." He grinned. "Of course, if any of your pretty boys wishes to claim his manhood by test of grappling with real soldiers, we stand ready to serve."

Gerritt laughed. "So it's to be a challenge of skills. On behalf of my sword-brothers, I accept." He nodded. "Honor, Ekurn."

Ekurn grinned. "Honor, Gerritt."

Gerritt then offered his report. "Captain, Horse will maintain forward and flank scouts, riding in twos. We will also maintain a rearguard. My men will rotate through their positions to keep them focused. My Second and I will ride on point with the main body. I will occasionally send my Second to check my scouts and to carry messages to them. They will return to camp at night only after Light has established their watch. This will ensure security during movement and at the halt."

Ardal nodded then addressed both Ten Leaders. "It's glad I am to have you along. As your sword-brother, I ask that you help me so I do not fail. While I am grateful for your support and seeming acceptance of my new role, I am fully aware that I am no true captain, and so will rely heavily on you. I lack skill and understanding as well as experience. Correct me as I require it. I only ask, for the men's sake, that you pull me aside when you do so. We should not be seen to be at odds. I accept responsibility for the success or failure of this mission. Now, I ask you to help me bear it."

"You are more a Captain than you seem to know,"

Gerritt told him. "You ask no more of us than any Thirty Captain should expect of his leaders. As this is our warband, I am for it."

Ekurn added, "Aye, Captain. Imagine I said this as nicely as Gerritt. I am your sword-brother, and the honor is mine." He looked away for a moment. "That's all the fine words I know."

So they departed, this sundry band. As they emerged from the pass near the end of the first day of agonizingly slow travel, they encountered a Thirty of Horse lying in ambush. They had been sent by the Captain of Three Hundred to locate the missing supply wains. Upon finding the remains of several, along with many soldiers, the Thirty Captain had sent a messenger back with word of what they'd found and his intent to ride for Stonebreak Pass, to see what might be done there. They had noted movement there and so had held up at its mouth, prepared to meet friend or foe.

Gerritt, Ekurn, and Ardal told their tale in much abbreviated form and informed the Captain that supplies at the caer were low and that fresh sword arms were much needed.

The Captain of Horse replied that Hugh Mor could not, by any means, require help, but that perhaps he would stop by to drink a bit of his old friend's tea. He then urged Ardal to request upon his arrival that the Quartermaster send a rapid resupply for a Hundred, followed soon after by a full month's stock.

That evening, while they established camp, Gerritt and his Second, Caleb, performed an astounding display of horsemanship. Caleb rode off and waited a hundred yards away. Gerritt dismounted, walked away from his mount, faced Caleb, and waved at him. Caleb rode swiftly toward Gerritt. Just as it seemed that Caleb would ride him down, Gerritt stepped to his side and raised his arm. In the blink of an eye, he was seated behind Caleb, the horse never breaking stride. Ardal asked the Horsemen to teach him.

Many of the men learned the flying mount and could be seen practicing it for the rest of their journey.

Later in the evening, Ekurn and his Second, Airt, demonstrated formal grappling maneuvers. After this, they went at it hammer and tongs so it seemed they might kill each other. Airt was massive, devastatingly strong, and faster than might have been thought. Ekurn was agile, blindingly quick, and stronger than he looked.

Their combat ranged throughout the camp and upset, among other things, a pot of beans and the good humor of the cook. Quicker than the eye could follow, Ekurn flipped himself onto Airt's back and snaked his arm around his neck. Then he locked his hold with his other arm, braced his feet against Airt's thighs, and squeezed and pulled with all his might.

Gerritt laughed. "I'd have given odds on the big fellow, but Ekurn has come out on top."

Airt scrambled and clawed until his face was swollen and discolored. Then he leaned forward and flexed his knees, as though done for. Instead of falling forward, however, he leaped back, throwing his feet into the air and coming down onto his shoulders, Ekurn trapped between his great weight and the ground. For a moment, neither moved. Then Airt rolled free, gasping, and crawled back over to Ekurn who was also gasping heavily. Airt helped him to his knees, and together they crawled to sit with their backs against a tree while they recovered.

Gerritt grimaced. "I'm confused. Who won?"

A voice rumbled from the gloaming. "We all did. No beans tonight."

That brought general laughter, and everyone went back to his business except a Horseman who sang in a well-trained tenor. Ardal went and squatted before Ekurn and Airt.

Ekurn grinned and winced. "I had him, Captain, but he cheated. Did you see that?"

"I saw him reach into himself after he was near

defeated and find a way to put you on the ground. I mean no insult to your considerable skill, Ekurn, but that was no mean feat. You are both animals. Are either of you damaged in any important way?"

"Damaged?" Airt seemed surprised. "Captain, it is good of you to remember that stomach trouble I got from last night's beans, but fear you not, the trouble passed with the beans."

Ardal shook his head and glanced at Ekurn. "Ai, Captain, it's ashamed I am that I allowed you to witness my distress. Truth be told, I am sore chafed. Haven't ridden much lately, you see. Not to worry, though, I'll have calluses soon and my arse'll be as hard as turtle shell."

Ardal stood. "I'll be out to check the perimeter shortly. Do you make certain I make no mistakes."

"Aye, Captain." Ekurn grinned. "As soon as I've recovered a bit from my 'saddle sore', I'll check the positions myself so you'll not need to make many adjustments. As a matter of fact, since Airt here's already recovered from his 'stomach trouble'…"

Airt attempted to leap to his feet and only just managed not to stumble over them. "Aye, Captain, I recover faster than the old man here. I'll see to setting the watch. Ekurn, if you'd be a good lad and lay out my bedroll, I'll be done with watch before either of you show for inspection."

"Don't be surprised if I leave a gift in your bedroll, lad," Ekurn growled as Airt pulled him to his feet.

"There's a good lad." Airt patted Ekurn's head, but as they went their separate ways, Ekurn tripped Airt.

Ardal turned to walk over to the Dearthman Thirty side of the encampment and almost ran into Partlan who was standing silently, waiting to speak with him. "Walk with me, Partie. Let's go see how our friends fare."

"Captain, they are prepared to stand watch along with the other soldiers. Also, they ask if they will be permitted to take part in the games."

"Games? Oh, I see, the horsemanship and grappling.

That was just a bit of a lark between Ekurn and Gerritt. I don't know if we need to involve anyone else at this point."

"You fear allowing such contests between men who scant days ago were killing each other? Do you also fear allowing them to serve as soldiers? They seem to believe so since you have not assigned them any duties as yet."

Ardal agonized for a moment. "Partie, go and tell Amir I want him to meet with me at the feed wain after the meal, when I meet with the other leaders. I'll need you there, as well. In fact, this will remain an ongoing requirement for both of you."

Partlan nodded. "Aye, Captain." He turned to leave.

"Partie, you, the both of you, will ride beside me as we travel. Be you careful to never forget that he is a Thirty Leader, and that if I could speak directly with him, I would. I want to engender no more distrust between us."

Partlan smiled slightly and nodded. "Aye, my Captain. I will remain aware of my words and manner."

"And I'll thank you for it, my friend." Ardal held his gaze for a moment. "As a matter of personal interest, Partlan, how do the Dearthmen treat you? Do they resent you?"

Partlan paused for a moment, clearly surprised, then recovered himself. "Thank you, my Captain, for thinking of such a thing. Many of the 'Forsaken…' That is how these men name themselves. They call me the 'Gelding' and say unspeakable things as I pass. Amir tells them that such behavior brings a curse upon them, but it only ensures he does not have to hear it. I remain subject to their derision."

"'Gelding?' Because you surrendered your weapon?"

"Captain, were it my decision, my hands would never have known a weapon. Laying it aside came easily. I told you when we met that I was a scholar."

"Aye, Partie, perhaps," Ardal chuckled, "but all men know that the wild Bracties are warriors from the cradle and that they live to kill. Are you not a Bractie?"

"Is that what 'all men know' of the Bractmen? Perhaps, Captain, one day you will know better." He sighed. "I am as true a Bractman as you will ever know. I was also a scholar, a scribe and a counselor to my king."

Ardal wondered at that for a moment. "Partie, how did you become a slave to the Dearthmen? A king does not allow men to simply make off with his counselors."

"On a day of days, a small troop of Dearthman traders passed through the lands of Clan Erc. They were strange in that they had none of their hump-backed desert beasts but instead rode sturdy northern ponies, and they carried none of the spices for which they are famous but instead relatively small quantities of metals which are plentiful in our islands.

"Intrigued, I watched them closely during their stay. I had given myself back then to studying Dearthman language and culture; so, I fancied I'd practice with these traders. Only two of them deigned me worthy to engage in conversation, but their dialect was one I'd not heard before, and neither was inclined to answer questions about their land.

"The daughter of my king had been taken by the wanderlust; so, I was unsurprised when she displayed a keen interest in the traders. Within a fortnight, Aedan was gone, as were the Dearthman traders.

"I approached the king in his great grief, bragged of my knowledge of the Dearthmen and their ways, and claimed I could find her. He offered me her hand if I returned successful. Marriage to a woman such as Aedan would make a man a king if he could survive it. I took upon myself an oath to bring her home or die.

"I traveled alone to a small Dearthman settlement on Thunderhead Bay where I made inquiries among the fishermen. The owner of a certain boat decided I was too inquisitive, or perhaps merely annoying, and denounced me as a spy to the local chieftain who paid a reward to the fisherman. There was no trial. I was sold to the next trader who passed through. He was told I was a meddling foreigner and treated me as such."

Ardal gave a slight wave of his hand to interrupt the Bractman's tale. "Partlan, you are under no onus here. You may return to your home at any time. You laid aside your weapons and are no longer an enemy of Tierasal."

Partlan grimaced. "How could I return to my king without his daughter? Where could I rest until I found her? My fate is with you, Captain."

"I'd not be rid of you so long as you'd stay. You're needed here – more than you know, because now you have a dull-witted student as well. I need you teach me their language and all you know of them."

"My honor, my captain," and Partlan nodded.

"The honor is mine, Partie. Hear what I say. I will teach these brigands to respect you."

"I thank you, my captain, but that is my task. No other man can do that for me."

"Whatever other men may think or say, you have my respect, Partie."

"Then, Captain, what they think or say matters not. With your leave, I will carry your message to Amir."

"Aye, Partie, that'll do, and my name is Ardal.

"Aye, Captain, that I know right well."

Ardal established a routine that worked the Forsaken into all aspects of camp life, including security and the games. They established procedures to ensure that they could live and work together and build trust.

Ardal formed the Dearthmen into Tens and assigned them to work with the Tierasalan Tens. Ten of them were mounted on captured horses. Eight worked with Light so that they were paired up. This left six of the Forsaken who were not assigned to train with a Ten. One was Amir, who was Ardal's shadow. Another was his messenger, Badur. Two were wounded and traveled in a wain along with one who offered to assist Hakov in tending to the wounded.

Ardal sent Partlan to find two suitable Bractmen translators from among the seventy-three surrendered Dearthmen who traveled with them. He assigned one to assist Gerritt, the other to Ekurn.

The Forsaken engaged heartily in the games and performed well, but they lacked a sense of fun and seemed to think that the point was only to prove who had the greater skill, strength, speed or agility. It never seemed to occur to them that part of what the Tierasalan soldiers accomplished in the games was to reaffirm their brotherhood. Again, Ardal wondered what damage had been done to them.

Amir and Hakov spoke with Nabal each chance they got. Ardal could not understand their words, and would not allow Partlan to translate. Nabal's response sounded less than respectful on each occasion.

Ardal checked on the wounded each morning before they broke camp, each evening before they bedded down, and at any halts along the way. Hakov and his assistant, Iasir, worked diligently under the tutelage of Dillon, the Binder, to change bandages, clean wounds, apply poultices, feed the wounded and dose them with the bitter herbs that made them sleep heavily.

Three days into the trip, Dillon informed Ardal that Elgin had called for him. Ardal went to him immediately, but he only muttered and began to claw wildly at his face. Dillon asked for permission to tie down his hands and dose him again with herbs. Of course, Ardal consented.

The next day they buried Enda. There had never been much hope for his recovery, but Dillon had fought valiantly for him. He had died in the night, and so they buried him the next morning and honored him all that day and into the following night. They departed the next morning leaving behind a cairn and a carved stone tablet that stated "Here Lies Enda – Honorable Warrior, Faithful Friend, One of Hart's Hundred Wounded in Defense of Hart's Pass - A Curse on Any Who Disturb Him". Ardal noted the location in his report.

They settled into a routine and wended their sluggish way toward the caer of the Three Hundred where, upon arrival, Ardal was summoned to the Captain's Seat. Ardal asked Ekurn, Gerritt, Amir and Partlan to accompany him to the door and then to wait until called inside at the Three Hundred's pleasure.

Before they left the unit, Ardal called Airt aside. "You're in charge. Your priorities are to get the wounded to the surgeon, prisoner secured, horses stabled, men housed, and requests issued to the quartermaster for supplies for our Hundred. You'll also want to ask them to secure the personal items of our fallen sword-brothers as well as the surrendered arms and armor. Make arrangements to keep these items separate until the Three Hundred has had the opportunity to inspect them. Before you go to the quartermaster, get a list from the men of any damaged, worn or lost items they might need to have repaired or replaced. Have I missed aught?"

Airt nodded. "That'll keep me busy 'til you get back, Cap'n."

"My thanks, Airt. We'll return as soon as we are able."

"Ah, we'll muddle through without you."

Ardal returned to the messenger and the men who were to accompany him. Without a word, the messenger walked away, and Ardal followed. When they got there, the Captain of Three Hundred himself stood outside the door, waiting to greet them. He looked grim. "Men and supply wains lost. A herd of armed Dearthmen in my caer." He eyed Amir and Partlan warily then shifted his gaze among the Ten Leaders and Ardal. "And I have a Captain of Thirty I've never heard of. Which of you is it?"

Ardal stepped forward. "Captain—"

"Hold a moment. Why have you brought these others?"

"They are here, Captain, so they may provide additional evidence and information to the report I bear." Ardal extended a bundle of folded pages that included his notes from the meeting before Hart launched the attack, Hart's notes, and Hugh's summary of the battle and outline of Ardal's mission to the Three Hundred, as well as his own notes on the mission so far.

The captain nodded and took but did not inspect them. He spoke to Gerritt and Ekurn. "As for you men and your friends," and he glanced at Amir and Partlan before indicating the messenger who had brought them, "Lorcan here will see to it that you are as comfortable as can be expected while you wait for your ... your captain to call you."

Lorcan nodded to the captain then walked away. Ekurn shrugged at Gerritt and followed Lorcan, along with the others.

The captain stepped inside and indicated that Ardal should follow. At the back of the office he opened a door into the next room where there was a large table surrounded by a dozen chairs. These he walked past to yet another door through which they finally passed into the Captain's Seat.

"Close the door." He sighed as he walked around his desk and sat in the chair behind it. Rolling his sleeves, the captain indicated a shelf to one side. "Port. Have a glass."

"My thanks, Captain." Ardal poured two glasses and set one before the captain where he now sat reading. The captain raised it to him in gratitude.

Ardal stood watching the captain's face for any reaction to what he was reading. Presently, the captain glanced up distractedly and waved Ardal to a seat. "Sit you down, lad." Ardal gratefully sat but maintained a rigid posture. The captain glanced over the papers at Ardal. "I'll read, then we can talk. Sit you back and take your port. There's another if you want it."

"Aye, Captain." Ardal gratefully settled back into his chair and continued to watch the captain's face.

It revealed nothing, and the captain only looked up

once, to ask, "You are the Ardal mentioned in this report?"

"Aye, Captain."

He read the report twice through before lifting his eyes again. Laying the papers aside, he lifted his glass in seeming acknowledgement of the actions they reported and drained it at one go. Leaning back in his chair, he propped his feet on his desk, rested his head back and closed his eyes. "Hart will be sorely missed."

After a while he addressed Ardal. "So, Light Footman Ardal of the Avinn Vale becomes Thirty Captain Ardal who commands his enemies and honors their vows. What would you have me do with you, lad?"

The question confused Ardal. "My Captain, that seems to me the easy part. Once you have determined what to do with the Forsaken, the Dearthman soldiers who would not break oath—"

"And instead swore one to you."

The thought of the oath left Ardal chagrined. "Yes, Captain. Once you have determined what to do with them, I would like nothing more than to return to my Ten as a Light Footman."

The captain chuckled. "And you think that feasible? Lad, it's not even possible." He considered for a moment. "Young Captain, this is no decision for a poor Captain of Three Hundred. This is a matter of State that will likely involve great men in Galantamhor and come before the High King himself. Lay aside any ideas you might hold of returning to your Ten … or to your smithy, for that matter."

Most of Ardal's company remained at the caer of the Three Hundred for three days. Before daybreak on the morning after their arrival, the rapid resupply mission departed with Gerritt's and Ekurn's Tens riding as escort. Amir supplied a guard from among the Forsaken, offering his own life in exchange for the prisoner if he were to escape.

Murtaw, Captain of Three Hundred, had added his notes to the report Ardal once more carried. Lorcan made two copies of the complete report – one for Murtaw's records and one for Hugh's. Murtaw handed Gerritt a sheaf of documents that included Hugh's copy of the report, Hugh's orders for permanent promotion to Hundred Captain, orders attaching the Thirty of Horse they had met en route to Hugh's Hundred, and orders for engineers to bolster the fortifications at the Caer in Hart's Pass.

Lorcan then handed identical packets of documents to Gerritt and Ardal. They included orders for Ardal's field commission as Captain of Thirty and transfer to the newly formed "Forsaken Thirty" as well as the Forsaken's orders to report to the caer of One Thousand.

During the three days they spent at the caer of Three Hundred, and through all their travels thereafter, Ardal focused on learning as much of the Dearthman language and culture as possible and on getting to know the men. Partlan taught him the rudiments of the written and spoken language as well as a fair bit about the culture.

The fact that the Dearthmen did not call themselves "Dearthmen" did not surprise him, nor did the fact that they did not know the Tierasalans as such. He was disconcerted to learn that they referred to themselves as the "Exalted" and to all others as the "Accursed".

Troubling in another way was the knowledge that the people he knew as the Dearthmen were composed of no fewer than seven races divided into nine nations, each of which encompassed any number of tribes and clans rife with internecine rivalries, shifting loyalties and wars.

He also came to understand that this particular band of Dearthmen was the remainder of a group of fifty men taken from seven villages of a people known as the Adnana. The Adnana had maintained their independence from the surrounding nations due mainly to their remote location on a high plateau surrounded by incredibly rough terrain, all surmounted by great craggy peaks. In addition to this, they also had a habit of ambushing any who attempted the road to their plateau.

When an unprecedented caravan of traders one day crossed the wastes and climbed toward their plateau, Amir, as headman of the first village the foreigners encountered, advised that the Adnana receive them as venerated guests. Things went well for a few days until the traders revealed themselves to be soldiers sent to "claim a tithe of the fighting men to serve in the army of the 'Protector of the Faithful'".

Amir consequently held a meeting in his home with the headmen of the other six villages. However, the soldiers raided the meeting and took the headmen and Amir's two sons. They then went to the homes of each of the other men and took their sons. Two men resisted and were emasculated in the street, then their wives were publicly taken by soldiers.

The commander told Amir to choose seven from each village to serve the Protector, saying that as soon as they had fifty they would leave the Adnana in peace. Of the seven village headmen they had already taken, two had been maimed in the street and so were considered unfit to serve. Of the fifty required, only eleven had been chosen: the five remaining headmen and six sons of headmen.

Amir selected from among the men remaining in the villages the most worthless he could find. The commander rejected them all, put his blade to Hakov's throat and told Amir to try again. He then sorrowfully selected the strongest and most capable. He attempted to distribute the tragedy as evenly as possible, but there was no way to make it fair.

He was cursed as a traitor by the affected families and finally by the people as a whole. His wife, Haziqa, accused him of "inviting wolves" among them and turned her back on him.

The commander stood the men before their people and

administered an oath against the souls of their families that they would serve him or his successor until death. That commander was the same whose head Ardal had carried to end the battle at Hart's Pass.

Throughout their ensuing service, each man had expressed a deep resentment of Amir for choosing him. Perhaps the most bitter of all was Nabal, Amir's recently married older son, who laid his losses at his father's feet. "If you were a stronger man, this would never have happened."

Amir responded with the only wisdom he had to offer. "Let us serve well. Who knows but that fate will reward those who act honorably?"

Nabal shouted each word of his retort as a hammer blow to his father's face. "There is no honor here, old fool." So it went until Hart's Pass and their new oath.

After three days at the caer of Three Hundred, the company traveled to the caer of One Thousand where they left two of the Tierasalan wounded in the surgeon's care. He demanded that the others stay as well, but Elgin convinced Murtaw that Ardal needed him and Cian as well to keep him out of trouble; so he took them along.

The Forsaken were adamant that their wounded travel with them. The personal items, including armor of the fallen, the wain load of armor and weapons taken from the surrendered, the surrendered themselves, and Nabal the prisoner, all went with them.

The visit with Torlough, Captain of One Thousand, was a rapid version of the one to Murtaw. Immediately upon arrival, he accepted Ardal's report, questioned Elgin and Cian, and endorsed Ardal's commission. He then summoned Amir, with Partlan to translate.

The next morning, Torlough returned Ardal's copy of the growing report with his own observations attached and sped them on their way to Shallowford where they reported to the Seat of Aindru, Captain-General of the Western Division.

Aindru repeated the process with the slight variation of summarizing the contents of all the reports. They then produced a number of copies of the complete document.

Aindru dispatched riders to deliver these to nine of the ten Captains of One Thousand assigned to the Western Division. One rider also carried a copy directly to the Seat of the Captain-General of the Armies of Tierasal in Galantamhor, the royal city of Tierasal.

After personally ensuring they were properly provisioned for the journey, Aindru sped the company on their way. As they mounted to depart, he handed Ardal a sheaf of documents that he said were greetings to one of his friends in Galantamhor. He admonished Ardal to "Deliver them immediately upon arrival into Flann's own hand".

"With a will, Captain-General." Ardal nodded in salute. The letter was addressed to "Flann, Chief Librarian, Galantamhor".

CHAPTER 9
The Royal City

"Nothing turns out to be so oppressive and unjust as a feeble government."
Edmund Burke

They moved onward toward Galantamhor, the great city that had begun as a simple entryway into the Keep of the High King. Amir and Ardal worked hard all the while to understand each other. Amir introduced Ardal to his Leaders of Ten – Daud and Ilyas. They introduced him to their Seconds - twin brothers named Fairok and Fasel who competed in all things.

By the time they crossed the Lower Frigid River, Amir was fluent enough in Tierasalan to ask Ardal a question. "We near a city. Many travelers on the road. They make – I do not know word – walk to special place. It is Royal City?"

"Pilgrimage?" Ardal asked.

When Amir shrugged, Partlan intervened. He and Amir exchanged words, then he assured Ardal that Amir had asked if the travelers who filled the road were pilgrims.

"Aye, we draw near to Galantamhor, the Royal City. Many of the people you see on the road have business there, but some are pilgrims who intend to enter the Keep and see the High King himself."

Partlan continued to translate: "Your High King allows his people to come to him?" Amir had been so shocked he did not even attempt to speak in Tierasalan. "How then does he have time to rule? How does he protect himself from assassins?"

"It's beyond me, Amir. I'm a soldier and a blacksmith. I know nothing of the ways of kings. I tell you that if ever I meet him, I'll bring you along. After all, he is your High King as well, now."

Amir smiled sadly, seeming to take Ardal's offer seriously. "That I would do with all my heart, my friend, but what have I to offer the great king?"

"I dunno, Amir. Do you know any good jokes?"

Amir smiled weakly and shook his head. "I have never been a humorous man. Does your great king esteem humor?"

"I dunno, brother, but I tell you that if he doesn't, I've no place there."

On approach, the vastness of the city was hidden from them by the terrain. They climbed from the river valley of the Lower Frigid and saw, looming atop the ridge above them, a high, fortified wall built of dressed stone the likes of which were not to be seen in the hinterlands. Beyond the wall, due to the angle of their ascent, all they could see were the battlements and slate roofs of two slender blue-gray towers.

The flagstone road from the river bridge to the main city gate was packed with people, carts and animals. They raised a din that made it difficult to think. Talking was not an option. The company dismounted to offer their horses a rest while they walked toward the gate.

When they came within view of it, a rider broke off from the detachment of the watch stationed there and cantered along the grass beside the road to meet them.

"Hail," he called as he neared. Ardal handed Partlan his reins and walked ahead to talk with the rider who had soon appraised him. "Are you Ardal of the Avinn Vale, Captain of the Forsaken?"

"Aye, friend. That I am, and these are the same here with me. What'll you have us do?"

"Captain, my orders are to conduct you to the barracks and to provide you all with what is necessary for your wellbeing. It is an honor to serve you, Captain," and the horseman nodded.

Ardal returned the nod. "The honor is mine. Is there a way through this press or must we wait the day through to enjoy the necessaries you offer?"

"The way stands open before you, Captain. He gestured toward a path parallel to the wall that was wide enough for two horsemen abreast.

Ardal called to Amir, who pushed toward him through the crowd, apologizing as he did. Partlan followed, holding the reins of all three mounts. Ardal explained the situation, and Amir returned to direct the men, leaving his horse with Partlan.

Ardal addressed the rider. "If we are to ride together, I'd have your name."

"Captain, I am Donal, son of—"

"Forgive me," Partlan said, "but is 'Donal' not a Bractish name?"

The man furrowed his brow. "Aye, friend. That it is. I've not known a Dearthman before who could distinguish Bract from Tierasalan, though. How is it you have that skill?"

"Because I am no Dearthman but as true a Bractman as you'll ever know, excepting your own father, of course. I am Partlan." The two grasped forearms in greeting.

"Partlan, I've some grievous news for you, friend: my own dad was no Bractman but a Tierasalan herald. My mam, now, she is a flame-haired and fierce-hearted daughter of the Mighty, known as—"

"Aedan," Partlan gasped.

Donal stared down at him, as though at a specter rising from the ground.

"Ai, Donal," and Partlan grasped the man's ankle. "That I might embrace you as my kinsman, I beg you to dismount." He dropped the reins of the three horses he had been holding and nearly pulled the young watchman from his saddle.

Donal managed to get to the ground without being pulled over and returned Partlan's exuberant embrace, if somewhat hesitantly. "Are we certainly kinsmen then, Partlan?"

"Aye, most certainly." Partlan held Donal at arm's length, tears welling in his eyes. "Before I say more, I must speak with our own dear, impulsive, sweet, savage Aedan, the Rose of Clan Erc and daughter of the great king Niall."

"There is some mystery here, Partlan, for my mother is a woman named Aedan, and your description of her is apt." He chuckled. "But her father, she told me, is 'A bee keeper, and a poor one at that'."

Partlan shouted his laughter, throwing his hands in the air. "Ach. That but proves it. Niall is a terrible beekeeper. He never failed to destroy a hive once he'd set his mind to caring for it. Your mother is right, lad. Niall has no skill with bees."

He embraced the lad fiercely again and wept freely. "Nay, lad, I'll own you as my kinsman whether you'll have me or no."

The Forsaken, assembled in a loose circle around them, were rather taken aback to see the former slave they knew as the Gelding receive such a welcome from a representative of the High King. The fact the representative was merely a member of the city watch only mitigated their shock a touch.

Fasel gave word to their thoughts. "See, the Gelding is held in great regard here. Surely this is where he will take his revenge upon us."

The Forsaken were surprised to hear Ardal respond haltingly in their own Alish language. "Nay, Fasel, son of Ibreem, there will be no retribution upon you. Neither will there be further contempt among members of our company." He gathered them all in his gaze. "As you are my brothers, so too is Partlan – I say Partlan rather than the Gelding – my brother. Therefore, he is your brother too, and that is the way of it."

"Aye, my captain," Amir responded in Tierasalan and nodded in salute. He gazed around the circle, looking each man fiercely in the eye, then raised his hands to encompass them all. In unison, the Forsaken responded, "Aye, my Captain."

Ardal mounted and turned to Donal. "I heard mention of mead, might there be ale available in this thirsty place?"

Donal laughed. "Aye, Captain. Here you'll find the best ale in all of Tierasal."

Ardal scowled. "Oh, lad, I'll forgive you, though all men know that the best ale in all of Tierasal is to be found at the Inn of Mag Petty in the Avinn Vale, but happily, I'll settle for second best today.'

Ardal gestured for Donal to lead the way, and the company followed at the pace of their heavily laden wain. Near on an hour later, they neared the place where the city wall came hard up against a sheer cliff that dwarfed it.

At the base of the cliff, the trail dropped into a steep-sided defile that formed a tunnel as it passed under the wall. Iron sconces held unlit torches, but enough sunlight entered the tunnel from either end to allow Ardal to make out some detail. He could see that they passed through a murder hole, rife with arrow loops and holes in the ceiling through which hot oil could be dumped or stones dropped.

Ardal also noted broad, straight lines that crossed the floor of the tunnel at regular intervals. As soon as they had left behind the echoes of their horses' shoes striking the cobblestone floor of the tunnel, he asked Donal about them.

"Captain, you have an eye for detail. Let us assume you are the commander of an invading army. You will, at some point, scout the trail and discover our tunnel. When you attempt to make use of it, though, we will employ all of the tricks you'd expect, but we can also raise rows of short, heavy spikes from the floor to slow your advance, making you easy prey to our bolts, shot and oil.

"If you are persistent enough," and he gestured toward a stone sphere, approximately ten feet in diameter, held at the top of a sluice cut into the stone floor above and to one side of the tunnel mouth, "I'll have that boulder released. It will then roll down and into the tunnel, getting faster as it heads downhill." He shook his head. "Nasty."

Ardal asked how one might affect its release. Donal gave him a sidelong glance and demurred. "Forgive me, Captain, but you cannot expect me to reveal all the city's secrets in one day."

When they arrived at the stable yard of the garrison, Donal called for the stable master and gave him charge of their mounts and wains. Before he could shout for the Provost, Donal found him at his elbow and remanded Nabal into his custody, instructing him to take care that no harm came to his charge.

He then invited the company to follow him into the common mess where forty or so city watchmen were enjoying a hearty meal. He indicated a basin, pitcher and soap beside a tapped cask of water. "Wash up, fellows. Then we'll tuck in."

The men stood as though waiting for something. Ardal told Amir, in his poor Alish, "Have them begin."

"My captain, would a soldier take his ease while his captain stands by?"

After a moment's consideration, Ardal understood. The Forsaken were accustomed to taking the remains after their "betters" had eaten their fill. Ardal looked to Partlan.

"Help me here."

"Captain?" Partlan stepped near.

"Help me explain that in our army a soldier washes first, eats first, sleeps first, receives his pay first, before his Ten Leader, then his Thirty Leader, then his Thirty Captain, and so on until all have received what they need. I wash last. I eat last."

Partlan translated and Amir grinned, bowing slightly. "Aye, my captain." The other Forsaken stood slack-jawed in amazement.

Ardal looked from one to the other. "Look you, lads. Understand that I shan't eat until I know all my brothers have enough. As I am hungry, I would eat soon." He called to the youngest of the Forsaken, "Hi, Badur, wash your hands and sit you down. From this time forward, whatever we do, you go first."

Badur looked askance at Amir who sharply told him in Alish, "Your captain has spoken."

Badur gaped at Ardal, bringing him to say, "Come, Badur, let me pour the water for you," and Ardal led him by the elbow to the basin and did just that. Ardal then handed him a towel and gave him a small shove toward the tables.

When he turned back to set the pitcher down, Ardal found another soldier waiting, his hands stretched over the basin. This went on until only Amir and Partlan had yet to wash their hands.

Amir gestured for Partlan to precede him, saying in Tierasalan, "Wash, my brother." Partlan nodded and washed. As he walked away, Amir washed then took the pitcher from Ardal and gestured for him to stretch out his own hands over the basin.

Ardal washed and accepted the towel from his friend. "Thank you, Amir."

"I did as you said, Captain."

"Yes, Amir. Thank you."

The captain and the leader of the Forsaken Thirty

joined their men at table, and attendants brought bread, soup, and water. As the men sopped their soup bowls, the attendants brought roast chicken, spiced potatoes, and cooked greens. After all had eaten their fill, the attendants brought wine and fruit.

Hunger sated, thirst slaked, heart content, Ardal's mind began to wander. He considered the road that had brought him to Galantamhor in the company of Dearthmen who had sworn their lives to his service. He mused on the surpassing strangeness of it all until Donal interrupted with a shout. "Hi, Partie. Have you no courtesy to offer for the Lady of Clan Erc?"

Partlan, who sat to Ardal's side, had been conversing animatedly with the Adnana when the shout had come from the stoop at the entryway of the hall. He was now silent, his face blanched. Looking stricken, he stood shakily and gazed incredulously over the heads of the seated Forsaken toward the entryway. His jaw worked soundlessly for a moment before a single croak escaped his throat. "Aedan."

Reviving, he attempted to clamber over his brothers but stumbled into city watchmen seated at the next table. Before he could right himself, a tall, pale woman with a conflagration of crimson and golden hair undulating down her back grasped his elbow and drew him into a prolonged clasp.

"Ai, my dear kinsman, how come you here with no notice, and arrayed as a Dearthman?" The lady pushed Partlan back to search his face.

He groaned. "Aedan. How could you be here so sound and hale with no word to your people of your whereabouts?"

She gazed around at the seventy or so men now staring openly at them. "I'd have your answer first, as it will no doubt require a shorter explanation and less privacy."

Partlan's eye found Ardal's, asking wordlessly for his leave. "Go, you fool. Why do you stand about like a gad while your noble kinswoman requires your attendance?"

The man's face shone. He crushed his cousin against his side and gestured for her to lead on. They soon passed through the door and out of Ardal's sight. Strange and wondrous it seemed then to him.

Ardal noted that Donal still stood in the doorway, and so he beckoned him over. "Would you not rather be with your kinsman and your mother?"

"My mother, Captain, made it clear that my presence is neither required nor would be appreciated just now. Aside from that, my duty is to you while you remain in the city."

Ardal gestured for him to take Partlan's recently vacated seat. Donal accepted with a smile. "Captain, is there aught you require to prepare you and your men for what is to come? There will be a meeting with the senior captains – perhaps with Dermot himself. Might I help to outfit you with more suitable clothing? I could provide you with any type of food or drink you may favor. Merely mention it, and I will do my best to provide it."

"Donal, I'm grateful to receive the provender due a soldier. The food here is hearty and savory. I'd not have anything you couldn't also offer my men. We would all benefit from new clothing. I'm concerned, however, that my Adnana friends might well be more comfortable in ragged robes than in new breeches and tunics. I will ask Amir what might suit them.

"There is one duty that weighs on me, though. I bear a greeting from Aindru, Captain-General of the Western Division, to Flann of the Library. I am charged to deliver it upon arrival. As you see, I am already remiss in this mission. I should have gone there before refreshing myself here."

Donal stood. "At your command, Captain, we may go directly to the library. I am certain that Aindru would approve your decision to ensure that your men were fed first."

Ardal stood and gestured to Amir to meet him in the

aisle that ran down the middle of the mess, then he and Donal made their way to meet him. "Donal, my lad, have you ever been privy to a discussion between a displeased Division Captain-General and the Captain of Foot with whom he is displeased?"

"No, Captain. I have not."

"Nor have I, but I sincerely hope never to be party to it." He stopped. "Donal, my name is Ardal."

Donal matched his gaze. "That I know well, Captain. All of the City Guard know your name as well as all who serve in the Seat of the Captain-General." If it would please you, I will call you Ardal, but in my heart, that word will come to mean 'Captain'."

Ardal scoffed. "You are certainly Partlan's kinsman." They then joined Amir.

"Amir, Donal will escort me to the library where I will deliver Aindru's message to the librarian. I might be detained there, so Donal will return to look after you all. He will also discuss with you the matter of new clothing and boots for the men, as you will advise him. Any questions?"

"You and Donal go to the library. I do not know this word, but it matters not. Donal will ask me about the things the men need. Is that correct, Captain?"

Ardal clapped Amir on the shoulder and said in Alish, "That is the meat. The sauce comes later," a phrase Amir had taught him.

Ardal checked his satchel and nodded to Donal. As soon as they had gained the privacy of the crowded street, Donal asked Ardal about his newfound kinsman.

"Partie, you mean?"

"Yes, Cap… Ardal. I mean Partlan, the man who is now alone with my poor, widowed mother. What can you tell me of him? Should I trust him? Should aught about him concern me?"

"I would and have trusted the man with my life. I see no reason not to trust him with my wealth or family.

Except that he might exasperate her with tales and exaggerations, I think Aedan will be safe. From all I've heard of her, Partlan will likely want protection from her before long."

Donal chuckled. "She is a formidable woman."

"Lad, you will forgive me. I did not imagine that your father had crossed over. Did he exact a great toll of his adversaries before he fell?"

The young guardsman released a sharp, sardonic bark of a laugh. "Aye, Ardal. He exacted such a toll that it became legendary throughout Galantamhor. He was a hero at his cups and overthrew countless hordes of them over the years before they overthrew him. He died awash in his cups as well as in his piss and vomit."

"I'll not mention him again then, brother."

"That is the highest honor you could pay him, Ardal." He looked away. "Perhaps, one day, I will earn the right to call you brother."

"Brother, you have chosen to serve honorably in spite of the lessons of your youth. Courage may be expressed in countless ways. Let the tongues wag. You are not the man your father was for he was no man at all.

"Now, let me tell you of your kinsman. I sometimes doubt his sanity, but never his honor... or his wisdom. Quite honestly, it's not his sanity I doubt when he is about; it is my own. How can a man have survived all he has yet remain so passionate – so unprotected from the agony that surrounds him? Have I lost or even killed a part of myself by protecting my innards from the suffering and madness? I cannot say, but Partlan makes me wonder if I could be a better man."

Ardal regaled Donal with tales of Partlan's exploits. Donal laughed loudly as Ardal quoted many of Partlan's strange comments then nodded thoughtfully as their meanings became clear to him. By the time they had arrived at the Library, Donal's opinion of Partlan had become a deep and rich respect, as his respect for Ardal had deepened.

"Ardal, this is the entryway to the courtyard of the library. I've no doubt you can find your way back to the barracks." He pointed to the gate towers. "Orient on those. Keep them to your left and walk downhill until you arrive in familiar territory. Thank you, Captain, for the enlightenment."

"It is I who am indebted to you. Please, see to my men. If we might find them suitable clothing, that'd be a great kindness. Now, away with you, Donal, my lad. I've a task before me."

The men clasped forearms and parted ways. Ardal approached the gatemen and requested admittance in the name of Aindru, Captain-General of the Western Division. One of the gatemen offered to escort him.

He glanced at Ardal then quickly looked away. "Captain, am I right in assuming you are Ardal, Captain of the Forsaken and Hero of Hart's Pass?"

Ardal halted abruptly, the gateman going on a pace before stopping. Ardal fixed him with his somber gaze. "I'm no hero ... but I've known a few."

The gateman nodded, and Ardal walked on again. When the gateman caught up, Ardal answered that he was indeed Ardal, Captain of the Forsaken by an indescribable fluke. "I was at Hart's Pass. If you desire to know more, I'll refer you to the reports that have been published. Now, where is this Flann?"

"My apologies, Captain."

The gateman opened a small door set into one of a pair of great doors that led from the courtyard into the great library. He gestured Ardal to enter then followed him in, quietly closing the door behind them.

Before them stood a broad staircase of dark wood within a tall atrium. The stairs rose to a landing, twice the width of the staircase. At each end rose a narrower flight of stairs.

Long, high-groined, wood-paneled hallways led off to

either side, along which tall stained glass windows faced out into the courtyard, throwing a colorful mosaic onto the inner walls.

"This way, Captain," and the gateman gestured into one of the hallways.

Ardal nodded but then said, "I would have expected the office of the Chief Librarian to be found at the top of these grand stairs."

"Aye, Captain. It is as you say, but I take you now to the Chief Librarian's secretary who will ensure you come before the Chief Librarian himself. I must soon return to the gate."

Ardal nodded and was led on, wondering why the secretary's office would be so far from the Chief Librarian's. Then the shifting flashes the dying sunlight cast through the stained glass onto the dark paneling drew his attention. He could almost make out the images portrayed in the windows by the patterns of light on the dark wood.

The gateman halted before a curtain and drew it aside, revealing an alcove furnished with a desk and behind which sat a rotund, beardless young man. He spoke in a high, peevish whisper. "What do you want at this time of day? It's—" Ardal stepped into the small space and the secretary raised an eyebrow. "Ah, we have a guest."

"This is Ardal, Thirty Captain of the Dearthmen known as the 'Forsaken', late of Hart's One Hundred, come here by way of the Seat of Aindru, Captain-General of the Western Division, with greetings from the Captain-General for Chief Librarian Flann himself."

The secretary appeared befuddled, as Ardal reckoned anyone might after such a verbose introduction. The gateman then said, "I thought the delivery of such an important greeting from such an important man to another such important man by hand of such a great Captain might require the involvement of the Chief Librarian's personal secretary."

The secretary's befuddlement deepened, and the gatemen began to sound exasperated. "Because I recognize the importance of communications from the western borderlands and because I know the severity of our master, I brought him directly here to you, his secretary, so you could ensure the proper delivery of the important message the captain bears."

The secretary's round face brightened noticeably. "Quite right. You are to be commended, Gateman" Then soon shooed him from his office.

The secretary cleared his throat and held out his hand, palm up. "You are so *young* for a captain. Forgive me." He fanned his hand before his face and took a deep breath then let it out in a protracted sigh, extending his hand again. "You have done well, Captain. You may hand me the documents with full confidence that I will place them into the hand of the Chief Librarian as soon as I may."

"I thank you for your offer of assistance, but I'm to place the documents directly into the hand of Flann himself."

"Oh, you soldiers. You're all duty and honor and rules and missions. I am the Chief Librarian's secretary and as such his right hand; therefore, when you give the documents to me you have placed them into the hand of Flann, in a manner of speaking."

Ardal only stared at the mewling, smooth-faced man before him. The secretary dropped his hand to the desk and sighed. "Of course, Captain, if you insist, you may wait here until the Chief Librarian returns tomorrow. It is late in the day, and he has gone home. You might return tomorrow to find him available. I will try my best to adjust his schedule so you may see him, but it is not as simple as it might seem to you."

He shrugged and smiled. "Or perhaps, Captain, you might find me worthy of your trust in this small matter. He extended his hand again, tilting his head.

"You give me your word of honor that Flann will

receive these documents as soon as he returns to his office?"

The secretary looked up, his smile broadening into a grin. "My word of honor, Captain. He will receive the documents as soon as I am able to present them to him."

Ardal took the sheaf of documents from his satchel and laid it onto the soft, sweaty palm of the secretary. He turned to leave then looked over his shoulder. "Upon whose honor have I entrusted these documents?"

The secretary seemed confused. "Mine, Captain. You have my word of honor."

"Yes, but whose word and whose honor? Who are you?"

"You know who I am. I am Secretary to the Chief Librarian."

"Yes, I know your title, but what is your name? The honor of a nameless man is not as valuable as some might think."

"Oh, well, I am known as Abban."

"Upon Abban's honor and therefore upon Abban's head be it."

"Upon Abban's head be it."

Ardal nodded and pushed aside the curtain. He stepped into the now torch-lit hallway and wondered what might linger in the shadows between their pools of light. He hastened to the entryway and back out into the dusk light, relieved to be leaving this business behind.

As he strode across the courtyard, a voice came from the darkness beyond the gate. "A good evening to you, Captain."

Ardal stopped to thank the gateman for his assistance but then realized it was the one who had remained behind at the gate. The other, it appeared, had been replaced.

"Is it standard procedure to change guards one at a time?"

"No, Captain, but we cannot have a gateman on watch who is too ill to carry out his duties."

"Of course not, lad. I hope he is able to return to duty soon."

"Likely he will, Captain. He did not seem overly ill to me. I call it malingering, but what do I know? I'm no healer. It was an honor to meet you, Captain. Do you know your way from here?"

Ardal oriented himself on the gate tower and raised his arm, pointing. "I reckon it's there."

The gateman grinned. "You've a deadeye, Captain."

"Nah," and Ardal grinned back. "The guardsman who brought me here showed me how to navigate by the tower. G'night, lads," and he ambled off down the hill and into the darkness.

CHAPTER 10
Debriefing

"The patriot volunteer, fighting for country and his rights, makes the most reliable soldier on earth."
LTG Thomas J. "Stonewall" Jackson

Throughout the following days, Ardal was summoned by various officials both military and civil to tell and retell his story, to answer questions about the Dearthmen and even about the Avinn Vale, which it seemed was of great interest to many even though, one official dismissed it as "a little-known and little-thought-of place."

The surrendered Dearthmen were questioned, Partlan and his fellow Bracties acting as interpreters. The Bracties were questioned separately. On the word of Donal, Partlan was accepted into court as an emissary of King Niall of Clan Erc of Bractland with an invitation from the High King for Niall to bring all who would come and dine with the High King in his home.

The arms and armor of the fallen were inspected then cleaned and mended then sent along with a packet of documents by messengers to the great library. A clerk prepared two vouchers for the family of each fallen man. One promised an amount equal to any pay owed the fallen man, and the other, the amount of an established death gratuity for his family. Included also was a statement releasing his parents, widow and children from the requirement to pay any taxes all their lives. Finally, there was a personal note purportedly written by the High King, himself. No one else ever read these but the families, and they never divulged their contents.

One day, Ardal was summoned to the armory. There, he met the master armorers of the Tierasalan army. There were a score of them who had been studying the captured enemy weapons as well as the damaged arms and armor of Hart's Hundred. The one who was most insistent to speak with him was called Brady – the chief metallurgist. He had studied the weapons of both the Tierasalans and of their foes and plied Ardal with questions concerning the performance of the Dearthman swords and armor.

Having done all they could to ascertain the qualities of Dearthman steel, the chief armorer and metallurgist made their reports to the Captain-General of the Armies of Tierasal – Dermot of Heatherdale. Ardal was invited to listen in. After the presentation of much technical information by the assembled experts, Ardal was called up to answer impromptu questions from Dermot, which generally touched upon the comparative qualities of Dearthman versus Tierasalan steel from the standpoint of their performance in combat. He gravely thanked Ardal for his time and service and then dismissed him.

As he walked toward the doors at the rear of the room, Ardal heard Dermot say, "It is imperative that we develop stronger, lighter steel weapons and armor, capable of countering those who threaten our realm. In order to better understand the qualities of our enemies' superior weapons, we must know more of their methods of production. We must send a team to spy it out. Now, tell me, Whom shall I send?"

The words barely had time to enter Ardal's mind before he found himself returning to the counsel table. "Captain-General, if I might speak for one moment more? A thought occurs to me."

The eyes of the Captain-General and all his senior advisors turned to Ardal expectantly. His own knowledge that he was completely unqualified to make recommendations to these men now overwhelmed him, but still they waited.

"Forgive me …" For what seemed like an eternity, Ardal vacillated between plowing on with his half-formed idea and excusing himself from the chamber. His gaze wandered around the table until he locked eyes with Dermot who nodded almost imperceptibly.

Ardal forged ahead. "It seems to me that we have a singular opportunity to answer the questions that plague us. Here in Galantamhor, we have a small unit of Dearthmen Soldiers sworn to serve Tierasal, led by a loyal Tierasalan who also happens to be a blacksmith rated as an armorer and blade-smith. Gentlemen, I know steel – from smelting to shaping to sharpening to wielding. The Forsaken know the terrain, the culture and the language. I do not yet know how this can be done, but I know who can do it."

Ardal's supply of words then ended. He now stood, slick with sweat and panting, as though he had just wrestled Ekurn, his former Ten Leader. At first, no one said a thing, but then Dermot favored him with a tight, crooked smile and a curt nod. "Thank you for your proposal, Captain. We will take it under advisement and inform you of our decision concerning its employment."

Realizing he had again been dismissed, Ardal nodded. "Captain-General." He turned on his heel and near sprinted from the room, thinking, "You are a fool, Ardal, and now the Captain-General has been made aware of the fact as well."

He intended to head straight to the barracks and lay

down for a good, long sleep, but Amir was waiting in the courtyard. "You had success?" he asked in Tierasalan.

Ardal shrugged. "I had success in making myself more of an ass than I already was."

Amir's concern was as evident as his confusion. Ardal peered sharply about. "Scrios. Where is this Partlan?"

"He is with his kinswoman, Captain, as you commanded him to be."

Ardal sighed. "Aye, he is and should be. Meanwhile, I've a tale to tell you that I'd rather not tell, but that you must know, and I lack the words for it. Let's find an inn, my friend, where we can talk at leisure and with no fear of interruption. I will tell you all as well as I can.

"Afterwards, I will lay me down and not stir until the High King himself requires it. Walk with me, Amir. I have done a thing that might give you cause to curse me."

Amir assented, and the two wandered on without speaking until Ardal spied ahead the welcome shingle of the Angry Cock. "Seems my sort of place," and he indicated they should make their way there.

They arrived early for dinner, so found themselves nearly alone in a large dining room. Without needing to consult each other, they chose a table in the back corner of the room, and sat so that each could observe one of the entrances to the room. The hunger they had until then kept at bay now renewing its insistence, Ardal called for food and tea.

He finally looked at Amir. "Thank you, my friend, for your gracious silence and for graciously allowing me my own. I owe you an explanation and will do my best in the absence of Partie."

The tea arrived, and Ardal nodded his thanks, but the lad who had brought it merely stood staring at Amir. With some agitation, Ardal asked the boy his name.

"Nevan, Sir. Is that…" and he swallowed. "Is that a Dearthman, Sir?"

Amir stood, and the lad leapt back, startled. The Thirty

Leader of the Forsaken extended his hand in greeting and addressed Nevan in Tierasalan. "Nevan, I am Amir, and I am at your service."

Nevan was wide-eyed, and glanced at Ardal then continued staring at Amir. "He speaks normally, Sir."

"No. Normally he is silent, but when he does speak, he speaks of normal things in one of two languages. Take his hand, lad, then bring us that squab I smell roasting."

Nevan grasped Amir's forearm and studied his face. "You are not so different."

There was a hint of moisture in Amir's eyes as he smiled. "You are also not so different." After a moment, he released Nevan and took his seat. "The Captain, here, can be difficult when he wants food. It would be wise to feed him before he becomes so."

"Captain?" Nevan searched Ardal's face. "But you are young for a captain."

Ardal peered sharply at the boy. "You are a smart lad, but a wise one would have my plate before me," and the lad skittered off and returned with two plates each bearing half a roast hen with a mound of mashed green peas. Then he came around with a ewer of fresh, cold water and two cups.

While shoving hunks of bird into his mouth, Ardal employed his best combination of Alish and Tierasalan to lay his proposal before Amir. He was prepared for the man to respond angrily, to tell him he had no right to volunteer his men and risk their lives in an ill-advised invasion of the Dearthlands.

Instead, Amir considered the proposal then responded thoughtfully in Tierasalan. "If you intend for this mission to succeed, you will need to greatly improve your grasp of Alish and perhaps spend more time in the sun."

With that settled, the men fell silent until Ardal rose and stretched. "Well, I've had enough of this."

Amir stood. "To the barracks?"

"Is there another option?" and Ardal led the way there.

CHAPTER 11
High Council

"If you know your enemy and know yourself, you will not be imperiled in a hundred battles."
The Art of War
Sun Tzu

Upon their arrival at the barracks, Ardal found a page awaiting his return. He briskly nodded in salute. "Dermot, Captain-General of the Armies of Tierasal sends his compliments and requests that you attend him in the council chamber at your earliest convenience, Captain."

"'My earliest convenience', eh?" Ardal wondered aloud, thinking on his longed-for rest. "My friend, can you divine for me what exactly is the ratio of 'earliest' to 'convenience'?"

The page cleared his throat. "In my estimation, Captain, since you ask, you would not be much mistaken if you were to run there as quickly as you can. The council has been expecting you for some time now."

"Right, then." Ardal looked at his Thirty Leader. "I'll ask you to come along, Amir, if you will."

"With a will, Captain." Ardal found himself sprinting to catch up, the page jogging along behind.

Arriving at the Hall of the Seat, Ardal yanked the front door open and strode through to the council chamber. He pulled the door open just enough to peek inside, finding all eyes fastened to the doorway.

Brady half rose and shouted, "Ardal. Stop dawdling. Get you into this chamber."

After stepping inside Ardal held the door for Amir. He glanced at Dermot who gestured for them to approach and invited the Dearthman into his counsel. "Amir of the Adnana, Thirty Leader of the Forsaken, you are welcome here. I trust your captain has advised you of his plan?"

Ardal leaned over and whispered to Amir as they approached the council table. "The man who addresses you is Dermot, Captain-General of the Armies of Tierasal."

Amir nodded a Tierasalan-style salute to the Commander of Commanders. "Captain-General." Amir then said slowly, attempting to fit Tierasalan words to his ideas, "Ardal has described the matter more as an idea than a plan. We have decided between us to develop a plan from this idea if this is required of us."

Dermot smiled broadly. "Perhaps, my friend, you will find that some in this room might assist you in developing such a plan. Please, take your seats and join our discussion."

"My honor, Captain-General." Amir nodded and pulled an empty chair from beneath the table, leaving the one to its right for Ardal who pulled a roll of blank papers from his satchel and sat next to him. After laying out the papers and opening a small bottle of ink, he sharpened his quill with the small knife he always carried and looked about to signal his readiness.

Dermot gestured to a lanky man with a circlet of white hair. The man fixed Ardal with his gaze after pointedly studying Amir for a moment. "Ardal, I am Rory, Captain-

General of Sensors. My duties include, among many others, studying our enemies and advising the Captain-General of the Armies of Tierasal concerning their likely actions in any given set of circumstances—"

"And he predicts the weather," the wide-set, thick-necked man seated at the opposite end of the table to Dermot said in a tone of facile credulity.

Across the table, another man waved his hands about in a frenzy of mock fear and shouted, "He's a witch."

Rory paused for a moment, allowing his colleagues to complete their antics. "As Captain-General of Sensors, the mission you propose would fall directly within my purview."

"But then, what doesn't?" The question came from the man at the end of the table.

Rory sneered without taking his eyes from Ardal. "I am terribly interested in knowing, Captain, how you might intend to accomplish the proposed objectives." He peered intently at Ardal, as though trying to hear his thoughts.

Ardal glanced about then looked back at Rory and squirmed beneath his intense gaze. "I, ah, had not actually thought about what I said when I said it. I merely saw an opportunity to assist in what seems to be an issue for our whole army and therefore of all Tierasal."

Warming to the topic, Ardal paused to focus his mind. "The unit that would undertake this mission must employ, at a minimum, one man who knows enough of steel production and the manufacture of arms and armor to identify the specifics of their materials and processes that might make Dearthman steel superior to our own. It is conceivable that I might fill that role.

"In addition, a deep knowledge of the language and culture would be required, in order to allow that unit to function within the manufacturing facilities long enough to gather the required information. Amir, of course, possesses such knowledge and can impart it at will to others." Ardal glanced at Amir who lowered his gaze to the table in deference. "The unit should also be large enough to ensure the success of the mission. Altogether, the Forsaken number two dozen.

"Based upon my discussions with the Chief Metallurgist," and Ardal glanced at Brady who nodded his assent, "it is my recommendation that we focus on the smelting process rather than the production of weapons. It is their steel that is superior rather than the weapons into which that steel is made, if you take my meaning. I believe that the most effective method of gathering the necessary information would be to station men inside a production facility as workmen, to observe and record the particulars of the process.

"My assumption, based upon all I have learned of the Dearthmen from Amir, is that the laborers in the smelters are likely to be slaves. Therefore, the most certain method for ensuring we gain such employment is for us to be sold to the manufacturers as such.

Rory scoffed. "You jest. What man in his right mind would offer to do such a thing?"

The man at the end of the table released a sharp bark of a laugh. "If I remember rightly what I read of Captain Ardal here, he is a Light Footman who became Captain to a Thirty of Dearthmen then led them to Galantamhor to face the Captain-General of the Armies of Tierasal where he proposed a small-scale invasion of The Dearthlands by his own Dearthmen, in order to steal their most valuable military secret. What about this man indicates to you that he is in his right mind?"

Rory stared at his antagonist without blinking. "Stefan, I do not doubt the Captain's fighting spirit, or even his ability to develop interesting solutions to merely tactical problems. I must ask, however, if either of you has considered the possibility – no, the probability – that it might seem suspicious that two dozen men of a certain Dearthman race are all offered for sale at the same time, and only to a facility that produces steel intended for the manufacture of weapons? What of the day when all two dozen throw off their bonds and run east –east, mind you – at top speed? What if they cannot throw off those bonds? Do you sincerely believe that these men have any chance of survival, not to mention success? And once they fail and die, do you harbor any doubt what the repercussions will be for the borderlands of Tierasal?"

Rory drew a deep breath then blew it out slowly. He laid his gaze on Ardal. "Thirty Captain, I do not doubt your skill with hammer or blade. Please believe that I do not doubt your courage. I do, however, suffer some doubts concerning your discretion, your subtlety, and perhaps," he smiled slightly and looked away, "perhaps your judgment."

Rory spoke formally to Dermot. "I cannot, in good conscience, endorse such a mad attempt at gaining the information we require."

Dermot nodded pensively. "Aye, Rory, I do see your point. You raise valid issues. I see you must be intimately involved in developing the methods for mitigating each of these issues, and any others you might foresee. I look forward to your briefing one week from today. If I might offer a recommendation, consider sending one of your best sensors along with the Forsaken to ensure that Captain Ardal, here, does not allow his courage to cloud his judgment."

Rory flushed crimson.

Dermot took in the assembled leaders and specialists with a gesture and his gaze. "One week from today, I expect to see the initial proposal for your plan. I am, as always, available for consultation in the meantime. My initial guidance follows." Each member of the counsel perked up and prepared to take notes.

Dermot pointed at Stefan. "Get them in, get them in place, keep an eye on them, get them out. Propose a timeline for the operation." Stefan nodded.

The man across the table from Ardal now got

Dermot's pointing finger. "Any necessary item we have or we can acquire or fabricate will be made available." The man nodded.

Dermot now pointed at Brady. "Provide Ardal with very specific, focused questions you need answered. Identify the critical points in the process. You have the captured weapons. Analyze the composition of their steel and determine as well as you can if the critical differences hinge on materials or process. This will allow us to focus Ardal's attention and activities." Brady nodded gravely.

Dermot's gaze then fell on Rory. "You have done an excellent analysis of potential impediments to this plan. Now, turn it around and develop methods for countering those impediments. Determine which of your techniques will provide Ardal with the greatest opportunities for success. Teach him. Teach his men if you can. Then select the one sensor you cannot risk losing and send him with Ardal to ensure the success of this mission." Rory kept his face neutral and nodded.

Spreading his hands to take in the whole room, Dermot then told them, "As we plan, prepare and execute, never forget that it is absolutely my intention to bring each of these men home as soon as they have done their job." All heads around the room now nodded solemnly.

CHAPTER 12
Chancy and Costly

"To know your enemy, you must become your enemy."
The Art of War
Sun Tzu

The next week was filled with questions, answers and challenges to those answers. A woman from Rory's staff made a day of plumbing the depths of Ardal's knowledge of Dearthmen in general and the Forsaken in particular. She seemed fascinated by the implications of the apparent factions and rivalries among their tribes. She implored him to take notes and to bring her any additional observations that might bear on such things. She was intelligent, insistent, and pretty. Ardal agreed to whatever it was she asked him to do.

The man who had sat across the table from Ardal during the meeting with Dermot – one Davin by name – carried him away from the Forsaken while they received training on sensing techniques. It promised to be interesting training, but Davin had come under Dermot's orders to ascertain Ardal's requirements for special equipment. His people displayed things such as Ardal had never dreamed of before. He could not imagine a slave carrying any of them and repeatedly made that point.

"Yes, Ardal, well and well, you've no appreciation for my beautiful toys. Well, fie on you then."

"I had hoped I could do more to assist you. Of course, I will supply all the standard equipment and supplies you need. You will have horses and food and weapons to get you as far as they will. Then you will have a caged wain to ride in and shackles to mark you as slaves until you arrive at the auction block. The cages and shackles are equipped with catches that will allow you to open them at will so you may fight if needs be. Beneath the wains are compartments where you will store your weapons.

"If between now and your departure any need occurs to you, ask. If it can be done, it will be. You have seen what my people are capable of. I am available to you at any moment." He grasped Ardal's forearm, looked into his eyes, grinned, and then turned away, admonishing his people to: "Pack it all up. The mighty Captain Ardal disdains the use of such poor implements as we can provide."

Ardal jogged back to where the Forsaken were training to find that Partlan and two of the other Bracties had joined the group. The Forsaken had been broken into three groups around the Bracties who were translating the instruction. At this moment, the discussion focused on ensuring that the whole team knew what each member knew. The instructor, a small, slim woman whose every word and movement was sharp and focused, had been asked why it was necessary for each to have access to all the information the team would gather.

"The answer is obvious, is it not? The information you seek is strategically important. You are only operationally important. The Captain-General has stated his intent to bring each of you back alive, but his purpose is to gather the information on the process of Dearthman steel production.

"If only one of you survives to return with all required information, we will all be very sad for the rest of you, of course, but will consider the mission a success. If all of you come back, but you fail to bring useful information, you will have failed, and something else more chancy and costly will have to be tried. How foolish it would be for you to do these things and gain the necessary information at great cost only to lose the man who held the key to the process.

"This man here," and she pointed to Fasel, "knows the proportions of the metals that must be alloyed. This man," and she indicated Fairok, "knows the process of heating. Which of these two holds the critical information?"

Through Declan, one of the translators, Fairok replied, "Both of us. You need us both."

The instructor scoffed, "I need neither of you." She smiled beatifically. "What I need is your information."

Fairok was transfixed by her beautiful malice. "So, you will send us as slaves to your enemies and are willing to abandon us there as long as you receive the information you need?"

"No, my friend." Her smile softened. "You have much to learn about your new home, much as I did when I came here."

"You are a foreigner?" Amir asked in Tierasalan. The question apparently mattered greatly to him.

"I am ... was a foreigner. My father, a Tierasalan, lived in the North – in the lands north of Tierasal. There he knew my mother. There I was born and learned to shape my life. Now, I am here, and I have learned that no one need remain a foreigner in Tierasal for long."

Turning back to Fairok, she addressed the doubts of all the Adnana warriors. "Know now, all of you, that you must no longer allow yourselves to be called 'Forsaken' for, in truth, you are not. It is with gratitude that your fellow Tierasalans receive your courageous offer to strengthen our position against the savagery to our west. Each of you will be known throughout Tierasal as mighty servants of our land, and of any man who chooses to bear the blessed burden of his own sovereignty…"

A loud whoop rang out in the courtyard. Partlan gestured toward the instructor with both hands and bellowed at Ardal. "This … this, Captain, is what I hoped to discuss after the battle when you told me not to speak." He fairly danced in agitation and joy. "That a man could choose where he might go, what he might do, who he might be. Think on it."

Bemused by Partlan's antics, Ardal told him, "Partie, 'tis a thing all men know. If you would go, then go. If you would speak, then speak. If you would not, then do not."

The instructor scoffed quietly behind him. "You know nothing."

Ardal turned to her, but before he could speak, Badur voiced his budding hope. "Is this true, Captain? May I earn such sovereignty by serving on this mission? May I raise sons who may do as they will?"

"Badur…" Ardal foundered for a moment. "Badur, you have that now."

"I do not, Captain. I have made a vow."

Almost frantic with frustration, Ardal raised his hand in declamation. "I release you." He attempted to look each of them in the eye. "Your vow no longer binds you. You are men. Do as you will. I am no arbiter between a man and his will or his conscience. None of you is bound to me or to this mission by anything other than your own sweet sovereign will. No one who does not willingly choose to go will be compelled."

"Badur, stay here, have sons and daughters, build an honorable life." That this was unclear to them seemed bizarre to Ardal.

"Aye, my Captain, as soon as we return successfully. Then the young women of Tierasal will know that Badur of the Adnana is valiant, and worthy to find a wife among

them. I will go with you of my own sweet, sovereign will."
He grinned and challenged his brothers. "I go first."

The others looked about, seemingly dazed. Amir spoke
quietly. "I go. This must be done. If we do not, others
must. We are best able to do what is required." He looked
about until he caught Hakov's eye. "I choose. I go."

Hakov nodded, "I choose. I go. Unarmed. I go as
binder."

"Thank you, Hakov." Ardal nodded. "We are sure to
need one."

By ones and twos, they volunteered, the last being
Ilyas, saying, "Of course we go," as he shrugged and raised
his palms before him.

Ardal turned to the instructor. "Now, where were we?"

She addressed the group. "Return here at sunrise. Now
go." Except for Amir, the Adnana dispersed. He and
Partlan approached Ardal.

The instructor acknowledged them with a glance.
"Captain, will you come speak with me when you have
done with them?"

"Aye. Where shall I come and when?"

"Where you find me. I have already told you when."
She lifted a small backpack from behind a pillar, threw it
onto her back and strode away.

Amir gestured to Partlan that he should speak first.
Partlan nodded. "Captain, I'll have a part in this adventure,
if you'll have me." He seemed almost hopeful a role might
be found for him.

"Partie, I think we're coming to a point where your
translations are not as needed as they once were. And were
you not dispatched to your king?"

"If you deny me, you turn my own name to dust in my
mouth. I will not shame my king by returning to him to tell
him how I left my brothers at the gateway to glory.
Besides, I am a free man. I will do as I wish."

"Partie, my lad, you have got to do something about
that pride of yours. Yes, brother, you may become a slave

again to the Dearthmen. Does this, then, please you?"

"Captain, I... You leave me speechless at times. Thank you. Yes, I will go."

"Amir, old man, did you hear that? Partie, speechless. Imagine that."

Amir smiled in his slow, cautious way. "It is beyond imagining, my Captain. Do you have a task in mind for Partie?"

"I believe I have a truly onerous one in mind, one that bears directly upon the instruction we heard today." Ardal turned to Partlan. "Aught else? Or might I be rid of you for a bit?"

Partlan released a short bark of a laugh and walked away, mumbling to himself.

"Amir, my brother, how may I serve you?"

"Captain, there are men among us who left wives and children—"

"And you want to know if we might collect them on this mission? I dunno, Amir. It does not seem likely to me. What does seem likely is that we would all die and fail if we attempted both missions." Ardal put his hand on Amir's shoulder. "But let's at least think on it, to see how it might be done."

Amir nodded and offered a slight smile. "Thank you, Captain."

"Aye, Amir, and thank you, my brother."

CHAPTER 13
Hide and Seek

"Many daughters have done well, but you excel them all."
Proverbs 31:29

As soon as Amir left, Ardal ran off to find the sensing instructor. Heading in the direction he had seen her leave, he soon found himself wandering through various training areas. He passed many that were vacant then came upon one that was surrounded by a small crowd of chattering onlookers. He pushed through the press to see that the edges of the training ground sloped down to a chest-deep pool in which two men were grappling sluggishly.

He studied the crowd, hoping to find the sensing instructor. He took a moment to study each person in the crowd then turned away disappointed. A man standing nearby was looking his way. Ardal approached him and enlisted his aid. "I am looking for someone. Can you help me?"

The man seemed interested. "Certainly, who is he?"

"I am looking for a woman."

"Have you tried the Brazen Standard? There's lots of

women there looking to make a soldier their mate." He quickly appraised Ardal. "You might do well there."

"I'm actually looking for a particular woman who, I believe, passed this way ten minutes ago."

"Right. Sorry. Who is she?"

"She's a sensing instructor."

"That doesn't help me. What's her name?"

"Ah, I dunno. She's small, sharp-minded and sharp-tongued, has her dark hair up in a very severe bun, furrows her brow quite a lot, and is dressed in a brown jerkin with green trousers."

"She sounds a nightmare, mate. You'd do better with a lass from the Standard. There's one I've seen there. She smiles like the sun on the water and never has a harsh word for no one. That's the sort you need, mate."

Ardal's grin looked more like a grimace. "Doubtless, you are right." He moved on, realizing he knew nothing about the woman he was pursuing except her appearance. He didn't even know her name. How was he to find her? When she had told him to do so, he had assumed she did not intend going far. He did not know if she was testing him or jesting with him. Knowing the little he did of her, he thought it best to treat this as a test.

He oriented himself on the gate towers, executed a half-right face and walked toward the barracks. From behind him, a woman's calm voice carried a hint of mockery. "Giving up so soon, Captain? I am disappointed. That does not sound like the Ardal about whom I have read so much."

He stopped in his tracks. "Actually, I was going to find Amir to ask him what he knew of you that might help me find you. I thought it might at least help if I knew your name."

Turning to face her, Ardal saw she had transformed. Her thick, wild chestnut brown hair now flowed in waves beyond her shoulders. The jerkin and trousers had been replaced by a plain blouse and skirt each of which was tinted a light red. She reclined against a column and considered him frankly. Something about her, though, suggested her body reclined without inviting her mind to do the same.

Ardal studied her for a moment. "I should have recognized you when I saw you in the crowd at the pool."

She raised an eyebrow and put her hands on her hips. He pointed to her feet. "Your boots don't match your dress."

She fumed, "I run better in boots, so I left my sandals in my bag."

Ardal nodded thoughtfully. "A valid concern when you're being pursued by the Captain of the Forsaken."

"You would do me no harm."

He grinned. "I am glad to know you trust me."

She laughed. "It is not you I trust."

She came to within a few feet of him. "If you care for them as I believe you do, then you will leave this word 'Forsaken' and all its connotations behind you. They must know that they have a home and a people. Isolation – especially the type that can happen in a crowd – gives a man reason to think monstrous things. From thinking them, it is but a short step to doing them."

"This seems a matter of some concern to you."

"I, too, am a foreigner."

"And a sensor who has gained the trust of the Captain-General of the Armies of Tierasal. Lady, I would have your name, and I will learn from you, especially since I apparently 'know nothing'."

A slight scowl flickered across her face, and Ardal prodded her memory. "I heard your comment earlier. So, teach me, if you will, beginning with your name."

"I am Laurelei, a sensor of the 'Veiled Encroachment'. That is the name of our organization within the Sensors of the Tierasalan Army." She seemed disappointed by Ardal's apparent ignorance of the Veiled Encroachment.

He extended his hand. "I am Ardal, a blacksmith of the

Avinn Vale, from a small village known as 'Taermun'. Of course, you know that and all that can be known about me because your work requires it." Laurelei grasped Ardal's forearm as he grasped hers.

She released it almost immediately, seeming embarrassed. That was the first time Ardal had ever noted the calluses on his own hands. "Forgive me, Ardal, for accusing you of knowing nothing. You know many things, of course. I asked to speak with you because I was surprised when you released your men from their vow. A Captain with a mission does not simply release his men from his service. I would know why you chose to do this, and why you chose to interrupt my instruction in order to do it."

Ardal's neck turned a deeper shade of red than it had when Laurelei withdrew from the handclasp. "I did not choose to release them from their vow during your instruction. I became aware of its necessity then and considered it wise to do so immediately. Forgive me my interruption."

"What do you mean you 'became aware of the necessity'?"

"I mean I was not previously aware that the Adnana agreed to execute this mission merely because of the vow. How could I know their motivation?"

"Fool. How could you not know?" The immediacy of her fury was breathtaking.

"So I understood," Ardal watched her closely, "from Badur's comments that the men still felt the onus of the vow even though I had called them 'brothers' and made it known I have no need of slaves."

Laurelei seemed to draw her ire within her. He could not say if she had released it or not, but her demeanor was now calm, focused, almost pleasant. It was unsettling.

She lowered her gaze. "I was wrong to call you a fool. You are merely naïve and arrogant, but not so much that the education of this mission will not bring you wisdom.

Many, perhaps most men, would revel to have twenty fighting men bound to them until death. Some could make a great name from such beginnings."

"Perhaps it seems a failure to you, but I'll not have my name written in the blood of other men."

"Tomorrow. Sunrise." She turned and strode away.

Ardal thought, as he wandered back to the barracks, "Women are a torture and a glory – this one more than most. Perhaps I should find her when I return from this mission. 'If' I should say. 'If I return'."

CHAPTER 14
Sensors and Plans

"I would rather be exact. Then when luck comes you are ready."
<u>*The Old Man and the Sea*</u>
Earnest Hemingway

The next morning, Ardal arrived at the training area well before sunrise and sat on the ground, his back braced against a wall. Above him, in the rafters, some small animal scrabbled about. Amir came a few minutes later, trailed by five of the men. Each bore a basket and a ewer. Amir opened a sack he carried and pulled out two stacks of tin cups. After directing the men to place the items on the ground a little way from where Ardal sat, he looked over. "Ho, Captain."

"Ho, Amir, and are you not always thinking of the things that should be done? I had not a thought in my head about feeding the men until you appeared."

"The kitchen has not yet opened for the day, but the cooks gave me fresh milk and yesterday's bread. I hope to take care of such things before they become a bother to you, Captain. You bear a heavy burden. If you will trust me with such things, you may spend your energy thinking on how we will do this thing."

"I thank you, brother, but sadly must advise that I'll need your help with the thinking as well."

Laurelei's voice came from nowhere. "Among all the captain's shortcomings, one could not add self-delusion, Amir." Amir looked up to a point directly above Ardal's head, and watched her drop lightly from her hiding place among the shadows of the roof beams.

"He openly admits that, for him, thinking is a weakness. Should we not, as good friends and comrades, relieve him of such a burden and allow him to employ his gifts, such as they are, to bluster about and make messes wherever he goes?" She laid her hand in a motherly gesture on Ardal's head.

Amir chuckled. Ardal bowed his head under her hand. "Aye, that'd be a kindness, for sure."

The import of her words settled into Ardal's thoughts, and he glanced up at her. "How do you intend to 'relieve me of such a burden' unless you are with us?"

A mischievous grin broke upon Laurelei's face, like dawn after a night of the new moon. "You see, Amir? Perhaps we *can* teach him to think a bit. It took him less time to understand than I thought it would."

Abruptly, the teasing tone left her voice. "Come, friends, we have much to discuss and less time than we thought to prepare for this mission." She thrust her hand out toward Ardal. He took it and she pulled him to his feet.

She grunted. "You could stand to miss the meal Amir has provided, and perhaps a few more," and she jogged away, Amir and Ardal on her heels.

Amir addressed her back. "What of the men?"

"My second is here and will continue the training I have laid out. Today, we learn to write coded messages. Tierasalan is not entirely unknown to the Dearthmen, so you must encode all our information by means of cloth steganography grilles sewn into your clothing."

Ardal looked in the direction Laurelei had indicated when she mentioned her second. He recognised the same man he had asked for help in finding her the evening before. The ease with which they had toyed with him both amused and disgusted him.

"He told you all I said of you?" Ardal asked between breaths.

"He reports to me." She flashed a grin at him over her shoulder.

They jogged on silently until they arrived at a stout wooden door banded with steel and set into a windowless stone wall. "Must be the treasury," Ardal panted.

"The treasures that reside here are far more precious than mere gold, Ardal." Laurelei drew her leaf-bladed dagger and banged on the door with its butt.

A small eye-level window opened in the door through which a gruff voice issued forth. "State your names, unit and commander's name. Speak the secret phrase. Sing the chorus to 'My Auntie Aegnes had a Pig', then go away 'til next Thursday."

Laurelei's dagger flew at the window which slammed shut in time to deflect it. There was a great deal of fumbling on the other side of the door before it slowly swung open. In one fluid motion, Laurelei recovered her blade, jabbed its tip onto the tip of the doorkeeper's nose, and roared, "Why must you be a trial to me, Fechin?"

Fechin looked thoughtfully down at the dagger, cross-eyed. "Because you need it." He now grinned, wide-eyed. "Because I need it. Because we both love it."

She sheathed her blade and gestured for Ardal and Amir to follow as she shouldered past Fechin, radiating disdain like heat from a forge. Ardal grasped the man's forearm and congratulated him on a game well-played.

"You are this 'Ardal'?"

"I am this Ardal. Perhaps there are others, but I am this one."

"You, my friend, have a long journey before you." He shook his head and closed the door.

Laurelei led Ardal and Amir to a spacious room dominated by a large, shallow, wooden box set on legs that brought it to waist height. It was filled with sand that had been shaped into the terrain of Tierasal and some of the surrounding provinces. Towns and major features of the countryside were clearly indicated by painted markers. A variety of people passed through the room or stood near the terrain table and talked.

Ardal ambled over to the table and traced the western boarder down to Hart's Pass. He stood for a moment, remembering. When he raised his eyes, he realized the room had become still, all eyes on him.

He glared ferociously about, and everyone returned to their tasks. He then asked Laurelei to show him the locations of known Dearthman steel production facilities and military towns.

She went to the northern end of the western border and indicated a town marked "Il-Hofra". "This is the best location for our operation."

"Laurelei, it's deeper into the Dearthlands than two other locations. See here? Qahl and... I cannot say the other one."

"I can see that, Ardal. This location was selected because it is believed to employ implements that are driven by the wind caught in turning towers, much as a mill might be driven by currents of water turning its wheel. It is the only such location we know of. It is our hope to gain technical drawings of the inner workings of these wind towers."

Ardal studied the terrain table for a long while before turning to Laurelei. "How much can we depend on the accuracy of this information?"

Laurelei bristled visibly. "I would trust my life to it."

"And she will." Ardal turned to the speaker and recognized Rory, the Captain-General of Sensors. "As a matter of bold fact, she risked her own life to gather much of the information before you."

Laurelei lowered her gaze. "You honor me too much, Rory. I have failed often and at great cost."

Ardal realized he'd given offence where none had been intended. "Forgive me. I merely asked what a Captain of Light should ask before committing his men's lives. Knowing that this information is valid and accurate strengthens my resolve."

Rory nodded then called across the room to Stefan, the Captain-General of Operational Plans. Stefan responded by waving distractedly at Rory while he continued a heated discussion with a younger man. "Come and tell me how difficult it was after you've done it. Yeah?"

The younger man nodded. Stefan stared hard-eyed at him and repeated louder, "Yeah?"

"It will be done, Captain-General."

"Yeah." Stefan laid his arm across the younger man's shoulders and punched his shoulder. "'It will be done, Captain-General'. That's the right answer."

The younger man walked away, and Stefan finally joined Rory and the others, muttering, "'Never been done before'. Scrios. Dead right. 'It'll be done, Captain-General'. Where do they find these simps?"

"Ardal," Stefan shouted from almost directly in front of him. "What do you think of all these geniuses talking in whispers and plotting to rule the world? Give me thirty dedicated men, and I can rule the world. This lot? They spend their lives dreaming up excuses for anything that looks aught like work. I say, you and me grab a cohort of Footmen, invade this nursery, and teach this lot to think like soldiers."

"Of course, Ardal, you'll remember Stefan, Captain-General of Operational Plans."

"I do, Captain-General." Ardal nodded in salute to Stefan who punched his shoulder by way of response.

"Now, if we could begin our discussion," and Rory

glanced at them all in turn. Ardal noted that over thirty people now filled the room.

Rory seemed pleased with the turnout. "Ardal, what you see here is an assemblage of most of the senior Sensing and Operational Planning teams. The sensing specialists will provide you the best analysis of the most current information we can get. The planning team will produce an effective, well-thought-out plan for this operation.

"Dermot's intent is for this team to provide you the greatest possible opportunities for success. If there is anything you do not understand, anything you disagree with, or anything you think we have inadequately addressed, please raise the issue for consideration."

Rory glanced around the room again, and Ardal understood that, although he had addressed Ardal, he had spoken to everyone in the room. "I will not waste our time by making personal introductions, but over the next few days, you will come to know most of the people here and perhaps a few others. When they offend you, as they surely will, by questions, inferences, implications, and demands, remember that each here has no thought but to make your mission successful."

Rory fixed Ardal with a searching gaze, and Ardal nodded. "I understand, Captain-General." He glanced around the room, meeting the eye of each of the staff members. "Thank you all for your efforts and concern. We will serve this plan honorably and hope to bring success for us all."

Ardal placed his hand on Amir's shoulder. "This is Amir. He is my brother and Thirty Leader of the For…" Ardal caught Laurelei's grim stare. "He is Thirty Leader for the Adnana soldiers who will henceforth be known as the 'Rectified'."

Amir raised an eyebrow to Ardal who now spoke in a low voice. "The new name means 'made right'. Is that well, Amir?"

Amir nodded slightly in approval but then sharply in salute. "My honor, my brothers," which gained him grins and nods from the around the room.

Rory gestured to one of the men on the far side of the room who launched into a lecture that was to end over four hours later. He began by addressing the general situation, including the geography, climate and political background of Tierasal. Ardal wondered why he wasted their time with this until he realized that Amir's attention had been riveted on the lecturer and that he had produced a pile of pages filled with flowing Alish script. When the lecturer switched to focus on the relevant points of Dearthman history and culture, he asked Amir to correct and clarify where necessary.

Over the course of the next five days, challenges, arguments and counter-arguments flew about the room like maddened bats. Rory and Stefan rode this chaotic beast, sometimes reining in the process with shouts, and at others guiding it with well-placed comments.

Ardal noted rancor on only one occasion. When Rory announced that Laurelei would be the sensor who would oversee the mission, sounds of dismay could be heard around the room. Blandly, Rory asked, "Has anyone aught to say of my choice?"

It seemed no one would respond. Rory's face and shoulders settled somewhat. "Well and good, then let's—"

"Captain-General?" A slim, dark-haired man stepped forward.

"Daley?" The tension returned to Rory's countenance. "What are your thoughts?"

"Captain-General, I do not question Laurelei's skills nor her abilities. It's just that she is a foreigner—"

"No, Daley," Laurelei attacked. "You'll not question my skills, but you'll question my loyalty. My skills are merely tools; my loyalty is my self. Rory, I request ten minutes to allow Daley to test my loyalty in the training area of his choice."

"As I believe I said," and Daley raised his hands in a gesture of surrender, "I do not question your skills—"

"Five minutes," Laurelei seethed.

Rory laid the full weight of his glare on Daley. "Dermot, himself, selected Laurelei for this mission."

"I understand that her assignment comes from the highest level, but that knowledge does not allay my concern. She remains a foreigner."

Rory looked toward Laurelei with a quizzical expression. She nodded and lowered her eyes while Rory told them, "Laurelei is the only child of one of the finest warriors who ever served in the armies of the High King. Her proofs of integrity and loyalty have satisfied me.

"If that is not enough for some of you, the Captain-General of the Armies of Tierasal assigned her this mission personally. It might be well for you to know as well that the High King himself approved her assignment." Laurelei looked up sharply at that and Rory nodded.

"Beside all of that, she is the only one who volunteered." It was Ardal's turn to look sharply at the Captain-General of Sensors who ignored him. He caught Laurelei's eye, though. Her grin reminded Ardal of the snarl of a feral cat.

In spite of all he had heard, Daley plunged on. "Forgive me, Captain-General, but who is she, then?"

"She is heir to the House of Killinchy." Rory let the statement stand with no explanation for none was required.

"Go, and sup. We reconvene one hour after sunset. This plan is near done. All that remains is to hear from the Chief Quartermaster and the Chief Armorer."

Everyone began shuffling from the room, discussing the day's revelation in hushed whispers, but Rory raised his voice above the din, "Daley, if you'll give me a moment…" This silenced the whispers and urged the stragglers from the room.

Daley watched until the last of the team had left then

brazenly accosted Rory. "Do you think it worked?"

"Aye, and how could it not?" Stefan said, clapping him between the shoulder blades.

"I believe the doubts were exorcised." Rory displayed a weary but pleased smile.

Laurelei placed a hand on Daley's shoulder. "That was well-done, my friend. Thank you for placing yourself in such a situation on my behalf."

"Ah, it's naught compared to where you'll soon be placing yourself on ours, madwoman. I had hoped your partner in this," and he jerked his chin toward Ardal, "would prove a counter to your recklessness; but, alas, I see he is like to incite rather than suppress your pursuit of risky ventures."

"I don't understand you lot," Ardal leveled at them all, "but feel it's my duty to inform you that I have always paid particular attention to taking all precautions. I cannot imagine anyone could fairly lay a charge of 'recklessness' on me."

Daley laughed aloud, "And yet you are the hero of Hart's Pass."

"Hundred Captain Hart is the hero of Hart's Pass. Do not speak of what you cannot know." Ardal's response came out harsher than he had intended.

"My apologies, friend. I misspoke." Daley's demeanor had become subdued.

"Ardal." Laurelei touched his elbow. "Rory determined long ago that there was some resentment against me as a foreigner in the sensing service, so he devised this plan to bring it out into the open, but in a controlled setting."

Ardal scowled. "Conspiracy."

"If you like." Her reply was pert and unabashed. "It is what I do, and now you are my co-conspirator," and she pulled a folded square of cloth from her sleeve. "This is more dangerous than any sword, Captain." She unrolled it on the table. "This simple square of cloth allows us to communicate vital information in a secure manner. You must master your new weapons, Ardal."

Ardal lifted and inspected the cloth. "Is this the grille you spoke of? It seems to me a worn handkerchief with bits cut out or torn from it. How do we hide messages in that?"

Laurelei snatched the handkerchief from his hand, laid it over a piece of paper on the table and wrote one character into each of the spaces left by its cuts and tears. When she lifted the grille, he could see she had written "Ardal is an ass". The letters were strangely arranged on the paper, but the message was clear.

After smirking at him, she filled in the rest of the paper with random letters, so the paper then appeared to be nothing more than that. "Orientation is, of course, critical." She indicated a small mark in a corner of the cloth. "Top, left."

She again laid the grille over the paper, so only "Ardal is an ass" was displayed. She stared at him until he nodded his understanding, then she folded the cloth and stuffed it into her sleeve. "Master your weapons, Ardal."

CHAPTER 15
Plans and Operations

"The best laid schemes o' mice an' men gang aft agley."
"Tae a Moose"
Robert Burns

A month of training and preparation later, the plan had been revised countless times before finally being signed off by Dermot. His signature transformed the plan into an order. Ardal briefed it in practiced but broken Alish to the Rectified with Amir interceding. They talked through it repeatedly for weeks

Each member of the team had primary and secondary responsibilities. The primary for one soldier was assigned to another as his secondary. This allowed double coverage on each task in the likely case that someone were lost.

Any of the soldiers was subject to being quizzed by any other at any time concerning any aspect of the mission plan. The penalties for failing a quiz were always challenging, sometimes embarrassing, and occasionally unthinkable.

Once, Badur challenged Ardal and announced the

penalty: "Steal a kiss from the Lady Laurelei."

Ardal was perplexed that Badur could so badly misconstrue his appropriate appreciation for Laurelei's obvious valor, intelligence and capability as mere sensuality. "Nay, brother. I am no thief. I'll not steal from her. I do not believe there is a man who could. Choose another penalty and let us hear the question."

Ardal earned Badur's latrine duty for the day. He spent that day weighing the threat of a humiliating death against the delight of stealing Laurelei's kiss. He finally concluded that a pilfered kiss would lack the deep satisfaction of a proffered one and set his heart on earning that moment.

A Thirty of Horse was tasked with escorting the Rectified to the border and awaiting their return. Ardal made a point of introducing himself to the Captain and Leader of Horse as soon as he knew which unit had been selected. Both were inexplicably replaced a few days later.

As it was imperative for Ardal to gauge the level of trust he could afford to invest in the newly assigned leaders of his escort unit he located it and asked a passing footman to point out the newly assigned captain and leader. The soldier indicated two men huddled together, their backs to him.

One hobbled away from the other, and Ardal became incensed. He cursed the Captain-General's staff who had taken away a perfectly capable leader to burden him with a cripple. He hoped the other made up for his friend's weakness.

Ardal approached the remaining man from behind, coughing to announce himself and then saying, "It's sorry I am to bother you, but it's time we met."

"Aye, I s'pose it is." The response was growled and slurred. When the speaker turned around, Ardal barely controlled his revulsion. One side of the man's face was a puckered mass of purple scars. A bandage covered the eye socket.

It took a moment for Ardal to realize he was looking at

Elgin, his former Thirty Captain. He relied on humor to regain his composure. "And the ugly fellow with the game leg?" He jerked his thumb over his shoulder in the direction the cripple had hobbled away. "Cian?"

Elgin grinned, the effect ghastly. "'Course. Old crank started threatening bodily damage to senior captains when they offered him his pension. They were gonna send me home, too, but the Thirty Captain for this mission begged me to take his place. It seems no one else could possibly replace him, and it only cost me half a month's pay." He grinned again - hideously.

Ardal crushed him in a wild embrace then stepped back abashed. "Elgin, I am…" but he could then only gesture at Elgin's ruined face.

"Ah, this?" He flicked the bandage over his eye socket with his thumb. "This is none of your doing, Ardal. On the other hand, the fact I now draw breath is very much your doing. Thank you, my brother. You saved me, and that was the least of your deeds that day."

"No, Elgin. Let's not speak on it." Fear and mourning knotted Ardal's guts. "I've duties to attend to. Will you and Cian find time to meet with Amir and me at the Inn of the Angry Cock, as soon after sunset as possible?"

"Yeah, alright." He laughed. "Sounds like the place for you. Sunset then."

They spent hours that night discussing the mission, their plans for afterward and the virtues of a settled life in a quiet place. Amir, who had no taste for any libation other than water or tea, ably guided each of them to their bunks by the end of Third Watch.

Three months from their arrival in Galantamhor, they again passed through the tunnel under the wall – this time, out into a light snowfall. Most of the ten-day journey to the insertion point passed like a blur for Ardal. He left all concerns for security, navigation and provision to Elgin, and thought only on the mission to come.

The Rectified quizzed each other repeatedly, and no

one had to be penalized. Each knew the plan, including the responsibilities of each of the other men, as well as his own.

For the insertion point into the Dearthlands, Ardal had selected a narrow canyon nearly a hundred miles south of the direct path from Galantamhor to the objective of Il-Hofra. His idea was to penetrate into the Dearthlands for a distance then turn north, to approach the targeted town from the south rather than the east or northeast. This ought to serve to misdirect any consideration of the true origin of the Rectified.

As they entered the canyon for the Dearthlands, Elgin called Ardal aside. Cian joined them, and Ardal waved Amir over. The Rectified and two Horse Soldiers continued to the west, the remainder of the Horse Thirty turning northward.

Elgin stood in his stirrups and raised his hands in declamation toward Amir and Ardal. "You men. You two men. Ach, my heart.

"I will give my remaining eye to see you return hale and triumphant, but will gladly see you return merely hale."

He paused. "No. That is what I wished to say, but it is unworthy of you. What I must say is that this is a wholly mad venture that lays a great responsibility on your heads. You must not think on that, however, unless you begin to waver. Then think on it only long enough to stiffen your spines but not long enough to break them.

"Think only on what you must do next or the magnitude of the thing will crush you. You are the right men, at the right time, in the right place to take this battle. You have the plan and the training that will carry you through.

"I will remain in the watchtower above Aislin Falls until your return. When you have met your objectives, head due east with all haste. When you can see it, orient on the tower. I will be there."

"Aye, Elgin," Ardal returned. "We know the plan. We

will come to you. It is an honor to serve with you, my Captain."

Elgin grasped his forearm. "The honor is mine, my brother."

Cian nudged his mount in between theirs and broke them apart. "Aye. Let's all dry our eyes and get on with it.

Ardal extended his hand, Cian grasping his forearm. "For a stupid ape, you make a pretty captain."

"Honor, Cian."

"Honor, Captain." He held Ardal's eye for a moment then broke contact and walked his horse over to Amir. "Listen, Amir, these young captains are sometimes too smart to do what makes sense. It's our job to let them know when their 'great ideas' are just so much spittin' in the wind. The way I tell my boy in front of the troops that his latest idea is barking mad is to say…"

"'That's a *great* idea, Captain'." Elgin interrupted Cian to quote him. "Never fails. I get the message, and the troops never know we had a disagreement."

"I will remember." Amir extended his hand.

Cian looked at it askance. "You know, Amir, I cannot clasp hands with you."

Amir slowly lowered his hand. "Honor, Thirty Leader Cian."

"We'll see, Amir. We'll see."

Elgin, though, walked his horse over and thrust out his hand. Amir grinned and returned a proper Tierasalan armclasp. "Honor, Captain."

"The honor is mine, my brother. Keep my lad here from losing his head … unless it becomes absolutely necessary."

"How shall I know when that is so?"

"I dunno, Amir. You're the Thirty Leader. Is that not a thing you must know about your Captain to become a Leader? Cian, tell him."

"Aye. You'll know. You're no fool. The problem is," he jerked his chin in Ardal's direction, "that one is."

Elgin and Cian rode north at a canter, to catch up with their column. Now, the weight of their venture landed on Ardal's shoulders. Amir rode alongside him and sang an Alish song of sliding tones and long vowels. It seemed half moan and half keen.

The Rectified meandered through the canyon until they reached its southwestern end where it widened into a small field. There they dismounted and secured their weapons and armor in the compartments built into the undersides of the wains. They then turned over their horses and anything that might identify them as soldiers to the two Horse Soldiers who had come with them. As the soldiers led their beasts away, the Rectified made camp and prepared to enter the Dearthlands.

According to the plan, Amir was a slave trader, and Laurelei his concubine. Except for his pale skin, Partlan's mastery of the language and culture of the Dearthmen would allow him to pass for one of them. Amir recommended that he blame his sickly pallor on his Bractie mother having been abducted by a Dearthman who had then sold him as soon as he was old enough to work.

Ardal's story was a bit more complex. Rory wanted to ensure that he would be allowed to observe work in the more sensitive areas of the armory where the Dearthmen would never admit someone who might be perceived as a threat. After much discussion, Rory recommended that Ardal give them reason to perceive him as a half-wit. Laurelei declared he was born to the role.

Amir assured them that the general assumption among Dearthmen was that Tierasalans were half-wits anyway, and that it would work in their favor. Ardal's halting Alish would add to the illusion as would the habit he developed of slapping himself and pulling his beard.

The two heavy wains, outfitted for prisoner transport, were each pulled by a pair of draught horses. Amir drove one, Laurelei seated next to him, Hakov and Ardal were chained to the bench of the other which Hakov drove.

The other men took turns riding inside the cages built onto the wains and walking alongside, shackled to their bars. All shackles and locks on the cages had hidden releases they could use to free themselves if need be.

In this manner, they followed a meandering stream in a generally westward direction, away from the canyon, now leaving the highlands of Tierasal far behind. The farther they went to the west, the more arid the land became. Ultimately, the stream petered out, and they turned north toward Il-Hofra, their ultimate destination.

Along the way, they stopped at a few small towns where Amir maintained their fiction by making half-hearted attempts at selling some of them. He would haggle a bit then throw up his hands and declare that he would "keep moving until he found serious buyers".

More than a few men offered astonishing sums for Laurelei. It began to sink in to Ardal how precarious was their situation. Amir could, if he chose, become an exceptionally wealthy man. Ardal had believed that Amir was beyond treachery until he began to realize what he could gain by it. What man would not be tempted?

The shackle began to weigh on his mind as well as his ankle. A fear he had never known infiltrated his mind. Logic could not counter, nor could courage dispel, the murky dread that grew in his thoughts. He could not take action against it, of course. All he could do was sit on that bench, day after day, held prisoner by it as he wondered how he would live if he remained a slave.

Hakov commiserated with Ardal's weak attempts at mocking the fear for a few days. Finally, he asked Amir to talk to him. Amir was merciless.

"So, you begin to see what it means to belong to another man – to have no life of your own. You despised us for not simply 'throwing off our bonds'. You think you are strong, courageous, free – that you have sovereignty over yourself as is your right. Know now what it is to be a tool in the hands of another man – bent to his will, broken at his behest — until all that is best in you, that which should belong to you for your use and as a gift to those you desire to bless, becomes a blessing only to your owner. He who will use your blessings to strengthen his hold on you until ultimately you will be so much his property that you will rejoice when your work strengthens his hand against you. This is but a small taste of what slavery means.

"He may do with you as he will. Think on that and despair."

He stared long and hard at Ardal then placed his hand on his shoulder and continued more gently. "And when you have savored your despair until its bitterness becomes the pattern of all your thoughts," and tears ran freely down his cheeks, "think on, my sons, and know my great love for you because of your mercy toward them. Then, in the name of all your men here — those who despite their deep knowledge of such bitterness willingly chose to follow you back into slavery," and he dug his fingers into Ardal's shoulder and shook him, "in their name, find your courage."

Amir allowed Ardal to consider his words for a few moments before, clearly shaken, saying, "You must do this alone because the men must not know of your doubts. However such doubts may gnaw the souls of the men, *your* certainty must be unassailable, or all will be lost."

Ardal shuddered then raised his eyes. "We will leave no one behind. I will die beside 'Joe' before I leave him behind."

Amir's grip loosened. "That is what we need to know. Know that you, too, are 'Joe'. We are your brothers. I am your brother."

CHAPTER 16
Il-Hofra

"The prisoner leaps to lose his chains. But his joy is short-lived indeed."
"Thoughts upon the African Slave Trade"
Reverend John Newton

By the time they arrived at Il-Hofra on a pitiless afternoon, blisters covered every inch of Ardal's exposed skin – that is to say, his nose, cheeks and the backs of his hands. The rest of him was swathed in light muslin that protected his pale skin from the sun and allowed for occasional breezes to cool him. There had been no breezes for many days.

Ardal's lips split, and blood seeped from the cracks. The air was so hot and dry that it seared the inside of his nose when he inhaled, and he could taste blood in the back of his throat.

The seemingly incessant winds over the past weeks had driven fine sand through the folds of his robes and deposited it over every inch of him. Anywhere one part of him rubbed against another, there the sand collected and chafed. Sand filled his ears; it coated his tongue and his eyes.

The first thing Ardal noticed as they drove into the market square of Il-Hofra was a handful of camels gathered around a trough. Before Hakov had the chance to halt the wain, Ardal leapt from his seat, intending to stick his head into the trough.

As a slave, he was, of course, shackled to the bench by his ankle. The chain went taut while he was in mid-air and snatched him back to strike his head against the wheel hub. When he woke, he could not decide whether his head or his ankle hurt worse. Fortunately, he didn't break either.

Amir later told him that he had assured the men that this was a deliberate action, intended to establish his role as a half-wit. Ardal knew the men knew better.

Once he was certain Ardal would live, Amir kicked him and told him to get up. He stomped around the yard, yelling about the "idiot making us all look like fools in the market place of the great city of Il-Hofra".

Hakov was unchaining the men from his wain and linking them together with a chain he'd pulled from beneath the bench when Amir ran over to Hakov, grasped the front of his robe, and backhanded him across the face, snapping his head back and bringing blood to his lips and tears to his eyes. He pulled Hakov forward until their noses nearly touched. "Now, you will know to keep your stupid ape under control."

Hakov hung his head. "It is as you say, Great One." Then Hakov grabbed Ardal's beard and pulled him to his feet, calling him "stupid, stupid, stupid". Hakov yanked his beard in the direction of the wain and kicked him. "Get over there, filthy monkey." He was careful to move the shackle to Ardal's other ankle before he connected the chain.

Hakov took an amphora from the wain and drew water from the well. After he had served Amir then Laurelei, he began to drink. Amir knocked the amphora from his hand, breaking it and spilling the water. "Look what you did, Stupid. You are no better than the ape. Now you will have to drink from the trough. I hope you don't mind the taste of camel spit."

Hakov lowered his eyes. "It is as you say, Great One." Then he knelt at the trough and scooped water up with his hands.

Amir stood behind him and placed his foot on the back of his head, pushing Hakov's face under the water. "I have helped you to drink. Why do you not thank me?"

Hakov lifted his face just above the level of the water. "Thank you, Great One."

Amir seemed to gain control of his anger. "Now, you will let the animals drink, then the slaves. The idiot may drink or not as you like. I go to find a decent meal.

"It will be as you say, Great One." Hakov shuffled toward the wains.

A small man from the knot of people who had gathered to watch the show approached Amir. "Welcome, friend, to Il-Hofra, the source of the Protector's great strength. Here we make the steel for the shields, armor and blades by which he keeps the Accursed at bay. I have a humble house here on the square where you can both refresh yourself and maintain vigil over these valuable slaves."

Amir smiled and bowed to the little man. "The hospitable stranger is an unforeseen joy."

The little man beamed at Amir then indicated the direction to his house. "Certainly, we will no longer be strangers after today."

Amir grabbed Laurelei's wrist and pulled her after him without ever looking her way. She stumbled along meekly behind him.

When the others had finished drinking, Hakov came for Ardal, murder in his eyes. He dragged and kicked him over to the trough. "Drink, idiot, so I won't be troubled with your carcass."

Ardal knelt by the trough and lowered his face to the water. Hakov placed his foot on Ardal's head and pushed it under. When he finally lifted his foot, Ardal's ears were ringing, his sight dim.

Ardal rolled over to sit with his back against the trough, raised his hands above his head and released a great belly laugh while waving his arms about. He started singing whatever words entered his head – a gibberish mixture of Tierasalan and Alish. Among the nonsense, he indicated that he was looking directly at the towers that housed the strange apparatus that Laurelei claimed caught the wind.

Hakov sneered his disgust. "Come, stupid monkey. We will sell you to the great Il-Hofra foundry where we can hope you will have an accident." He reached down to pull Ardal to his feet, but Ardal avoided him and crawled under the wain, then curled up like a dog in the shade.

Hakov ran the chain through the loop on Ardal's shackle, linking him to the other men and to the wain. He took the ration box from the wain and issued a portion of bread to each man, demonstrating who his favorites were by pointedly issuing them with greater portions. Finally, he threw a small portion of bread on the ground in front of Ardal.

There they stayed through the afternoon and into the night. Before nightfall, no one spoke for they were under constant observation by potential buyers and other curious townsmen. Besides, it was too hot to think, much less speak.

After sunset, as the heat became less oppressive, the men began encouraging each other, for in the morning they were to be sold.

CHAPTER 17
Sold

"This creed of the desert seemed inexpressible in words, and indeed in thought."
<u>Seven Pillars of Wisdom</u>
T. E. Lawrence (of Arabia)

In the morning, Amir led the Rectified onto the auction platform and chained them there. He hung signs written in Alish script around their necks. Each of them had been trained to perform a specific step in the Tierasalan process of steel weapons production. They had also been trained to distinguish and record the critical differences in the Alish method. The signs identified the skills and threshold price for each of them.

Hakov was identified as a record keeper and priced at a premium. Ardal's sign stated that his skills included vermin catching and filth removal. It did not state a minimum price.

For Partlan, Ardal had devised a complex role that exposed him to a high level of scrutiny. His hope was that Amir could sell Partie's abilities as an observer and scribe to assist the master of the production complex in inspecting and recording the process. If it worked, he would be able to provide an overview of the whole process and might be at liberty to communicate with the teams stationed throughout the complex.

Even before they were properly assembled, the square began to fill with people who might have been interested in a household or field slave, but when they saw the prices Amir asked, they shouted questions at him, in answer to which he presented his sales pitch.

It was a complex business. Amir had to maintain the illusion that his only motivation was to sell slaves and make money. His true intent, of course, was to infiltrate the men into the foundry.

It did not take long for some clever soul to run off in search of Karim, the armory master. Within the hour, a donkey cart driven by a slave entered the square. Riding behind the driver was Karim – an enormous fat man displaying a wispy beard on his tired, sad face.

Amir set him up to bid against the master of the armory near the village of Qahl. Amir had him bidding against a phantom by convincing him he could just take his highly capable workers to Qahl, where the production rate was so high they could not find enough slaves, and that he had only come first to Il-Hofra merely as a courtesy.

Karim ultimately acceded to the general scheme after he had gained some concessions on price and asserted his independence by removing one man each from the foundry and forge teams and reassigning them to the smelter where he required more workers.

In order to insert Partlan and Hakov into the required positions, Amir appealed to the master's vanity. "How would it be if the master of the great armory at Il-Hofra were attended by slaves who could alleviate the tedium of inspecting, counting and recording? This would leave him at liberty to think and plan as a great leader should." He also had to take a bit less than he had hoped, but dismissed the loss as nearly equal to the cost of continuing to feed so many slaves for the time the journey to Qahl would take.

Ardal was another matter altogether. Karim asked Amir, "And what need have I for a slave such as this?"

"What is that to me? Kill him. Adopt him. Make a spittoon of his head." Amir seemed to consider the idea for a moment. "As for me, my friend, I would put him under the supervision of that one who is the son of the same father," and he indicated Hakov.

Karim noted Hakov's disgust and tittered. "Yes, I will take him. He will entertain me, but you will not receive one copper more, and you must pay for our feast this night. Such is our custom here."

Amir paused to do a tally in his head then agreed to the deal. He beckoned to Hakov who produced a bill of sale from the notes he had taken.

Karim perused the document and chuckled. "I hardly think it was necessary to include the fact that you invited me to a feast to celebrate the success of our business."

He assessed Hakov. "You did not lie about the efficiency of this one. Let us hope his idiot, half-breed, accursed brother does not distract him from his duties."

The men were soon parceled out to their respective departments within the armory compound and assigned to sleeping quarters and workstations. Because the departments were separate and self-contained, Ardal lost track of most of the men. He and Hakov remained in constant contact with one another. Fasel, Badur, and another Adnana named Gullam were assigned to the forge, to which the master's office was connected, so they saw each other often in the evenings in the sleeping quarters.

That night, Amir secured Karim's goodwill by inviting him to bring the leaders of his departments to the feast. This allowed Amir to establish friendly relationships with each in turn. Over time, he would be able to exploit their jealousies to maneuver among the departments.

The next morning, Amir announced he had found Il Hofra to be a pleasant town with friendly inhabitants and that he might stay for a time. Karim asked if Amir did not have a wife who awaited him. Amir nodded, a far-off look in his eyes. "Yes, my friend, I do. At least, I believe I do."

Karim tittered, thinking he understood the joke in Amir's comment.

As long as she was always seen two paces behind Amir when he was out in public and restricted herself to the quarters open to women when he was not, Laurelei was free to look about as she liked. At first, the women would have nothing to do with her. When they discovered that her Alish was good and that she was both gentle and willing to share details of her master's life, they began sharing their own details with her. She was able to gather a great deal of useful information about people and events in the town and armory while disseminating a great deal of false information about the Rectified.

Ardal discovered that slave society was somewhat more complex than he had at first imagined. He had thought to find a tight knot of men united against their oppressors and dedicated to survival, if not resistance.

These men seemed willing to sell their honor very cheaply for a slight increase in food, a lighter work assignment for a few hours, or even a word of approval from a guard, here known as a "rhys". Ardal held these men in highest contempt – even after circumstances revealed him to be one of them. The debasement of his honor was a greater blow to his courage than the loss of his freedom.

Each indignity, each slight, each moment of his life that he lost forever became a stick of kindling that he stacked in his heart, storing them up for the day when he would ignite a balefire of rage within himself. Occasionally, larger slights or even injuries would occur, and he would add a log to that stack. He was very careful for some months to douse any sparks that might come near the pile. An inopportune outburst could endanger the whole mission and the lives of his men. Over time, he had built a massive pyre of resentment, awaiting a moment when his will would be unequal to the task of snuffing out errant sparks.

On a day of days, when he was exasperated with playing the fool, and fatigued with anxiety for his men, another slave stole his bread. For a moment, he tried to douse the spark. He shuddered with the effort to control his rage, then gave in to it utterly.

He broke the man's arm then his other, and was making progress toward killing him when Hakov flew at Ardal, knocking him to the ground. Ardal flipped Hakov over, knelt on his shoulders and reached for his throat. "Ardal, please," Hakov coughed in Tierasalan, and the conflagration died as quickly as it had started.

Ardal fell to one side and patted Hakov on the chest. "Forgive me, brother," he said in Tierasalan, keeping his tone low.

"Idiot," Hakov spat in Alish. Panting hard, he rolled over and slapped Ardal. "All will be well," he whispered in Tierasalan.

While Hakov splinted the arms of Ardal's unfortunate opponent, Ardal regained control of himself and slipped back into his role. He grabbed the stolen bread from the floor where it had been trampled and held it above his head. "Ha." He danced about and shouted, menacing the broken thief, then shoved the filthy bread into his mouth in apparent triumph. Pouring his soup in behind the bread, he allowed it to dribble through his beard.

Much of the kindling had burned away, but now the logs smoldered.

The next day, Karim called an assembly of slaves in the courtyard. The Rhys had a team of slaves push the central podium aside to reveal a slope-sided, circular pit. The man who had stolen Ardal's bread was sent flying headlong into it, trying to break his fall with his broken arms. He rolled about, shouting, then tried to stand. Ardal pushed forward to help him, but a Rhys struck him in the throat with the butt of his whip. He dropped to his knees, gagging, and watched dogs leap into the pit from behind the podium.

The mongrels circled the bread thief, snapping and feinting. Once they had determined he was defenseless, they tore into him. It took longer than it should have for him to die. It was a great relief to Ardal when one of the dogs finally ripped out his throat and so silenced his cries. They continued to fight over the scraps for half an hour more.

The thief's name had been Hassan. He had never spoken to Ardal. He never did him a kindness. He stole his bread. Ardal was to mourn him every day until his life's end.

Karim, from his seat on the platform on the far side of the pit, clapped and tittered then stood. "My friends, you can see what I must do with slaves who become useless to me—"

"He would have healed." Hakov received a whip butt to the gut for his impertinence.

Karim glowered at him. "Do not allow yourself to become useless to me."

A pair of Rhys led the dogs on short chains from the pit and stood with them before the platform.

Karim raised his arms, taking in the entire assembly with sweeping gestures. "My friends, I am aware of the dullness of your poor lives. As your benefactor, I have determined that this is unacceptable and have decided to offer you opportunities to escape your dreary labors, to entertain yourselves, improve your prospects ... and perhaps, get some exercise." He again tittered. "Beginning today, any slave who distinguishes himself in his work may be offered all these opportunities in the pit. Any who fails to distinguish himself in his work will most certainly go to the pit."

Beaming his goodwill at them, Karim issued a seemingly gracious invitation: "Who'll go first?" A man Ardal had never seen before stepped forward and glared a challenge at the world as he descended into the pit. He stood a head above the men around him and had a chest like a wine cask. Someone shoved Ardal from behind, and he stumbled into the pit. He attempted to scramble back up the slope, but his opponent was on him in the space between a gasp and a cry.

From behind, he stuck his arms beneath Ardal's own and linked his hands behind Ardal's head, then shoved it forward until his chin ground into his chest. Remembering Ekurn and Airt's demonstration, Ardal bent forward, lifting the big man from his feet, then leapt backward. His opponent hit the packed clay floor of the pit with their combined weight, breaking his hold, Ardal's head snapping back to strike him on the nose. Ardal jumped up and attempted to clamber out of the pit. The crowd pressed in, shoving him back amid cheers and jeers.

In a desperate attempt to surprise his opponent, Ardal turned and ran straight at him. Running almost into his embrace, Ardal sidestepped but continued forward. Placing his hand on the man's shoulder, he leapt up and descended with the full force of his weight behind his fist as it connected solidly with the side of the man's neck. He dropped. To keep him down, Ardal stomped his heel into the man's inner thigh. It proved unnecessary as the man was already out cold.

Panting hard and hurting badly, Ardal too dropped to kneel at the head of the unconscious man. He poked his closed eyes, twisted his nose and moved his lips. When he lifted the man's head by the ears and moved it from side to side, Karim shouted, "Get that idiot off him."

Ardal jumped up and ran around the pit, yelling vile insults in Tierasalan in every direction and apparently enjoying himself immensely. A Rhys brought four slaves down to remove the huge man while Karim shouted for someone, anyone to take the idiot apart. The reward would be double rations for a week. Ardal heard a man whoop behind him and spun to face his attacker.

It was Partlan. In a mad rush, he was on Ardal: all fists,

feet, elbows, and knees. Each blow was enough to bruise but no more. Ardal took him down and they grappled. "What are you doin', Partie?"

He laughed wildly. "I've dreamed of this day. I've something special for you." He clapped his hands over Ardal's ears, making them ring, and reached for his throat.

Ardal felt something slide into the front of his robe before he broke Partlan's hold on his throat and fell forward, shoving his forearm under Partlan's chin. Partlan struggled for a moment but then apparently passed out.

Ardal leaned in closer. "Good job, my lad. Brilliant. Brilliant." He dragged Partlan around the pit by his ankle and whooped in a mocking imitation of Partlan's first challenge. Ardal then dropped Partlan's ankle, threw his arms over his head and ran around in circles, whooping, until Karim sent Hakov to restrain him.

Hakov grasped the front of Ardal's robe and slapped him. Ardal became subdued and allowed Hakov to lead him away. "What was the meaning of that, Ardal?"

"The Mad Bractie passed me a note. It's inside my robe. We'll read it at rations. See if you can have Fasel join us. I am betting my sanity that he has good news for us. The note is good news in itself. We can communicate." Ardal threw his hands above his head and whooped again.

"Yes, and all it requires is your allowing yourself to get beaten occasionally."

"Beaten? Beaten, lad? No, that was sport. I've not had such fun in a camel's drink."

"Still, Ardal," and Hakov turned to face him. "You must not allow yourself to 'become useless'. The dogs offer no honorable death."

Ardal shuddered. "Aye. Not that. Never."

They moved on, Ardal considering their next step. "We need to figure how to communicate with Amir and Laurelei."

As it turned out, they had no need to figure it out. The next week, the platform was filled with local dignitaries, including Amir who recommended they allow his lovely concubine personally to congratulate the winner. Karim readily agreed.

Maybe he understood the incredible power a woman's recognition had to spur a man on to exert himself. Perhaps he was amused at the prospect of teasing slaves with a glimpse of something they would never again know. It might have been that, in his piggish dimness, he had merely acquiesced to a strange request from a man he hoped to impress.

What he could not know was that Laurelei was establishing communications with her field operatives. The woman was indeed formidable.

Ardal tried to win as often as possible. He and Partlan developed a popular rivalry that had the slaves as well as the visitors clamoring to see them fight each week. They began betting their rations on the outcome. To keep the rivalry alive, Ardal occasionally allowed Partlan a victory. Partlan, of course, made the same claim.

They had a few setbacks, however, such as the time Fasel's note fell through a hole in Ardal's robe. To avoid drawing attention to it, Fasel flipped Ardal over and slammed his face to the ground. Ardal came up with a mouthful of clay, threw Fasel from his back and spit the clay at him, keeping the paper in his mouth.

Once they'd established this system of passing their coded messages, the operation began in earnest. The men had gathered much of the information required of them and could now communicate it. Sometimes, the information led to a new question requiring an answer. On a day of days, Ardal received a note from Laurelei with a new requirement. "Draw wind towers."

Karim effectively ignored Ardal unless he was in the fight pit, and so he was allowed to bumble madly about, chasing rats and removing filth throughout the facilities. During his ramblings, he was able to view and sketch the apparatus from all angles. Once, while he was intent on his sketching, a Rhys surprised him and demanded to know what he was doing. Ardal proudly displayed his sketch which depicted a hastily drawn stick figure with a large misshapen head. He had written "Rhys" above it. The Rhys snatched the paper from his hand and, without looking at the other side, wadded it and threw it into a coal bin. Content that the paper would soon be shoveled into the furnace with the coal, Ardal allowed himself to be kicked and chased from the area.

The two coal-fired furnaces of the smelting facility were a hundred feet long with doors at either end. A pair of level, smooth stone tracks ran inside the furnaces and extended a hundred feet beyond each end. A series of long, low stone skids slid along the stone tracks, bearing a number of earthen crucibles loaded with iron and charcoal. The skids were pulled through the furnaces by means of a pair of massive carved stone chains, drawn through a series of gears by power supplied from the wind towers.

Ardal knew the system well, having once been sent in to remove the crucibles from a jammed skid some way into the furnace. He had overheard the smelting master shout to his second to "disengage the drive before the towers come down."

After a cooling period, a Rhys had sent him in wearing a hooded leather long-coat and thick gauntlets. Even after the furnace had cooled for hours, the heat almost killed him. It took him days to recover, with Hakov's care.

Once he had completed his sketches of the wind towers, Ardal directed the men to collect certain samples and advised Laurelei and Amir that it was time to execute their extraction plan.

They had been slaves for over eight months. They had accomplished the objectives of their mission, and had an excellent extraction plan that should allow them to put a couple of hours behind them before their absence would be noted. Ardal was now possessed of an anticipation almost as wild as the hot winds that spun the towers.

Amir sent him a note. "Hanging shadow brings abaddon to fool."

Ardal read the note twice. It made no sense unless Amir had intended to say "abandon" rather than "abaddon". In which case, it made very little sense rather than none at all. He handed the note to Hakov.

Hakov looked it over. "I do not know 'hanging shadow'. 'To fool' means 'to deceive' – which is Laurelei's specialty."

"Yeah, it's also what she calls me. Maybe she is bringing me abandon. It's sweet, but now is no time for flirtatious notes."

"What is it she calls you, again? 'Fool'? I wonder why. Why do you say that Laurelei is the one who will bring abaddon?"

"She once hid in the shadows above me to listen to a conversation between Amir and me."

"Yes, I see the meaning, now. So, Laurelei intends to bring you abaddon. That is ominous, indeed. It could well endanger our escape. Of course, done correctly, it might facilitate it."

"Scrios, Hakov. Speak plainly." It seemed to Ardal that Hakov was teasing him about something important.

"Ardal, I speak as plainly as you, for 'Abaddon' is the name the Adnana give to your 'Scrios'. Laurelei says she will bring you 'utter annihilation'."

"She intends to destroy the armory." The woman's audacity appalled Ardal. "We've done the job. It's time to go. Nothing further was required of us. She has no authority to risk the lives of my men."

Hakov shrugged, "According to you, we are our own men. Which of these, having learned to own himself, would not desire the destruction of this place? When will we have another opportunity to do this? I say she is right. You know she is right. I only wonder how she will do it. 'Abaddon' implies 'fire'.

"There's plenty of that around here, but something else

here would be more likely to cause 'utter annihilation' than a mere fire. What if the crucibles were ready to pour and, instead, broke loose and spilled?"

Hakov considered this. "No. Not catastrophic enough."

Ardal gave a harsh bark of a laugh and shook his head. He had never heard anything referred to as "not catastrophic enough". "As you say, Hakov, one way or another, we must warn the lads to prepare for extraction."

By means of their steganography grilles, Hakov and Ardal rapidly wrote notes to each of the teams, directing them to prepare to execute the extraction plan and advising them that the signal would be a catastrophic event in the armory.

Ardal ran from workshop to workshop, asking if they required his services as rat catcher. At each, he contrived an excuse to pass a moment with one of his men there, so passing the coded instructions.

CHAPTER 18
Fire, Steel, and Blood

"It is not light that we need, but fire…"
"What to the Slave is the Fourth of July?"
Fredrick Douglass

During the wee hours, Ardal roused Hakov, and together they woke Fasel, Badur, and Gullam. The five men worked their way silently through the sleeping shed and across the armory to the smelting facility. As they passed the well, Ardal ripped the pouch of powder from his trousers and dropped it into the water. Once inside the smelting shed, they quickly dispatched the two snoring rhys with the hammers used to break the earthen crucibles. Drawing the weapons of the dead foemen, they cornered the slaves working the ovens. Badur and Gullam held vigil on the slaves while the other three ran to the wind tower controls.

Hakov and Fasel disengaged the pulley system from the wind towers, then opened wide the gates that controlled the volume of wind passing through the towers, and so the speed at which they turned. The sound of the turning spindles increased in pitch from a low moan to a high whine. On Ardal's signal, Hakov and Fasel engaged the pulley system.

A moment later, he heard a series of loud clangs – metal on metal. Above the din, Ardal shouted, "To the pit, my brothers!" There was a cacophony of rending, splintering wood, screaming steel and what seemed to be hundreds of frantic smiths hammering cold steel. The hammering petered out, and for three heartbeats, the only sound was the deranged wind, then a horrible creaking came from two directions at once.

Looking over his shoulder as they ran toward the fighting pit, Ardal saw both wind towers fall inward toward the furnaces. The crash as they burst through the roof was deafening, but when they crushed the furnaces, there was a sound like a man makes when punched in the gut, but ten-thousand-fold.

A wave of incredible heat rolled outward from the furnaces in all directions knocking them to the ground. Clambering to his feet, Ardal grabbed Hakov's elbow to turn him about and together they followed Badur, Fasel, and Gullam to meet the others at the platform beside the fight pit.

In his headlong dash, Ardal crashed into someone, knocking him into the pit but Ardal continued running toward the platform until Hakov shouted his name and he heard a snarl from near at hand. Two of Karim's dogs were now menacing the man in the pit.

Hakov threw stones at the beasts, drawing their attention, and Ardal joined him. The man laboriously crawled out at the far side of the pit. When he stood, silhouetted against the light of the now raging fires, they recognized Karim. As he ran away, the dogs leapt from the pit and chased after him.

Ardal and Hakov briefly looked at each other, then both ran to meet their brothers.

Without warning, Ardal found himself on his back, having run into someone else. Standing over him, gibbering with his bloody fist raised, was the enormous slave he'd bested in that first fight. Hakov translated: "He says he is Hasim and he's going with us because he knows you have a plan." Ardal nodded. Hakov spoke to Hasim, and he held out his massive paw. Ardal grabbed it and jumped to his feet, and together they ran on.

At the platform, each section leader reported to Amir that all of the men were present and a few had acquired weapons. Hakov explained the brute's presence. Ardal gave orders, and the Rectified sprinted toward the section of the outer wall nearest the furnace complex.

Their semblance of order drew others to join them, and their group grew as they crossed the compound. By the time they had arrived at the wall, they now numbered some fifty men. Ardal directed the few with weapons to guard their rear and sent Hasim with five of his fellows to rush any guards remaining on the gate. The rest he ordered to gather flaming brands from the burning wind towers, so the gates could be burned down, but Hasim was already opening one when they arrived.

They were now nearly a hundred in total as they rushed through. The majority scattered, but the Rectified were soldiers and so knelt in a loose circle in the shadows just outside the wall, allowing their eyes to adjust to the darkness, listening to the sounds around them. Hasim punched Ardal in the shoulder and disappeared into the darkness.

Two Tens of Rhys sprinted through the gate with two dogs on chains. They ran straight on, pursuing the scattering slaves. Ardal's intent had been to let them pass, but Badur clearly had other ideas.

He leapt from concealment and rushed them, laying open the first he met, whirling about to impale another, and finally striking the head of a third before anyone could react. As the rest of the Rectified entered the fray, Badur fell.

Ardal squatted beside him and Fasel helped Badur

climb onto his back. Ardal stood and shouted for the men to break contact, but it turned out to be unnecessary. The Rhys had been prepared to hunt scattering slaves not meet a disciplined military unit.

Three of the Rectified had lost ragged chunks of flesh to the dogs, but the curs now lay whining and thrashing, like their masters.

The Rectified took up the weapons of the fallen rhys and jogged on.

Before long, they stumbled into the market square and found Amir and Laurelei with the cart horses hitched and stamping the ground. Amir ran to Ardal and helped him lay Badur in the wain. Before Amir could speak, though, Ardal pointed to Fasel. "Find a horse. Meet at the east gate."

Fasel sprinted away. Laurelei and Hakov jumped into the wain with Badur and a few other wounded men. Amir and Ardal then drove east from the village. At the small square before the gates they found Fasel mounted on a tall horse, facing down two footmen, but the arrival of the rapidly approaching heavy wains distracted them. The kick of Fasel's horse gave them something else to distract them as they hurriedly retreated.

Fairok leapt from the wain and ran to the gates, four gatemen before him. Laurelei released a shaft that skewered their leader, then Fairok's team scattered the others. Ardal shouted to Laurelei that she should mount and waved the folio of notes and diagrams at her. Fasel brought the horse beside her wain and slid to the ground. Laurelei then vaulted into the saddle and shouted for Fasel to lash Badur into the saddle behind her.

Ardal bellowed, "Mad woman, leave him and fly."

"Shut you up, great beast." She guided the horse alongside Ardal's moving wain and leaned over to snatch his roll of papers then kissed him hard. She sat bolt upright in her saddle, looking as astonished as he. By the time she had regained her wits, Badur was secure behind her.

Fasel shouted for her to "Go, go, go," and she went, Ardal thinking he would never see her again.

Fairok's team swung wide the gates. Amir called in the rearguard. The men caught up with the wains and slipped the pins that secured the cages. When they slid off and crashed to the ground, the men leapt aboard and Amir and Ardal whipped up the horses. They aimed for the sunrise and pushed their horses hard.

When the beasts eventually began to puff and blow, Ardal ordered all but the injured and Hakov, their caretaker, off the wains. He and Amir also dismounted and walked alongside the horses until they judged them rested enough. The men piled again into the wains and rode a while until the horses required a rest. And so this became their rhythm through the next day and into the following night.

CHAPTER 19
Dust and Death

"... the dreamers of the day are dangerous men..."
Seven Pillars of Wisdom
T. E. Lawrence (of Arabia)

The waxing crescent moon was high when Ardal's wain jolted off the road and woke him. The horses were ready to drop. Ardal ordered the wains off the road and placed men to keep watch. Fairok took two to scout a hide position where they could rest in relative security.

Amir offered to take charge so Ardal could rest. "I have been resting, old man. That's why I ran off the road."

"I allowed some of the men to drive for me while I rested a few hours."

"Why did that not occur to me?"

"Perhaps Laurelei could answer that question, Captain."

"Amir, you're mocking me."

"Yes, Captain. Take your rest."

"Aye, but wake me when Fairok returns or if aught else passes."

Amir nodded and shoved him toward the wain. "Good night, Ardal."

Just after midnight, Amir woke Ardal to advise him that Fairok had found a dry stream bed with high banks, where they could rest in relative security. Ardal roused himself enough to say, "I want security on any trails in, and observation on any high ground," then he passed out.

He awoke with the sun well above the horizon and dust caking his throat. He willed his mind to focus and called for Amir. The Thirty Leader rushed over, laid his hand on his Captain's mouth and spoke directly into his ear. "They are studying the point where we left the road. They will be here soon."

"Why didn't you wake me?"

"You were the only one who did not rest at all yesterday. I left you while I established our defenses. I was just coming to call you. Do you need anything?"

"Water, an orientation to the situation and a latrine, in that order."

Amir handed him a water skin and led him to a point behind a boulder while describing the situation. He continued talking while Ardal took care of business then led him toward the observation point. One of the men on duty looked back at them and signaled that enemy soldiers were moving along a line parallel to their own positions. Amir advised Ardal of a parallel dry watercourse that had branches connecting it to the stream bed in which the Rectified hid. He said that two men were there to secure that approach.

"Leave these two here, displace six from the perimeter to reinforce the two at the stream juncture. Tighten the perimeter if you can. I am going to the stream juncture."

Ardal approached the two sentries there from behind. One glanced back and gave him a shushing signal. Slowing to a stealthy walk, Ardal then lay on his belly and peered between the man's feet to see around the bend.

He watched the approach of the enemy point man for

a few moments then signaled to the man beside him to kneel. Ardal whispered, "Reinforcements coming. Meet them. Ambush at choke point." Ardal jerked his thumb over his shoulder to where the watercourse narrowed.

The sentry nodded and dragged his partner away. Ardal looked back at the enemy raiders who hunted his men. Fortunately, their movements were intended for stealth rather than speed, and so allowed time for the Rectified to establish their ambuscade. Ardal heard small scuffling sounds coming from behind him as the men worked their way to their positions.

When the scuffling ceased, Ardal slipped away from the observation point and returned to the chokepoint. Here, he scouted a position that would give him cover and a clear view of the enemy's avenue of approach, as well as allow him to communicate visually with at least one of his men.

Daud stepped out from his concealed position as Ardal approached and indicated the position he had selected for him. Ardal nodded and whispered, "Not guards. Soldiers. Ten." He felt the tension pass from one man to the next as word passed around the perimeter.

He slipped in behind a column of stone right beside the chokepoint and glanced around once more to ensure all was well. Daud waved then pointed up. Ardal looked up to see Fasel's backside a few feet above him. Fasel had suspended himself with his back against the wall of the watercourse and his feet braced against a boulder perched precariously on top of the column that hid Ardal. It took a moment for Ardal to understand why, but then he nodded at Daud.

Ardal stopped breathing when the first Dearthman rounded the bend fifty feet from where he hid. The second and third came in quick succession, indicating that their fear of separation outweighed their fear of the men they hunted. Ardal shook his head and spoke under his breath: "Foolish."

Ardal counted the Dearthmen as they passed him. When he reached ten, he looked up to Fasel and nodded. On that signal, Fasel strained mightily to shove the boulder off its pedestal.

The last Dearthman in line glanced up at the scraping sounds. Ardal slid his blade between the man's ribs under his raised arm, and he dropped. The other nine spun and charged. Ardal dodged out of the path of the descending boulder and into the path of the descending Fasel. By the time Fasel and Ardal had regained their feet, the Rectified had dispatched the remaining Dearthmen.

Daud laughed while one of the other men bound a gash on his arm. "Ardal, you look funny when Fasel falls on top of you."

Ardal grimaced. "I reckon Fasel is the funny one, Daud." He checked the wrap and nodded his approval. "Who wants to ride horses rather than wains to the tower?"

"We will take the horses of these men?" and Daud grinned.

"Aye, I reckon we can trace this streambed back to where they dismounted, deal with the guards they left, and then ride out of here. Yeah?" Ardal glanced around, receiving nods in return.

"Yeah," and Fasel spoke for them all. "Let us ride."

"Fasel, you are on point. Track them back to their dismount point."

The one youngster the Dearthmen had left to guard the horses was not prepared for the sudden appearance of nine enemy soldiers. Fasel disarmed him before he could raise his blade in challenge.

"How many men and horses remain on the road?" Fasel demanded, indicating that the young man should kneel.

He did, then blubbered, "Do not kill me. I have done nothing against you."

"Except guard their horses, allowing your friends to

attack us. They are all dead, and you will join them unless you tell me how many men and horses remain on the road."

"The captain and eight men remain. If they know I told you, I am dung."

"Before long, they will know nothing and be dung themselves," Ardal assured him.

"I have another question. Why do you pursue us?"

The boy looked confused. "Are you not the slaves who destroyed the armory at Il Hofra?"

"I certainly hope so. It is only that, and nothing more? There is no other reason we are pursued?"

"What else have you done?" The boy took on a shrewd look.

Ardal indicated Fasel. "This one was well known for writing poetry to the lady who awarded the winners of the weekly fights. You heard naught of that?"

The boy spat. "I am a man of name, so I have no interest in the affairs of slaves or of concubines. You will die because you destroyed the armory. Is that not enough? Do you also wish to die for wooing a whore?"

"'Whore'?" The veins on Ardal's neck stood out. "Choke him," Ardal instructed Fasel through clenched teeth, and Fasel complied.

It took a long time for him to stop struggling. While Fasel bound him, Daud laid his head on the boy's chest, listening for his heartbeat. He grinned up at Fasel to indicate that the boy still lived. "You are an artist, brother."

"I was, once. Now, I choke children and steal horses."

Ardal inspected the horses and grinned. "Right. Think on this, brothers. Eleven horses here. Nine on the road. Four that pull our wains. Twenty-four horses for twenty-two men and two to bear burdens. We leave the wains behind. We might then move quickly enough to win this race. The trouble is that four of the beasts are slow draft horses."

Ardal looked around to nods and grunts of approval. "Well and good. It is worth our lives to take these other horses. Fasel, get you up to Amir. Tell him all you can as quickly as you can. Have him lead the men from his position to attack the Dearthmen on the road. This is the diversion. We ride out from the streambed while they are preparing to face Amir. They will not expect a mounted attack from a quarter they believe to be secure.

"Once Amir has captured the Dearthmen's horses, we will withdraw to our original position at the wains. There, we will loose the carthorses and head east as fast as possible. This delay will allow the pursuit to gain on us but will soon allow us to gain more ground over time.

Fasel repeated all that Ardal had told him then rode back along the watercourse to Amir, the captured blades bound together in the coat of the Dearthman lad. Daud was already moving the men to the horses. Ardal fell into the file behind Daud, trusting him to lead the men into good positions. Upon arrival at the assault position, they took up concealed positions in the streambed and waited for Amir to initiate his attack.

They did not have to wait long. Amir had foreseen this possibility and had the men drop non-essential items near the wains, so they could move more quickly. He only had to raise his blade above his head, and the men rose and ran, ululating across the fine sand to engage the Dearthmen on the road.

The surprised Dearthmen mounted to face Amir's assault only to discover they were engaged by a mounted foe from the flank. Ardal slashed the nearest Dearthman across his back before he could find his stirrups. Daud charged the next. Fasel dodged the swipe of a blade and thrust into the horseman's armpit.

The other Rectified had more trouble, for their targets had had more time to respond, but in relatively short order, the Dearthman horses and captain fell into Rectified hands.

Ardal stripped the captain of his arms and armor and bound him while Amir and his men returned to the wains. Fasel recovered the lad they had left behind and dropped him beside his captain. That done, they rode away to link up with Amir at the wains.

Ardal's section rode up just in time to see Amir's men roll the wains off a high embankment, to smash them into the dry rocky streambed below. They slowed only enough to allow the other men to mount and catch up with them. Amir rode alongside Ardal and handed him his sword that had been stored in in the box beneath one of the wains. "I am sorry to have left them so much useful firewood, but it was preferable to leaving them useful wains."

Before Ardal could return a witticism, a shout arose from behind them. "Dust cloud. They are coming." There was nothing for it but to ride until the horses were lamed then run until the men were, too.

They pushed the horses harder than they would have liked, but dismounted and jogged alongside each time they found it necessary to slow the horses to a walk. During one of these periods, Ardal looked towards the east and spotted the tower where Elgin was meant to wait for them.

About this time, a scout in the tower called for Elgin. Laurelei went with him to receive the scout's report. When they looked out over the Dearthlands, they saw a small cloud of dust approaching, behind which a vaster dust cloud rapidly appeared to be devouring the distance between them. Neither of them heard a word the scout said.

Laurelei flew down the stairs and into the paddock, shouting, "Bridles. Bridles only. No time for saddles." Men leapt to obey. Elgin sprinted into the paddock, carrying Laurelei's bow and quiver. She snatched them from him, mounted the first available horse and rode down into the pass alone.

Elgin mounted and shouted to Cian that he should

send men with fresh horses as soon as they were bridled. Cian nodded. Elgin gave his mount a kick and shot from the paddock after Laurelei.

The exhausted and parched men each led an equally exhausted and parched horse while the tower appeared to recede as they walked. The dust cloud behind them, however, seemed to grow like a storm.

Ardal scanned the almost featureless landscape for a place to make his final stand, but then noted a thin trail of dust rise from near the base of the tower. Clearly, a single rider had crossed the border into the Dearthlands to stand with them against the coming storm. "Elgin," he thought, "is stalwart. He could not stand in a tower and watch us be slaughtered. He comes to be slaughtered with us. I love that fool."

A few moments later, another dust trail appeared from near the base of the tower. "Cian," he thought, "has joined Elgin's mad rush to defy the entire Dearthman army. Ornery old bull."

Ardal directed the men to mount and speed toward the tower. As they closed the distance to the first of the approaching riders, Ardal realized the figure was far too small to be Elgin. Before long, he recognized it as Laurelei, and thought, "A woman of valor is splendid beyond imagining."

She rode straight to him, as though she knew him alone among the Rectified, shouting, "Fresh horses coming soon. Ride."

As she drew near him, she grinned. "You are a stubborn beast."

"Aye," he grunted, "and are you not the maddest of all women?"

"Ardal, I will find a hide from which to send arrows into their vanguard. I should have time to take only a few before they would overwhelm me, so I will need your sword arm to ensure my escape."

"Find your hide. I will inform Amir." Ardal called for Amir and briefed him while he kept an eye on Laurelei's back. Amir acknowledged Ardal's instruction, and shooed him off in the direction of Laurelei.

As he parted with the Rectified, Ardal heard Elgin boom his encouragement. He raised his arm in acknowledgement and rode hard after Laurelei. Elgin shouted to Amir. "Where is that ass going?"

Ardal had time to raise a dust-choked whoop when he noticed the dust cloud of the approaching fresh horses. Riding down into a dry streambed, he saw Laurelei lead her horse around a bend. He dismounted and led his horse the same way, spotting Laurelei scrambling up a slope to the base of a gnarled tree atop the bank.

Ardal caught Laurelei's eye and indicated where he intended going to ground. He slowly poured the last of his water into his hand and placed it under his horse's nose then left her behind to find a concealed position from where he could observe the approach of the Dearthman army, and ensure that he had a secure route to Laurelei's position. He could no longer see his men, but rested in the surety that Elgin was with them.

Not long after taking their positions, Ardal saw a Ten of Dearthman scouts far out ahead of their main body, closing rapidly on the Rectified. A shaft appeared in the throat of the lead horse. It went down at a headlong gallop and rolled over its rider. The second horse threw its rider as it stumbled over them. By the time they too were down, Laurelei had already released her second arrow but it glanced off a Dearthman's helmet. She was already nocking a third.

The Dearthmen spread out in search of their attackers. The third arrow ended its flight in the gut of a soldier who had pointed in Laurelei's direction. She loosed another shaft, but her target managed to raise his buckler in time to deflect it.

Laurelei leapt up and shouted, "Go."

Ardal's poor horse balked when he tried to mount. Laurelei rode past behind him, repeatedly shouting "Go!" Ardal finally mounted and slapped his mare's hindquarter with the flat of his blade.

They galloped along the floor of the dry streambed until the eastern bank fell away to reveal the plain. As they climbed out, the mare went down. Ardal tucked and rolled when he hit the ground, then crawled over to check his mount.

An arrow protruded from her flank. She tried to rise, but she rolled screaming onto her side. Two more arrows struck her belly. She screamed and flailed wildly. Ardal scrambled away to avoid being kicked or crushed, taking cover behind a boulder.

When he chanced a look, Ardal saw the scouts were now working their way down the western bank of the streambed. He resolved to hold them until his friends could mount the fresh horses and make for the tower.

The sound of hoof beats approaching from behind startled Ardal, but he grinned when he heard Elgin bellow his name. He stood, and watched Elgin gallop toward him. Remembering the technique that Gerritt and Caleb had demonstrated, Ardal ran toward him, arrows and curses following behind.

Elgin rode straight at him. They clasped hands, and Ardal leapt as high as he could, throwing his leg over the horse and his arm around Elgin's waist, leaning hard to keep his seat. Now secure, he shouted, "Good. Go."

Elgin reined in and wheeled the horse then kicked him into a gallop. A thrill passed through Ardal when, in the distance, he saw Laurelei enter the pass behind the Rectified. Two of Elgin's soldiers galloped toward them, leading two fresh horses. Elgin's valiant mount was blowing loudly when they finally met.

They dismounted, and Ardal dropped to the ground, no strength in his legs. A soldier held the lead for him while he fumbled around, trying to mount. Elgin hurried his horse over, offered Ardal his foot as a step up, and pulled him up with a hand under his arm. As soon as he had mounted, they were off.

The ride to the mouth of the pass was a dead gallop over rough terrain. It was a wonder that none of the horses stumbled. As they entered the shadow of the pass, Ardal glanced to one side and saw Laurelei sighting along a nocked shaft.

A moment later, he heard the "Thrum" as she released, followed immediately by the clash and shouts of battle. He turned to join the fight only to find it was already over, Laurelei and the Rectified having taken care of the remaining scouts. At long last, they could ride up the pass toward the tower and its relative safety.

Ardal hoped to sleep for ten hours and enjoy a couple of good meals as well as a great quantity of water. As soon as he could, though, he wanted to be off again to Galantamhor, to present his report to the Captain-General.

When he dismounted, Laurelei ran to him. He prepared for another kiss, but instead, she stopped a few feet from him and lowered her head. "Badur the Brave is dead."

"Ach, my heart. But I didn't think it so bad as that."

"He told me to tell you he went first, like you taught him. I don't think he meant ill by it."

"No. No, I understand what he meant." Ardal sank slowly to his knees, threw his head back and howled. Amir and a few others ran to discover what the matter was.

Laurelei told them, "Badur the Brave is dead."

Amir lowered his head and moaned. He remained so for a while until spurred on by the needs of his men. "Will the burial wait for the morning?"

"It will be well to bury him early tomorrow." She lifted Ardal's chin. "What sort of man loves his enemies – those who killed his brothers – so they too become his brothers?"

"I canna answer that, Lady. I only know that he is my brother and that his loss hangs heavier on me than any other before. I have no strength in me to bear it."

Amir helped Ardal to his feet and embraced him. "Then we will become stronger together until we can bear it. It will be well, my brother."

He turned Ardal toward Laurelei. "Go and wash yourself. We will care for the men and horses."

Laurelei called for grooms. Elgin had dispatched most of his Thirty to guard the approach to the tower. The remainder had watched the conversation from the perimeter of the bailey. At Laurelei's call, they all rushed forward to help. The Rectified dropped whatever they had in their hands and followed Ardal to the barracks.

CHAPTER 20
The Long Road Home

"The life of the dead is placed in the memory of the living."
Marcus Tullius Cicero

The panic of their flight had given way to momentary exhilaration upon their arrival, but that had been quickly dashed by their anguish at losing Badur. Reclining in a shallow pool of hot water, Ardal knew only emptiness.

In the morning, they buried Badur. Someone had inscribed a white stone marker with both the Alish and Tierasalan words for "Badur the Brave", below which read "He went first". Ardal reckoned it was enough.

Elgin prompted Ardal to speak. He said the only words he knew at this point. "You are our youngest, and you went first. Honor, my brother."

The Rectified responded in unison: "Honor, brother."

Amir caught Ardal's eye and nodded. When he returned the nod, Amir began a wild, high keening lament that tore at Ardal's soul though he could understand few of the Alish words. The others joined in while Ardal stood, feeling empty.

The journey to Galantamhor turned out to be unremarkable except in its somberness. The magnitude of what they had done began to settle in on Ardal's mind, and he finally admitted to himself the extreme implausibility of their desperate plan. He shuddered so hard he nearly fell from his saddle.

Upon their arrival, Dermot, Rory, Stefan, and Brady met them at the city gate and escorted them to the planning center. Laurelei offered a formalized general report of the mission then called on each of the Adnana in turn.

When only Ardal and Amir remained to report, Rory addressed Ardal. "If you wish to release your men, please do so now."

Ardal turned to Amir who spoke a few words in Alish. All the men except for Fasel and Partlan headed for the door. Amir gazed at Fasel, then looked to his captain with a raised eyebrow. Ardal gestured to the seat next to Partlan. Fasel took his seat, and the discussion continued.

Ardal and Amir reported as cogently as they knew how with Laurelei prompting them to remember details that had seemed unimportant at the time.

Each member of the assembled staff had opportunities to address the leaders of the Rectified. Each expressed gratitude for their success and sorrow for their loss of Badur. Understanding the importance of their accomplishment and receiving the appreciation of these people strengthened them enormously.

After they had discussed the mission to Dermot's satisfaction, he nodded to Rory. The Captain-General of Sensors displayed papers that his people had acquired. They bore the seal of Majid Kahn, the king of the Dearthmen, known among them as the "Protector of the Faithful". In those papers, the Protector offered freedom to any slave and wealth beyond imagining to any freeman in exchange for the head of "any who had taken part in the cowardly act of destruction against the Il-Hofra farm implement production facility". The man who produced "the head of the bandit leader" would have the hand of the Kahn's own daughter, Qamrosh.

Rory's only comment was that the Protector's daughter could have been born no more than ten years before. He then offered a position on his team to any and all Adnana who would have it. Fasel leapt from his seat but remained tensely silent.

Addressing Elgin, Cian and Ardal, Rory said, "Stefan, Captain-General of Plans, has expressed an interest in having the three of you on his team, but then Chief Metallurgist Brady has some ideas for you, Ardal."

As it fell out, Fasel became the captain of a new unit of Sensors who specialized in deep infiltrations and included a Ten of Adnana from among the Rectified. Hakov became apprenticed to a great surgeon in Galantamhor. Amir became a "spice merchant" in Rory's employ.

Ardal was assigned a post under Brady as a metallurgical researcher, equipped with the best available tools, and allowed two weeks' leave to arrange for lodgings in Galantamhor.

Elgin and Cian were ostensibly retired due to their injuries, but nonetheless remained armed and ready nearby Ardal.

Amir, in his role as a spice merchant, visited Ardal often with interesting tales of things he'd seen in the Dearthlands and things he'd heard in Galantamhor. Often, when he came, he would carry some metal oddment or arcane sketches for Ardal's consideration.

Even Nabal was able to settle down. He abandoned his quest for vengeance and took up an altogether different one: for his wife. Dermot granted him a pardon in the High King's name as well as leave and resources to return to the villages of the Adnana. Seven of the Rectified, including Amir, accompanied him. They returned with all who were willing and settled in Galantamhor. Amir discovered that his wife had found some peace in the home of a neighbor. He resolved not to trouble her more than he already had and returned to Tierasal without her.

Something about the armory must have appealed to Laurelei, for she regularly discovered a reason to make her way there. At least as often, Ardal determined that he should visit the Captain-General's Seat to offer a personal explanation to Brady of some detail or other of his work. Somehow, once he'd seen Brady, Ardal always found himself calling on Laurelei. Sometimes, each of them found a reason to visit Ardal's home in Taermun.

For nearly a year they carried on this way until one day at the inn in Taermun, Ardal broke the spell. "I've a yearning to stay here and live out my days as a village smith. How do you suppose that would be"?"

Laurelei displayed no surprise, but Ardal knew she only let her face show what she wanted it to. "I suppose that I could visit you here on occasion."

"Nay, lass." Ardal's frustration made his voice gruff. "I'd have you come along."

She gave him a small smile. "What would a woman of my skills and…. ah, temperament do in a place like Taermun, Ardal?"

"I've put some thought into just that question, Laur. You could hunt wolves or teach the daughters of rich folks to dance or sit about poking barbs at the poor village smith. I reckon you'd be a fair hand at any of those occupations." His grin beamed encouragement.

Laurelei lowered her gaze. "There are no rich folks in the Avinn Vale. What is it you want of me, Ardal?"

"Only as much as I'm willin' to offer, Lady. We've a sayin' here:

'Laughter by day
And warm hearth by night
Withstand the Fey
And winter's blight'.

"You are a smith, so I know you keep a warm hearth, but I must inform you that I find your buffoonery a sight less amusing than the lads do."

"Oh, Lady, you misunderstand me. It's you who makes me laugh." Laurelei looked askance at this assertion, drawing from him a hearty deep laugh. "My heart's so merry when you're about that I forget there ever was a Hart's Pass or an Il-Hofra."

"Oh, lad, is that a thing that should be done? To forget? I cannot, nor would I have you do so. Only tell me you'll not forget Gallant Hart or Brave Badur, and I'll come to Taermun.

"And as I am the woman I am, I'll lay a heavy task on your shoulders - that you wait for me until we are wed. A harder task I will lay at your feet, though, that you also ask my father's blessing before we do. Even harder than that, once we are wed, you must love the one I am even as I become another, and you'll love her too all your days."

Ardal leapt to his feet. "Aye, m'love. With all of me I will love all of you until I am naught but dust." He scooped her up and reeled about the inn, kicked the door open and leapt over the threshold to continue his reel outside where there was more room for it.

Finally, flushed and panting, he stood her before him and took her hands in his. "Now, tell me, Lady, where would a poor smith find the great king who is father to such a bright lady?"

Laurelei stared hard at Ardal's red face. "You jest, of course. That is the challenge. I told you it was a hard task. You must help me find him."

"Lady, if *you* know not where to find your own sweet da, how can I be expected to? Surely, you are better trained at discovering mysteries than this brute of a footman."

Ardal rarely experienced embarrassment, but this moment was exceptional in every way. He ducked his head and asked as gently as he could, "Do you at least know his name, Laur?"

Laurelei scoffed, "You hear nothing. Do you not think? Can you not solve a puzzle whose pieces are all arranged before you? Did Rory not tell everyone present exactly who my father is? Ardal, I held you away from me for many long weeks when we first returned to Galantamhor because I feared your interest might be in whose daughter I am rather than in who *I* am, but you... You never even thought about it. Did you? Ai. Which of us is the greater fool? Well, speak. Answer me, you great clown."

"I don't believe I've ever heard you say so much all at once. I believe you're becoming a woman of Taermun already. Will you continue to do so once we're married? Talk, I mean."

"Ardal. We won't be married if I don't find my father. Can you not help me?"

"I'll help as I can, Laur. I'll track him over the sea if you'll just tell me: who is the man?"

Laurelei growled her exasperation then sighed. "Do you remember how Rory responded when Daley challenged my right as a foreigner to go on the mission to Il-Hofra?"

"Yeah, Laur. He said your da was a great soldier."

"And?"

"And that you were..." Ardal's flush deepened. "He said you are 'heir to the House of Killinchy'."

Laurelei smiled and patted Ardal on the head. "You *were* listening. Good. So, we're going to find my 'own sweet da', as you say–"

"Your da's Fintan, Prince of the House of Killinchy." Ardal choked on his incredulity.

"If he is, Ardal, will you love me the less?"

"'Love you less?' What? No."

"Will you love me more?"

"What? No."

"Good. Let's go find my da so you can ask for my hand."

"Right. Yes. So, what does he look like?"

"I have no idea. I've not seen the man since I was a babe in arms."

"And now, you are a woman at arms. What do you know of him? One moment… if you've not met the man, how can you know he is your father? Why would Rory call you Fintan's heir without good reason?"

"My mother, Mairyam, is the daughter of Dieterick, Lord Nordhelm of the Northern Marches. I rode into Galantamhor mounted on a white horse that bore the livery of the House of Nordhelm. To those who know my father, this is enough to establish that I am indeed his wife's only child and so, his heir."

"Lady, you are heir to two great houses, granddaughter to a king and to a lord. Why would you have such a rough lad as I am?"

"'A great lord and a petty king' as my mother has often reminded me."

Laurelei shook her head. "Ardal, you great ass, I will answer this question once and become angry if you ever ask it again. You are the truest man I know. The nobility of a man who can overcome his enemies only to preserve them, make his slaves into brothers and his brothers into princes, is far greater than any title inherited or bestowed by even the High King. You ennoble yourself and those around you and then perceive yourself as the least among them. How could I not love you?"

She drew a breath. "Speak, man. You look as though you've heard naught I've said."

Ardal stared stupidly at her grinning. "It's as I feared. All the lovely terseness has been purged from you." He sighed. "Ah, well. Let's to it, then," and he rubbed his hands together. "Where can this lost warrior prince have toddled off to, eh?" He dodged Laurelei's fist and caught her forearm.

Pulling her toward him, he wrapped his other arm around her waist and drew her against him. He kissed her hand then released it and enfolded her in his arms. His solemnity struck a sharp counterpoint to his previous levity. "Were you a washerwoman and I the High King, I'd have none other than you for my queen. You are faithful and valiant, honest and wise; and, even though you disbelieve it, you are gracious and kind.

"When we find your father, if he will not own me as a son, even so, I will serve at your side because I cannot become the man I should be if your light fades from my heart." Ardal leaned down to kiss Laurelei's forehead, but she lifted her face and his kiss found her soft lips.

Laurelei recovered before Ardal. She sighed and shook her head. "Oh, my lad, I find it my sad duty to inform you that I am heir to naught. Dunglaun has fallen, and Lord Nordhelm has disowned me. Your bride comes to you with no dowry at all."

"Well, that's a small matter. At least you have the horse."

Laurelei's shoulders rose and her eyes closed. "I borrowed him from the stables when I left Nordhelm."

"You stole a horse?"

"I borrowed him from my grandfather. I returned him. Rory insisted. In fact, he sent a retinue to escort the horse home with all the honor that one can give to a horse. The retinue carried a letter from Rory to my mother stating that he had been honored to receive as his apprentice the daughter of such an excellent family. He included a great deal of flowery language. I called it 'asinine'; he called it 'prudent'. My cousin is heir to the House of Nordhelm, not I."

Ardal grinned. "Lady, we are heirs to the fruits of our labors," then he looked down, "and of our loins. What could be nobler than that?"

CHAPTER 21
Lofty Accommodations

"I walk to the horizon, and there I find another."
"Anywhere is"
Enya

Ardal and Laurelei invested the next week in preparing for their journey to Galantamhor. She informed him that she had little enough to bring with her to Taermun, but what she had was important. Rory and others deserved a personal goodbye before she disappeared into the hinterlands with a mad footman. Besides, she had to resign her commission with the Sensor Corps.

Meandering cross-country to avoid larger towns in favor of smaller inns and houses, they filled the uneventful trip with warm jests and small graces.

Laurelei offered warm empathy but no sympathy when Ardal spoke with her about Hart's Pass. She offered no judgments of his actions, calling him neither "hero" nor "fool". Her only comment was to remind him that Elgin had so overcome the loss of his eye that he had managed to lead an emergency extraction from enemy territory with an entire Dearthman army approaching at a gallop.

When Laurelei described her childhood in the house of a great lord, her clear longing for her absent father struck deeply into Ardal's heart. Her mother's cleverness, combined with her self-indulgence, had trussed Laurelei in a web of manipulation and guilt until the day they celebrated her sixteenth birthday.

Her mother, Mairyam, had entered Laurelei's dressing room and shooed away her attendants, saying that on the great occasion of her entry into womanhood, a young lady should be attended by her mother. Laurelei had bristled when her mother entered, then deflated utterly when her friends left.

The lady crossed the room to stand behind her seated daughter and spoke to her in a sing-song voice while braiding her hair. "Laurelei, my dear. Today, you are to be presented as an adult to the nobility of the Realms of the Fair – as a lady, a young woman of substance and value. That substance and value is derived from the House of Nordhelm. Your loyalty and your obedience belong to the Lord of Nordhelm."

Laurelei sighed. "And what command, Lady, would my fair lord have me loyally obey on this the great occasion of my entry into womanhood?" She stifled the laughter inspired by her mother's befuddled expression.

Mairyam recovered her poise. "I am glad you listened so closely you were able to throw my words back in my face. Child, where did you learn to speak with such vitriol?"

Laurelei stared into her mother's eyes, reflected in the polished brass mirror on the wall before her.

Mairyam continued braiding Laurelei's hair and speaking as though the moment had not only passed but had never been. "You are not an unattractive young lady, so we may assume that young men in attendance will seek your favor. Your grandfather, my own beloved father and the honorable lord of Nordhelm, asks a boon of you."

Laurelei responded warily, mindful that a boon asked by the imperious lord of Nordhelm was in truth a command issued in a soft voice. "How may I serve my lord, Mother?"

Mairyam stepped around her daughter and stooped, to bring her face on a level with Laurelei's. "There is emptiness behind her eyes," Laurelei thought as her mother smiled winsomely.

"Lord Nordhelm invites you to join him in diplomatic intercourse this eve. This shows his great faith in you, his heir to enact the realm's duties."

"What form will this intercourse take, Lady?"

"There is a young lord of a small realm that borders our own. He is proud but weak, and foolishly refuses the counsel of our wise lord..."

"Our wise lord would have me devote my attentions to this young fool; and failing to sway his will, maneuver him into a position that might compromise his honor, therefore making him vulnerable to Lord Nordhelm's demands. Have I assessed the situation aright, dear mother? Was your choice of the word 'intercourse' intentional or merely a slip of the tongue?"

For the second time in their conversation, Laurelei had clearly dismayed her mother. "It is not as though he wishes you to act a whore."

Laurelei shook her head. "No. He merely wishes me to become my mother."

Before either of them knew that it would happen, Mairyam's hand had shot out like a striking viper and bruised her daughter's cheek, her thumbnail left a cut on Laurelei's eyelid.

Mairyam was visibly shaken. "See what you've made me do. This was unnecessary. In five minutes, I will send your attendants to finish dressing you and to make your face more presentable. In half an hour you will be at Lord Nordhelm's side, smiling eagerly while he presents you to our guests."

The moment the door closed behind her mother, Laurelei changed into riding clothes and sprinted to the stables. If her attendants were to see her leave, they would suffer as though it were their fault she had left.

***

When Laurelei had finished her tale, she searched Ardal's face for traces of pity. She found, instead, deep admiration. Here, finally, was a man she would not despise.

They rode on, meandering from topic to topic, as the terrain rose through the Frigid Mountains. The land seemed limitless, as did the possibilities that filled it. A small copse of alder beside a swift stream invited them to leave the road.

They neared the stand of trees, and a murder of crows rose at their approach. They dismounted and loosened the girth straps then, after Laurelei had taken a cheese and a brown loaf from one of the saddlebags, turned the horses loose to graze. Ardal carried their water skins to the nearby stream.

After they had eaten and drunk, Ardal refilled the skins and packed the food. As he fastened the flap of the saddlebag, Laurelei approached him from behind and reached around his waist. She laid her head on his back and muttered, "We need to find my father before I go mad."

"We should take turns. We'll never find the duffer if we're both mad at the same time. I get to go first."

Laurelei released her hold and leapt onto Ardal's back. She wrapped her arms about his neck and bit his ear then whispered into it, "One day, we'll go mad together, and the world will be a better place for it."

Ardal reached back to squeeze her thighs and chuckled. "The children who come of our two-fold madness will make it so."

Laurelei and Ardal traveled so for over a month.

Nothing changed but the terrain and the weather. The pleasant monotony of performing necessary tasks established the foundation that would one day allow them to build a strong home.

On a day of days and in the gloaming, they halted atop a rise. From the relative darkness in the valley below rose the sound of a turbulent mountain river. "Can't see it, Laur, but sounds like a lot of water. Our road should intercept the Great Bend of the Frigid River, about a day's travel from the gates of Galantamhor. Reckon that's it?"

"It is. I've stood here before with the valley full of snow and the sunlight on the water. The slopes are populated with tall conifers. Back then, only the tops of them were visible above the drifts. I'd a pursuer on that occasion but he passed the valley by. I had found a space under the trees that was mostly clear of snow and slept there, for the first time in days confident that the still falling snow would cover my tracks.

I found his camp site in a dingle the next day, and at a distance, followed him into Galantamhor. Never did I determine who he was or why he had pursued me."

She stared for a long moment down into the valley while they both kept their peace. "We should keep to the ridge line. The valley narrows and steepens farther up." She guided her horse around Ardal's and back onto the trail.

Ardal remained for a moment, gazing into the valley and imagining his Laurelei sleeping beneath a snow drift, hunted, alone, freezing and exhausted. He shuddered and turned to follow.

A few hours later, they encountered a way station. Ardal stripped the saddlebags from the horses and dropped them inside the door then walked the horses around to the stable.

Laurelei found the barman. "Have you room for two tonight? We've two beasts that might like some oats."

The barman nodded. "I've just the room. It's no

wedding night bower, but it'll do, I reckon."

Laurelei's normally pallid face became ruddy. "We aren't married … not yet."

The barman seemed unaffected. "Well, lass, I reckon that's between you and him. None of my business, except to know if you'll have the room."

Her ruddiness became crimson as Laurelei explained, "We'll need two rooms if you have them. Please alert the cook that the lad eats twice what another man would."

The barman looked down and chuckled. "I'll alert the cook as you say. I'm sure that when you are married you'll manage the lad well enough. But for tonight I've the one room and no more, I'm afraid. There's space in the barn above the stalls, though. If he'll take that, I'll not charge him for it or for the extra victuals."

"He'll not complain. Thank you," and Laurelei lifted her saddlebags to carry them up the stairs.

The barman pointed. "End of the hall's a bath. I'll draw water and have some heated for you. Should be a pot of soap on the shelf next to the towels. Your room's the first on the right."

Laurelei halted on the first step but did not look around. "Thank you. That is a kindness." She continued to her room.

After she had dropped her gear, she went back downstairs to find Ardal laughing with the barman. "I hope the arrangement suits you, Ardal," she said.

"Oh, aye. Such lofty accommodation suits me well enough. And you, my Lady? How are you accommodated?"

"With kind words and strong deeds, my lad."

CHAPTER 22
Resignation

"He who overcomes himself is mighty."
Tao Te Ching
Lao Tzu

Upon their arrival at the Seat of the Captain-General of Sensors for the Armies of Tierasal, they were ushered into an anteroom and offered cool water and apples to refresh themselves while they waited for Rory. Laurelei accepted the water with a nod.

Ardal took two apples, bit into one, and held it with his teeth, then accepted the water and nodded. He glanced at Laurelei, his hands and mouth full and apple juice running down his beard. She seemed displeased about something. "Hunh?" he grunted by way of asking what was troubling her.

Laurelei took the apple from Ardal's hand and placed it in his satchel, all the while shaking her head and muttering to herself. She removed a handkerchief from the satchel and offered it to Ardal, but his free hand was now filled with the apple he had removed from his mouth. Muttering again, she wiped his chin and returned the handkerchief to the satchel.

"Hullo, Rory," Ardal tried to bellow around a mouthful of apple.

Laurelei composed her face before turning to the Captain-General of Sensors, her overseer, trainer and foster-father. "Rory…"

"Laurelei, Ardal, come inside." Rory stepped aside to allow them to pass.

Rory's outer offices bustled with "Readers" – a section of Sensors who specialized in studying the reports the office received from the Sensors in the field.

The atmosphere of Rory's inner office, however, was muted in all ways. Thick carpet, large tapestries and heavy drapes absorbed the sound. The drapes allowed only slivers of light from the courtyard to enter through the windows.

Ardal felt as he had whenever he had stepped directly from his clamorous smithy into the shade of the large oak that grew in the lea of the slope above his home. Peace settled on him like a mantle. He placed the remains of the apple he had been gnawing into his satchel and drew his sleeve across his mouth.

Rory took Ardal's beaker and gestured toward a chair. Laurelei wandered about the room, fondling the spines of leather-bound tomes and lingering before framed sketches and documents. After she had made a full circuit, she took a seat beside Ardal. Rory returned Ardal's beaker, now filled with cool mead, and offered Laurelei a glass goblet half full of dark red wine. He relieved her of her own beaker and placed it on his desk.

Rory then took a seat facing them. "Tell me, my friends, how such an honor comes to my door unbidden and unanticipated."

"Rory, we sent a letter weeks ago requesting an audience with you." The news that a letter from a Sensor to her Captain-General could be waylaid clearly disturbed

Laurelei. The letter itself bore no critical information other than the fact that Laurelei and Ardal intended to visit, but its disappearance was of concern.

Ardal had kept a nagging thought at bay since his initial arrival at Galantamhor with the Forsaken. The knowledge that Laurelei's letter had not reached its intended recipient caused the nagging to become insistent. He had once been entrusted with the delivery of a message himself, from the Captain-General of the Western Division to the Chief Librarian of Galantamhor. Aindru had called the sheaf of documents "greetings to one of his friends", but had insisted Ardal "deliver them immediately upon arrival into Flann's own hand". Ardal had instead, for the sake of convenience, placed the documents into the hand of a smiling man who had been introduced as the personal secretary to the Chief Librarian.

He knew he should be whipped for his failure to follow Aindru's exact instructions, but it had seemed unimportant compared with the larger matters afoot at the time. He had since learned that "larger matters" often proved to be mere distractions, allowing subterfuge in "smaller matters". He had also since learned that failure in any duty can prove dangerous.

Ardal determined he would go and find this Flann as soon as he left Rory's office. Only if he found that Flann had received the letter from Aindru would he be able to enjoy his time in Galantamhor.

While Ardal fretted, Rory and Laurelei had been talking, but the Captain-General now interrupted his thoughts. "Is that the way it stands, Captain?"

"My apologies, Captain-General. Is that the way what stands?"

"As Laurelei has just explained, you two have been making plans."

"We have. Of course, we have to locate Laurelei's father so I can ask his permission to marry her."

After a tense pause, Rory responded. "Actually, we

hadn't yet reached that point in our discussion."

By the fire in Laurelei's eyes, he knew that had they not been in Rory's office, she would have called him a "great ass". He could hear her voice clearly in his mind, but could not clearly ascertain the reason that should have done so.

Rory broke the tension that had quickly filled the room. "Captain, perhaps you are unaware of the fact that I have considered myself a sort of father to Laurelei since she rode into Galantamhor at the age of sixteen. I did not intend to presume, but apparently I did, and you have drawn attention to my presumption.

"Because of this, she believes you have given me cause to feel slighted and that the perceived slight could have been avoided had you cared to pay attention to the guidance she no doubt gave you before entering this office. Laurelei values her relationship with me and would do nothing that might damage it, so her perception that your naïve action might threaten that relationship has given her cause to become angry with you."

He shifted his gaze to Laurelei and continued, "I am not, in fact, offended. I am not your father. I am concerned, however, that you have chosen to delay your happiness while you look for a man whom the best trackers in three nations have been unable to locate. Do you think it wise?"

"I cannot say it's wise, Rory, but it's as I'll have it."

"Would you be swayed at all by my opinion? I know Fintan well and believe he would give the lad a hard time by demanding some impossible service of him then laughing at him when he agreed to it. He would approve, and that most gladly, to a proposed union between his daughter and such a man as Ardal. I know this as I know my own mind on the matter."

Laurelei smiled. "What is your mind on the matter, Rory? Have you aught to say against my intended? Will such a one as he do for such a one as I?"

Rory demurred. "As I said, Laurelei, I am not your

father."

"You're as like it as I've ever had. What say you?"

The two of them turned to consider Ardal, as though they had never seen him before. Laurelei rendered judgment first. "His beard needs trimming."

Rory agreed. "That might help with the apple juice problem."

"He's impetuous," and Laurelei appeared to consider this flaw to be fatal.

Rory, though, pulled Ardal back from the brink. "And yet it seems his impetuosity might also be called audacity."

"You refer, of course, to the Battle of Hart's Pass."

Rory seemed surprised that Laurelei had mentioned the battle. "Well, yes. I suppose the observation could be applied to his actions in Hart's Pass as well."

Laurelei's grin betrayed her immense enjoyment with the game she and Rory were playing at Ardal's expense. "Perhaps you refer to his mighty exploits on the Il-Hofra mission. You cannot mean that you attribute them to his impetuosity."

"No. I do not attribute his deeds to impetuosity alone but also to his tenacity, courage and so forth."

"'And so forth', eh, Captain-General? Yes, I've noted the 'and so forth' of which you speak and am convinced it bears further study."

"An excellent idea. I approve. I suppose I should assign my finest sensor... No. No, he's currently unavailable. Laurelei, it is your idea. Perhaps, if you are willing, you could conduct a long-term study of our young captain. The intent is to learn three things about him.

"The first is to determine what characteristics contribute most to his success – especially as evidenced by his apparent success in his most daunting endeavor. The second is to determine the durability of those characteristics. I'm afraid this will require intensive, long-term study. Finally, I'll need to know if the specific set of attributes that have made a great captain of our friend the smith can be replicated. In short, can they be reproduced in any meaningful way?"

The blush that burned on Laurelei's cheeks amused Ardal for a moment. When it struck him what the blush implied, his admiration for her expanded within him like a sunrise.

In a bid to relieve her of further discomfort, Ardal said the first thing that came into his mind. "Rory, what did you mean by my 'most daunting endeavor'?"

Rory somberly eyed Ardal. "Captain, if you do not now consider the possibility of marriage to this woman to be your most daunting endeavor, you soon will.

"She will have convinced you that she is indomitable, Captain, but I assure you that she needs looking after. She's a darkness comes over her at times. I'm certain you'll find the answer to it; though, I'll admit I never have."

Laurelei stood. "As I've heard the mighty Captain of the Rectified say on occasion, 'That'll be enough of that'." She laid her hand on Ardal's shoulder. "So, he'll do then, Rory?"

"Oh, he'll do. Only have him trim that beard and teach him some table manners. Then he'll do."

Ardal stood and was about to cross to the door when Rory said, "I believe that you intended the marriage discussion as an introduction to the one about resigning your commission in the Sensor Corps. Is that not so, Laurelei?"

"Well, yes, but since you've made it clear that we have your approval, I must assume you will also approve my resignation."

"No, Laurelei. You must not assume unless you then take steps to validate your assumption."

"Well and good then," said Laurelei standing to attention. Ardal followed suit out of habit.

"Captain-General, I, Laurelei, daughter and heir of Fintan, Prince of fallen Dunglaun, do now tender the resignation of my Sensor Corps commission, effective immediately for the purpose of marrying this great ass and living with him in our ancestral lands." Laurelei smirked at Rory.

Rory stood for a long moment, studying Laurelei's smirk. "Laurelei, daughter and heir of Fintan, Prince of fallen Dunglaun, your resignation is now denied by order of Dermot, Captain-General of the Armies of Tierasal."

While Laurelei's jaw worked soundlessly, Rory turned to Ardal. "Captain, I believe you would receive the same answer were you to attempt your own planned resignation."

Rory opened the door and stepped aside, gesturing through the doorway as he smiled. "You're dismissed. Thank you for stopping by. Come by again before you leave the city. I will have orders for you, Laurelei. Captain, your orders will come, of course, From Stefan through Operations Branch."

Rory signaled a passing staff member who hurried to his side. Rory smiled. "Please convey my compliments to the Chief Reader with an invitation for him and the Lead Readers to join me for our scheduled meeting. Offer my apologies for the delay. Thank you."

The young man scuttled away. Rory nodded to Ardal and Laurelei and went back to his desk. Laurelei stood in the doorway, flummoxed, until the participants began to arrive for the meeting. Ardal touched her elbow and led her through the outer office toward the hallway.

"That was a shot in the gut. Laur, I'm as stunned as you are, but we've business to attend to. How would it be if we were to separate now, take care of business and meet up at the Angry Cock for supper?"

Laurelei glanced up. "Yeah. Right. See you at the inn."

"Right, then." It was a while before Laurelei had recovered enough to wonder why Ardal had been in such a hurry for them to part company.

CHAPTER 23
Loose Ends

"A fool may talk, but a wise man speaks."
Ben Jonson

Ardal jogged up the hill in the general direction of the Library until he finally had to admit to himself that he was well and truly lost, or "tactically mis-oriented" as he preferred to say. He stopped a water seller and had two beakers of tepid water before asking the man to direct him to the great library.

The water seller grinned at him. "You're 'avin' me on then, eh?"

Ardal gazed at the man while he tried to make sense of the sounds that had just come from his toothless mouth. "I'm uncertain what you mean by that. I'd be grateful if you could just point me in the direction of the library."

The water seller shook his head and muttered then hitched his thumb over his shoulder toward the high wall that stood a few yards behind him. Ardal could not understand much of what the man said afterward, but it was apparent that he didn't approve of "ejacated folk".

Around the next corner, Ardal spotted the gate through which he had previously entered. He approached and noted that neither guard seemed familiar. He extended his hand to the nearer. "Hullo. My name is Ardal. I'm captain of a thirty of light foot. I've business with your chief, Flann, but I've no appointment. It's somewhat urgent. I come in the name of Aindru, Captain-General of the Western Division."

The gateman clasped Ardal's forearm in greeting. "Come with me, Captain. I'll show you to Flann's offices."

The gateman looked to his partner and received a nod before leading Ardal across the courtyard, through the front doors and directly to the top of the massive central staircase. On the third landing, a tall pair of deftly carved heavy wooden doors stood open.

Through the doorway, Ardal saw a venerable gentleman seated behind a colossal desk, apparently engrossed in a stack of documents. The gateman gestured for Ardal to enter then returned to his duty. Ardal strode across the room and tapped on the desk.

The old man continued reading but gestured vaguely to a high-backed tawny leather chair set in front of the desk. Ardal sat down and studied the man. He was frail, pale and squint-eyed, and so conformed exactly to the image the term "Chief Librarian" would have evoked had Ardal taken the time to imagine him.

Ardal became more agitated as time passed and it became clear that his presence was not the most important fact in the gnome's mind. He settled into his chair and allowed his mind to drift to Rory's strange declaration that Ardal and Laurelei would not be released from service. Each had exceeded the minimum time requirements of their inscriptions. Would they be required to take up residence in the city, or worse, posted far from both Taermun and Galantamhor? Was it possible that they would receive separate postings? What did Dermot have in mind for them? What if there were another mission like the last one?

Ardal started then stood when the old man shifted and cleared his throat. "Forgive me, Chief Librarian, for coming unbidden and unannounced—"

The man had held up both his hands. "Young man, I am Abban, secretary to the Chief Librarian. Flann will return shortly from… Lad, what could the matter be? You've gone pale."

Ardal sorted through the wreckage of his thoughts until he found one undeniable fact, and latched fiercely onto it. "Oh, Abban, I am a fool and a wretch. I have done a thing that proves me so." He lowered his head and drew in a deep breath.

"Tell me your name, lad, then tell me what you've done. When Flann returns, we will explain it to him."

Ardal released his breath and began to pace the room. "I am Ardal, Thirty Captain of a band of—"

"I have heard your name, Captain, and know of your deeds. You may be assured that Flann knows you as well. What could you have done to put you in such a state?"

Ardal stopped, to consider how best to begin, then paced again as he spoke. Abban leaned back in his chair, steepled his fingers and closed his eyes. His expression never changed, nor did he move until the flow of Ardal's words had halted.

He gestured for Ardal to take his seat again, then spoke in low, measured tones. "Captain, I cannot alleviate all of your concerns, but I can assure you that Flann ultimately received the packet. Of course, we might never discover what was done with the documents during the lapse of time between their delivery to a false Abban and their final arrival in this office.

"Considering what I know of the information conveyed in them, though, we could be in a tenuous, perhaps even a dangerous position. I cannot imagine how we might mitigate the damage. The culprits have had ample time to make use of the information."

Ardal sat with his elbows on his knees and his hands supporting his head until Abban spoke again. "Captain, I hear footsteps on the landing. Here is Flann."

Ardal stood and faced the door. A moment later, a tall, sharp-eyed man with thinning black and silver hair entered, surrounded by four younger men engaged in earnest discussion. The older man halted and stared at Ardal as the younger men continued talking for a few paces before they too came to a halt, looking from the Chief Librarian to Ardal.

Ardal introduced himself, whereupon Flann crossed the room and offered his long, angular hand. Ardal grimaced and clasped it. The librarian studied the footman's eyes for a long while then turned to his retinue. "We will continue this discussion tomorrow. The Captain requires my attention."

The young men bowed to their master and turned to leave, but then one turned back and bowed to Ardal. The others immediately followed suit before they all left. Flann gestured to a door in the back corner of the large office and directed Ardal toward it with a hand on his shoulder. Abban took up his writing tools and followed.

They entered a workroom furnished with many shelves, bins, racks, and tables covered and filled with oddments and documents. The soldier's habit of studying any new environment allowed Ardal to take in the entirety of the room on his first glance, then to begin focusing on interesting details. His gaze locked onto a table against the wall to one side.

Flann had been watching him. "Captain, if anything here interests you, I invite you to study, handle and ask any questions you wish about it."

The soldier made his way to the table and surveyed what it held. "These are some of the Dearthman weapons we captured and the broken Tierasalan blades recovered from the field. Brady was to study them."

"So he has, Captain. I requested that he loan them to

the library and provide copies of his notes to be included in the archives. He has graciously complied."

Abban scoffed. "He had no choice. When the Chief Librarian requires something—"

Flann raised a palm to his secretary. Abban covered his mouth with his hand.

"Captain, did you note any other item of interest among the weapons?" Flann smiled, as though at a child opening a gift.

"These papers." Ardal selected a dirty, torn bundle from among those that lay on the table. "They might be the ones I carried."

Flann grinned. "That is, indeed, the report you carried, beginning with your notes from the meeting with Hundred Captain Hart and continuing through the handwritten commentary by Dermot himself, from your first meeting with him. And on my desk," he gestured vaguely toward the far wall, "you would find your notes from the Il-Hofra mission. This is a treasure for an archivist. Would you like to peruse them, Captain?"

Ardal returned the bundle to its place on the table. "Flann, I've a thing to tell you. With all my heart, I wish I did not. Here it is. I carried, with these notes, a message for you from Aindru, Captain-General of the Western Division, and gave it over to a contemptible lout. I cannot in any way excuse myself and so place myself in your hands."

Ardal stared at the center of Flann's chest, waiting to hear his judgment until he felt the librarian's hand on his shoulder and looked up. Flann spoke as though Ardal were his favored son. "Ardal, that was bravely said. Now, what shall I do with you?"

He did not allow Ardal time to consider. "Put your mind at ease. All that could have been correctly surmised from that letter was that it was written by Aindru and addressed to me. Our adversaries already suspected we were in communication or they would not have positioned their agents within our organizations.

"The letter was, as he told you, a greeting. It was also an invitation for me to join the harvest jubilation at his family's villa. The other, more inflammatory, information was included in such a way that it would mean nothing to anyone other than the two of us.

"Captain, you will absolve yourself of your prior breach by delivering a letter from me straight into Aindru's hand. What questions do you now have of me?"

The color began to return to Ardal's face as he considered this. After a moment, he unclenched his jaw. "I've two that matter, Flann. May I speak of this to Laurelei? And shall I take you to the lout who claimed to be Abban?"

"By all means, invite the sensor to assist in your mission. I trust her as well or perhaps better than I do you. She is as honorable as you and likely more circumspect.

"As for the other, I would not forewarn our adversaries that we have become wise to their ruse. Let's not make a show of confronting their agent.

"I cannot hide the fact that Ardal, Captain of the Rectified, came to visit me today, but I can give their spies reason to believe that I suspect nothing. I will escort you to the door, and there thank you for ensuring that I received the letter you carried. I will assure you that all is well, and we will say our goodbyes. You will finish your business in Galantamhor and go to Shallowford, where you will deliver my letter directly to Aindru."

He smiled. "I think you will also find that the orders you and Laurelei will receive this evening have you posted to Shallowford for the foreseeable future."

Flann gestured toward the table and spoke in a casual, almost friendly manner. "I would be greatly honored, Captain, if, at your convenience, you would come here to interpret for me some of the more arcane passages in your notes. You see, I am neither a captain nor a sensor; so, I am afraid much of the nuance is lost on me."

Ardal nodded a salute. "It would be my honor, Chief Librarian, though based on our conversation today, I am of the opinion that you are well suited to either capacity."

He glanced toward the door. "Laurelei will be lookin' for me. I'd best go meet her."

The librarian and the captain left the secretary to his now continued furious scribbling.

CHAPTER 24
The Jumble

"Affection is responsible for nine-tenths of whatever solid and durable happiness there is in our lives."
<u>The Four Loves</u>
C. S. Lewis

As soon as Ardal had briefed Laurelei on the situation and the mission he had received from Flann, she showed him the orders she had received for him from Stefan as well as her orders from Rory. Each had separately been assigned to the caer of the Western Division in Shallowford and ordered to travel in disguise.

"Right." Ardal grinned. "It seems our betters have mapped the situation out for us."

Laurelei took charge of preparations and guided all their movements. Her work thoroughly bemused Ardal. She planned every move and interaction such that each portrayed some aspect of the ruse she had developed for those who were watching them.

Five days after he had spoken with Flann, Ardal loaded three chests and seven crates of Laurelei's belongings into the wain. When all was secure, he tied the two saddle horses to the rear and drove to meet Laurelei at the great central marketplace.

He pulled up next to where she sat atop two additional crates, both filled with new items she had bought to make their home more comfortable. "Ai, m'Love," Ardal said, "I'll be back in an hour."

"Where is it you think you're goin', then?"

Ardal shrugged and spread his hands. "Lamentably, love, we've no room for your new purchases in the wain. I'm for the poor house where I'll leave the two crates filled with the most useful items. The folks there will be glad of them, and you'll be glad to have the room in the wain for your new crates."

"If only you worked your back as much as your lip, we'd be for the gate by now." She lifted one of the crates and tottered toward the wain.

"I thought you liked my lips." Ardal leaped from his seat, went to the rear of the wain and attempted to take the crate from her as she struggled to lift it into the bed of the wain.

She pushed the crate against him. "Get back, oaf."

While she continued to struggle, Ardal hefted the other and tossed it into the wain. He slid a hand under her own crate, enough for her to get a corner into the wain.

"Get back, I said." Laurelei finally shoved the crate into place and secured the tailgate.

"I like your lips," she told him, "but sometimes your back is what I need. Because of your foolishness, we are now behind schedule." She climbed onto the bench and looked back at Ardal, grimly amused at his amazement that she had managed to lay the delay at his feet.

"My foolishness?"

"Which is currently delaying our journey yet further," and her tone brooked no argument.

Ardal was known for his audacity rather than discretion. "Madam, I would have had us begin our journey three days ago."

"There it is." She smirked. "As I said, 'foolishness'."

Ardal secured a canvas tarpaulin over the bed of the wain and mounted the bench. He did not stop muttering until he had released the brake, then he clicked his tongue to stir the draft horses on.

Laurelei embraced his upper arm. "So begins our new life together. It seems a dream to me."

The journey from Galantamhor through the northern wilds to the ruined watchtower beside the ancient, overgrown north-to-south highway was uneventful and pleasant except for the occasional moment of frustration between the couple. These almost always ended with Ardal apologizing and wondering why he had done so.

As they neared Shallowford, they rehearsed the tale that would provide context to the roles they played. Ardal's portion was simple. He was a blacksmith. That was evident from his dress, the tools he carried and the work he was able to pick up along the way.

Laurelei presented herself as a school teacher. That explained the crates filled with books and her casual manner of disdain. Her appearance marked her as a northerner, but everyone knew that Galantamhor was filled with folks from throughout the lands.

Their reason for traveling was also easily explained. They had left the teeming city in search of a quiet life in the warm south where Ardal could ply his trade and Laurelei could find students. The elegant tale provided ready answers that fitted easily into the framework of everyday life for many a citizen of Tierasal. As long as they could keep their weapons out of view and remember their roles, they should have no trouble.

Along the way, they met a newly married couple who had been granted acreage by the local governor. Ardal considered them interlopers, but Laurelei saw them as further camouflage; so, they traveled together as far as the southern edge of a treeless undulating plain dotted with massive boulders known as "The Jumble".

They drove away leaving the hopeful farmers to determine how thin soil and enormous stones could be made to give life to their dreams. Ardal tried to reassure Laurelei that their new friends would thrive. "They'll get by. Orin's a lad who knows how to work, and Keva's a stout lass."

"If they survive the shock of discovering how barren is their land, they'll get by, but what of children? It won't be long before they'll need to feed children." Laurelei looked over her shoulder and spoke to the friends she could no longer see. "We'll return to ensure you're well."

Ardal drove on.

CHAPTER 25
Dark Riddles

"The important thing is not to stop questioning."
Albert Einstein

At the Seat of the Captain-General of the Western Division in Shallowford, Aindru formally and cordially received the pair in his outer office, accepted the packet Ardal offered and thanked him for delivering the requested report on the status of Dearthman units along the border. Ardal opened his mouth to inform Aindru that the documents actually contained a letter from Flann, but Laurelei's glare stunned him into shutting it.

Aindru nodded at Laurelei then waved an orderly over and told him to take them to their quarters and to provide anything they might require. The Captain-General returned to his inner office and closed the door without further comment. Ardal fumed as they followed the orderly but had enough sense to keep his thoughts to himself until they had a moment alone together.

When they arrived at the barracks, the orderly indicated where their rooms were and the route to the common mess then excused himself and left them to settle in. As soon as the outer door of the barracks building closed, Ardal gave vent to his spleen. "And how is it we have traveled so far and laid aside our own plans for so long to arrive here and be treated as though we carried a note to the baker 'round the corner?"

"Shut you up, you great ass." Laurelei's response did nothing for Ardal's wounded pride, but it did shut him up. Laurelei took his hand and led him into her room. She moved a wooden chair from beneath the casement window of the small room to up against the wall opposite and indicated that Ardal should sit on it. He complied but opened his mouth to speak. "Shut it," and she jabbed a sharp finger at him.

Ardal's anger had been fuming, was now smoldering, and would soon enter the realm of raging. Laurelei leaned forward and tapped his lips with hers then with her finger. A small, bemused smile flitted across her face when she noted his befuddlement. She watched his face until his ire had dimmed and then turned away and strode to the window.

She lifted its latch, taking great care to make no sound, then shoved it open and leaned on the sill, as though enjoying the fresh air. After glancing about, and even leaning far out over the sash to admire the flowering shrubs growing along the wall, she turned back to Ardal and noted with satisfaction that he had opened the door just long enough to allow him a glance down the hallway. He quietly closed the door and returned to his seat.

Laurelei took a seat on the bed. "Clear?"

Ardal's frustration had dissipated. He nodded and matched her soft tone. "Clear."

"You have no doubt ascertained that Aindru suspects members of his own Seat."

"And how, bright Lady, was I to ascertain such a thing?"

Laurelei stared at Ardal as though attempting to

understand the question. The mild gaze he returned only confused her more. "Say you jest or I shall reconsider our betrothal. Did you not note the diffidence with which Aindru received us? His utter indifference to the information contained in the documents we carried?"

"Aye, sure I noticed, and wondered at it."

"And did you not think, 'Perhaps the canny Captain-General has determined it unwise to allow someone present to ascertain the origins of the message we carried'?"

Ardal snorted. "A commander must trust his men, especially those who serve within his own Seat."

Laurelei forgave Ardal, but found it necessary to instruct him. "This sort of naivety is unseemly and dangerous to a man with the responsibilities you bear, beloved. Do you truly believe that all soldiers live by the same warrior ethic you serve with all your heart?"

"It's a surety, is it not? What man would take upon himself the duties, burdens and oath of a soldier if he did not mean to serve them? If Aindru cannot trust the men who serve here in his Seat, the men who surround him, how can the Western Division itself serve?"

"It cannot—"

A sharp knock at the window drew curses from their mouths and their blades from their scabbards. Ardal crossed the room in two strides and lifted the latch. He eased the window open enough to allow his voice to pass through, but before he could speak, a thin, broad piece of wood slid between the frame and the sill. Ardal opened the window farther to accost the man, but he had already moved away through the shrubbery.

Laurelei laid her hand on his arm to stop him then stooped to pick up the wood. "It's a message." She drew a lace handkerchief from her sleeve and wrapped it around the wood. Ardal recognized it as a grille like the ones they had used in the Dearthlands. She turned so he could look over her shoulder.

"Throne," Ardal breathed just behind her ear. He moved toward the door.

"Where are you going, then?"

"You read the message as well as I. We're goin' to the Throne. Come on, then. Don't dawdle. Just like a woman to dawdle when there's work to be done."

"I'll not move from this spot until you explain the meaning of this message."

Ardal grinned half-idiotically. "Ah, so, the stupid footman knows a thing the brilliant sensor does not. If I tell you, then you will know and I will never again have a bit of knowledge you lack. I think you should just trust me and do as I say."

"I'll not move, I tell you. Besides, all men know that I love your mind above all else about you."

"If all men know it, then I lose naught by telling you that the Throne is the name given to a high, flat hill to the east of Shallowford. During training, all recruits into the Western Division run around the town once each week. Late into the Light Footman's specialized training, we ran halfway 'round the town then surmounted the Throne before completing the circuit. Aindru apparently wants us to meet—"

Laurelei had snatched up her cloak from the bed and now opened the door. He sighed. "Now you're harried to leave."

A sliver of moon had risen before they left the road that encircled the city and onto a path that ascended the hill known as the Throne. After thirty minutes' climb, the pair saw a break in the tree line ahead. Ardal pulled Laurelei to one side of the trail and they proceeded the last few yards under the cover of the trees. They again halted when they arrived at the edge of a roughly circular clearing that Ardal knew to be just large enough for a company of Light Footmen to assemble.

From the far side, a low voice called to them. "I'm here, you two, on the bench behind Iron Murcad."

Ardal stepped from the trees and led Laurelei to a low plinth topped by a statue of the legendary Light Footman. The voice came again from behind the plinth. "Come. Have a seat. We haven't long."

"If you are the man we hope you are, you'll forgive our suspicion."

"On the contrary, Captain, it would be unforgiveable if you were not suspicious. Test me, if you will."

Laurelei and Ardal stared at each other in the wan moonlight until she said, "Who sent us to Shallowford, and why?"

Ardal nodded at her choice of test. If the man behind the statue could answer correctly then either he was Aindru or they were already lost.

"Flann, Chief Librarian of the archives at Galantamhor sent you to deliver a message to inform me that your foolishness had compromised our communications." He chuckled. "The Chief Librarian also asks me to show you mercy in his name. It seems he thinks you ... both of you might become a valuable addition to our company."

Sure now that they spoke with Aindru himself, the two approached the bench where he was sitting and took seats on either side of him. "What do you want of us?"

Aindru stared straight ahead and spoke as though to the most intimate of friends. "Ardal, Laurelei, we – that's all of Tierasal – are hanging on the edge of a precipice. I would... We – a small group of those who know this – would turn the tide to save our land. We want you to join us. We need you to join us.

"Flann and I are members of this small group. Upon our recommendations, the group has agreed that I should invite you to help us turn Tierasal from the brink. However you decide, our respect and friendship goes with you, but you must decide based only on what you now know, and I will require your answer before you leave here."

"'Based only on what we know?' But we know

nothing—"

"Hush." Laurelei's soft voice cut through Ardal's like a razor through wool. She then asked him, "What do we know? What can we surmise? What has brought us to this point that might lead us farther toward a decision?"

"I am certain I know naught that might guide us in this matter."

The tone of Laurelei's voice sharpened. "I am certain you know naught of what you know or do not. Still your mouth and think, Ardal. What *do* we know?"

"We know that Aindru and Flann have maneuvered us into an untenable position."

Laurelei drew a sharp breath. "Not only they, but Rory and Stefan as well."

Aindru chuckled.

"Rory and Stefan are complicit in this conspiracy to retain our services," she reminded Ardal. "They blocked our plans to resign and transferred us here to Shallowford so we would remain accessible and therefore useful to them."

Aindru, who had never before met Laurelei, grinned in her direction. "You are as bold and skilled with your mind as the Captain with his arms. I had heard of you, heard you were a formidable woman but was in no wise prepared to see your mind at work."

"No one is prepared to meet her," Ardal informed him. "She is the most honorable, the wisest and the most valiant of women. Do not doubt her skill with arms, either, for there she is formidable indeed."

She leaned forward to look past Aindru at Ardal. "What say you, Captain? I will as you will."

"If there is no threat to the land, then the Captain-General of the Western Division is lying. That fact, itself, would betoken a grave threat to the land. Were he behind such a threat, it seems to me that he would lie to convince us that all was well or else simply keep silent on the matter."

Laurelei was silent herself until it seemed Ardal would say no more, then she prompted, "On the other hand, does it not seem exactly the sort of thing one would tell a warrior to enlist his aid in fomenting the very threat of which he warns us?"

"Aye, Lady." Ardal shook his head. "Yet it seems to me that the fact that Aindru is here talking with us indicates that, one way or another, there is a threat. It seems that either Aindru's group confronts that threat or is that threat. We have no option but to engage it, either by joining as conspirators or as infiltrators."

"You do realize I'm sat between you two, Ardal?"

"That I do, Captain-General, and you knew before we spoke that I would have these thoughts. Here is my proposal if it meets with the Lady's approval. From here, we return to Taermun and marry as though naught has changed. There, we'll winter over then come here to Shallowford where we will live according to our established roles. When you are prepared to provide details, you will know where to find us."

A long silence passed between them as they each stared toward the graying horizon, then Ardal stood and offered Laurelei his hand, which she took although she remained seated. "Ardal, we've no right to give the Captain-General an indefinite answer."

Aindru sighed. "You've as much right to answer me as you have as I have to ask you as I did. Go, you two. Marry. You will raise up such a throng of the mighty between you. Perhaps this is what Tierasal requires of you in these dire days, that you provide the heroes who will carry us through the darker days to come. If our need becomes great, we will ensure you know all you need, so you may commit fully to our cause."

CHAPTER 26
Not Anymore

"I would rather walk with a friend in the dark than alone in the light."
Helen Keller

Ardal and Laurelei returned to their barracks rooms and employed the campaigner's discipline of sleeping when the opportunity presented itself. They woke a scant two hours later when the orderly knocked on their doors to inform them that breakfast was served. They washed and dressed then headed there with all their gear.

After they had eaten, Laurelei convinced the kitchen steward that he would not miss a few loaves, some vegetables, a wheel of cheese, a bushel of apples, and a small basket of boiled eggs. He convinced himself he could live without the firkin of wine he added to their provisions. Ardal muttered that he wouldn't mind a firkin or so of ale, but Laurelei shushed him and asked him to bring the wain to the scullery door and load the supplies.

When he arrived, Ardal was surprised to discover a cask of ale had been set beside the firkin of wine. Laurelei came to help him load. "I see your beauty and smooth words have won me a cask of ale. I am grateful, but would prefer knowing that your beauty and smooth words are for me alone."

Laurelei gave him a hard look. "You are too good a man to debase yourself so. I am too good a woman to allow it. Your name won you that ale. I merely told it to the steward. He decided that sharing his ale with the renowned Captain would be for him a great honor."

Ardal saw himself for the fool he was and nodded while looking at the floor. "Aye, Lady. Forgive me. You merit better of me – the steward, as well. I'll go offer him my gratitude."

Laurelei nodded and turned her attention to carrying the supplies. When she had returned from her second trip out to the wain, Ardal and the steward joined the effort. They made short work of the job and thanked the steward one last time before climbing into the wain. Ardal snapped the reins and guided the horses out of the kitchen yard.

An hour later, they crossed the ford for which the town of Shallowford was named and drove until they arrived at the southern edge of the boulder-strewn heath known as the Jumble. There, they followed a small track that lead off to the west from the main road to a sod house. Beside it, a woman was turning the earth to plant a kitchen garden.

Laurelei alighted from the wain before Ardal had set the brake and ran to greet her friend. While they talked, Ardal unhitched the team. He led the horses to the trough and drew water for them then bellowed to Keva, "Where's that layabout lad of yours? We've ale that needs drinkin'."

Keva waved her arm toward the wooded hills, where Ardal spotted a figure loping in their direction along a stream. Ardal jogged over to meet him. When they clasped arms and caught their breaths, Ardal noted that Orin's characteristic good nature was greatly dampened. As they walked back to the house, Ardal peppered Orin with questions about the prospects of farming such stony soil.

Each answer weighed Ardal down a bit more. By the time they reached the wain, Ardal had decided to leave the ale and other supplies with the struggling family.

Keva and Laurelei were still talking by the wain, but Keva glanced at Orin as he unstrung his bow. He shrugged in reply and her shoulders drooped. "Ach, my friends, we've naught to offer you but roasted oats and cool water from our babbling burn. There's poor cheer for you, but it's such as we have."

Laurelei hugged her friend. "Today, we bring the cheer with us." She raised her eyebrows at Ardal who smiled and began unloading the supplies from the wain. He noted that she slipped her purse into the egg basket, and he grinned.

After dinner, Orin and Keva offered Laurelei and Ardal the only bed they had – their own. The travelers gratefully declined and chose to lay their bedrolls out on the dirt floor. As she lay next to him, Laurelei drew an invisible line with the edge of her hand between them then shook a warning finger at Ardal. He grinned and turned away, but it was a long while before he managed to sleep.

In the morning, they invited Orin and Keva to visit them in Shallowford. Ardal elbowed Orin. "If you tire of plowing stones from the ground, you might choose to stay a bit. There is good bottomland along the Frigid that needs plowing."

Orin seemed to consider it for a moment. "My lad, that good bottomland likely belongs to another man. As I cannot buy it from him, I reckon we'll work the land that's rightfully ours and make a farm and a home of it."

Keva shrugged at Laurelei then embraced her fiercely. "When you pass this way again..."

Laurelei returned the embrace. "We will. We will. Come to us when you can or send a message, and we will come to you."

The travelers boarded the wain and drove down the track. They looked back once or twice but said nothing. Laurelei leaned against Ardal who pulled her closer.

The journey to Taermun continued apace, and the conversation turned often to their proposed plans for locating Laurelei's father. When they eventually arrived, they stopped first at the Inn of Mag Petty and asked for the room that Laurelei had occupied on her previous stays. Mag shook her head. "I'm sorry, lass, but that room was taken by a traveler just yesterday. He asked for it 'specially', 'the one under the dormer that looks out over the valley' he said like he knew it. The request seemed odd to me…"

Laurelei looked pensive. "Hm. I suppose I'll need the other dormer room then."

"Of course, that one's on the opposite side of the inn, though, so has no view but of the stables below and the hillside a quarter mile off."

"It'll do well." Laurelei lifted her gear and followed Ardal who was already climbing the stair with a crate of her books. She halted and turned back to the innkeeper. "Mag, did he tell you where he had come from … or was going to?"

"No, Laur. He didn't mention it."

Laurelei nodded and carried on to the stairs. Ardal heard her mutter, "No, he wouldn't mention it to anyone. Would he?"

Laurelei was distant and distracted during dinner and for the rest of the evening until Ardal rose from the table, stretched and announced he was going home. He leaned forward to kiss her cheek, but she turned her lips toward his and grasped his upper arm. When she released him, Ardal had a foolish grin across his face. "Lady, I–"

"Ardal, will you break fast with me in the morning?"

"Sure, and how could I not after that?"

"You'll have to come early, at sunrise I would think. Please don't fail me. Our quarry is sly, and he has the advantage of us. G'night, m'love."

"G'night, m'love," and Ardal lumbered home, raising his hand a few times to acknowledge greetings from friends but allowing none to engage him further. At home, he dropped onto the bed his parents had once shared and soon gave himself over to sleep.

The next morning at sunrise, Ardal woke and ran to the inn with Laurelei's admonition echoing in his mind. "Please don't fail me," she'd said. He paused only long enough to draw water and splash it on his face then have a drink. He burst through the front door of the inn and found Laurelei seated against the back wall of the common room, wearing a fawn colored skirt and a white blouse, her thick, dark hair braided and still damp from the washing it had received the night before. He plopped down next to her, and she wrinkled her nose.

Laurelei sighed. "You slept later than you intended then ran here without a bath so you would not disappoint me. Is that not so?"

"Aye, Lady. I've clothes in the wain out behind the stable. I'll change quickly and regain my seat before it has had time to cool."

"My bathwater has not yet been tossed out. Perhaps you'd care to—"

"I will smell of lilacs and springtime when I return," Ardal said as he stood and jogged out the back door of the inn to get his change of clothes.

When he returned, he sat across the table then leaned in closer to Laurelei. "See? 'Lilacs and springtime' as I said."

Laurelei scoffed. "At least you no longer smell of the mingled sweat of horse and footman." She patted his head. "You'll do."

They fell silent and Laurelei became tense as the sound of shuffling, punctuated by a rhythmic tapping, descended the stairs. When it reached the bottom, an ancient man came into view. His eyes were bandaged and his sparse white hair shot out from his head in all directions. He tapped around him with a thin rod before shuffling forward two steps at a time.

Laurelei and Ardal watched him silently as he

circumnavigated the room. Ardal wondered at Laurelei's growing agitation as the old man neared them. He was astounded when her foot shot out from beneath the table in an apparent attempt to trip the poor fellow.

The shambling blind man leapt nimbly aside, and landed in a fighter's crouch holding his cane out in front of himself with both hands. For a moment, none spoke, but Ardal laid his long knife on the table, keeping his hand on it.

Laurelei scoffed and moved along the bench, away from the man. "Take a seat, old man. We've been waiting for you."

The man spoke in a low, resonant voice. "I'll not take my ease until the proper pleasantries have been exchanged." He removed the bandage from his eyes, stood his stick against the wall and hung the bandage from it. He seemed to focus his entire self into the gaze he now laid on Laurelei's face. "It is *good* to see you, lass. Long have I dreamed of standing before you. Forgive me—"

Laurelei was already on her feet, her arms around him. "My own dear dad, how can I not forgive what had to be? And yet I wonder why it must have been." He slowly enfolded her with his own arms, as though savoring the movement.

Ardal stood and sheathed his blade. Laurelei pulled away from Fintan but kept her arm around him. She gestured to Ardal, "Fintan, Lord of Hebron Heath, rightful king of shattered Dunglaun, founder of Taermun, and father to a willful daughter, I want you to know this man. He is Ardal ... *the* Ardal of the Avinn Vale, the hero of Hart's Pass—"

"Hundred Captain Hart was the hero of Hart's Pass."

While Laurelei studied Ardal's face, a tender, fierce look crossed her own. "The Captain of the Rectified is a man who loves his enemies until they serve him, then calls them his 'brothers'. How can such a man live long in the land without the wisdom of a good woman to watch over his heart?"

Ardal bowed slightly from the waist. "Fintan, I offer my life as surety that I will serve her needs before my own, that I will honor her both in our home and before all men, and that I will remember how precious is her valiant heart even when she is at her most difficult, demanding and dismissive. I swear on my head that I will do these things and more if only you will allow me the honor of doing so."

The couple stood breathless, awaiting Fintan's response. He seemed to be far away in his own mind but then cocked his head to one side. "And what, lad, would you do were I to withhold my approval?"

Ardal looked at Laurelei as she had looked at him while speaking of him. "Were you to deny me the opportunity to love and honor her in our home, Fintan, I would continue to love and honor her before all men. Were you to say that her destiny is higher than marriage to a village blacksmith, I would agree and would do all in my power to clear the path to her high destiny for I do indeed treasure her valiant heart."

Ardal drew himself up with the air of a condemned but honorable man awaiting the axe. Fintan raised an eyebrow at him then looked at Laurelei. "He blusters a bit, doubts the value of a good blacksmith and smells of lilacs. Are you certain this is the one you want?"

Laurelei grinned. "None other will do. There is no help for your first complaint. The second, though, I will correct. The third is my own fault, and I assure you it's only temporary. I'll have him, Dad."

Fintan pulled the two together and embraced them. "This is the day promised so long ago to a desolate and desperate young fool." He wiped his eyes and shouted for Mag. "Bring tea and eggs and toast and cheese and honey and milk and porridge and bacon – I have a son, Mag. I have a son." The old warrior and crownless king danced and shouted, waving his arms above his head while tears trickled like a burn down the crannied terrain of his face.

Mag bustled into the room in a right fury. "Quiet, you mad fool. You're disturbing the other…"

The expression on her face bore testimony to her consternation. "You're blind."

"Not anymore." Fintan danced over to her and drew her into his jig.

She resisted. "You're the Lord of Hebron Heath," and she attempted to curtsey while he danced her around the room, filling it with his laughter.

"Not anymore."

Mag finally broke free and Fintan continued to caper about. "You're dead."

He stopped dancing, faced Mag with his arms outstretched and said solemnly, "Not anymore."

CHAPTER 27
Lifelong Binding

"My most brilliant achievement was my ability to persuade my wife to marry me."
Winston Churchill

Fintan dispatched wains in search of the finest of everything that could be found for the wedding of his only child. Mag Petty's larder, cellar and scullery were so filled with casks, crates, bags, and pitchers that scant space remained to move among them, but the finest thing Fintan supplied was the battle standard that he had secreted away since his return to fallen Dunglaun.

On a clear evening in early spring, a cool breeze rustled the small, green leaves of the fruit trees that surrounded the greensward at the heart of Taermun. The residents of the village and of many far-flung farms stood silent while Cavan, the old Teshak of Taermun, prepared to speak the words of lifelong binding over Ardal and Laurelei.

Ardal stood facing him fidgeting with the knot in his sword belt. Cavan gestured with his chin, and Ardal turned to see the crowd parting behind him. At the end of the aisle that had opened in the crowd stood the most valiant, wise, and comely woman that Ardal had ever known. Her unruly dark hair was plaited at the temples with the plaits pulled back into a thick braid behind. The remainder of her voluminous locks fell free to be teased by the same breeze that lifted the tail of her linen shawl like a pennant. The sun shone off her dark tresses like an auburn corona.

She locked her gaze on his and strode forward at a stately pace. When at last she stood beside him, she glanced at him eyes gleaming and winked. Looking down at her hand she twitched it in a beckoning motion then looked up at him and raised her eyebrows a bit. "Go on, Ardal, take my hand."

Ardal engulfed Laurelei's lithe hand in his great paw and grinned like a loon. The corners of Laurelei's mouth lifted then she faced the teshak. Ardal, however, continued to grin at Laurelei.

Cavan opened his mouth but snapped it shut again as Laurelei spoke before he did. "Teshak, I must speak before we continue. Will you give me leave to do so?"

Leaning forward, Cavan replied. "It *is your* wedding, Lady. Do as you will."

Laurelei faced Ardal directly and took each of his hands in one of hers before she spoke. "I need to know, Ardal." She looked beyond his shoulder into the distance and her voice became a chant.

"Who will cross the river with me, in the shallows and the deeps? Will you?

Who will descend with me the valleys and climb then to the peaks? Will you?

Who will bear me up when I am weak? Who will shout bold truth when I cannot speak? Will you?"

She turned her head slightly to focus her eyes on his and repeated fiercely, "Will you?"

Ardal absorbed the impact of her fierce gaze for a long moment before he responded. "Aye, my love. I would feed you my last morsel. Clothe you as I stand naked. I would shield you with my body. I will carry you though I can no longer walk. You are more precious to me than my very self. I have naught but that I am, and it is yours. As Wisdom guides me I will."

Utter silence reigned as the two stood among the many intent upon the moment until, once again, the corners of Laurelei's mouth turned up, and she nodded then turned to Cavan.

"I thank you, Teshak, for allowing me a moment to know this man. Please continue."

Cavan cleared his throat then muttered, "I hardly think it necessary to speak my paltry words, but we will plod on if you wish."

Laurelei graced him with an encouraging smile and a slight nod.

The teshak cleared his throat again and began the ancient Ceremony of Lifelong Binding. "Ardal, son of Ivor, will you bear the burdens and build the walls that will ensure for Laurelei and for your children the security and provision your family will need to prosper and to uphold our traditions and standards?"

"Aye, Teshak. That I will and more."

Cavan nodded then addressed Laurelei. "Laurelei, daughter of Fintan, Princess of the Ruined Land, will you speak with wisdom and grace that will ensure for Ardal and for your children the compassion and strength your family will need to become a blessing to each other and to Taermun?"

"Aye, Teshak. I will as I can as I will that I can more."

Cavan instructed the groom to take the bride's hand then wound the battle standard around their hands and forearms, binding them together. He then held up a two-handled cup filled with wine. With their free hands, each took hold of a handle and together they drank.

Cavan addressed the crowd. "I present to you Ardal the smith, son of Ivor and his bride Laurelei the tutor, daughter of Fintan of the house of Killinchy, Prince of Dunglaun and Lord of Hebron Heath. He gestured to the couple. Ardal wrapped his free arm around his bride and leaned forward. Laurelei placed her free hand behind her husband's head, and they kissed while shouts, cheers, whistles, and hoots erupted around them.

Cavan lifted his hand above the couple, and the noise abated enough that he could be heard. "May they be as fruitful as they are bold."

The cheers broke out again in full force. Laurelei and Ardal stood bound together and flushed until Alistair, Ardal's brother, stepped forward, waving his arms and bellowing, "Aye. That's all very nice. Yes. Lovely. All this cheering has worked up in me a powerful thirst. I see there a rank of kegs and casks. Who will help me tap them?"

A rank of musicians who had prepared for this moment struck up a reel and the village began to dance. Ardal unwound the binding cloth so he might dance with his bride then folded it and offered it to her.

She demurred. "You, too, are of the House of Killinchy. It's now your standard as well as mine."

Ardal shouted over the music, "Does that make me, then, a prince?"

Laurelei grasped his tunic and pulled his face down to hers. With an impish grin she replied, "Prince Consort, shall we say?"

"Aye, m'Love, and when shall I have the pleasure of consorting with you?"

Before she could respond, Ardal pulled her into the center of the common and made a poor attempt at dancing a reel with her while she ignored his cloddishness in favor of his gallantry.

The celebration went on into the wee hours, but Ardal

called his bride away not long after darkness fell. They slipped unnoticed to the house beside the smithy where, earlier in the evening, the matrons of Taermun had scrubbed and swept, then burned incense, poured wine and strewn roses petals while they sang the songs and spoke the rhymes that would bring joy and children to the couple.

A great tub sat half-filled in the center of the room, and a great pot full of hot lavender-scented water sat on the grate. On the bed lay a freshly stuffed mattress covered in soft linen and rose petals.

Laurelei indicated the pot of scented water with her chin. "It'd take a mighty man to lift such a pot full as it is and hot as well. How nice for me that I have such a man."

Ardal grinned and walked to the grate where he donned thick leather gloves and lifted the pot. When he turned around, he almost lost his hold on it for there stood the most comely woman in the world with her wild hair and her bodice loosed. After carefully pouring the scented water into the tub, he glanced up through the steam and noted that the bodice was gone and the skirts with it, and all that remained to protect Laurelei from his thirsty eyes was a long pale blue chemise. He set the pot on the hearth and turned expectantly but was disappointed to discover that the chemise remained firmly in place.

His bride's small smile and downcast eyes drew him to her. Laurelei placed her hands on his chest and murmured, "M'love, perhaps you could help me with the stays."

Ardal looked up from kissing her neck. "Stays?"

Laurelei looked mildly chagrined. "Yes, love. The stays on the back of my frock. Help me remove it or never see me without it."

Ardal stepped back, and Laurelei turned so he could unfasten the closures and allow her to remove her chemise. Once he had completed that task, he tugged the cloth from her shoulders and the undergarment fell to the ground. Wrapping his arms about her waist, Ardal began again kissing the side of her neck. Laurelei reached back and placed her hand behind his head pulling him in closer for a moment. Then she lowered her hands to his and gently broke his hold on her then stepped away.

She lifted a bowl of sweet wine from the table. When she turned around and Ardal caught his first glimpse of her unveiled glory he lost the capacity for speech. Pushing him gently backwards into a chair, she held the bowl to his lips. "Refresh yourself, m'love," and he took the bowl from her hand before she stepped into the tub, "while I do the same."

Ardal spilled his wine.

CHAPTER 28
Conspiracy

"The nation that forgets its defenders will itself be forgotten."
Calvin Coolidge

The couple stayed in Taermun through the winter and began preparations to return to Shallowford as soon as the snows began to melt. They spent the week before their departure assuring friends that they would return to visit. They also discussed with Ardal's brother, Alistair, what was to be done with the smithy and cottage that had been left to Ardal by Ivor. Alistair had definite plans for the house and shop, but acknowledged Ardal's right to speak in the matter. Entering through the shop, Alistair found the pair seated at the table engaged in intense discussion.

"Lover's spat, eh?" Alistair swaggered over and plopped down on a stool.

Laurelei's face flushed crimson, and her eyes flashed.

Alistair chuckled. "Ah, lass, it's naught to embarrass you. Mam and Da had them often enough while Ardal was out adventurin'… right up 'til the day Da died and Mam not long after. Of course Ardal don't know that 'cause he was out adventurin' as I said."

Ardal shook his head. "Alistair, my lad, my brother, my childhood companion, it's not embarrassment that colors her face so. That's rage. There's a fury there you likely can't imagine. You'd do well to note it."

"I've no fear of a woman's distemper. Not this one nor any other, and I'm not like to take advice from any lad who has."

Laurelei stood, and Ardal raised a hand to forestall the imminent torrent of invectives, but she took his hand and spoke gently. "M'love, by your leave, I'm for the inn and tea with Mag Petty. Do you require aught of me?"

Ardal kissed her hand then released it. "Thank you, m'love. Wish Mag well for me."

Laurelei leaned forward, laid her hand on his cheek and kissed him slowly and firmly then walked out the door.

Alistair chuckled again. "Well, I can see you've got her under control. A wave of the hand and she's demure…"

"Ach, Alistair, were you always such a fool? Look you, nothing excuses your walking without invitation into my house to insult my wife. It will not happen again. Do you ken?"

"Oh, little brother, I ken sure enough that you think you're a great hero come home to reign over the wee folk in quaint Taermun, but I'll have you know that your sword and your high-born woman make you naught but my little brother playin' at bein a man.

"As for me walkin into 'your house', I'd say it ceased to be yours the day you walked out of it to kill folks that never bothered you.

"In hopes that you'll one day come to your senses and settle in at home to serve Taermun as her smith, I'll not sell the shop nor the cottage, but I've a fellow will travel up from Culverton for a week each month to serve the needs here in the village. I'll let him the shop and the cottage for the times that he's here. I only need to know if you've a mind to take the tools with you or no."

Ardal shook his head. "It's a worthy idea. I'd not thought on how to get a smith to Taermun in my absence."

"No. You don't think on such things."

"The armory will provide me a full complement of equipment in Shallowford so I'll need none of what's here, but I will take with me Da's cross-peen for a memory."

Alistair scoffed. "The armory? So, you're not a real soldier? You're naught but a smith for the army? I might've known. A smith, but you'll carry yourself about like a man at arms and your woman looks on you as though you saved the world. The lads carry on about the things you must've done, but I'll set them straight. All men will know you're naught but an ironmonger for the real soldiers.

Ardal thought how best to correct his brother's misapprehensions then thought better of it and extended his hand to him. "Alistair, it is my house. I state that now. The smithy also is mine. You let it. You keep the money for your trouble, but when the time comes that we need it, this is our home. My family lives here although we must for a time be elsewhere."

Alistair clasped Ardal forearm. "Aye, little brother. It's yours, and the benefit of it is mine and Taermun's until you return."

"Good enough then." Ardal released Alistair's forearm.

Alistair turned to go, but Ardal was not yet finished with him. "Alistair, brother or no, if you ever again speak disrespectfully to my wife or of her or if you enter our home unbidden, you will discover what I learned in Hart's Pass."

Alistair grunted as he suppressed a shudder then turned and left.

After he had given Alistair enough time to amble to the end of the alleyway, Ardal made his way to the inn and found Laurelei chatting over tea with Fintan and Mag Petty. As he approached, Mag stood and offered him tea.

Ardal slid into the seat she had vacated next to Laurelei and shook his head. "Ach, no, Mag. Tea'll do naught for me now. I'll have a pint if you will though I know it's early. Alistair has just that effect on me."

Once Mag had shuffled off, Fintan sighed. "Ach, my son and my daughter, it's to Aindru you must go, and tell him you're with him. He's born more of this than any man should, and needs those he can trust in his camp."

Ardal and Laurelei considered Fintan's words for a long while. Finally, Ardal broke the silence. "I *am* a fool. Why did I not think that you were party to the conspiracy of which Aindru spoke? How else did you know to meet us here?"

"Lad, just to be clear, Stefan told me of your intent to marry and your posting to Shallowford. It was then that I followed you to Aindru's Seat and learned of that you forestalled him. He and I decided that I might be the one who could earn your trust in the matter."

Mag returned with Ardal's ale. "So somber you all are. Have you not just been married? And you, Fintan, was it not you who reeled me about in your joy just a short time ago? What is it that could have darkened your thoughts?"

Mag looked from Ardal who shrugged apologetically to Laurelei who merely drew down the corners of her mouth. Fintan stood and took Mag's arm. As he escorted her toward the scullery, he explained to her that they were discussing family matters and begged her forbearance to allow them to continue in privacy.

Glancing over at Laurelei, Ardal noted that she seemed agitated. "Look you, Lady. If this is a thing that involves Stefan, Rory, Flann, Aindru, *and* your Da, it must be right, yeah? There's not a one of 'em I mistrust. In fact, I trust each of them to no small extent."

"Ardal, it's no longer a question of whether we are involved or not. The question is: What risk are we taking? What do we stand to lose?"

Fintan spoke from behind them. "Our lives, our

fortunes, our honor." He walked over and took his seat. "Children, there's a rot at the heart of Tierasal, and the whole land is beginning to feel the effects of it. I will say it once more. Get you to Shallowford. Make it soon but not in haste. It wouldn't do to draw unwanted attention. Take your orders after you arrive from Aindru. Your children and theirs will thank you."

"What if we have no children? What if we lose the lives we risk before those children are born?" Laurelei spoke to her father but looked at her husband.

"'Twould be better to die childless than to allow this rot to grow unchallenged." Fintan leaned back and grinned. "But that'll not happen. I have it on good authority that I'll become a grandfather in due course."

Leaning back and lifting his pint, Ardal laughed. "Well, that's settled then." He drained his mug and sighed deeply. We'll visit Orin and Keva on the way then, eh, Laur?"

She smiled. "What a lovely thought, m'love."

CHAPTER 29
Seedlings

"Be at war with your vices, at peace with your neighbors, and let every new year find you a better man."
Benjamin Franklin

The journey from Taermun to Shallowford was far more enjoyable than the previous one primarily because they were able to enjoy the intimacy that came with being married but also because the question of joining the conspiracy had been settled.

Upon their arrival at the home of their friends, they were heartily welcomed and fed from the fruits of Keva's garden and of Orin's weir. They spent the evening recounting the tale of their wedding and sipping cider that Laurelei had brought from Taermun.

Once the tale had been told and bits of it re-told, Laurelei looked askance at Keva and smiled as though they shared a secret. "How long have you known?"

Keva lowered her eyes and placed her hand on her belly. "Not long. I only told Orin a few days ago."

"Told him what, then?" Ardal smiled benignly at Keva

who merely smiled back at him.

Ardal shifted his gaze to Orin. "Right. So I'm the idiot. Let's have it, and everyone can laugh at the stupid smith."

Keva chuckled, "You're no stupid man, Ardal. You're just a man. I'm with child. Orin will have a son."

Ardal sat for a moment wondering how Laurelei had guessed such a thing before he realized that he was expected to respond. "Well done, lad." He lifted his cup to Orin.

Laurelei rolled her eyes. "Yes 'well done, *lad*' indeed." She took Keva's hand and grinned at her. "We are very happy for you."

The friends continued talking late into the night until Ardal stood, stretched and yawned. "Look you, Orin. You're a fine lad, but you're sitting in my bedroom, and I've a need to lay me down."

Orin and Keva wished their friends a good night and felt their way to the bed chamber. Ardal and Laurelei laid out their bedrolls on the dirt floor and settled down together.

In the morning, Orin took Ardal out to show him where he had built a wooden box and filled it with soil in which were growing about fifty small plants. "I planted the seeds from the apples you brought before. Only about a third of them sprouted then I lost a few to critters. I'm preparing to plant them on that hillside when they've grown into saplings. I'll build a cider press over there."

Ardal grinned. "Aye, lad. The hardware for your press will be my first project when I re-open the shop. I'd be proud to do it for you."

The ladies walked over arm-in-arm talking earnestly. When they reached the patch of seedlings, they halted and Laurelei announced her decision. "In five months, Orin and Keva will come to Shallowford and stay there with us until the baby is born and Keva has recovered."

She looked at Ardal and raised an eyebrow. "Well, of course they will," he said as though he had been thinking it all along.

Orin gestured at his seedlings. "But what of my apple trees?"

Laurelei fixed Orin with a diffident gaze. "Do you as you will, Master Orin, but the lady and her child will be snug in our cottage within reach of a quality midwife."

Turning to Ardal, Orin lifted his hands in a silent plea for help. Ardal punched his shoulder. "Ah, lad, it's for the best. Build a fence to keep the rabbits and deer out of your seedlings. The sun and rain'll take care of the rest."

***

Upon arrival in Shallowford, Ardal and Laurelei immediately reported to Aindru's seat and soon established a plausible cover story that afforded them regular access to the Captain-General and allowed him to task them with missions as required. Ardal was assigned to the armory and Laurelei as tutor for Aindru's three daughters.

Over the next months, they settled into a rhythm punctuated by occasional meetings with Aindru until the day Laurelei informed Ardal that the time had come to bring Keva to their home. They hitched the team and drove the half-day trip out of Shallowford, across the Frigid and into the Jumble.

Orin met them as they drove up and offered Laurelei a hand down from the wain. "Keva's inside. She'll be glad to see you."

Laurelei stepped past him toward the house. "I've been looking forward to this day. Let's go check on our girl."

Ardal and Orin walked around discussing what might need to be done about the farm before Orin would be needed in Shallowford. "Lad, you've been busy. I like to think I'm a worker, but you make me look like a layabout."

The men went inside and brought out Keva's things. While they arranged a comfortable spot for her in the bed of the wain, the women came out. Keva cried quietly while she hugged Orin; then he and Ardal helped her to climb into the bed of the wain.

As Ardal helped Laurelei climb into her seat, Keva looked over her shoulder and winked. "So, how long have you known?"

Laurelei grinned. "Not long now. In fact, I haven't yet told Ardal."

Ardal pulled himself up into his seat and reached for the reins. "Haven't told me what, then?"

Orin laughed. "Well done, lad."

Ardal stared at Orin. "What are you on about?"

Orin shook his head still laughing and waved. "Drive safe. Watch for bumps. If my Keva becomes uncomfortable you pull over and let her walk about for a moment."

Ardal shrugged and lightly slapped the horses' rumps. As he guided the team down the drive, he looked back and saw Orin grinning at him in a manner he considered to be half-witted. He glanced over at Laurelei who was engaged in animated conversation with Keva. She paused for a moment and favored him with a smile like the first warm day of spring. Again, he shrugged. Whatever it was she hadn't yet told him couldn't be a bad thing. He'd ask about it later.

A short while later they turned onto the high road and began to make good time toward the ford. A bit farther on, a thought struck him. "Laur... are we havin a baby?"

"We are, m'love," she said primly.

"Well, you might have told me."

"I might have..." She grinned, "but it was more fun this way."

He drew the team up and leaned over to kiss her then took up the reins again. "Perhaps we'll have twins."

Laurelei looked shocked. "Bite your tongue."

Keva giggled from behind them.

***

On a bright morning just before mid-summer, Laurelei came to Ardal's shop and stood in the doorway until he looked up from his work. On his way to the door, he splashed water onto his head and face then washed his hands. Stepping outside, he found Laurelei standing in the shade of a massive oak.

Gently placing his hand on her rounding belly, he asked about Keva. "It's time, eh?"

"Aye. Time to fetch Orin. Not yet time to fetch the midwife, though I might have her over just to have her opinion."

"Right." Ardal kissed her quickly and stepped away. "I'm off then." He leaned in and kissed her once more but slowly this time. As he backed away from her, he grunted apologetically and gestured at the marks he'd left on her clothes and face.

Laurelei shrugged and smiled. "I married a blacksmith."

Ardal glanced over his shoulder as he walked away. "There was a time I was more than that."

She raised her voice as he jogged off. "You're my child's father. That's more than enough."

***

The night that Keva labored with their child, Orin paced beside her. Laurelei sent Ardal to fetch the midwife then prepared a tea of raspberry leaves as the midwife had instructed her. Upon her arrival, the midwife spent a few minutes alone with Keva then recommended that Orin take her for a walk saying, "She's an active woman and this waiting's making her mad.

***

Orin and Keva named their daughter "Ciara" and began to conjecture on the sort of woman she would become. A few days passed with no sleep for anyone in the house then Keva informed Orin that she and the princess were ready to go home. The next morning, Orin eagerly began packing their gear and some freshly laundered blankets that Laurelei had given them.

As they loaded the wain, Ardal walked around the corner of the house with a crate full of pullets that he placed into the bed of the wain before he jogged off behind the house again. A moment later, he appeared again this time with a milk goat whose lead he tied to the wain.

"No. Lad, no," Orin shouted from the driver's seat. "We didn't come here to beggar you. I'll say thanks for half the hens, but put the rest back along with the goat."

Ardal laughed and ran behind the house again then returned a moment later with a crate filled with metal bits. "The hardware for your cider press." Ardal stepped over and grasped Orin's forearm. "Drive slow. Don't kill the goat."

Laurelei climbed up to kiss the baby once more on the forehead then the mother as well. "They'll make a pretty pair. Your lass and my lad."

Keva grinned. "Now, that *would* be lovely."

CHAPTER 30
Ban Shee

"Grief does not change you, Hazel. It reveals you."
The Fault in Our Stars
John Green

On a dark and bitterly cold winter solstice, the wind shrieked and wailed like a cohort of ban shees had descended on Shallowford hunting a lost soul. The sun which had made only a cursory appearance during the day had gone again into hiding by the time Ardal arrived home from the armory. He found it necessary to drag the door against the wind to shut it and was beginning to remove his outer coat when Laurelei stirred in her chair beside the fire.

There was a raw edge to her voice. "Get the midwife, m'love. It can't be long now. I *am* sorry."

"Right. Do you need anything? Tea? A blanket?"

Laurelei grunted as she repositioned herself. "The midwife, you great ass."

Ardal ran out into the malevolent night. When he turned the next corner, sleet flew horizontally into his face.

He gasped and leaned into the gale so he could move up the street. Arriving, he found it necessary to kick the door to gain the attention of the inhabitants.

Faintly above the storm, from the other side of the door he indistinctly heard a woman's voice. He shouted Laurelei's name, and a moment later the door opened a crack. He shouted again this time into the crack, "Laurelei needs the midwife."

The door opened wider, and Ardal shoved his way into the house. He pushed the door shut behind him and stared intently at the young woman who had opened it for him. "Who are you? Where's the midwife?"

The young woman was obviously cowed and responded too slowly for Ardal's need. He raised his voice. "Get the midwife."

From a doorway on the far side of the room came a woman's husky voice. "Quit shouting at my second and sit you down. I'll be out directly."

Ardal quit shouting at the young woman, but was too agitated to sit down. He paced the length of the room a couple of times before he recovered the presence of mind to ask the midwife's second to forgive his rudeness.

She replied pertly, "Quite understandable under the circumstances."

A few moments later, the midwife shoved a bag into Ardal's hands. "Sure and the streets are slick with mud. The wind is a terror, and I'll not soon arrive at Laurelei's side if you don't shield me from the wind and give me an arm to lean on."

Ardal shoved her bag back into her arms. "I can do better than that. He turned his back to her and knelt. "Mount up. I'll carry you."

The younger woman snickered behind her hand, but the midwife climbed onto Ardal's back and indicated that her second should open the door. The way was treacherous and the old woman heavier than he had expected, but the wind was at his back. In due course, they arrived at the door to his house. Ardal pulled the latch, and the wind yanked the handle from his hand. The door banged open. Ardal ducked inside and allowed the midwife to dismount before he wrestled the door shut.

Turning around, he saw Laurelei and the midwife disappear through the doorway into the bedchamber. He carried the lamp into the room and set it on the table beside the bed.

The midwife grunted, "Bring the lamp and the table to the foot of the bed. It's not her face I need to see."

Ardal complied then asked, "What can I do?"

"Stay out of the way and silent until I say otherwise."

Ardal stood in the doorway and employed all of the discipline he had learned as a soldier to keep his silence. After muttering and pottering about for a few moments, the old woman had Laurelei in a position that allowed for a thorough examination. She glanced up at Ardal. "Bring the lamp in closer. I need more light."

Ardal again complied. The midwife made a closer examination then began prodding and pressing. Each time she touched her, Laurelei grunted and shifted. Her husband knew her well enough to understand that her modest response was the equivalent of a cry of pain from most women. Completing her examination, the midwife allowed her shoulders to slump.

She looked up to Ardal. "I'm not sayin we must, but *if* we must chose, which of them shall we save?"

"Baby!" Laurelei shouted.

"Both!" Ardal shouted half a second after. He refused to consider the idea of losing either his wife or his child.

"Might lose them both. Fetch my second." The urgent note in the midwife's voice impelled Ardal out of the house and into the storm without his cloak.

When he and the second returned, Ardal was soaked and half frozen but strode straight to the bedside. The foot of the bed was covered in what seemed to Ardal more blood than Laurelei could afford to lose, but she was contentedly nursing the largest newborn he had ever seen while the midwife massaged her abdomen. The second placed her hand on the midwife's shoulder signaling her readiness to work. They switched places, and the older woman motioned to Ardal that she needed the lamp. He kissed his wife's forehead then picked up the lamp.

A few moments later, Laurelei began laboring again and the placenta plopped onto the bed. The midwife held it up to the lamp and inspected it. "It's deeply torn, but the delivery was so fast that the child might suffer no ill effects."

Ardal screwed up his face. "'Might suffer no ill effects'? What could you mean? He…" He glanced to Laurelei who smiled wanly and nodded. He continued sure now that he had a son, "He looks hale enough. Look at him. He's a bear."

Laurelei groaned, and her arms fell to her sides. Ardal was just able to catch the child before he tumbled from the bed. The midwife cut the umbilical then shooed Ardal and the baby from the room. For hours father and son paced before the cold hearth. The child's unending wails became to his father one with the ban shee scream of the storm.

***

Ardal woke to a weight being lifted from his chest. Gazing blearily about he saw a young woman walking into his bedchamber carrying a burden while an exhausted looking older woman lowered herself into Laurelei's chair. Laurelei! He was on his feet and into the bedchamber before he could think why he must go there. The young woman laid the child beside his mother who then cupped the back of his head and brought him in to nurse.

Ardal knelt beside the bed and kissed Laurelei. "You did well, lass. A boy that size should have teeth." He studied her pinched, wan face. "How are you, then, m'love?"

She attempted a smile. "Be a good lad and lift me so they can change the bedding?"

Ardal helped his wife to roll onto her back and laid their son on her chest then gently slid his arms under her and stood. He carried his little family to the hearthside and thanked the midwife's second for the roaring fire. Then he sat in his chair and held them while they slept.

***

Laurelei did not rise from her bed for a month, but in that time she progressed from wan and weak to irked and irritable. "Ardal, can you spare a moment?"

"Half a moment, m'love," he called from the other room where he was scrubbing clothes. Walking into the bedchamber, he found Laurelei sitting up and fidgeting with the pillows.

She looked up and shouted at him, "Get me out of this bed, Ardal, or I'll go mad."

He knelt to lift her, but she would have none of it. She pushed him away. "I want to stand. I'm going for a walk today. In a few days, we're going to see Keva."

"Ach, m'love…"

"Don't you, Ardal. I'll not have you, great lout, tell me what I may not do."

"I'll to Keva's with or without you. Now, give me your arm."

***

It was another month before they made the half-day journey to Orin and Keva's farm. By the time they arrived, Laurelei was exhausted. She managed to hand her baby to Keva. "We call him 'Mathan' – our bear. Then she slept through the night in their friends' bed while Ardal described the harrowing ordeal to them.

At the end of the tale, he sighed, "If I had lost her, sure

and I would have lost myself as well." As an afterthought, he added, "The midwife says there'll be no more children for us. Truth, it's a relief. I couldn't do that again."

***

For eight years, Laurelei and Ardal instructed, corrected, and entertained their only son. When Aindru sent them on missions, the boy would stay on the farm with Orin and Keva and their growing brood. He always complained when they left him at the farm because he wanted to go on their adventures, and he always complained when they picked him up because he'd been having adventures with Ciara and her brothers.

Mathan grew into a lusty lad with a quit wit and a quicker mouth. He was a good humored child but intractable. His mother often commented that he was "very polite about his disobedience". His father's opinion differed slightly. Ardal called his only son "a Footman in the making."

Laurelei scolded him saying, "Don't encourage the boy." Ardal was never quite sure whether she meant that he should not encourage the boy in his mulishness or that he should not encourage him toward the life of a soldier. Either way, it amounted to the same thing.

***

On a bright autumn day, having returned by way of Galantamhor from a long mission into the Dearthlands, Ardal and Laurelei busied themselves at home. Around noon, they heard Orin calling his team to a halt in the street outside their house. Laurelei flew to the door and whipped it open. Mathan crashed into her and would have knocked her down had Ardal not stood directly behind her.

They embraced for a long moment before Laurelei

stepped back to study her son. "Sure and you've grown, lad," she averred.

"That's what happens, you know," Orin quipped from behind Mathan. "You feed 'em, and they grow,"

He glanced past the mother and son who remained in the doorway to Ardal. "Lad, I know you've a need to see your boy, but I'm three hours late on deliveries. With a bit of help, I might complete my rounds…"

Before Ardal could respond, Laurelei pulled Mathan from the doorway and stood on tiptoe to kiss Ardal's cheek. "Take your gloves. We won't expect you for dinner."

Ardal took a knee to hug his son. "Welcome home, lad. Tomorrow, it's you and me."

"I'll come and help, Daddo. I can near lift a cask on my own."

Ardal felt his son's bicep. "Ach! I'll bet you could, but your mam would have my hide if I took you from her now. We'll have to make do without you this time."

Ardal mounted the wain and started a bit when his wife slapped his thigh with a pair of worn leather gloves. He took them from her and leaned down to kiss her. Orin spoke to his team and they started forward on their accustomed round of Shallowford inns delivering casks of "Orin's Stonefarm Jumble Cider".

The lads passed a lively time as they drove around the town. Orin maintained a running banter with each of the innkeepers that seemed to pick up where it had left off on his last visit. As they stopped for the final delivery, a fussy, rotund man stepped out the door wiping his hands on his apron and began upbraiding Orin.

He shook his head. "I had begun to think I'd not see you, Master Appleman. If you cannot come earlier, I will find another supplier and advise my fellow innkeepers to do the same."

Orin grimaced. "Now, Mainchin, I *do* regret arriving late, and I'll not try to excuse it. In future, I'll rearrange my route so you're earlier in the rotation."

Mainchin simpered. "*If* I decide to keep you as my supplier, I'll need a guarantee of your good will."

Ardal growled, "You've got the word of an honest man. What more could you require?"

Orin held up a hand to Ardal then climbed into the bed of the wain. Wading amongst the empty casks, he lifted the one remaining full cask and handed it down to Ardal. Hopping down from the wain, he smiled at the innkeeper then took the cask from Ardal and carried it into the inn.

When he returned, he offered his hand to Mainchin and explained, "The extra cask'll ensure you'll not run out if I am ever late again. It'll not happen, mind you, but just to be certain, you've an extra cask."

Mainchin grasped Orin's forearm and gave him a sly smile. "Good evening, Master Appleman. It is good to know that you appreciate the value of my business." He began to turn away but instead offered the sly smile again. "I have veal tonight and a very nice cider to complement it..."

Ardal spoke up before Orin could reply. "Ach, it's a pity we can't stay. My wife expects us soon for a bowl of pottage." He slapped Orin on the shoulder. "I know you'd rather stay, lad, but you know what a fright she can be."

Orin shook his head and climbed up to the driver's bench in the wain. As Ardal climbed up next to him, he looked back to the innkeeper. "Next time, perhaps, Mainchin. Thank you for the invitation, but my friend here lives in fear of his woman. She is a bit of a terror, to be honest with you."

Driving away, the two men controlled their mirth until they had passed out of earshot of Mainchin's inn then released a prolonged bout of roaring laughter that left them weak and breathless. Orin had found it necessary to halt the team long enough to allow him to catch his breath. He spoke to the horses, and they stepped off.

Orin maintained his focus dead ahead as he spoke.

"You know, that last cask was for you." He drove on chuckling, but Ardal was sullen.

Entering the district of the city where Laurelei and Ardal made their home, Orin turned away from their house and toward the Inn of the Drowsy Bear. "Look you, Ardal. I heard what you said to Mainchin, but I've a need for something more savory than pottage."

Ardal nodded. "Ah, there's no pottage. I just wanted to give the fellow my back without putting your business with him on a bad footing. A good meal will do much to alleviate my grief over the lost cask of cider."

The friends passed such a pleasant evening that Ardal was in fine spirits as Orin drove him home. Turning onto the lane that led to his house, both men went still and silent as a child's scream ripped through the cool evening. Before the echoes had passed away, Ardal had leapt from the wain and was almost home.

As he rounded the corner, two men disappeared into the shadows at the far end of the alleyway that ran beside their home. Two others lay on the ground within a few feet of where Laurelei lay still. One of the men attempted to drag himself toward her. Ardal dropped to his knees at her side and began frantically checking her wounds. Orin rushed past him, took up the hammer Laurelei had apparently dropped, and smashed the head of the man who crawled toward her. Mathan's screams filled the night.

Orin dropped the hammer, scooped up Mathan and ran into the house. A few moments later, he carried the screaming boy and a sack out of the house and placed them into the bed of the wain. He then jogged over to where Ardal knelt rocking in the mud with Laurelei cradled against his chest. Orin touched his shoulder, and Ardal howled a wordless defiance of the horror his life had become.

Placing his hands under Ardal's arms, he attempted feebly to raise him to his feet. Ardal stood with his wife's limp body in his arms and followed Orin to the wain. He climbed onto the wain with Orin pushing him from behind and sat on the bench. Glancing back, he saw his disconsolate son sitting mindless with fear and wailing like the ban shees that had roamed the town the night he was born.

Ardal croaked, "Mathan, my lad…" Orin climbed into the bed of the wain and lifted Mathan over the back of the bench to sit alongside his dad then clambered onto the bench and released the brake. As they drove away, Ardal noted the faces of his neighbors in the windows of their homes — each had been watching intently but doing nothing to help his poor Laurelei.

CHAPTER 31
What's Necessary

"Until our duty becomes to us common as breathing, we are poor creatures."
The Wise Woman and Other Stories
George MacDonald

Sabia sat silent for a long while before extricating Mathan from the horror of the moment in which her tale had left him. She stood from her seat on the dais and knelt on the ground before the grieving young man. "Forgive me, Love, for speaking of her loss, but you must think on it at times, and you must remember well."

She kissed his forehead. "Only one person lives who saw the men who did this. Their identity is the key to discovering who sent them as well as to learning the nature of the threat against the land."

She stood and tugged on his hands attempting to pull him to his feet, but he remained seated and mourning. "Mathan," she spoke insistently, "You now see why it's to the High King you must to go. You must tell him what you saw. Share your loss with him. He will hold accountable not only the murderers but also those who sent them. You cannot and should not bear the responsibility for retribution. Their crime is not against you, alone, but against the High King and the land, itself."

Mathan gently removed his hands from Sabia's grasp and stood. "Lady, the High King, if there is such a person, and the ministers and rulers of this land have, for a dozen long years displayed naught but apathy toward my mother's death. Two of the killers died that night. That is all the justice she is like to get if I don't take a hand in it. The High King has abdicated his responsibility; so, vengeance is now mine to take as I will. I will take it up and move the gates of Galantamhor, itself, to fulfill this obligation."

He placed his hands on her shoulders and looked into her eyes. "I thank you, Lady, for the tales you've told me today. They have strengthened my resolve immeasurably.

Sabia displayed her disdain openly. "Do not patronize me, my brother. Remember your father's deeds, and your mother's words."

"My father's deeds call me to be a man. My mother is long dead and what I know of her words calls me to take action in response to that fact."

"*Wisdom* calls you. She has claimed you as her own." The words fairly leapt from Sabia's mouth, as though they had for years been dammed by her patience.

The exasperated young man rolled his eyes and shrugged. "Sabia, who made you wisdom's mouth? I too know wisdom—"

"Look at me." She so rarely raised her voice that Mathan was shocked into obedience. "This is no mere puzzle, beloved. It is a matter of deciding who you are and what you will become ... of other men and how they will live or die ... of nations and kings ... and of concerns far more important than any of these."

He opened his mouth but she raised her hand. "Do not interrupt. You must understand, and you must decide wisely. Much will be lost if you fail to consider wisdom."

"Sabia, I *will* go to the Keep," Mathan averred, "as soon as I have done what's necessary. My first act after learning the use of my blade will be to turn it toward the Dearthlands. There will I hunt the monsters who trouble my dreams. Then will I turn my steps to Galantamhor and the Keep where I will lay my bloody blade at the High King's feet and demand an answer." Mathan's placating smile and soothing tone would have charmed a maddened badger.

Sabia, however, remained uncharmed. "A plague take Galantamhor. Oh, you great and proud fool, know you not that your vengeance will consume you?"

"Vengeance, aye, and justice also." Mathan's grim-faced demeanor would have cowed a brave man.

"There is no justice in your wrath, child. It is but the fear of a motherless boy and the hubris of an angry young man. The burden of your wrath has not yet stolen your promise. Lay it down, and pursue truth."

"The truth, you nattering harpy..." but Mathan paused to regain a modicum of his presence of mind, then started again.

"Forgive me, Sabia, but the truth is that my own sweet mother was mangled and murdered to protect me from the hands of foul creatures. The truth is that my father has lived with a hideous burden on his heart and I have lived without the comfort and wisdom she would have offered me."

Sabia kept her peace while he considered his next words. "The truth is that I've been released. I am my own man. I'll choose for myself the path I'll take. I have decided. I will become a soldier and so learn to destroy evil creatures. As soon as I am able, I will pursue the cowards who took my mam from me. When I have found them, I will employ the skills of a soldier to ravage first their minds then their bodies until I decide it is time for them to die."

He paused to catch his breath. "That, my oddly

tenacious foster-mother, is the truth I will pursue. Once I have served that truth, I will with all due haste hie me to Galantamhor where I will, by any means necessary…"

He grinned maliciously. "Who knows? Perhaps I might be the plague you called down on the city." He chuckled. "I will, by any means necessary, gain audience with the High King himself, and demand to know why we suffer great loss and inevitable death while he hides himself away from us."

A long, deep silence passed between them. Mathan eventually smiled tenderly. "Do you see, Lady? You do not need to coax, cajole or demand. I will make my way to the Keep. Are you not satisfied?"

"No," and Sabia's quiet, firm negation of Mathan's plan was absolute. "You speak forcefully of 'Truth', but you know naught. Those men who died with our Laurelei that night were not her killers; they were her brothers. You think to find those responsible in the Dearthlands, but Hakov and Nabal followed the assassins from Galantamhor and died for it.

"Hakov would be alive today but that Orin mistook his intent and hammered his brains out. Can you live with the burden of a mistake so costly? Have you any idea how a man can die piecemeal from guilt and regret? No, fool. You know nothing yet speak vainly of truth and duty. Why would you choose to pursue wisdom *after* vengeance? "

Looking mildly perplexed, Mathan explained his intent to her. "Why do you speak of guilt and regret? I'll do naught that I should then regret. I will find the men who killed my mother, a woman you call your friend. Once I have found them, they will suffer until they tell me who sent them. Then, I will find the man who sent them, and he will suffer. When I have determined that it is enough, they will die."

"Child, do you think it so simple as that? What of the damage you inflict on yourself while you inflict suffering on him? Is that nothing to you? It is everything to me. I beg you, love, lay aside your lust for vengeance. Instead, come with me to the Keep. Dine with the High King himself and lay your complaint before him. He will hear you. You need not 'gain audience' with him; he invites you.

"Now. Now is the time, Mathan. There is much to do. Much is lost, much is imperiled by the negligence of fools. Do not make yourself one of them. There is no need for further preparation. Your life has prepared you. The High King has prepared you."

She laid her open hand on his open mouth. "Do not pretend to be surprised. Before you were born, he chose you, and you have seen him with your own eyes."

Despite the indignation Mathan displayed, she kept her hand over his mouth. "Beloved, if only you would listen and consider my words, you would remember and know that none of them are foreign to you.

"In fact, your mother nursed your soul with my songs, and your father has told you my tales each day of your life. You are my son, my brother, my apprentice, my defender, my darling, and my friend."

She lowered her hand and, smiling shyly - winsomely, grasped his hand in hers and tugged him toward the King's Highway. "Mathan, come with me now. There is *work*, love ... work to be done. Do not delay. Night fast approaches."

Mathan loosed a bemused chuckle, shaking his head. "Sabia, it is near night already. This fact argues against my immediate departure. I will not delay overly. My departure is imminent. I will go to the Keep and lay my complaint before the High King as soon as I have done what's necessary."

Sabia displayed little of the ocean of her frustrated disappointment. "All that is necessary, Mathan, is for you to go where you are called, to remember the lessons of your youth and to find me wherever you travel. This is the sum of your duty."

Mathan pulled his hand from Sabia's grasp and raised it in a soothing gesture. "Sabia, sweet, maniacal Lady, I will do as you say ... soon. Tonight, though, I will say my goodbyes and depart in the morning for the inscription office in Shallowford. Do you not see, Sabia? I too have wisdom."

"If only you would shut up and let *that* be your wisdom." A warning flashed in her eyes; then she sighed and tried once more to convince him. "The High King has made all provision for the journey—"

"I'll not travel on another man's means while I may earn my own. His provision is for those who go directly to the Keep. I have other business before I accept his invitation. Good night, Sabia. I will see you tomorrow." Mathan turned on his heel and strode to the cottage by the smithy one last time.

Sabia addressed his retreating back. "No, beloved, you will not."

CHAPTER 32
Sendoff

"Never fear quarrels, but seek hazardous adventures."
<u>*The Three Musketeers*</u>
Alexandre Dumas

Sabia's tales had taken a day in the telling and would take the night to digest. Mathan was left with a sense of wonder in his newfound knowledge of his parents. His anger had now been focused; his doubts answered; his purpose forged.

One question remained, though. Mathan addressed it while packing his gear. "Daddo, why would you return here to Taermun when the men who sent the assassins would surely know your home and send assassins for you here as well?"

"Ah, it's me you're thinkin' they were after? No, lad. It was yourself. They didn't want to kill Laurelei or myself. They wanted to torture us; they wanted to take you from us."

"Well, then, the question remains."

"This is the safest place I know. It was before. It is

288

more so now. Remember, lad, that 'safe' is a relative term. Since that day, other precautions were taken. Elgin and Cian formed the town watch. Regular patrols were mounted, and a truly dangerous man now abides in King's Valley to greet any who might pass that way."

"One man?" Mathan scoffed.

"He will suffice. When I reported to Dermot after Laurelei's murder, we decided that the report would reflect that you had also died in the raid, and that I had become a hopeless drunk. The latter was true, at least for a while, and my behavior, while in Galantamhor; would have been enough to start the rumor if *we* hadn't.

"We took these precautions at Rory's insistence because he believed that someone with knowledge of the situation had accepted the Protector's coin and sent the killers our way."

"A Tierasalan? Sabia implied as much."

"Aye, and one with rank and position. That one is my business. You have work to do in Shallowford.

"You would be remiss not to take the roundabout trail down to the Shallowford Road. Meander up through the Avinn Vale to the King's Table and down through the King's Valley and then to the high road."

"What of this 'truly dangerous man' who 'abides in King's Valley'?"

"Aye, it's he who'll be waiting for you. Go you now, lad. Quit you like a man. Remember your father's words; never forget what you learned at your mother's knee."

"The last bit sounds like somethin' Sabia once told me."

"Only the once, eh? I'll warrant you weren't listening the other thousand times."

Ardal stood and Mathan took his cue. "Well, Daddo, I'm off to make the world a better place."

"Nay, lad. You're off to make yourself a better man. I'll see you at my leisure." Ardal embraced Mathan and clapped him on the back. Mathan squeezed until Ardal choked. They broke contact, and Mathan slipped his head and arm through his sword belt so the blade hung diagonally across his broad back. He turned to leave.

Ardal quietly spoke his name. Mathan turned and accepted the arm clasp his father offered. "Honor, brother."

Mathan responded with a catch in his throat. "The honor is mine, my Captain."

After a long moment, Ardal released him. Mathan lifted his pack and lumbered to the door. Outside, the sun had set and a chill, dense mist was rising. It mattered not for he would have known the way blindfolded. He had a bit of thinking to do before he was prepared to deal with the lads at the inn, so he ambled over to the green. At the dais, he dropped his pack and laid his scabbard against it, then sat on his accustomed third step and wandered the halls of his mind.

Sabia pervaded his thoughts, supplanting for the first time his enthralling dreams of vengeance and battlefield glory. Her presence there suggested something he needed but could not name. Prosaic in appearance, her slight figure concealed beneath an unadorned white cotton shift, Sabia projected a potent presence that saturated Mathan's mind with a deep and solemn gladness.

He meditated on a plethora of tales in which the strangely earnest woman had woven the fantastic and the commonplace into a single tapestry, as if they were threads spun of similar substance. She had always spoken gravely and plainly, often of things so lofty that Mathan had never considered them, and often of things which seemed to him so axiomatic that they required no mention. He had known her all his life, but their recent interactions had changed everything he thought he knew.

Events had revealed that the quietude of the twelve years since his sweet ma's murder had comprised no lasting peace. Instead, a legion of change had employed the intervening years in massing to assault him over the course of the past few days. The myriad epiphanies inspired by his consideration of these phenomena had harassed Mathan into withdrawing to the common. Certain things must be settled in his own mind before he could finally set foot outside the vale.

After filling his bowl from the pouch at his belt, he rummaged through the gear that lay at his feet, lifting a small tin-lined hardwood box that contained his flint and some char cloth. After lighting his pipe, he replaced the flint and shut the box but did not repack it. Instead, he sat holding it while he pondered the tales that Sabia had told him.

After the mists inside his head had cleared a bit, he repacked his gear and ambled to the inn to spend a few minutes with his friends before leaving Taermun behind. They received him as the conquering hero that he hoped one day to become, and the few minutes stretched into many hours. Mag offered her finest room in honor of his imminent departure, and he gratefully accepted.

The following morning, the sun rose but Mathan did not, due to the insistent hammering in his head and the ceaseless motion of his bed. A while passed before he had assembled the bits of his thoughts, one of which rose preeminent. Today, he would leave home to pursue his destiny. He rolled to the edge of the bed and struggled to sit on its edge.

Suddenly, he needed to be outside. Bumbling down the passageway in the dark, he tripped over a basket of potatoes outside the kitchen door. He reeled and fetched up hard against the wall then continued toward the door, his shoulder rubbing along the wall.

He fumbled with the latch for a while as his need to escape became yet more insistent. Once outside, it was difficult to prioritize his needs, so Mathan tried to do it all simultaneously. He stumbled as quickly as he could down the slope to the outhouse while pausing occasionally to surrender portions of last night's meal.

An eternity later, he stepped from the outhouse, fairly certain he would survive but not yet grateful for it. Fighting his way uphill, he noted that Mag Petty stood in the doorway. "Ah, Mag, it's sorry I am that I woke you with my foolishness."

"You didn't, lad. I was in the kitchen baking apple dumplings."

Bile rose in Mathan's throat at the thought of food.

"I don't know that I should allow you any," she said, "seein' how you've treated my roast."

Mathan glanced at a puddle he had left behind on his way to the outhouse. "It was a fine thing goin' in, I tell you, but was unruly thereafter."

Mag stepped aside. "Cool water is what you'll need. Then perhaps tea. I'll wrap a dumpling and some other things for you to take on your way."

An hour later, Mathan stepped out the front door and realized he'd not yet seen Anyah. "Mag, where's Anyah?"

"On one of her rambles. I can't say where."

"So early?"

"Finished her chores and left me with a kiss on my forehead."

"Did she leave a message for me?"

"No, lad." She smiled hopefully. "Do you have one for her?"

The young man considered the possibilities for a moment. "Yes'm. Tell her, if you would, that I'll see her in Galantamhor."

"Mathan, it might take a while for either of you to get there. Would you not like to see her before?"

"Oh, aye, but I've a need to go."

"So it is with men. Go you then and see if you'll not think yourself a fool for it someday."

"Aye, Mag, aye. More likely than not, I'll prove myself a fool on many accounts, but I'll not let it vex me so long as I may taste your apple dumplings from time to time."

She smiled. "Come as you will, Bear. As long as it's the

Inn of Mag Petty, there'll be apple dumplings and a place at the table for you."

Mathan strode forward and enfolded the slight, wan woman in a fierce embrace. After a moment, he stepped away and ambled up Market Street.

For days, Mathan wandered the Avinn Vale, visiting the places where his soul had been fed. He meandered among the laurel and boulders, intentionally gathering the bits of his life that lay strewn among them. Following the river, he worked his way toward the head of the valley, to where springs fed the languid cataracts of the Dolewash. With his feet, he remembered the paths he'd explored as a child on his first ramble along the river with Ardal.

While Mathan's feet ambled about the vale, his mind wandered among dark images he thought he had long ago interred. The memories he had intended to entomb he had instead enshrined. He continued so over the ridgeline past King's Table until he entered King's Valley. His focus vacillated between the sunlit terrain about him and the misty, twilit ones within. The internal ultimately absorbed him, and he settled on a convenient boulder.

A cavalcade of mental vestigia, beginning with his earliest recollections, inundated Mathan. The wave of memories receded, though, and eventually left as a bequest a single ubiquitous image – the gravely merry mien of a small, plain woman.

CHAPTER 33
Troglodyte

"...a wise man should so write (though in words understood by all men) that wise men only should be able to commend him."
Of the Life and History of Thucydides
Thomas Hobbes

"**G**ood evening, my lord," a voice like a punctured bellows, startled Mathan from his woolgathering. He fell from the boulder as he spun to locate the speaker. Drawing his blade, he then squatted, peering cautiously over his perch. A wizened man stood a few yards away grinning toothlessly at him. "Sabia sends her greetings."

"It is not evening, and I am no lord." Mathan stood, extended the blade and glared at the rangy kobold. "Sabia would never be content merely to greet me; she would proceed from there to advising, then to lecturing, cajoling and threatening me. Finally, she would fly away like a sparrow to her roost on the mountain.

"On these three fallacies, I doubt your character. Skulking this trail in ambush speaks ill of you as well. State your name and business."

The old man had grinned and nodded as Mathan spoke. This angered Mathan further, and he advanced upon the old man. "How do you answer me, gnome?"

"My lord, more graciously than you ask." The grin had been replaced by a stony mask punctuated by glittering eyes. "My name, lord, is Fionn, and my business is to wait. The trail leads to one of the great treasures of the age... in my mind, at least. I 'skulk this trail in ambush' for those foul creatures who would delight to despoil such treasure.

"In the twelve years of my skulking, few have come this way. Fewer still have passed. My character is vouchsafed by a far greater lord than you, and I daresay the Lady has lectured me on more occasions and topics than she has you; though I will admit perhaps that her threatening was a bit less effective with me."

The gnome smiled at Mathan, as though they had long been co-conspirators. "As it *is* evening, you *are* the lord of whom Sabia apprised me so long ago. Evening comes early in this hollow, and your lordship comes late."

Fionn sighed deeply and stepped closer, studying Mathan as he would a market foal. "Truth be told, I dinna need to hear you speak. Your da's grit and humor, your mam's grace and temper - they're all writ plain and large 'pon your large and plain face. That face whispers a tale I'd hear in detail. And now you're here and sadly all alone."

Deep solemnity settled over Fionn, and his gaze drifted to Mathan's feet. "Where is she, lad?"

Mathan took a deep, ragged breath. "I mocked her and turned away from her. She told you she'd come here?"

The old man's face mirrored Mathan's. "No, she told me you'd come. It seemed to me she'd come with you. I've not seen her in a hound's age."

Mathan dropped his head. "I've the voice of two women callin' my heart. One has every right to my life. The other thinks she owns me."

Fionn chuckled ruefully. "Well, lad, you've had my name. I name you 'Mathan – the Bear of Taermun'."

"As you say, I am Mathan. And true, some call me 'Bear'."

Fionn nodded, as though his suspicions had been confirmed. "As well they might for all your hulking and sulking. At least you don't skulk as I've been accused of doing."

He turned on his heel, lifted his hand, index finger raised, and spoke over his shoulder as he wove his way among the trees along the side of the trail. "Food and rest. Then we talk of all that is, has been and should be."

Mathan lumbered along on the trail beside him but came up short at Fionn's quiet insistence. "Hold."

Mathan halted in his tracks. "What is it?"

Fionn beckoned him silently and did not speak again until Mathan had stepped off the trail. "Never walk a clear trail, lad. 'The easy way is always denied'."

"Denied? How do you mean that?"

"Open your eyes. Can you not see what's in front of you?" The old man gestured toward a portion of the trail that would have led Mathan to pass between two large trees.

Mathan stood silently studying the trail and then recognized a deadfall, arranged to crush anyone approaching along the trail from the opposite direction. He stepped into Fionn's footprints and gestured for him to lead the way.

A short while later, they halted in a small dingle, and Fionn stepped over to the vine-bedecked stone face of a hillside. Grinning, he pulled back a handful of vines to reveal a large, oval opening. "Stow your gear inside, lad. We'll have a stew soon enough."

Mathan ducked inside, allowed his eyes to adjust to the gloom and took five steps to the far side of the cave. He dropped his gear and opened his sack to rummage for something to add to the dinner, but exhaustion soon overtook him and he slumped against the wall.

CHAPTER 34
The Cave

"What sort of knowledge is there that would draw the soul from becoming to being?"
<u>The Republic</u>
Plato

Mathan gradually woke, rising through dense, hazy layers of sleep to find himself curled on his side, aching and shivering. Clamping his eyes shut, he rolled about for a while in search of a comfortable spot then finally gave up, sat up and opened his eyes to almost complete darkness. Awareness began to dawn upon him and he at last recognized his surroundings. He recalled that the cold, uneven surface on which he now rested was the floor of Fionn's grotto home. This realization came to him more through the scent of loam and the dampness of the air than by any information his eyes could gather in the darkness.

Before him, a rough oval of faint green, shifting light marked the cave's mouth. Two voices spoke in hushed and strident tones just outside, but Mathan could not comprehend them. Rolling to one side, he steadied himself against the wall as he stood. He blundered forward, occasionally kicking or stepping on some unseen object, until he was close enough to recognize the voices, although he could not distinguish their words.

Fionn spoke with Sabia just outside in the dingle. His agitation at realizing Sabia had come while he slept drove him fumbling toward the light.

The voices ceased just as Mathan reached the opening. He stooped to pass through but was knocked back when Fionn ducked into the cave and struck Mathan's nose with his head. Mathan pinched his nose and muttered mild invectives while Fionn sat heavily on the ground and held his head in his hands.

Fionn grunted. "For twelve years I have entered so without ever once encountering another body coming through."

Mathan snorted, blood flecking the front of his shirt. The blinding pain began to subside to a dull ache around his eyes. His nose was broken. It wasn't the first time. As he covered his face with his hands and rubbed his eyebrows, he hoped it was the last. Finally, he dropped his hands and stepped past the old man, through the vine curtain into the clearing.

After a moment, Mathan shoved his head back into the cave entrance. "Where's she gone?" He spoke more harshly than he had intended.

"Where does Sabia ever go?" Fionn asked dismissively.

Mathan sighed heavily and attempted to moderate his agitated tone of voice. "I need to speak with her. Now," he insisted. "Where has she gone, Fionn?"

"Lad, she left words for you but made no sign that she cared to speak with you at the moment."

"I'd hear those words from herself rather than a mad, ancient hermit, if you don't mind." Mathan immediately regretted his crass words but continued his assault on the old man's resolve nevertheless. He hefted the curmudgeon off the floor by the collar of his cassock and hauled him outside.

He touched the tip of the recluse's nose with his own bloodied one and bellowed, "Where has she gone, Fionn?" The fierceness of his face would have cowed a panther, but Fionn only returned a hazy, beatific smile. Staring intently into Fionn's sharp eyes, Mathan realized they were focused on a point far beyond him.

Mathan gently set the aged sage on his feet and stepped back, his head dropping. "Fionn," he said through his chagrin, "I've a desire to speak with the lady. You know this. When we parted, I was... She deserves an apology. She finally comes and you fail to wake me. What words did Sabia give you?"

"Mathan, she told me I'd done well, and that I could rest. She said she'd tend to my affairs after I'd gone" Fionn seemed awed.

"That is good news, mad, old gnome. But what did she say of me?"

Fionn graced him with that beatific smile once more. "She says you go to the Keep to know the great High King."

"I'll to the Keep when I will, and I'll know if there *is* a High King and, if so, what excuse he makes for his disregard of those who call him 'High King'."

Mathan ducked into the cave and returned a moment later, his gear in hand. He strapped his blade across his back, threw on his pack and strode for the far side of the clearing.

Fionn's strident call brought him up short. When Mathan turned to face him, Fionn hobbled near and, in a conspiratorial tone, said, "'Great King' she called you ... and with reason, I'm sure. 'Lord' I called you, and you can be sure I know what I say. Whom do you serve, lad? Yourself or others? A lord, a king, does not live for himself."

He held up a hand to forestall Mathan. "You'll protest

that you are no lord, no king, but surely you know that no man is a man who is not in some measure warrior, poet, prophet, priest, and king."

Mathan again turned to go.

"Do not leave, Mathan. Stay yet a while." Fionn seemed almost desperate. "I'll not vex you longer than a day more. Only stay one day. I would speak with you."

"I've waited over half my life to go to Shallowford. I'll delay no longer. If you've aught to say, you've had ample time to say it. Meanwhile, the lady appears and you've no thought for me. Now, you ask me to stay a day. You've waited twelve years. What difference can one more day make to you? I'm no waiter. I've things to do, and I'd make peace with Sabia while I can, if I can. Now, where has she gone, Fionn?"

"I do not know which way she went. I *do* know, however, that she will find you. I also know you cannot pursue her on your own terms. Do not leave. We do not know but that she might return tomorrow."

Mathan turned his profound pity and mild contempt on the hermit sage. "Again, I thank you, old man. I don't know why, but I thank you." With that, Mathan once again began to leave. Fionn darted back into the cave and came out again before Mathan had crossed the clearing. The sage caught up to him and grasped his wrist. Mathan jerked his arm up in annoyance but took the fiercely clinging ascetic along with it. He bent his arm enough to bring Fionn's eyes in line with his own and raised his eyebrows.

Fionn stared unblinking back into Mathan's feral eyes. "I have something for you. Take it with you, please."

Mathan roughly brought his arm down and indecorously dumped the elderly man in the mud at his feet. He pointed at Fionn's forehead, as though his finger were a weapon. "Make it quick." Then he extended his open hand to receive Fionn's gift.

Fionn laid into Mathan's hand a large, dirty bundle of

odd-sized parchments, all tightly bound into a folio of worn goatskin. Then he watched Mathan expectantly. Mathan eyed the book then tucked it into his belt at the small of his back.

The old man looked disappointed. "Lad, that book is my life. Please carry it safely and keep it close to you. Perhaps it will have some value for you along the way."

"If it is as full of vague ramblings as you are yourself, I doubt it, Fionn. If it is as important as you say, why not keep it here with you?"

"You've heard nothing I've said." Fionn shook his head sadly. "I'll not be here tomorrow. Take it, lad. When you've naught else to occupy your thoughts, open it."

"Aye, Fionn," and Mathan sighed. "I'll keep it close … just in case. When Sabia returns, if she returns, kindly inform her that I will look for her along my route to Shallowford. Greet her for me and offer her my apologies. I should not have parted with her so."

As Mathan strode away, Fionn called, "I'll not be here when she comes."

CHAPTER 35
Shepherd's Blessing

"He was a dreamer, a thinker, a speculative philosopher... or as his wife would have it, an idiot."
<u>*The Restaurant at the End of the Universe*</u>
Douglas Adams

Mathan located Garald by the wave of dark blue if somewhat monotonous maledictions mixed with smoke that poured interminably over the wall of the fold where he had formerly kept a small flock of sheep. His curiosity piqued, Mathan entered the fold through its gate. Garald whirled about with an axe in his hand and murder in his eye.

Mathan raised his hands, half in surrender and half in warning. "Friend," he declared, chuckling to disperse the tension. He nodded toward the disheveled stack of splintered bedroom furniture which lay at his friend's feet and joked, "Though I am tender, I'll not burn so readily as that which you have at hand."

Garald's murderous expression softened into a deeply muddled one. He lowered his axe. "Go 'way," he said then stooped, wobbled and stood again before steadily stooping once more and lifting a piece of wood from the pile he had been battering and tossing it into the fire. "Go 'way."

"What are you doin', Gary?" His concern for his own safety had transferred to concerns for Garald's sanity.

"Burnin' her, or what's left to me of her." Mathan barely understood his slurred response.

His concern escalated into alarm, and he skewered the angry drunk with a scrutinizing glare. "What do you mean to say, Gary? What's happened to Maia?"

"She always said she was gonna find her a better man and let him take her away from here … away from me. She always said I liked the solitude of the high pastures so much, why didn't I just stay there? Well, she's done it, and I'm getting rid of anything of *hers* that I find in *my* house. This here's the bedroom furniture that her pappy made and give to her on our weddin' day. Cordin' to *her*, I never matched up to her dear ol' pappy … not half as good as him…"

Garald ranted on into a confused mumble. He threw a few more pieces of shattered bedstead onto the pile. "I hauled this trash up here from the house by way of the sheep path. Jack-a-ninny, my old ass, was wheezin' and stallin' the whole way up, but I wheezed alongside him and we made it here yester eve."

Mathan chuckled and hefted the entire dressing table onto the top of the mound. It slid down the far side, coming to rest on the hand-carved trim along the edge of its top. Bemused, he brushed his hands together, turned to Garald and clapped him on the back.

Mathan shook his head in commiseration. "I *am* sorry to hear you have troubles, Gary. When you're done here, I'll be in the cottage, makin' us some dinner."

Mathan turned away before Garald had a chance to consider. He heard a strangled gurgle from behind him and turned back in time to watch Garald hit the ground face down and lie still. "Garald! What are you doin', man? Are you all right?"

Kneeling at the man's side, Mathan heard a wet wheeze escape Garald's throat. When Mathan rolled him onto his back, he could see that Garald was laughing. The laughter was only a small choking sound at first but soon grew into an unrestrained roar.

Studying his contorted face, Mathan saw that his neighbor was now crying. Tears and laughter fought for control until neither could be discerned alone. Garald flailed on the ground, tearing up tufts of grass then gagged and released a fountain of vomit. Afterwards, he lay very still.

Mathan had leaped out of the way of Garald's slop, but now cast about for a container of water. Instead, he found a glazed clay jar half full of an aromatic clear liquid. He figured the harsh jenever would work at least as well as water to remove the filth, so upended the jar over Garald's upturned face before wiping away the remaining bits with his fingertips. Once he was sure Garald still breathed, Mathan hefted him over his shoulder and lugged the poor cuckold toward his shepherd's cottage.

Climbing the stile that led from the pasture into the garden was a hazardous affair. Mathan lost his balance and almost dropped his burden onto the low stone wall. He opted to hop down instead. The jolt caused Garald to groan loudly.

Mathan paused for a moment, listening, but no commentary followed. He hitched Garald's dormant form higher onto his shoulder and strode toward the stone-lined well at the center of the dooryard.

Laying his burden as gently as he could beside it, Mathan repeatedly lowered the bucket and brought it up to douse his befouled friend. He then removed Garald's filthy clothes, doused him once more and again slung him over his shoulder. After laying Garald on his bed, he rolled him onto his side and propped him with pillows.

Mathan tied the door curtain back to allow the sun in

to the dusky interior of the cabin, enough to peruse the larder for suitable victuals. He found only four spongy potatoes, a few measures of roasted barley and a couple of stale bits of bannock. Sighing, he sighed and stirred up the coals then carried the kale-pot out to the well.

When he returned, Mathan found Garald had rolled onto his back and was now snoring heartily. Rolling him again him onto his side, he propped the sleeping man a bit more securely with a bolster he found shoved between the bed and the wall. Returning to the ingle, he hung the pot over the fire. While the water was heating, he diced the potatoes and dropped them into the pot. When it began a rolling boil, he dumped the stock of barley in.

While the potatoes and barley boiled, Mathan stepped outside, cut some kale and pulled a few leeks from an overgrown garden patch near the harness shed. Passing the well on the way back to the house, he drew some water and washed the vegetables.

Stepping back inside, he again checked Garald only to find him sleeping soundly. Mathan laid the vegetables on the table, sliced them crudely then threw them all into the soup. He pulled a chunk of potato from the pot and blew on it. When it had cooled, he popped it into his mouth and found that it had softened considerably. He gave the kale and leeks a few minutes to cook into the soup then looked over his shoulder at the inert form of Garald.

"Don't worry, Gary. I'll save you a bite or two." He ladled a large bowl for himself then took the larger of the two pieces of stale bannock, dipped it into his soup and gave himself for a while to his hunger.

After a second helping, Mathan set the bowl aside and shuffled over to find Garald resting more easily than he had before. As he sat again, Mathan realized that the discomfort he had earlier ignored in favor of his keen hunger was caused by the thick, goatskin-bound sheaf of parchments still in the small of his back. He leaned forward and withdrew the folio, setting it on the table. He peered at the book through slit eyes and chuckled as he remembered the crazy old man who had pressed it upon him.

He soon began to nod.

Mathan gradually became conscious that the afternoon had slipped into late evening and that the fire had died down. He peered through the gloom in search of the source of the sounds which had roused him. A deep voice spoke from the far side of the darkened room. "I owe you much, Bear, and I thank you." Garald stood there, buckling a wide leather belt about his plain cotton tunic.

"You owe me nothing, Gary. How are you?" Mathan said in a friendly but gruff manner.

"I reckon the mass of pain in my head is almost enough to distract me from the void in my heart. At least I had clean clothes laid by. What business brought you to such a comfortless place as my old cabin? Did you come here to find me?"

"Nay," Mathan replied thoughtfully. "I did not think to find you here as I know you've not kept a flock for a while."

"That's right. I sold the last of 'em nearly two years ago for that roan mare my Maia had to have." Bitterness crept into his voice. "Not that she's *my* Maia now." He paused, and again asked, "Why are you here, lad? Not that I don't welcome you, but it does seem a wonder that you'd be here just at this time."

"Gary, I'm for Shallowford, to present myself to the Inscription Officer. It's the army for me and I for a soldier, as is right and good and worthwhile. I'll have none gainsay my plans, so do not try."

Garald shifted in the darkness. "No need to insist, lad. I'll not deny your right to stand at arms. Who is it that gave you reason to speak so?"

"That Sabia who confounds me in all things I would do, that's who. She would have me bow to the High King who was nowhere doing nothing while my sweet mam was murdered by Tierasal's enemies rather than train my sword arm to extract payment for their crimes. A man might see wisdom in laying my complaint before the High King, but there is wisdom also in punishing evil men. I'll follow the wisdom that leads me to peace with my conscience."

"Wait a moment, will you? I'd say that such discussion requires some light."

Mathan nodded in the darkness. "Aye, Gary. In truth, it requires much light."

There was more shuffling as Garald lifted down a lamp that hung on a peg near his bed and carried it to the hearth. Mathan caught glimpses of Garald in the flashes of light from the coals he stirred. After a few moments' effort, a flame kindled on the wick of the oil lamp, and Garald set it on the table where it lit the center of the room. In the light of it, he saw the book and looked from it to Mathan. "What's this to do with your journey, lad?"

Mathan glanced at the book as though he had forgotten it. "Ah, no. No, that's another thing altogether. I got the book on the way up here. It was given to me for safekeeping by an old gnome in a cave."

Garald's answering guffaw rang loud, deep and long in the shepherd's small hut. When he was again able to speak, he needled Mathan. "You visited a gnome, did you, Bear? And he gave you a gift? Do you not ken that gnomes are long lost to this world? Why would you mock a poor man like me with such tales of fanciful creatures? Did he promise you gold if you'd release him? No? I see. He gave you the book in return for his peace. Poor ol' gnome. Not a coin to his name. Harassed by a passing ruffian. Gave up his only book." Garald lost the ability to talk as he crumpled into a prolonged fury of laughter.

At first, Mathan was vexed that Garald found his story absurd, then he began to see how it must have seemed preposterous. "Well, he was just a man, an old hermit, anyway, and he made me promise to keep the book before he'd release me."

"Keep it? Is that all? He didn't ask you to deliver it to anyone?" Garald seemed keenly interested.

Mathan noted that a measure of his friend's misery had dissolved in his curiosity. Hoping to distract Garald for a while, he told his story, beginning with his last encounter with Sabia. He sometimes paced the space between the bed and the hearth, gesticulating and bellowing wildly, and at times stood bowed and spoke in a whisper.

Mathan purposefully omitted a few personal details which might have proven a bit embarrassing, but Garald knew him well enough to guess at them. For hours, Mathan spoke while Garald prompted him with questions, exclamations and assertions.

When the flow of words had ceased, Garald stood without a word and walked outside. Mathan sat for a moment in awkward silence then turned his attention to the hermit's codex, still on the table where he had laid it.

Garald had expressed a severe exasperation with Mathan's apparent disinterest in the old man's testimony. It now seemed to Mathan that it might be worth his time to peruse the documents, to determine the value of continuing to carry their burden. At the moment, he had naught else to occupy his thoughts, so he moved his stool closer to the lamp and sat to read. He opened the book near the middle, to a page titled "Fruition" and read:

"The desire to be somewhere else possesses me like a phantom
And each time I experience it,
it carries a bit more of me away.
The dormant souls who surround me will mark my departure
only at its culmination.
They will view it as my abduction
by a raptor which swoops from the sky.
The Raptor, alone,
will know it as the fruition of decades –
A lifetime of tiny steps."

Mathan was more than a little surprised at the passion contained in those few words. Where had Fionn learned this verse? The fact that Fionn would recognize the value of such a thing raised Mathan's estimation of him considerably. He turned back some twenty pages to a stained linen napkin upon which someone had printed the word "Sabia". Deeply interested now, Mathan read the words that followed:

"Her incandescent innocence stands iconic in the wasteland.
Her elemental eloquence shouts essential knowledge of what is and ought to be.
Her quintessential quiescence aptly quells my interminable rant.
Her blessed benediction subtly breaches my impregnable barriers.

My gratitude for her existence absolves my mindless fear."

Mathan sat in sweet wonder, thinking that the words expressed exactly a truth he had known but had never attempted to articulate. So deeply did he marvel that he nearly overlooked the note crammed into the bottom corner of the napkin as he flipped to the next page. He turned back and squinted at the napkin, to decipher the scrawl:

"Today, came this woman to the Laughin' Donkey. She was plain and severe in aspect and even more so in comportment. I thought, 'If ever a woman needed a draught of the aqua vitae, it's this one.'
  "She caught my eye, strode over to me as bold as you like and said, 'Finnbarr son of Uvar, you will come out of your cups, lad, and into the path which is laid before you.' She then turned on her heel and sauntered from the lodge as though she'd discharged a solemn duty and had pressing business elsewhere that must not be delayed by such a one as I.

"How did I not know her as the Sabia? Could I have been that deep into my cups?"

Mathan dropped the book onto the table and laughed long and loud at the idea that Sabia had tortured some other lad much as she did him and apparently that lad had been the dissolute crown prince of fallen Taermun who, according to Sabia's tales would have been Mathan's own grandfather.

He hefted the tome and opened it to a new page. "Affirmation" was the legend atop the column of script he found there:

"Carnal and not quite bestial,
Spiritual and surely not spiritualistic,
Holy and never yet religious,
Groping through the darkness
Blinded by the light
Perceiving reality
And stumbling on illusion
Violent and controlled
Intelligent and faithful
Questioning and certain
Not hero, not martyr,
But man
Mortal and eternal
Dons the face of Omnipotence
Patiently stalks the darkness
And makes it his own."

This one had no meaning that Mathan could divine. He laid the book aside with a mental shrug as Garald swept back the curtain and reentered the hut. "If I'm to remain here any time, I'll need to dig a new dump hole and build a new outhouse. The old one's not worth movin'. Your help would be welcome."

"Sadly," Mathan's smiled, "I'll not be able to help you

dig nor build. I do wish you luck, Gary. You should stock your larder before you work on other chores. A bit more of the roasted barley and a bit less of the brewed might serve you well. I must retrace my steps."

"Where are you bound in the dark, lad?"

Mathan sighed. "I'm goin' to speak with the man who gave me this book. I need to know who he is. For this, I'll delay Shallowford for a day."

He gestured toward the ingle. "There's a drop of soup and a hunk of bannock for your dinner and my hand for your friendship." Mathan thrust his hand toward Garald and offered him a melancholy smile.

"Get yer great paw out of my face!" Garald shouted in feigned indignation. "Is my hospitality so poor you leave it to go you ken not where in the full dark of a heathen night?"

Mathan chuckled, "'Heath-en', eh? Ai, but you're clever, Gary. A dark night on the moor would be 'heath-en' indeed, but you'll note that the moon is full and I know my way. As for your hospitality, my requirement is for good company whatever the accommodation or provision. I'll take my leave of you, satisfied that our friendship is firm."

"Aye, Bear, I am cleverer than you for I'll not leave my caer until full daylight shines on my face." When he spoke again, it was a bit morosely. "Bear, I greeted you with an axe and a curse. How can you leave before I've made restitution?"

"My friend, your hasty greeting was born of great pain and fear inflamed by a flood of jenever and was recompensed with the gift of all you had in your hand. I ate and slept and am refreshed. All I lack now is a blessing for my journey, and 'all manner of things shall be well'."

Garald made a great show of sighing loudly and rising from his seat upon the bed. He tottered over to the younger man and laid his hand on Mathan's heavy, shaggy head as he raised his other in declamation.

"May you ever know battle. May your strength be a bulwark and your compassion a comfort for all but yourself. May you never claim honor for aught that you do. May your greatness be measured in small things. When your heart and spirit and body are broken beyond mending, may you find all you long for and more."

Mathan swept Garald's hand from his head. "Ai! If you continue, you will bless me to death. Write your words for me and title them 'The Drunken Shepherd's Blessing'. I will publish it throughout Tierasal in your name and the whole land will be blighted by it."

"And yet it remains a blessing. You'll become a great man, Bear. And what makes a man great but suffering, and suffering well? Accept my poor words for the hope they offer."

"I hear no hope in them, Gary. In its place I receive your hand and wishes for my safe journey." Mathan again offered Garald his hand.

Garald grasped Mathan's forearm and did not release it until he had bestowed upon him one last bit of wisdom. "A blind and deaf teacher once said that she regarded security as a superstition."

Mathan gently but firmly removed his hand from Garald's grip. "So, I'm to be advised by a shoeless madwoman, a senseless gnome, a sheep-less shepherd and a sightless teacher. Gary, I *must* go now. There is much to do, and I seem always to be occupied with exactly the wrong thing." He granted his friend a solemn smile and stepped out into the moonlit night.

CHAPTER 36
Wisest Among Us… and Fair

*"Son of the dragon, of night and the slaughter whose wisdom his
unshaven youth will belie…"*
"Kingsword"
Heather Dale

Tufty tussocks aside, Mathan encountered no
impediments as he loped across the heath. The air began
to cool and he lost the moon before the ground began to
slope down into the vale. Upon arriving at the edge of the
valley, he stared into the deepening blackness below and
shivered as his sweat cooled. His good sense spoke to him
in a shrill and strident tone, telling him to wait for the sun
to rise before he descended the steep trail before him.
Mathan, however, preferred the low confident tones of his
imagination which told him that he could handle the
descent quite nicely as soon as his eyes adjusted to the
waning light.

He advanced along a footpath which led by way of a
series of switchbacks onto the floor of the valley. There,
he could travel parallel with the King's Run a short

distance upstream to a ford he had crossed earlier. This late in the autumn, the burn was low and he was far upstream from most of its tributaries, so he should have no problem crossing it in the dark. Mathan gained confidence as he passed the first couple of switchbacks. He could feel the air cooling and hear the din of cascades as he descended.

His mind wandered to Fionn. Would the old man welcome him? If not, Mathan could easily make a show of his regret over having left as he had. He would explain that reading from the book had helped him understand that Fionn's apparent lunacy was simply a function of his solitary vigil. He well understood how Sabia's chiding and insistence could affect a man. Fionn would have to receive him.

In pursuing this thought, Mathan took his mind off the task of carefully placing his feet. He had a moment to savor the horror when he realized that his foot hung in empty space before he fell sideways then tumbled headlong down the slope. At one point, he regained his feet for a moment but was moving too quickly to avoid being thrown onto his shoulder and tumbling on. Finally, he fetched up against a boulder and lay still for a long while.

**

Sabia's voice floated into Mathan's disjointed thoughts, seemingly from the far side of the mountain. "You *are* impetuous, dear one. You are like to kill yourself. What would I do then with no Bear to smash the faces of my detractors?"

"I th-thought you didn't need—" but Mathan's whispering croak gave way to a sharp gasp as he attempted to get up and pain seared his ribs. He fell back and lay still, his eyes tightly shut and began reviewing the states of his various bits.

"I do not, Mathan, require the services of a defender." Sabia's bemused voice lilted through the still night air. She paused. From quite nearby, she said, "It *is*, however, a wonder to be offered the services of one."

As the silence lengthened, Mathan opened an eye and perceived a point of bright incandescence above him. He opened the other and the point resolved into the gravely merry mien of a small, plain woman who stood peering across the valley, no doubt wandering the passageways of some bright memory from her distant past.

Presently, she shuddered, seeming to shake off the dust of centuries. Shifting her gaze to Mathan, who still lay at her feet, she spoke again in an amused tone. "Now, to have a man fling himself down a hill in fear of missing my passing is another thing altogether. Were you so sure I would not wait for you that you had to become a bird and fly to intercept me?"

Mathan chuckled but then groaned. "I did not think to find you. I came in search of Fionn. He is other than he seems." He smiled fetchingly up at Sabia. "I suppose I also hoped you might find your way back to Fionn's cave."

"Get up, Mathan. You are well. A lazy messenger is worse than an irritation to the one who sends him." Sabia's small hand encircled Mathan's large thumb in a vicelike grip and pulled him to his feet. He grunted feebly and swayed before leaning back against the boulder.

"Lazy am I?"

"No, love. Never lazy. Although often impetuous and sometimes petulant, you are never lazy." There was a smile in her voice, but Mathan knew she spoke the truth.

He sighed, perhaps petulantly. "I don't know what to do or say, Lady. I only want to be a good man. I can't deny my failures. Does my desire amount to naught?"

"Aye, Mathan, aye. Your desire amounts to all as far as it goes, but you must add wisdom to your desire."

Mathan grinned. "I came here for just that purpose. Reading from Fionn's book, I realized that in spite of his madness he possesses a wisdom I want."

The anguish Mathan perceived in Sabia's bright eyes stole the words from his mouth. Wounded silence hung interminably between them like an obscenity.

A phantasm of screaming guilt now assaulted Mathan's mind. He fought to breathe through the shame which bound his chest. "Oh, Sabia–"

"Do not speak, beloved. Surely, foolish words will fill your mouth, and I will hold you accountable for them. Do not speak. In your arrogance, you left my dear friend, my faithful one, to walk the cold, dark valley alone. You will not speak. I will not soothe your heart. It will break, and you will be a better man for it. The loss is real."

Mathan slid down until he sat on the ground, his back to the boulder. Bitter recriminations settled on him like vultures on a carcass. He had left an old man – one who had offered him hospitality, one who had waited twelve years to do so – left him to die alone, uncomforted, unmourned, forgotten. Mathan had never before known he was capable of betrayal. Fionn had tried to tell him. He had almost begged... In fact, he *had* begged Mathan to stay with him. Mathan had treated him shamefully and left him alone.

His shame and sadness deepened until surpassing all description. Mathan's thoughts became incoherent, and for the first time he mourned for someone else. In his despair, he was drawn from himself enough to see from Fionn's own perspective.

Tears washed Mathan's muddy cheeks. He threw back his head and howled as if he were being torn in two.

"You do well to mourn, my love. This grief is born of your first glimpse of yourself from the perspective of another, a better man. This sorrow will lead you to become a better man, yourself, and that will save you from unending regret. This is almost the beginning of wisdom."

"Ah, Sabia," Mathan moaned, "am I not yet wise?"

Sabia chuckled ruefully, "Child, your cleverness has

sometimes been mistaken for wisdom, but you have only today learned enough to realize that you are not at all wise."

Sabia turned to leave but cast a glance over her shoulder to the mound of a man slumped at her feet. "Take heart, my champion, for today you have taken a small leap across a narrow chasm. It is only the beginning, but it is more than most men do."

Mathan clambered to his feet, to bar Sabia's path, and pled in a husky bluster, "Ach, Lady, surely you'll not leave me again?"

"Would you stay me by force?" Sabia queried, arching an eyebrow and setting her mouth firm.

Mathan missed the challenge in Sabia's voice. "I would go with you, Sabia, and never again go without you."

"When you have mourned sufficiently to purge the self-pity from your guilt, you may follow me to a place where we can talk and rest."

"I am ready. Lead on."

"Come then, great Bear, that we may dine on bitter herbs." Sabia swept Mathan from her path and strode away.

Lumbering along behind her, Mathan wondered on the densely packed changes of the past few weeks. It seemed to him that he had been raked from the tidal pool of Taermun into the fathomless ocean of a vast and indecipherable world, though he had only just left the Vale.

"I, ah, realize, of course, Sabia, that you never left me..." Trudging behind her he could not see if she reacted. Ten paces later, having perceived no response, he plunged on. "I know that when we were apart, even when it seemed you had walked away, I was the one who had separated us. If only by not going along with you—"

In a single motion, Sabia swung around and caught Mathan in the steel clasp of her arms. "My love, you have espoused wisdom. Her embrace is not warm, but her hold is firm." She pressed her face against his chest and kissed his heaving heart.

In a heartbeat, she was once more striding along at a furious pace, leaving Mathan to catch his breath.

When later, in a cold dawn light, they arrived at Fionn's cave, Sabia ordered Mathan to awaken the fire in the pit and to build a bier on the far side of the clearing. She slipped through the curtain of vines across the mouth of the cave, and without a word, he did her bidding.

He took Fionn's axe and his long knife then set out to find a stand of green saplings. He cut a few then limbed them and tied them all together with strips of bark. Hefting the bundle onto his shoulder. He winced for the hundredth time at his bruised ribs and returned to Fionn's cave.

Once there, he chose an area for the bier and pounded medium-length poles into the ground with the flat side of the axe head. Then he fixed two longer poles along the sides and cut shorter ones to lay across them. Having built the platform, he turned his attention to building a flat-topped pyramid beneath it from Fionn's store of firewood and kindling. Now satisfied with his construction, he went to the nearby fire pit.

He knelt by the pit with a handful of dry tinder and stirred its dark ashes but found not a single live coal. Muttering to himself, he went to the cave to retrieve his flint.

"Could you not draw a flame, blacksmith's son?" Sabia teased as he entered the cave.

Mathan ignored her as he waited for his eyes to adjust to the darkness. Her kneeling form coalesced from the gloom, and he realized she was bundling something together. He recognized Fionn's supine figure before her and drew a sharp breath. Kneeling beside her he asked, "Shall I carry him outside?"

"Gently, Mathan, gently on his kite."

"His kite?" He glanced about before Sabia pointed to a

crevice in the wall behind Fionn's sleeping pallet. Mathan reached in and withdrew a long teardrop-shaped shield, a serpentine strap affixed to its back. He reached across Fionn and laid it between the pallet and the wall, where it rocked gently on its curved face.

Sabia stood aside and intoned a mournful ayre which thrilled in Mathan's blood as he knelt beside the pallet, lifted the remains of the old man and arranged them on the shield. The song continued as she glided to the mouth of the cave and held aside its vine curtain. Mathan could not say if she merely hummed or if she sang words in a language he did not know. He hefted the kite-shield onto his shoulder and solemnly bore his burden out into the morning light.

He laid Fionn's shield beside the bier then lifted Fionn's shell onto it. As he struck his flint, the fire burst into life and Sabia burst into song. In a heart-piercing soprano, she sang:

"I followed my king
To a war in a far southern land
Where men said he should prove his throne.
I stood with my king
And was ready to strike them all down,
But my king stood tall
and reached out, and took sword of his own
And as we departed, he said to me there,
Before warring and feud could begin,
If I am afraid to be beaten
Then where is the pride when I win?
I followed my king
To the door of the vigilant squire
But a guardsman stood and barred the way.
I stood with my king
And was ready to strike the man down
But my king took stall
And reached out, and shook hands at the gate.

And as we departed, he said to me there,
Before warring and feud could begin,
If I won't clasp hands with a neighbor
Then how can I ask it of him?
I followed my king
From his place at the mead hall's high seat
Where the hungry sat in grim array.
I stood with my king
And was ready to strike the cook down
But my king stood tall
And reached out and he shouldered a tray,
And as we departed he said to me there,
Before warring and feud could begin,
If I cannot serve in the kitchen
Then how can I serve them as king?
In word and deed
I follow my king,
The wisest among us and fair.
In word and deed
I follow my king,
The wisest among us and fair."

"I Follow My King" – *Heather Dale*
(Reprinted with Permission)

While she sang, Mathan stood transfixed by her sorrow and joy. When she had finished her song, she intoned a blessing in a forgotten tongue then sat silent. Mathan shifted his gaze to observe the conflagration. Slowly, Fionn's fists rose above his chest, as though he were ready to face his next adversary. Mathan offered the man a grim smile and stood witness as the flames inexorably consumed Fionn's corruption.

Glancing her way, Mathan asked, "This great man who died alone in a cave... Who was he, Sabia?"

Keeping her eyes fixed on the flames, Sabia silently pointed with her chin to the kite shield that lay near the bier. Mathan flipped it to reveal the ensign of the ruined house of Killinchy, the ruling house of fallen Dunglaun. He drew in a breath and shook his head. "Fintan. Fionn. They are one and the same. He is my granddad, the father of my own sweet ma and the man who stood watch over me for a dozen years from his home in a cave." He shuddered. "Ai, my heart. Sabia is there no depth to my foolishness?"

Sabia maintained her vigil over her old friend as she spoke to his grandson. "If there is, Bear, we've not yet plumbed it."

Then descended a silence so complete it seemed a wall about them. So they remained while the ashes of Finbarr, son of Uvar rose on the breeze with those of Fintan, father of Laurelei, and of Fionn, grandsire of Mathan.

After the embers had died, Sabia and Mathan scattered the ashes and found the charred bits of bone that remained. Sabia placed them gently into a silk purse. She sighed then took Mathan's hand. "I'll ask you again…"

"I'm for Shallowford." He looked grimly into her eyes.

"That you are, m'love. I go to Dunglaun to bury these relics among the ruins." She hung the purse from her belt. "The book and the shield are yours. He always intended them for you."

"Sabia…" Mathan gathered her into his arms. "I do love you."

"I know right well who you are and what you love. You will see me again when you've forgotten to look for me." She turned on her heel and was gone.

CHAPTER 37
Stolen Water

"Suspicion is the companion of mean souls and the bane of all good society."
<u>Common Sense</u>
Thomas Paine

The terrain opened out onto a broad plain below the low hill where Mathan rested on a boulder. For as long as he cared to remember, his world had been bounded by the mountain to the west, its arms to the north and south and the high moorlands of Hebron Heath to the east. He'd never before seen such a wide expanse of earth and sky.

He levered himself off the boulder and worked his way downhill. There was a village ahead on an east-west road he could see crossing the plain. The village likely boasted an inn. He lumbered forward with his mind fixed on savory stew or maybe some tender mutton.

After an hour of hard walking, Mathan arrived at a farm and stopped for a drink. Climbing a stile, he looked around and shouted, "Hallo? I'm a traveler hoping for a drink from your well. I mean no mischief."

Receiving no answer, he continued across the barnyard to the well. He dropped its bucket in and had begun to wind it back up when from behind him, a small, high voice demanded he pay for the water he drank.

He turned and saw a slim lad holding a crossbow and staring him down. "There's no call for that. I'll not steal or damage anything. I only hoped for a wee drink of water."

"That you was gonna steal."

"Steal? What? No. Just drink a bit."

"You're gonna pay for the bit you drink."

"What's the cost of it then?"

"What you got?"

"Less than you might want, and more than you deserve. You'd charge a traveler for a drink at the point of a bolt? Your hospitality is poor. In my home it is a disgrace to require payment for a drink of water. Aim the crossbow in a safe direction and take two dadas for your trouble. I'll have my drink, fill my skin, and leave."

The lad lowered the weapon but kept it ready. "Where you goin', then?"

Mathan laid two dadas on the stone wall that encircled the well. "I discuss my travel plans with my friends. May I drink now?"

The lad slung the crossbow across his back and shrugged. Mathan dropped his pack and laid aside his shield, then picked up the bucket and drank long and gratefully.

"I'm Bronach."

Mathan set the bucket aside. "You're a lad."

"Am not. I'm a woman as sure as the sun shines." Her indignation amused him.

"I'd not say so. You've the look and manner of a lad." He again lifted the bucket. "But no matter. I will drink again and be gone if you'll agree to maintain your aim on something less precious than myself."

"Where d'you go?"

"Shallowford, to become a soldier. Why do you think

323

you should know?"

"I'll be going along."

Mathan guffawed loudly. "You'll not. You'll stay here and feed your ma's chickens and pester me no more."

"I've no ma and no chickens. I'll to Shallowford, and you'll keep me from the bad 'uns."

"What makes you think I'm no 'bad 'un' myself? And how would you pay?"

The young woman bristled. "I'm not that sort. I'll pay you in coin," and she glared fervently. Mathan laughed and she turned crimson. "You're no bad 'un. I know. I've met a few. You'd not have that great cleaver strapped 'cross your back if you couldn't use it. You're the sort that'd keep me safe even if you didn't wanna."

"I reckon I can't keep you from walking the road behind me. But what of your farm?"

She chuckled, "It's none of mine. I planned to sleep in the loft tonight and have a few eggs for my dinner."

"You said there were no chickens."

"I said that I have none."

Mathan grimaced and took the coins from the well wall. "Aye. You said just that. And I'll have my two dadas back that I paid you for the water you do not own."

"We'll say it's an advance on your pay."

Mathan snorted. "It's not yours, as the water was not. Besides, in my home it is a disgrace to require payment for companionship. You'll owe me nothing, and you'll steal no eggs. The village below must have an inn. I've had my drink and am leaving. Stay or come as you wish."

He slung his shield across his back. In lifting his pack, Mathan was reminded of the remainders of the food Mag had packed for him as well as what he'd scavenged at Fionn's cave. He lowered the pack and drew out a dumpling but then replaced it and drew out the hard cheese instead. "I've a thing you'll like better than stolen eggs."

Bronach considered him for a moment then took the

small bundle he had proffered. Mathan stooped to secure the mouth of his pack. "Bro, I'm Mathan. That cheese was made from the milk of the happiest sheep in Tierasal."

In one motion, he stood and slung the pack around to strap it onto his back. "You'll note it's fine texture and rich flavor…" He glanced over and saw that Bronach's mouth was now full and her hand empty.

"Bronie, that's not the sort of thing you swallow whole. 'It requires rumination and pontification to augment its appreciation'. That's somethin' my mam used to say. Besides, I had hoped to share it with you rather than give it to you and do without myself."

Bronach spit some of the cheese back into her hand and stared at Mathan. He dropped the bucket into the well again and drew it up. "You'll want a drink with that, I warrant."

She nodded and smiled then reached for the bucket. Mathan dumped it over her head. Bronach threw down the cheese she held and sputtered through what was still in her mouth. Mathan laughed, adjusted the straps on his pack and strode away.

A short time later, he heard Bronach's footsteps on the road behind him. Without looking behind, he said, "It is good to know you've an appetite; for if you threaten me again with that bolt launcher of yours, you will eat it."

"I might've been wrong. You could be a bad 'un."

A farm cart turned into the roadway a short distance ahead. Mathan ran after it and asked the farmer for a ride to the village. "I can pay you for a ride to the inn."

"And your lad?"

Mathan scoffed, "He's none of mine. If he wishes to ride, he'll pay for himself."

"I'm not a lad," and Bronach was again incensed.

Mathan clapped her on the shoulder. "That's right, lad. Practically a grown man now, yeah?"

The farmer chuckled. "Up you get, and neither pay. 'Twould be a disgrace to require payment for a ride when I go that way without you."

Mathan clambered onto the bench next to the farmer and hitched a thumb over his shoulder to indicate that Bronach should climb into the back. She eyed the chicken droppings that covered the planks then glanced back at Mathan. The farmer shrugged. "Hup, Sive. On with you," and the horse began to move.

As the cart pulled away, Bronach finally decided she wanted to ride and vaulted into the ubiquitous chicken scat.

Ignorant of her ignominy, Mathan had already engaged the farmer in animated conversation. After a while, he glanced back to find Bronach staring fixedly at his back. "Comfortable?"

She shifted her position to enjoy a view of anything other than Mathan's face, but she couldn't escape his laughter. The cart rumbled on.

***

When they arrived at the Cross Keys Inn, Mathan thanked the farmer and ambled inside. Bronach stood alone outside for a long while, thinking, looking at the stars that now peeped from the darkening sky, and allowing her deep anger to subside. When she finally made her way inside, she pushed through the crowd until she found Mathan seated alone at a table but speaking with a man at another.

"I reckon I might be able to take you," Mathan was saying, "but here's the problem. I don't have enough money to lose. So, if you were able – *if* you were, mind – I'd then be without a bed for the night, and maybe even my dinner. I've a feeling you're a pretty accomplished arm wrestler, so I've no call to risk it."

The man, larger than most but by no means as large as Mathan, went to sit across the table from him and placed his right elbow on the table. "I'll go you for a pint. I don't want your money – just the pleasure of drinkin' your ale."

"I reckon no man could argue with such wisdom," and Mathan too set his elbow on the table, but his left one.

The other man seemed flummoxed. "You're not a lefty, are you?"

"Ah, no. But if you're goin' to injure an arm, I'd rather have it be the left one."

The man grinned and switched arms. Mathan had to move his elbow back a bit to accommodate his opponent's shorter reach. A wiry fellow with a crooked mouth called out, "Last bets," and there was a scramble as men handed him money.

Mathan glanced over and saw Bronach pull a small purse from inside her shirt. He shook his head. She made a show of deliberately placing the money into the odds-maker's hand.

Mathan's opponent squeezed his hand to get his attention. "You ready?"

"Aye. Begin."

The contest raged for over ten minutes. Each man had moments when he owned the advantage. Great beads of sweat rolled down their faces and the veins in their temples stood out. Each crouched over his stool rather than sitting on it. Finally, with a great cry, Mathan's opponent threw the last of his strength into an all-or-nothing push and drove Mathan's hand to the table.

Mathan dropped to his stool and bowed his head. His opponent leapt to his feet and clapped his hands over his head. There was a massive uproar from the crowd, and money changed hands. Mathan stood and offered the victor his right hand.

"Your right is considerable stronger than your left," the victor said beneath the din.

"I'm a blacksmith."

"If you'd challenged me with the right, I don't know that I'd have stood a chance." There was a question in his eyes.

Mathan smiled and called for ale.

After the crowd had quietened and each returned to his own company, Bronach sat across from Mathan who was now enjoying a large serving of roast mutton his opponent had bought to show his friendship. "You owe me dinner and a bed, and much more than that, oaf," she told him.

"And how have I come into such indebtedness?"

"I bet all I had on you, and you lost."

"I told you not to bet. Besides, only a fool would bet all she had."

"You are huge. How could you lose?"

"The other fellow was no stripling lad. He is more practiced in this art than I."

"You used your weaker arm and threw the game."

"They are my arms. I may choose between them. I fought with all I had in that arm. You chanced losing all you had on something you could not affect. The loss is yours. The fault is yours."

Tears collected in the corners of Bronach's eyes. "What can I do?"

"I dunno, Bro, but then again, I can't be expected to know anything; as you said, I'm an oaf." Mathan sopped some of the juice from his roast with soft, white bread and shoved it into his mouth. He grinned, and the juice ran down his beard.

"You mock me."

Mathan caught sight of something across the room and pushed his trencher to Bronach's side of the table. "Shut it, lad."

"I'm not a lad. I told you."

"You are while you travel with me. Don't like it? Pester someone else. Now shut it. They've a harper."

The musician tuned his clarsach while the crowd settled down. Once people had taken their seats and Mathan could see the bard clearly, he abruptly stood, knocking his stool over. "Tigue," he called over everyone's heads.

Tigue acknowledged him with a nod and a smile but continued strumming. The music built to a thrumming crescendo then immediately dropped to an almost inaudible sighing. Tigue now sang.

> "I sing a sacred lullaby
> To the pale child of the night.
> Her luminous eyes reflect
> My harsh and glaring light
> As a secret, knowing glow.
> She is night;
> I am day;
> We are one.

> "She is constant
> And constantly changing,
> Always here
> in perpetual motion.
> In her subtle shifting,
> My passions neap and ebb.
> She is pale and cool and lovely who Saunters through my night
> Who, when she stands before me, Eclipses my great light.
> In all the cosmic night,
> There is only she
> Whose face absorbs my light
> And offers it back to me.

> "She reminds me that I am alive."

Tigue delivered the last line with his eyes closed. For an interminable moment, it seemed he barely breathed. Then he rose silently and wound his way through the patrons toward Mathan. His food arrived as he did, and he placed it on Mathan's table before sitting down. The other patrons resumed their meals and their conversations.

Mathan grinned. "Tigue, it is good to see you, but…" He noticed that Bronach stared wildly at Tigue, as though he had a blade to her throat. His gaze bore into her and she cowered. Mathan's bemused chuckle, though, drew Tigue's eyes away from her.

"Mathan, what is this woman to you? Why does she pretend to be a lad?"

"Ah now, Tigue, I've been wonderin' that myself, and also why she's following me to Shallowford. Women are inscrutable, are they not? But what are *you* doing here? How did you come here before me? Was it bardic magic that brought you mounted on the wind? As for what she might be to me, she's a nuisance and a bother; she tends to steal things, and she gambles."

The exasperated tone of Tigue's voice came as an echo of the teasing tone of Mathan's. "I rode a horse. I took the road. I am here to see you. Yes, they are, and this one in particular is difficult to understand." He again laid his sharp eye on Bronach. "You said she intends to follow you to Shallowford, and you intend to allow that?"

"Tigue, I've no call to prevent a body walkin' down the road. She asked me to protect her."

Tigue snorted. "Sorry. Go on."

"She said she needed protection. It seems to me that's why she travels as a lad. I reckon she figured, since I'm protectin' her, she can become a woman again. Way I figure it, I'm more likely to survive if it's not general knowledge that I'm travelin' with an attractive young woman."

Crimson flooded Bronach's face.

"So, from here on out, long as she's with me, she's a lad. She don't like it, some other rube'll take her on."

Tigue clearly considered Mathan's reasoning. "It does seem best for now, especially as she insists on traveling with you."

Bronach pounded her fist on the table.

Tigue smiled, "I'll come along as well. After all, you've no call to prevent a body walkin' down the road."

Bronach blanched. It was a wonder. Now she was cotton white where a moment before she had been scarlet.

"Dad, no."

Her vehemence shook Mathan a bit until he realized what she'd said, then he became profoundly confused. Bronach puffed like a horse after a wild ride while she stared at Tigue. Tigue watched Mathan placidly as he glanced between the two of them, until understanding dawned.

"Mo croi, Tigue. Why did I never know you had a child?"

"Perhaps you never asked, Mathan," and he then turned to Bronach. "You'll not travel alone with this one. Not that I worry for your honor, more because he cannot offer protection to himself much less others."

"Only look at him, Dad. He could handle any bad 'un that comes along. And he's got that great sword. Who would be fool enough to challenge him? I'll maintain my disguise, only don't come and save me."

"I didn't come to save you. I didn't know I'd find you here. I came to meet Mathan, to travel with him to find something I've been looking for all my life."

"The Undefeated Man."

"Yes, Bronach." Tigue seemed mildly surprised. "The Undefeated Man. So, you are a spy as well as a thief and a gambler."

"I am none of that. I heard you talking with mam. You said you were going to find him and that when you wrote his tale you'd become the man you once were."

"That's almost what I said."

"Mam said you'd left Galantamhor for Hebron Heath to find your myth, and now, all these years later, you're lookin' for him elsewhere. Then she said some very unkind things. I didn't know you'd look for him here."

"I'm not lookin' here. Sabia told me that in following Mathan I would find him."

Mathan chuckled. "I'll not lead you to him, Tigue. Sounds like nonsense to me. Likely no such man exists. On the other hand, I owe you a pint. If you remember, I as much as promised you one if you could sing a 'sweeter song of Sabia'. The song you sang that last night at Mag Petty's – the one about the wise queen - that was about Sabia. Well I know her effect on a man."

Mathan raised his hand to call for ale, but Tigue gently pushed his arm back down. "I thank you, Mathan, but the stuff's lost its enchantment for me."

This ale-free fellow, this father of a grown woman, this chaser of myths was so different from the familiar dissolute mendicant Mathan had known that the man before him seemed a stranger.

Tigue looked at his daughter. "I am not such a fool to think I was ever a dad to you, but I am your father, and you'll not have another, so hear me. This lout," he indicated Mathan, "is as friendly and honorable a traveling partner as any dad could want for his girl, but do not let his beard and deep voice fool you. He is a child, and a mischievous one at that. He'll not protect you from real dangers. That sword was a gift he carries as a burden until he learns to wield it. One day, this Mathan might become a formidable man, but for the now, he's naught but a child in large boots."

He glanced again at Mathan. "Besides, for the now, his path is mine. Whether it is yours or not, you must decide."

Tigue lowered his gaze to the unfinished food before him. "I do love you if you'll have it or no." He lifted his clarsach and meandered to the fireside.

Mathan had watched him, slightly awed, walk away then turned to see Bronach devouring the remains of her father's meal. Mathan stood. "I'm for my bed."

Shoving the last of the sop into her mouth, Bronach also stood then wiped her hands on her trousers. "Aye. Let's go," she mumbled around the bread in her mouth.

"I thought you were none of that kind, Lady."

"I'm not. I'm your lad. My place is with my master. You'd not have your lad sleep in the smelly stable when there's a cozy chamber in the inn?"

Mathan muttered to himself as the master of the house led them up the stairs. Across the passageway from the door to Mathan's room was a rude bench with a thin cushion. "Wait here," and he pointed to the bench before stepping into his room and closing the door.

A short while later, he opened it a bit and threw out a folded blanket, hitting Bronach in the chest. "Good night, Bro. Sleep well," and he closed the door again.

The next morning, Mathan tripped over Bronach's supine form on the floor of his room. He poured water into the basin and washed his hands and face, using a cloth lying next to it to clean up as best he could, then he dumped the contents of the basin over Bronach. She shot to her feet with a gasp.

Mathan picked up his gear and walked out, humming as he went downstairs, where he found Tigue moping over a cup of tea. "A fine good morning to you, my friend," Mathan said. "You look as though you've spent the night wrestling your bed. I prefer to surrender to the thing and have an end to it. Doing this helps me avoid appearing a decade older in the morning, as you now do."

"Ach, my Bronach; I had hoped I might become a friend to her during this journey, but she left in the night. I'll not have the chance again."

"Tigue, Bro's upstairs in my chamber. She slept with me last night."

Tigue flew off his stool and across the table, straight into Mathan's face. Before either knew it, Mathan was stretched out on his back across the table behind him. He covered his face with his hands. "Half a moment, Tigue. I can explain."

A swarm of blows and curses, kindled by the guilt of eighteen years' of a father's failure, flew from Tigue's heart and into Mathan's face. "My daughter is the only precious thing left to me in all the world. You, the only lad I might ever have trusted with her, have betrayed me."

Mathan uncovered his face so he could wrap his arms

around Tigue. He crushed the bard to him. "Hush. Hush now, Tigue. She slept on the floor. I dinna bother the lass. She is well."

Tigue slowly relaxed. "Release me," and Mathan complied. Tigue stood and then helped Mathan up. "Forgive me, Bear. I lost myself."

"Nay, Tigue, I say there is more of you here than I've ever seen before. I'm for the kitchen to find a steak for my eyes." He stumbled away down the passage.

"Dad." Tigue raised his gaze to see Bronach cascading down the stairs. She flew to him, searching him for any injuries. "Dad, what happened? What passed between you?"

"The only thing that could cause me to strike one I love so well as Mathan. But he assured me there was no reason for my anger. He said all is well between you two."

"Did he, now? I suppose he would lie to save himself from the walloping you laid on him. Dad, you were somethin' to see."

Tigue's ire rose again. "He lied?"

"Yes, Dad. He did terrible things to me. Then, this morning, he left me poorly used and gulping for breath while he walked out the door, humming. *Humming*, I say."

Tigue clenched his bruised fists. "Tell me quickly what he did that left you so."

"Dad, that pig dumped a full washbasin on me as I lay sleeping, and I was in a dream of such beauty."

Tigue grasped Bronach's shoulders and shook her. "He did what, Bro? He poured water on you and naught else? Tell me," and he shook her more insistently.

"It was dirty water, Dad, that he'd used to wash himself. But that's not the sum of it. He also told me to sleep on a rickety bench in a drafty passageway with naught but a seedy blanket for warmth. Go you and thump him again for me, Dad."

The tension drained from Tigue and he slumped onto a

stool. He bowed his head and braced his elbows on his knees, shuddered, then threw his head back and laughed long and loud, as he had not done for almost two decades.

Bronach flounced off, no doubt to find Mathan and teach him to fear her displeasure even if her dad would not.

On the way out of the village, the trio stopped by a livery stable where Tigue had apparently made arrangements for the horse he had borrowed to be returned to its stable in Taermun. The groom asked if they wished to take horses for the three of them as far as Shallowford. Mathan looked to Tigue who said that they wouldn't mind a bit of a walk.

Three otherwise uneventful ten-hour days of walking brought them to a narrow drive that rambled through boulder-strewn rolling grasslands toward the rising foothills. Beside the head of the drive was a well-maintained, sturdy wooden sign that was both carved and painted to read, "Stone Farm – Home of Orin's Stone Farm Jumble Cider".

Mathan halted beside the sign and waited for the others to stop as well. "I've a need for some cider."

Bronach scoffed, "I thought that you had a 'need' to get to Shallowford…"

"Hush, Bronach." Tigue spoke to his daughter but stared intently at Mathan. "It's not cider he wants here."

Mathan started up the drive with Tigue following, but Bronach shouted, "I'm goin' to Shallowford, not to some lost farm."

Mathan glanced back. "As you will, Bro," he said with a shrug then ambled forward.

Bronach scoffed again then jogged to catch up with her dad who remained fixated on Mathan. As she flounced up to him, he glanced over and said, "We're goin' to *the* Stone Farm, to meet *the* Orin along with *the* Keva."

Bronach replied succinctly, "Humph."

CHAPTER 38
Sharp and Sweet

"Lay this unto your breast.
Old friends, like old swords, still are trusted best."
<u>The Duchess of Malfi</u>
John Webster

Nearing the rustic house at the heart of Stone Farm, Mathan noted a great deal of activity all around. The farm was a busy place. A young woman approached from the direction of the cider mill. She seemed nervous as she spoke rapidly to Tigue, obviously the oldest of the three travelers. "Good day, gentlemen. Would you be interested in our fresh cider, or would perhaps prefer some that's aged a bit? We make it both sharp and sweet. Either way, we're happy that you've come to Stone Farm. We've a wash house if you've need of it and a bunkhouse as well. It looks as though you've traveled a good distance afoot."

None of them replied immediately. While Tigue awaited Mathan's response, Mathan stared stupidly at the hostess, and Bronach glared at her. Finally, Tigue jabbed Mathan with a sharp elbow prompting him to speak.

Mathan lowered his gaze and stepped forward. "Hullo, Ciara," he mumbled.

Ciara grinned. "I didn't think you would know me."

"Then why did you act as though I were a stranger?"

"Oh, Mathan," she took his hands, "I wanted to at least allow you to know me." She released one hand and began walking toward the house. Mathan followed meekly along. "Mam will be very pleased to see you."

"Yes, well, I'll be glad to..." He stopped walking and pulled her toward him. "Ciara, I have forgotten so much of myself."

She embraced him and laid her head on his chest. "Welcome home, Bear. We've not forgotten you." From somewhere behind him, Bronach scoffed, but it reached no further than his ears. He wrapped his arms around Ciara and felt something inside him tear loose.

A long moment later, Mathan broke the embrace and wiped his eyes as he introduced Tigue and his daughter. Ciara embraced each of them and welcomed them to Stone Farm then invited them all inside. Grasping Mathan's hand again, she took off running for the house. When they arrived, she dragged him across the threshold and directly to a willowy woman seated at a table and doing sums on parchment.

Mildly startled, the older woman looked up. "Ciara, what is..." She realized that her oldest daughter was holding hands with a young man. Her surprise quickly became disdain then wonder. She looked at her daughter who grinned in response. She came to her feet "Is't our Mathan? Our young Bear? Come here to Stone Farm?"

She stepped around the table and reached as far around him as she could. "Oh, lad," she moaned. Pushing away and looking up at him she asked, "Where's Ardal then? Is all well with him?"

Though disconcerted by the emotions his visit had elicited both in his hosts and in himself, Mathan replied, "Dad's well. He's at the smithy as he always is."

He again felt moisture in his eyes and distracted himself by offering to introduce his friends to Keva. As she walked toward the door told Ciara, "Fetch your father and the boys." Ciara was out the door like a shot. Keva squeezed Mathan once more and said, "Let's go and meet your friends."

Stepping outside, they found Tigue and Bronach sipping cider and chatting with a young man. Something had worked a profound improvement on Bronach's attitude. Perhaps it was the cider, or it might have been the company of the young man.

Keva eyed Bronach somewhat dubiously and said to the young man, "Garvan, go you, now, to the cook house and tell them we have guests."

"Yes, Mam," the lad replied then he grinned at Bronach. "Come along, Bro. I'll show you about."

Grinning in return, Bronach moved to follow him but Keva brought her up short when she said, "Ai, no, Lad. I've not yet met our guests. There will be time later for showing them about... all of them, together, mind you. Go you now."

Garvan jogged off, and the pout returned to Bronach's face. Keva extended her hand to Tigue. "Welcome, friend. I am..."

"You are Keva, wife of Orin, of Stone Farm, the Jumble." He spoke as though reciting an incantation. "And the young woman who passed by a moment ago is Ciara – your firstborn."

Keva fixed the bard with a hard stare and demanded more than asked, "And who might you be who knows my family as no stranger might?"

"Fantastic," Tigue said while staring at her like a man beginning to understand a foreign tongue. "Amazing. A sharp blade concealed beneath fine muslin." Easing his intense study of her for a moment he smiled.

Keva had no patience for a stranger on her farm who knew her family but would not give his name. She turned to Mathan for answers. "Who is he, then, that you bring him here? And this girl, what is she to you?"

Mathan gestured at the older man. "He is Tigue, a bard." He jerked a thumb at the bard's daughter. "She is Bronach, his daughter and a nuisance."

Bronach snorted. "And he," she leaned forward and sighted along her pointing finger at Mathan. "He is a brute and an ass and acts as though he had no mother to teach him civility."

Tigue's head fell forward until his chin rested on his chest.

Mathan and Keva locked eyes, and a lifetime of loss reverberated between them. A long while later while maintaining her gaze on Mathan, Keva responded. "He hadn't."

Bronach had the decency to be embarrassed but not to keep her silence. "That *is* too bad, but it's no excuse for him to act as he does."

Keva turned her studious gaze on Bronach. "What then, is your excuse? Had you a mother?"

Tigue grimaced. "Aye, Lady, but sadly, she had no father."

It was Keva's turn to become embarrassed. "Forgive me, Tigue, I…"

"Nay, Lady. It is I who ask forgiveness of all present and of many who are not."

The uncomfortable silence was broken by Keva's announcement. "Here's Orin, then."

Running toward them from among the apple trees on the slopes above the farm, was a tall, lean man with a slight hitch in his gait. Mathan grinned. "Orin."

When he arrived, Orin attempted simultaneously to embrace Mathan, look at him, welcome him, and catch his breath. Finally, he grasped his forearm, wrapped his other arm around behind him and said, "Oh, lad. Welcome home."

Keva joined them in their embrace. "Come to the

cookhouse," she urged, "where we can sit and talk."

***

The talk ranged over every topic imaginable other than Mathan's plans. Remembering, reliving, and honoring all that had gone before, the friends laughed often and occasionally cried a bit. Tigue sat writing the whole time only looking up to ask for clarification at times. Bronach sat very close to Garvan and kept her thoughts to herself. Orin and Keva's other children joined them as the afternoon became evening. Someone prepared a meal and served it, but Mathan was so intent on the conversation and on the warmth and peace that seemed to emanate from the young woman at his side that he barely ate.

They talked late into the night, and the others all found their beds, but Orin, Keva, Mathan, and Ciara remained. During a lull in the conversation, Keva smiled warmly at Mathan. Then tugging on Orin's sleeve, she stood. "Take me home and into your arms," she proposed.

Orin grinned, slapped his hands down onto the table, and pushed himself up from his chair. To Mathan he said, "A man doesn't often get an offer like that from a good woman. G'night, lad. It is *good* to have you here."

Mathan watched the couple walk to the door then fixed his eyes on the lamp burning in the middle of the table. His heart seemed to be vibrating as he heard Ciara's soft sigh. He covered her hand where it lay on the table with his own then slowly shifted his gaze and found her staring wide-eyed at him like a startled child.

Sliding from the bench to kneel beside her, he held her hand in both of his and looked up too her. She seemed terrified. "Ciara, I…" His voice cracked. He cleared his throat and began again. "Ciara, come with me to Shallowford. I want you to be my wife."

Ciara pulled her hand back. "Oh, Mathan. You've no… What are you doing? I haven't seen you for a dozen years.

I can't... I'm not ready, and neither are you."

Shoulders slumped and head hanging, Mathan stood. "Aye, Ciara. You are right, of course. I am impetuous. Forgive me." Walking toward the door, he discovered his body to be more of a burden than it had ever before been.

Behind him, he heard the bench hit the floor as Ciara stood. "Bear," she called softly. He stopped. "Mathan, where are you going?"

He glanced back, but not far enough to see her, and spoke into the darkness, "I have to get some sleep. Need to get moving in the morning. Going to Shallowford."

A moment later, he reached for the door, but she spoke again. "What takes you to Shallowford, Mathan? What could mean more than what you have here? Can't you stay a while?"

"Nay, lass. I've promises to keep. Those promises take me to Shallowford and the army. Perhaps when I've done what I must, I'll stop by for a sip of cider."

He walked out the door.

***

At first light, Orin had the team hitched and ready to take the trio to Shallowford. Mathan somberly thanked him, but refused his help. Keva filled the travelers' satchels with bread, cheese, apples, and nuts; then gave Mathan a motherly kiss before wishing them all good travels.

Orin clasped hands with Mathan and grimaced. "Anytime, lad. You are always welcome here. Be safe. Come back soon."

Keva's tears flowed freely as she embraced Mathan. "We *all* love you here, Bear. Come home as soon as you may."

CHAPTER 39
Fording the Frigid

"Let us cross over the river and rest under the shade of the trees."
LTG Thomas J. "Stonewall" Jackson

Cresting a rise, they caught their first glimpse of the palisade that surrounded Shallowford. The setting sun sparkled off the Frigid River as it flowed before the town's gates. After an hour's walk, they drew near enough to see that the gates were being closed. By the time they arrived at the river's edge, a guard stood before the secured gates.

Mathan jogged across the low wooden bridge and spoke with the watchman. "Lad, we've walked a ways and would be glad for a meal, a bath and a bed."

"Gates are closed," the guard replied.

Mathan sized him up then asked, "And you're to be out here before the gate all night, then?"

The guard snorted. "'Course not. At the end of my watch a lad comes out and replaces me."

"And would this lad who will replace you pass through that gate behind you?"

Fixing Mathan with a shrewd gaze, the watchman

replied in a measured tone, "The gates are closed and will remain so until sunrise. You and your party are welcome to camp on the field there across the ford."

In the last rays of the sun, Mathan saw a number of tiny wooden huts arranged haphazardly about the field that the watchman had indicated. Each seemed to be little more than an arrangement short planks stood on end and leaned against each other to form a low but steep roof above a small patch of bare earth. He thanked the guard and ambled back across the bridge to where Tigue and Bronach awaited him.

After explaining the situation, he hitched up his pack and walked toward the scattered huts. The nearest huts seemed to be occupied, so they moved on to the next, away from the town, until they found some that were unoccupied.

They had all been expecting to sleep in a bed that night, at an inn in the town. Each handled the disappointment in a unique way. Mathan selected a hut that seemed to be in good repair, crawled inside, laid out his bedroll and went to sleep. Tigue tuned his clarsach and hummed a new tune he'd been composing on the road. Bronach complained vociferously for a while about the shortage of beds then complained about the shortage of interested recipients for her complaint. Before long, they were all asleep.

Waking before sunrise, Mathan was shocked to see the road full of people, carts and animals. He woke the others then rolled his blankets. While the others gathered their things, he had a word with the guard at the gate before returning and packing his gear.

Tigue held Mathan's knapsack so he could more easily pack it. "Will they require us to join the throng or does our arrival last night play in our favor?"

"When I told him we'd spent the night in the shacks, his exact response was 'I hope you found one free of vermin. I'd get into line soon, if I was you'."

Tigue chuckled and shook his head. "I fared well in

reference to vermin. How about you?"

"My hut was home to a family of mice, but we let each other be."

A moment later, the men were accosted by a disheveled and angry Bronach. "Did you sleep well?" her father asked.

Bronach snorted and walked toward the road, scratching at various parts of her anatomy. Mathan came alongside her and informed her that they would need to join the rear of the column if they cared to enter the town. She stopped and stood rigidly, staring ahead at the road. Every inch of it from the gate to a hill that blocked further view of the road, was packed with people, carts, and animals. She slumped and walked toward the hill.

Cresting the hill, Mathan was glad to note that the column extended only a short distance beyond its base. A while later, the gates opened and the queue moved steadily forward bringing the travelers to a small guardhouse just inside the city wall.

"Step forward. State your name, location of origin, intended duration of stay, and business here." The guard was obviously bored and spoke in a disinterested tone.

Mathan hesitated, so Tigue stepped forward. "The young gentleman is Mathan, son of Ardal of Hart's Pass."

The guard looked up from his notes and studied Mathan. "Welcome, Sir. It is an honor to have you here. Is your father likely to join us?"

"I don't know that he has plans to come. I'm here to sign into the army. I don't know how long I'll be here. I hale from the village of Taermun–"

"In the Avinn Vale." The guard breathed the words as though speaking of a mystical place.

Disconcerted by his behavior, Mathan responded. "Aye, Taermun of the lovely Avinn Vale."

"And who are these with you, Sir?"

"Look you, I'm no Sir. I hope to be a light footman much as my father was before me."

"As your father was. Yes, Sir."

Mathan was befuddled by the guard's response. Tigue no doubt remembered that a befuddled Mathan was rarely a polite Mathan, so he cleared his throat and said, "The lad is Broghan, Mathan's page, and I am Tigue, his bard. We hope to lodge nearby the training post and occasionally communicate with Mathan in order to send word of his progress back to his father."

"Of course. I will have a man escort you to suitable lodgings and show you the way to the post." He then addressed Mathan. "I, myself, will escort you to the inscription office. And my apologies, Sir, for turning you away earlier. If you had only told me who you are, I would have welcomed you in immediately."

"Told you who I am? Who am I?"

The guard shook his head and chuckled, "As your father, indeed, Sir."

He stepped away and gestured for two guards to join him. After giving them his instructions, he returned. "Calva, here, will escort you two to the Drowsy Bear where, I am certain, you will be comfortable. If you need anything, the barman knows where to find me.

"I am Quinn, a ten leader of the Guard," he then said to Mathan. "Gladly, Sir, will I escort you to the inscription office when you are ready."

Mathan glanced at Tigue then at Bronach. "I reckon I've waited long enough. Lead on, Quinn."

GLOSSARY

Terms:

Alish – The common language of the Dearthmen

Caer – A fortress

Clarsach – A hand-held harp

Common – The public space in a village

Release – The public rite by which a father declares his son independent

Seat – Capitol or headquarters

Wain – A heavy wagon

Warband – The small army of a petty king

Weir – A fish trap

Titles:

Binder – A person who binds or bandages wounds

Captain – Any low- to mid-level officer of the army or of the watch
Commissioned Officer

Captain-General – Any high-level officer of the army or of the watch
Flag Officer

Chief Librarian – Maintains the Royal Library at Galantamhor and manages the smaller libraries throughout Tierasal. The libraries are archives as well as museums.

High King – the rightful ruler of all Tierasal

Leader – Any Soldier who is not an officer but is responsible for other Soldiers
Non-commissioned Officer

Light Footman/Heavy Footman/Horseman – Any Soldier as designated by his unit of assignment

Primate – The High King's Chief minister
Believed, by some, to rule in the stead of the apparently absent High King

Provost – The detention officer at any army post

Rhys – Any Dearthman guard

Sabia, The – The Wise Woman

Second - Assistant

Sensor – Loosely, any spy

Teshak – The chieftain of Taermun

Warder – A city guard

Watch Leader – The warder responsible for one of the three "Watches" or shifts of the Dunglaun city guard

Locations:

Avinn Vale "the vale" – A narrow valley on the Eastern slope of Mount Doleram

Bractland – The island home of the Bractmen off the western coast of Tierasal

Carragaener – A small city east of Hebron Heath
Rival to Dunglaun
Ruled by Fardorcha

Dolewash – The river that runs from the slopes of Mount Doleram through the Avinn Vale

Dunglaun – A small city west of Hebron Heath and east of Mount Doleram
Rival to Carragaener
Ruled by Uvar of the House of Killinchy

Galantamhor – The "Royal City"
Sprang up at the gates to Maldren Keep
Purports to administer Tierasal in the name of the high King

Hart's Pass/ Stonebreak Pass – Site of an historic battle

Hebron Heath – A high heath situated east of Mount Doleram

Il-Hofra – A Dearthman city
Home to an advanced forge and foundry for the production of excellent weapons

Maldren Keep – The home of the sequestered High King of Tierasal

Mount Doleram – The dormant volcano near the center of Tierasal

Shallowford – A military town situated near a crossing point on the Frigid River

Stonebreak Pass/Hart's Pass – Site of an historic battle

Taermun – A village in the Avinn Vale established by refugees from Dunglaun

Tierasal – The great land

Groups:

Adnana – A tribe of Dearthmen

Bractmen/Bracties – The inhabitants of the island known as "Bractland"

Dearthmen – The inhabitants of the great desert known as the "Dearth"

Fair Ones – The pale skinned northern people

Foot/Horse – A unit of Soldiers designated by mission and equipment
Light Foot is rapidly mobile Infantry.
Heavy Foot is armored Infantry.
Horse is Cavalry

Forsaken/Rectified – A unit of Adnana
Fought at Stonebrake Pass

House of Killinchy – The ruling house of Dunglaun and Hebron Heath

Rectified/Forsaken– A unit of Adnana
Fought at Stonebrake Pass

Ten/Thirty/Hundred/Three Hundred/One Thousand/Division – Echelons of the Army of Tierasal

Individuals:

Aedan, the Rose of Clan Erc – Daughter of King Niall of the Bracties
Mother of Donal
Kinswoman of Partlan

Agrona/'Grona – First Watch Leader of Dunglaun
Daughter of Fardorcha

Alistair – Cartwright of Taermun
Son of Ivor
Older brother of Ardal

Amir/Kaff – Spice merchant of Taermun
Leader of the Forsaken
Father of Nabal and Hakov

Anyah – Daughter of Mag Petty
Mathan's best friend since childhood

Ardal – Blacksmith of Taermun
Captain of the Forsaken
Husband of Laurelei
Father of Mathan
Son of Ivor
Brother of Alistair

Brady – Chief Metallurgist of the Armies of Tierasal

Cavan – Teshak of Taermun

Cian – Leader of the Light Thirty at Hart's Pass
Guard Leader of Taermun

Davin – Quartermaster of the Armies of Tierasal

Dermot of Heatherdale – Captain-General of the Armies of Tierasal

Dieterick – A lord of the Fair Ones of the Northlands
Father of Mairyam

Donal – A Leader of the City Watch in Galantamhor
Son of Aedan

Ekurn – A Ten Leader of Light Foot at Hart's Pass

Elgin – Captain of Light Foot at Hart's Pass
Captain of the Guard at Taermun

Evan – A herald sent throughout the land with an invitation from the High King

Faelan – Third Watch Leader of Dunglaun
Son of Mawnus

Fardorcha – Lord of Carragaener
Rival of Uvar
Father of Agrona

Finnbarr/Fintan/Fionn – Son of Uvar
Rightful lord of Dunglaun/Hebron Heath
Husband of Mairyam
Father of Laurelei

Flann – Chief Librarian at the Royal Library of Galantamhor

Gerritt – A Ten Leader of Horse at Hart's Pass

Glendon – Captain of Horse at Hart's Pass

Hakov – One of the Forsaken
Son of Amir

Hart – Hundred Captain at Hart's Pass

Hugh/Hugh Mor – Captain of Heavy Foot at Hart's Pass

Ivor – Northman warrior and smith
Helped Fintan to establish Taermun
Father of Alistair and Ardal

Kaff/Amir – Spice merchant of Taermun
Leader of the Forsaken
Father of Nabal and Hakov

Karim – Dearthman
Manager of the Forge and Foundry at Il-Hofra

Keva – Wife of Orin

Laurelei – A Sensor of the Armies of Tierasal
Daughter of Fintan and Mairyam
Wife of Ardal
Mother of Mathan

Mag Petty – Innkeeper in Taermun
Mother of Anyah

Mairyam – Daughter of Dieterick
Wife of Fintan
Mother of Laurelei

Mathan – Son of Ardal and Laurelei

Mawnus – Captain of the Watch in Dunglaun

Nabal – One of the Forsaken
Son of Amir

Nikko – Son of Cavan

Orin – Husband of Keva

Ossian/Oss – Second Watch Leader of Dunglaun

Partlan/Partie – A Bractman
Translator for the Forsaken
Kinsman of Aedan

Rory – Captain-General of Sensors for the Armies of Tierasal

Stefan – Captain-General of Plans for the Armies of Tierasal

Tigue – The bard of Taermun

Uvar – Lord of Dunglaun and Hebron Heath
Father of Finnbarr